Sandy McC
New Zealan
mainly in Au
jobs, from _____ ....yee and
swimming pool painter to actor and theatre director.

Although he is best known as the host of 'Australia Talks Back' on ABC Radio National, Sandy is also the author of more than twenty plays. He has travelled extensively in Africa, Asia and Europe as well as living in Finland and Austria. He has twice won awards at the New York Radio Festival for radio documentary making and been awarded the International Kalevala Medal by the Finnish Government for services to Finnish culture.

A practising Buddhist for the last twenty-five years, Sandy is a passionate campaigner for social justice and human rights and is a strong supporter of Community Aid Abroad and Amnesty International, with a special interest in the issues of self determination for Southern Sudan, East Timor and Tibet.

He currently lives in Brisbane where he plans to continue his radio work while attempting to find the time to complete two more thrillers featuring the life and times of Savva Golitsyn.

IN WOLF'S CLOTHING

SANDY McCUTCHEON

HarperCollins*Publishers*

HarperCollins*Publishers*

First published in Australia in 1997 by HarperCollins*Publishers*
ACN 009 913 517
A member of the HarperCollins*Publishers* (Australia) Pty Limited Group

HarperCollins*Publishers*
25 Ryde Road, Pymble, Sydney NSW 2073, Australia
31 View Road, Glenfield, Auckland 10, New Zealand
77–85 Fulham Palace Road, London W6 8JB, United Kingdom
Hazelton Lanes, 55 Avenue Road, Suite 2900, Toronto, Ontario M5R 3L2
and 1995 Markham Road, Scarborough, Ontario M1B 5M8, Canada
10 East 53rd Street, New York NY 10032, USA

National Library of Australia Cataloguing-in-publication data:

McCutcheon, Sandy.
  In wolf's clothing.
  ISBN 0 7322 5770 0.
  I. Title.
A823.3

Cover illustration by Vivien Kubbos/The Drawing Book

Printed in Australia by Griffin Paperbacks, Adelaide

7 6 5 4 3 2 1
99 98 97

DEDICATION

For Brian David Parry who has been working undercover in Australia and New Zealand since 1949. And for all those who have attempted, unsuccessfully, to track him down.

Kiitos myös muille ystävilleni, ja tovereille, jotka ovat osallistuneet teoksen syntymiseen tai muuten kannustaneet minua työssäni. Kiitos kaikille.

PART

I

CHAPTER

ONE

WHEN Savva Vasilyevich Golitsyn finally decided to go home he was sixty-four years old, though he looked and acted like a man at least ten years younger.

In June, he discreetly sold his house in Melbourne and, surprised at how much it was worth, was able at the end of July to put $100,000 into a special account. Another $10,000 he changed into traveller's cheques. He bought two complete sets of new clothes, an expensive suitcase and a fine pair of thick-soled German walking boots.

Back in his temporary accommodation at the Luxor Hotel, Savva Vasilyevich laced the boots and put them on. For a moment he paced the room, feeling the leather stiff around his toes. It would soften soon enough. There was still the question of what to do with the additional money. After a while he turned on his bedside light and emptied his money belt onto the table. He placed $5000 in fifties to one side, then divided the remaining $40,000 into two neat bundles. Savva had been with the one bank since arriving in Australia in 1949. There had been no questions asked about the large withdrawal.

From a plastic shopping bag he took two padded post bags and after writing a couple of short notes, placed $20,000 in each and sealed them. For a moment he sat looking out into the Melbourne dusk. It had been a busy few months and now they were nearly over. He picked up the phone and dialled nine. Why was it always nine in Australian hotels?

"Room Service, Gerard speaking, can I help you?"

"Thank you, yes . . . Room 1117. I would like an open sandwich, salmon, pickles and a bottle of white wine. Chardonnay, oh, and I have two parcels I would like posted. Thank you, Gerard."

Monday morning. Temple Beth Israel, Alma Road, St Kilda. Rabbi Schiff was used to a spirit of *tsedakah* or charity in his congregation, but the bundle of currency that had spilled out onto his desk was extravagant to say the least. It was only as he counted it again that he came across the note.

"For the community, with thanks."

It was signed "Leon Silbert".

Rabbi Schiff jotted a memo to his secretary to look through the records for a Leon Silbert, and locked the money away in the safe.

It was not until Tuesday that the second note was opened. It was simply signed "Leon".

> Dear Amelia, I am going home.
>> This does not and can never repay the friendship.
>> Maybe one day I can explain.
>> With love,
>> Leon.

Amelia Lippmann read the note several times. She cried quietly for a while; the money, scattered, forgotten, on the floor.

Savva Vasilyevich had spent the weekend walking the Melbourne streets in some sort of ritual farewell. He strode with his head down, avoiding faces; keeping to the back of cafes when he stopped for his favourite short black coffee. His walk was not around the landmarks of the city's tourist routes but rather the back streets; the tree-lined streets – the small parks and gardens. He sucked these images in as though storing them up for future use. He hardly paused, but kept on the move; driven by a ticking clock that reminded him that each street was feeling his footfall for the last time. It was a grieving . . . his unspoken *Kaddish*.

Monday he spent laboriously destroying his past. He went through his remaining possessions one by one, scrutinising them. His Australian passport he put to one side but the rest of his identity he shredded by hand and flushed down the hotel toilet. Notes, phone numbers, business cards and an address book soon followed. In the dusk he caught a tram to Lygon Street and spent the evening in a cafe. For a while he glanced at magazines and thumbed through a leftover *Weekend Australian*. At nine o'clock he field tested his new walking boots all the way back to the Luxor.

The next day he took a taxi to the airport and bought a one-way ticket. On a whim, to treat himself, he changed his mind at the last minute and smiled at the Qantas ticket clerk. "Make that first class."

At the same time Amelia Lippmann was reading the note, Savva Golitsyn was on his way to Canberra.

The secretary placed the information about Leon Silbert on the rabbi's desk along with her own short note about Silbert's friendship with her friend Amelia Lippmann. The rabbi had been in a few minutes ago, but it appeared he had slipped out again. More cake and coffee, she thought to herself. In some things he was so weak.

The scrap of paper was soon buried under a copy of the Melbourne edition of *Jewish News*. Later in the day there was a squabble over the new Lubavitch *Mikvah* – a ritual bathhouse that was causing dissent, and then there was the trouble about a divorce that was civil and not religious; all in all, Rabbi Schiff felt he should have stayed down at St Kilda Road drinking coffee. By the end of a wearying day he had forgotten about Leon Silbert. He didn't ask his secretary about him again.

On the flight he sat next to a Liberal Party Senator from Tasmania who spent the entire time reading Vincent Cronin's *Catherine, Empress of all the Russias*. Savva recognised it, disliked it and spent most of the flight musing about *Imperatritsa Ekaterina*. At one point the Senator noticed that Savva was watching her read.

"You know, I admire Catherine so much."

"Sorry, Senator, I didn't mean to stare."

The Senator smiled her professional smile. "I think one can learn so much from history."

"So did Zavadovskii. He also . . ."

For a moment the book was folded over one hand.

"Zavadovskii?"

"Oh, I am certain you will come across him in the book. He was one of Catherine's lovers; a Ukrainian."

"So you, too, admire Catherine?"

Normally he would have opted for diplomacy but, after all, he was leaving. He would never have allowed himself the luxury otherwise.

"No, Senator, I admire Zavadovskii."

That was it, he thought, as he watched the Senator turn back to her book, he felt empowered.

The aircraft banked as it prepared to land and he held his nostrils closed and blew into them, helping his ears to adjust to the change in cabin pressure. A car ride away, he thought, just a car ride away. He flexed his toes inside his new walking boots; he wouldn't be doing much walking, but now the leather felt just fine.

He was a bastard, like all the others, she thought. Poor little refugees; off the boat, handouts from the Jewish Welfare, and then, within a few years, they take the money and run. Of course he had fooled her. Sweet talk, little favours and, after her husband died, well she had needs, so did he ... bastard! Twenty thousand dollars for what? Amelia felt soiled; an over paid prostitute. Why didn't he say he was going? They had talked about it; a small house in Tel Aviv. They could have gone together. They had planned a holiday in Israel for Pesach one year, but nothing had come of it. She became aware of her tension and anger and slowly unclenched her fists and willed her jaw to stop grinding her teeth together. The bastard didn't know when he was well off! I mean, he was lucky to have found a young widow like her. Forty-seven, and what was he now? Sixty-two? Sixty-five?

Amelia Lippmann had known Leon all her life. She was barely two when he came to Australia; a young Russian refugee with poor English and not a living relative. Her family had sponsored him for a time. "Uncle Leon" with his dark hair, dark eyes and dark silence was part of family history. He had disappeared for a few years, and when they met again he was involved in policy analysis, computers or something, in the Premier's Department. Her husband had actually introduced them at their wedding.

"Amelia, I would like you to meet Leon Silbert."

They had both carried on the pretence in front of Michael, but later, after supper, Leon had come up behind her and put his hands on her shoulders and said very quietly, "Ringed with the azure world, he stands."

"Azure means blue," she replied. It was an old and private joke.

She had liked the power in his hands on her shoulders. She felt about him as she had done about her father . . . the bastard, he was bloody old enough to be her father!

She folded the note and put it in her desk drawer. For a moment she looked at the money still at her feet. Then, with a sigh she bent down and started gathering it up.

Savva Golitsyn collected his bag and waited until the rush of people had subsided. There was still a taxi waiting outside. He felt almost light-headed as the driver put his bag in the boot.

"Where to, mate?"

"76 Canberra Avenue, Griffith, thanks."

★

"He clasps the crag with crooked hands;
close to the sun in lonely lands,
ringed with the azure world, he stands.

"The wrinkled sea beneath him crawls;
he watches from his mountain walls,
and like a thunderbolt he falls."

Amelia clapped her hands in delight.

"Well done! But it is my homework, and I think the idea is that I am supposed to learn it, not you."

"Uncle" Leon sat and took the book from her lap.

"Good, then you recite."

After a time he looked up again. "What is 'azure'?"

She liked it, that she could teach him things. She liked him, too. He was funny and wise at the same time, and he was so quick. He had read the poem only once and then some minutes later had stood and recited it in his careful English.

She was thirteen, he thirty.

For a moment he looked at her; his face gaunt, but with eyes that flashed and glinted like polished onyx.

"If azure means blue why do they not say blue?"

They laughed; she tall and blond, belying her Jewishness, he dark and only marginally taller.

For several weeks he had been coming every Saturday for the Sabbath meal, then staying to baby-sit while her parents went out. They didn't talk a great deal at first. She, though relaxed in his company, had been preparing for her Bat Mitzvah, and he, for his part, seemed content to devour the books in her father's

10

library while she studied. As the weeks passed they talked more and more, but often it was Amelia who talked while he listened, stopping her every now and then to ask her about an English word or Australian custom. He never spoke of the suffering in Europe, or his decision to come to Australia. His earlier retreats into what she had always regarded as a dark silence appeared to have progressed to occasional reticence.

Leon Silbert vanished from Amelia's life for three years and turned up again just once, on her sixteenth birthday. He gave her a small present and after speaking with her parents for a while left the house without saying goodbye to her.

Apart from the meeting at her wedding reception when she married Michael Lippmann in 1973, she saw nothing of him and soon forgot all about her "Uncle" Leon.

In 1985, Michael dropped dead on the back lawn of their Melbourne house. He had been mowing when he was hit with a massive heart attack that didn't even give him a chance to sit down, let alone call for help. In retrospect, she was glad it had happened like that. The autopsy showed that his heart was diseased and the family doctor explained that although it had not come to light in his check-ups it would have deteriorated, causing a series of strokes and prolonged illness. Michael had left her wealthy but childless, yet she thought of neither of these things for months.

She quit her job as a librarian in the local library and spent her time between the house in Melbourne and her preferred option, the shack on the Mornington Peninsula. The grief seemed to go on forever and at times she thought she was having a breakdown; long hours of sleeplessness, tossing around in beds that were too big, too cold and too empty. Family and friends tried to distract her, some even suggesting that it was now "time to pull herself together and get on with her life . . .". She vaguely remembered throwing a vase at one of her would-be helpers.

For several months she became a virtual recluse, going out only when she had to, and when she did go, she found herself frightened of contact with people. She would stand in the checkout at the supermarket wondering what she had come for; tongue-tied at the bank and having to turn and flee. Scared of causing an accident, Amelia garaged her car and walked everywhere.

It was June 1986, ten months after Michael's death, when she met up with Leon Silbert again. She was sitting on a park bench amongst the fallen leaves, lost in her daydreaming when she became aware of a man sitting beside her. He had aged and, though still slim and fit, his once jet black hair was silver and thin. For a while they sat in silence. When he did eventually speak, his accent was now just a faint trace amidst the Australian vowels.

"Who wrote that poem?"

She looked at him, searching for a clue to his intentions, but he just sat staring at the leaves at his feet.

"Tennyson."

"I have often wondered about the last line. It seems strange . . . 'and like a thunderbolt, he falls.' It seems to me an eagle would dive, and a thunderbolt? Strike, maybe?"

There was silence. A child pushed an empty stroller in front of them. A mother, laden with plastic shopping bags, followed.

When Leon spoke again, it was not with the soft hesitancy her friends adopted, but with a strength and passion she had never heard from him. He still didn't look at her but raised his eyes to watch the edge of the park and the circling traffic.

"I understand grief for the motherland and lost ideals, but not for people. Would you explain it to me?"

Amelia smiled at the weighting he gave the words. The emphasis was foreign. She pushed her hands deeper into the pockets of her coat and stretched her legs, flexing her toes in her shoes. Then she started to talk. In all her grieving he was the first person who seemed to want to listen. Oblivious to the stares of passing strangers, oblivious to the fading of the day, she let the tears and words pour out.

It was dark when he walked her to her door, and it was only after he had said goodnight and vanished into the cold Melbourne evening that she remembered she hadn't thanked him. She flipped through the phone book but found no "L. Silbert".

For Amelia Lippmann it was the turning point, and so when Leon rang two weeks later she was pleased to hear from him.

CHAPTER

TWO

"I AM afraid that the Ambassador is in Sydney for several days, Mr Golitsyn, but the Third Secretary can spare you a few minutes."

Savva Golitsyn had already been sitting in the small office for over an hour and a half. He had not expected it to be otherwise as he knew they would need time to check their files and verify his identity. Eventually, a middle-aged woman brought him a cup of tea. She made no attempt to speak to him, not even pausing to ask if he would like milk or sugar.

Feeling suddenly weary he drained the cup and stood up to stretch his legs. The last couple of months had tired Savva more than he realised, and added to this was the tension and expectation of this moment for which he had waited almost forty years. At first it was the fantasy of going home the hero who had done something decisive and pivotal to world events. Later it had drifted more into his subconscious, but the traces always remained. Home was not a concept easily eradicated.

There had been other times; times flashing with laughter and friendship, when he imagined never returning. Always, though, he came back to his desire to go home, taking with him the good memories to tell his grandchildren. Of course, there would be no grandchildren, it was too late for that. For a moment he thought of Amelia, knowing that she would feel betrayed. Well, it had all been lies. No, that was not true, he had – did – love her, not that he recalled ever having said it. His knowledge of what lay ahead of him had tempered everything he had done for years and also with Amelia it could not be otherwise.

"May I have your passport, please?"

The man standing in front of him was obviously the Third Secretary. He was casually dressed in jeans and a T-shirt, and looked as though he probably played squash three or four times a week, in between working on his tan in the embassy's security compound. The messages abounding in the media about melanomas had not penetrated the ragged fence that faced onto Canberra Avenue.

Savva withdrew his Australian passport from inside his jacket and passed it across the desk to where the man had seated himself. There was something about the man, an air of someone with much more authority than just a Third Secretary. Those who were fighting their way up the diplomatic ladder dressed sharper, too. Savva had seen it before, years ago, when attending a cultural evening. The so-called Cultural Attaché had the same studied casualness but his position had been given away as soon as the Ambassador arrived. When he entered the other members of the post, in suits, had all inclined their heads in a slight bow of acknowledgment, yet the Ambassador had himself nodded in deference to the Cultural Attaché in polo-neck sweater and Levis. Like the man behind the desk he had "spook" written all over him.

"There is something I don't understand, *Gospodin* Golitsyn." The man's English was passable. "Why have you got a passport in the name of Leon Silbert?"

"It was my cover name."

"And now you want to go home?" The Third Secretary flipped the passport onto the desk.

"Yes."

"I will have to ask you some questions."

"Of course."

It had been late when he had arrived at the embassy and by the time the questions finished it was dawn. The Third Secretary, who never volunteered his name for the entire time, spoke only in English. He was very good at his job. He took Savva Vasilyevich back to his family, his schooling, and he seemed particularly interested in his recruitment.

"Let me understand this. You are saying that it was simply because of your school grades; your aptitude for English, not family connections?"

Savva sighed. "I've told you."

"No uncles in the army, no political connections?"

"No."

"This approach was made and the next thing you knew you were whisked off to – not one of the regular training institutions, not one of the academies, but to . . ." he glanced down at the notes in front of him, ". . . an old house in the country. Do you understand that this sounds . . . er . . . irregular, to say the least?"

Savva stood up and put his jacket back on. The tiredness was making him feel cold. He began to pace.

"It was explained to me that any other way of doing it would be open to compromise. There were worries about leaks . . . nobody knew who could be trusted. I was young. I was excited by it all. I went along with it. Look, ask for the file, it will all be there."

The Third Secretary yawned and turned his attention to the desk. The way he hunted through the drawers showed it was obviously not his own office, and he took several minutes to find what he was looking for. He had not smoked all night, but now he fished in a drawer and pulled out a black packet of

John Players. He removed one and lit it from a book of matches, then tucked the matches into the cigarette packet and slid it over the desk to Savva, who shook his head. He hadn't smoked for fifteen years and yet the craving still came occasionally.

Savva Golitsyn stopped pacing and sat again. The Third Secretary, it appeared, was not a regular smoker. He switched the cigarette from hand to hand trying to feel comfortable with it. He said nothing all the time he smoked; just sat, watching Savva, and playing with the cigarette. He was waiting for something, thought Savva, and what would have been his next unspoken question was answered by a door opening to his right. A diplomatic assistant, a *pradavyet*, dark haired, dishevelled and looking as tired as Savva Vasilyevich felt, stuck his head around the door and gestured to the Third Secretary, who stubbed out the cigarette butt, before excusing himself and following the man. He closed the door behind him, and for a moment Savva imagined that he had been locked in.

After a while Savva tried the door. The handle turned freely and the door swung out. The Third Secretary and his assistant were standing in a wide, arched hallway. They look a little surprised as Savva appeared.

"Toilet?"

The dishevelled *pradavyet* smiled broadly and pointed to the door opposite them. Savva nodded his thanks and, marvelling at the lax security, took himself off to relieve his tea-filled bladder.

When he had completed his toilet he dried his hands on a paper towel and went back past the two men to the office. They paused in their conversation and he felt their eyes follow him until the door was shut again. Savva gave in to a growing desire and helped himself to a cigarette. He lit it and felt the mixture of relief and nausea that comes with the first smoke after a long time.

The office was small; just the one desk set back into the corner furthest from the door to the hallway. Behind him was the door from the reception area through which he had first entered. Two other chairs, a coffee table and a print of a bleak and rather nondescript rural landscape, were the only interruptions to an otherwise drab room. On the desk was a tray and two cups. Savva saw that the Third Secretary had removed his notes when he answered the other man's summons. The book of matches caught his attention. The grey cover had a small red symbol at the top under which the words "Acropole Hotel" were printed in white flowing script. He turned it over and found a list of fax and telex numbers and the names "Lex" and "Spiros" scrawled in biro. He opened the cover and was informed that his every whim would be satisfied at the Acropole Hotel, Khartoum.

Khartoum? It took him a moment to recall, but then he remembered it was the capital of Sudan. What on earth could be the connection between the Russian Embassy and the Islamic Republic of Sudan?

Any link seemed highly unlikely . . . but then again, the convolutions and twists of political game-playing could lead to the strangest bedfellows. Savva pocketed the book of matches as he heard the door open. The Third Secretary had lost his relaxed mood. He handed Savva's passport back to him.

"I'm sorry you have been playing games with us, Mr Silbert. My *pradavyet* has just had exhaustive checks run and re-run in Moscow and I am afraid that there is no file on anyone remotely like Savva Vasilyevich Golitsyn. I do not know what you intended with your little charade, but I would advise you against repeating such foolishness. In earlier days we might have rewarded you in a less friendly way for your attempted deception."

Savva used all the control he could muster to hide his reaction. He stood up very slowly and returned the passport to his jacket pocket.

"Comrade Third Secretary," he spoke in Russian for the first time all night, "you have done your job as I have been doing mine in this country for the last forty years. I have no doubt that a grave mistake has been made. I do intend to return home. This means simply that I will have to do it without your assistance."

He turned and opened the door to the reception area. The dishevelled man was standing holding Savva's bag. He had a broad smile on his face.

"Goodnight, Mr Silbert." His English was flawless.

The sneer in his voice was too much for Savva. He took the bag and spun around to face the man who was a good twenty years his junior. There was something about him that struck Savva as unusual. Then he realised. The man wasn't Russian, he was a Chechen. No wonder he was still a *pradavyet* – despite his command of English. The Chechens had been deported en masse from their homeland on 23 February 1944, Red Army Day. Thousands were sent to the north of Kazakhstan, and never trusted again. Stalin had believed they had collaborated with the Germans; true or not, the Chechens were in the wilderness for a long time. And given their recent attempts to set up their own breakaway state, it looked as though they would remain in the wilderness for years to come. It would certainly make this man's future less than bright. Savva spoke to him in Russian.

"If this mistake is caused by you, Comrade Chechen," he spat the word out, "then I would be watching my back. The *Istrebiteli* live long and have longer arms. Kazakhstan would seem like paradise."

His bluff was rewarded as he saw the sudden hesitation sweep across the man's face. It was only a bluff though. The old NKVD hit men had long vanished into legend. If any of them still existed, or had modern counterparts, there was certainly no way that Savva could harness their skills. He took the moment however, and, holding himself erect, walked from the Russian Embassy into a chill and misty Canberra dawn.

CHAPTER

THREE

IT was not in Savva Golitsyn's nature to have mental blanks, but when he looked back on it later, he found he had very little recollection of the next twenty-four hours. Somehow he must have dragged himself to a bus station and been sufficiently *compos mentis* to buy a ticket. He could never work out why he had chosen the rural town of Orange in New South Wales, but the next day he woke to find himself in the Hotel Cannington. He spent the day in his room, waking only to put a "Do not disturb" sign outside his door.

The following morning he rose feeling as though he had returned to some kind of recognisable reality. He was also very hungry, so he dragged himself down the corridors until he found the dining room and treated himself to a dreadful breakfast: tiny packets of cereal, sliced processed bread, toasted and spread with the contents of plastic sachets containing sugar attempting to masquerade as raspberry jam. The caterer's blend instant coffee with Long-Life milk was the final straw. He signed for the meal and, leaving the hotel, turned left into the main street and eventually found himself outside an Italian cafe. He went in and had a second breakfast of hot bread rolls and real coffee.

Though it was now mid-morning it was still too damp and chilly to walk the streets so, cursing himself for not having thought to keep his battered old laptop, Savva bought a pad and biro and hurried back to his room. He had just sat down on the edge of the bed when the ringing of the phone caused him to start. He froze. No one knew where he was. He let it ring for a moment, then picked it up. To his relief it was the hotel receptionist inquiring as to the length of Mr Evans' intended stay.

"Oh, several more days . . . make it a week. I have some business that needs attending to; I'll let you know by the weekend a little more clearly."

That, it seemed, was no problem, as they had no overcrowding at this time of the year. Savva Vasilyevich found it hard to imagine the hotel booked out. The first breakfast should stand as a firm warning to anyone. The hotel itself, though, was actually quite pleasant, if one liked being closeted in a time warp complete with swirling blue and red disco carpets that looked as though they were designed to be improved by having things dropped on them. From outside and certainly from most of the interior one was assailed with reminders of what it must have been like in the 1930s . . . and the answer was, not much different. He had, however, seen a neon sign advertising a nightclub, and towards the back of the Cannington was a modern courtyard that looked as if it would be a pleasant place for a beer on summer evenings, so there were some attempts to marry the thirties with the nineties, but Savva smiled to himself; as a marriage, it was de facto rather than legitimate.

After placing the "Do not disturb" sign on his door again, Savva began to make notes of everything he had said to the Third Secretary. He went through his story several times.

He had been questioned mostly about information concerning his recruitment and training. Obviously this was not seen as orthodox, yet, to Savva, it seemed logical that if you were going to place an agent in a foreign country for an extended period then his identity must be known to as few people as possible. Maybe that was where the problem lay. Maybe too few people had known about him. Because he had no one else's experiences to judge it by he had always assumed that his training was standard; identify the agent as young as possible, isolate him, and immerse him in his false background until you put him in the field.

He had been a young teenager when they had taken him from his Moscow orphanage which had, ironically, been foundered by "Iron Felix": Felix Dzerzhinsky. His uncle, who had been keeping an eye on him since his parents' death, had signed a consent form for some rather nebulous training program, and that was it. Into the mist. The first move had been to Leningrad; not to some swanky training establishment but to a squalid apartment in the *dom-vashen*, the old town. Here he had spoken nothing but English for an entire year. Every now and then people were brought in to play cards with him or have a party but they were conscripts whose hearts were not in it. Savva Vasilyevich had also enjoyed occasional trips into the country, but they were few and far between.

He also spent the year studying in English. He still had no clear idea of what result his trainers were after and was often surprised by the subjects thrust in front of him: accounting, English law, business management and political theory. Politics was the strangest inclusion for it was not the Marxist–Leninism that he was used to, but rather a country-by-country study of Western democracies. Then, just when Savva thought he was building some picture of a possible outcome, he would be taken out of the city for two days of tree pruning or to learn to strip a diesel tractor engine.

"In case you ever need to talk about it," laughed one of his teachers, "you can claim a very varied childhood."

At the end of the first year they moved him to the country. Though who "they" were, he was never sure. Family names and patronymics were banned with only first names or nicknames allowed. The only time he pressed one of the conscripts for information he was pulled in front of a panel and informed that it was his first and last mistake. Any more trouble-making and he was on the scrap heap.

He arrived at a small secluded farm house and was told, at last, what his training was for. He was going into an area of the world where he could be of great service to his country. He was going to be taught very few of the tricks of the spy trade – only basics like how to recognise a tail and then reverse the roles, how to organise a *tref* or clandestine meeting using dead-letter boxes – which added up to nothing much at all. His childhood ability to remember a scene image-by-image was remarked on, but they insisted that the less his behaviour was that of a trained agent the better his chances of survival.

A sleeper was expected to blend in; to build a life in the new society. If he could work himself into a position of influence, so much the better. But even that was not essential. His real role was to be the man on the spot should circumstances ever require it; the wild card that could be called up in a crisis; the local eyes and ears. Help would not be available if anything went wrong and, above all, he was not to attempt to contact any other Russian agents, visitors or embassy staff. When, and only when, the time was right he would be asked to perform certain tasks. In the meantime, would he please go upstairs and meet Mr and Mrs Silbert.

The Silberts were Jewish, and for the next two years they were his life, except for the English lessons that occupied three afternoons a week. They schooled him in *Torah* and *Talmud*, *Seder* and *Shema*, *Kiddush* and *Kaddish*. They taught him the dietary laws and the history of their people, and Leon, as he was now being called, was a good student.

In what turned out to be the last year of his training, a regular string of visitors was paraded in front of him, all giving him different perspectives on the importance of the Pacific Region to the Soviet Union. From this Savva/Leon began to think of the United States of America as his possible destination. His visitors appeared to have no idea who he was, and some seemed singularly put out to have been dragged from their *dachas* or Moscow offices to deliver their speciality address to some kid, wet behind the ears. The highest ranking was a Lieutenant-General Engineer, M. Lobanov, a specialist, who bored him with two hours of the theoretical possibilities of radio electronics, and ended up with the splendidly scientific suggestion that wherever he was going, "Keep your ears open!"

Then came what Savva Vasilyevich remembered as the diet stage. It was starvation really. Over a period of what seemed like months, his food rations were gradually reduced. The Silberts would try to slip food to him but after being caught they vanished from the house and Savva never saw them again. He imagined that, having performed their task for the motherland, they were probably now buried beneath it, or living somewhere in Siberia. Savva felt sorry for them, as, for a while, he had actually felt part of a family for the first time in his life.

The reason for his starvation eventually became evident. His emaciated frame was bundled into a car in the middle of the night and he began his life as a homeless, Jewish refugee.

Overland through Finland, Sweden, then to Denmark and a freight truck to Hamburg. Just before they drove into the docks area the previously taciturn German driver pulled into a parking area and, handing Savva his forged papers, addressed him in perfect Moscow Russian.

"You have done well, Savva Vasilyevich. You are going to Australia. Build your cover slowly, we have all the time in the world. And remember, don't attempt to contact us. When the time is right, contact will be made. Good luck."

Australia? It had never occurred to him. By the time he was marched up the gang plank of the ship he was feeling as genuinely displaced as the hundreds of other refugees.

That, thought Savva, was my graduation.

The MBR, the Russian successors to the old Union KGB, had been through a rough and rocky ride during the last few years. Places had been tightly controlled, people had been scrapped, and the former Union KGB personnel had to fight to be included in the revamped organisation. Though many of the titles had changed, the functions remained. A few of the old guard still thought of themselves as maintaining the same roles, and in fact did so.

The signals clerk, at what had been the KGB First Directorate (Foreign Intelligence) Headquarters at Yasenevo, was one of the old guard and his daily habits had not changed. But market forces now played a more important role, so he was in a hurry to leave work as there was a rumour around of a load of shoes due into the market and he didn't want to miss out. The request from the embassy in Canberra for information on a person named Savva Vasilyevich Golitsyn and the report on the subsequent failure to verify his existence were still in his "in" tray when he left the building.

A short time later, a woman came through from the newer 22-storey building to deliver a folder of documents. She paused over the signals clerk's desk and casually removed the Canberra papers before continuing with her other deliveries. On her way home that evening she took the papers to the Special Projects Research Institute near Vnukova 2 Airport.

Next morning, as the signals clerk walked from the carpark off the Moscow Ring Road, through the entrance gate and past the ornamental lake to the main entrance his feet were smarting. In yesterday's rush he had grabbed the wrong size shoes. In Moscow nothing seemed to fit any more.

Early the next day the phone calls began.

Was it Flaubert who said that anything becomes interesting if you look at it long enough? This was not true of Savva's room at the Cannington. You lied, Gustave! The longer he sat there, the more prison-like it felt. During the last few days his feelings had gone through the spectrum from anger to confusion and had now settled into a debilitating depression. His anger had been at the waste of it all; almost a lifetime spent preparing for a call that had never come. It was true that he had enjoyed his life in Australia, but he had never let himself settle into it fully, living as he had, with the knowledge that it could all change at any moment.

His confusion was full of "what ifs?". What if they had simply lost his file? What if that had happened years ago? What were the chances of them finding it again? What if it were something more sinister? Though what that might be, he had no idea. Should he return to Canberra and try again? Should he give up his ideas of returning to Russia and simply go back to Melbourne and pick up where he had left off? Ask Amelia to marry him? Accept his Jewish identity as real and have one final adventure with Amelia and go to Israel?

The depression left him powerless. For hours he castigated himself, listing the mistakes, the stupidity of what he had done. He had failed to keep to the rules of the game. He had broken cover by going to the embassy. He was certain that all movement around the embassy would be monitored and it would take very little checking of taxi drivers and flight details to establish who he was. He went down to the bottle shop in the hotel driveway and bought a Bloodwood Merlot and returned to his room. The wine cheered him for a time. He realised at one stage that he was actually chuckling out loud to himself.

"I'm blown!"

For that moment, at least, it seemed funny.

What was not so amusing was the question of what to do next. He reasoned that he was secure enough in Orange, at least for a while, as he had not supplied his name at the Canberra bus depot and, anyway, why should anyone want to trace him? He had checked into the Cannington as Michael Evans from Brisbane and had enough cash on him not to need to use his passport to cash a traveller's cheque – all of which was fine but led him inevitably back to the issue of his next move.

Very early Saturday morning, Savva went down the street and bought a selection of newspapers. He was no closer to making a decision about the future, but the depression had lifted enough for him to realise that the time to move was fast approaching. His small forays around the town had exhausted every cafe and pub, and the lack of phone calls in and out of his room was making his supposed business in

Orange look pretty thin. Twice the hotel manager had asked him how business was going and Savva realised he was beginning to feel a twinge of paranoia about being drawn into a lengthy conversation. He was not certain how convincing he could be in creating a brand new legend at this stage.

Returning to his room he tossed the newspapers on the bed. They were a treat for later. I'm working on the Sabbath, he smiled to himself and started reviewing his notes on the questioning at the embassy yet again. He certainly could not return to his old identity. A blind Russian doorman could locate him in less than an hour if he attempted that, let alone any Australian or other unfriendly security service that might have been monitoring the embassy. He flushed the notes into the safety of the Orange sewerage system.

Several times Savva had considered telephoning Amelia Lippmann, but he suppressed the urge and rewarded himself with the thought that between now and whenever hunger drove him out in search of a half-decent place for lunch, he could relax with the weekend papers. His earlier disgust with the hotel's instant coffee had resulted in his purchase of a small single-cup plunger and a bag of medium roast Kenyan. So he made himself a cup, rearranged the room's furniture so he could sit in the rather awkward armchair with his feet on the bed, and picked up the Melbourne *Age*.

He nearly missed the small paragraph on the bottom of the page and was in the process of folding the paper when the word "synagogue" caught his attention. He read the item quickly and then again carefully; trying to tease out more from the scant description of the outrage. The Temple Beth Israel had been ransacked in the first incident of its kind since the spate of synagogue attacks that had followed the most recent skirmishes in the Gulf. The police were puzzled as there had been no arson and no anti-Semitic daubings as on previous occasions and only the office records had been rifled through. A large sum of money, not usually on the premises, had been scattered around the building – investigations were proceeding.

Savva picked up the phone and dialled for an outside line. Amelia was not orthodox and so would usually answer the phone on the Sabbath. He reached over for his cup of coffee and as he put the phone back firmly to his ear he realised it had stopped ringing.

"Hello? Amelia?"

He recognised the voice that answered him. It was the *pradavyet* from the Russian Embassy.

"Ah, Mr Silbert, you must be ringing in response to our advertisement in the weekend newspaper? For your health and that of our mutual friend you would be advised not to contact the embassy again."

Savva dropped the phone down on its cradle as though it had burnt his hand. When he finally took a sip of his coffee, it was cold and bitter.

CHAPTER

FOUR

THE grounds of the *dacha* at Arkhangelskoe were like a scene from *Dr Zhivago*, thought the man from Moscow. He had been on a posting years before in London and had attended the world premiere there. The British national anthem was played before the screening and the Soviets had dutifully stood up with the rest of the audience. To his surprise it was followed by the Soviet anthem, and to his disgust the rest of the audience had sat down, leaving him and his eight comrades standing, feeling both patriotic and foolish.

The silver birch glade and freshly opened spring flowers may have been straight from the set of

Zhivago, but what was emerging from his paint brush certainly wasn't. He had been struggling with the watercolour technique all week. Each morning when the light was, according to his guest from the Academy of the Arts, "just right", he had set up his easel and started on the background washes. Each lunchtime he had returned to the *dacha* with the morning's work screwed up, ready to be tossed in the fire.

"More colour and much less water," his tutor kept repeating.

The clouds in the background were not as ethereal today; that was better, he felt competent with their solidity, and moving slightly to the right of where he had stood yesterday he placed the largest of the birches in the left-hand third of the paper. What was it that Radishchev had called it? The "golden mean"? Anyway, it did look better, having the tree off-centre.

He was feeling rather pleased with himself now, which was a distinct improvement. When his doctor had suggested taking a couple of weeks off and doing something to bring his blood pressure down he had thrown the man out of his office. It was true, he reflected later, he could do with a rest. Then when his secretary, Anna Petrovna Florensky, suggested her art teacher friend as a companion and intimated that she, herself, would also enjoy spending time with the Colonel, he had rung the doctor and thanked him for his diagnosis.

It was a moot point as to the benefits for his heart and blood pressure of screwing the tail off Anna Petrovna each night, but it had certainly lifted the gloom that had descended on him in autumn and remained all winter. Part of it was seasonal, his doctor had insisted, but Colonel Victor Ivanovich Danilov knew it was also to do with the bunch of loonies in the Kremlin who seemed so intent on reforming the new Russia out of existence.

Pausing, he rested his brush on the easel and surveyed the almost completed painting. Apart from the fact that the clouds had moved a considerable distance closer since he started, it was actually the best so far. He would be proud to take it back to his Katya in Moscow, and show her the results of his "therapy".

Art teacher Radishchev, his house guest, shouted from the veranda that there was an urgent phone call for him. Danilov swore under his breath and, forgetting his promise to the good doctor in Moscow, lit a cigarette and drew back heavily, letting the acrid smoke fill his lungs before making his way to the house. Why didn't the party give him a cellular phone like his counterparts in the United States?

"Another fucking crisis, most likely," he snarled at the comrade artist. "Why can't those sissies in Moscow sort anything out for themselves?"

Twenty minutes later he was still on the phone feeling that he had said nothing but "*Da* Comrade Primakov" for the entire conversation. For a long time he had been aware of how much he resented deferring to Andrei Petrovich Primakov; a jumped-up opportunist without even the military training that sorted men out from fucking goats, though Primakov had set up the Special Projects Research Institute and hired him. But who the fuck insisted on being called "Comrade" any more?

"*Da* Comrade Primakov, I understand how serious this is and I'll get to work on it right now. This Golitsyn, in Australia, you can forget about him."

Long after he had hung up, Danilov stood as though gazing out the window, but his eyes saw nothing. A long way away, on the far side of the chessboard, a piece had made the wrong move. It was only a small move, but in the delicate balance of the present, this pawn from the past could bring attention from the wrong quarters to focus on the quiet moves being made. The pawn must be eliminated. He glanced down at his long-dead cigarette and let the butt fall to the floor. He sighed. His depression was back and when he looked up again he noticed that his less than ethereal clouds had started to deposit a very substantial rain on the landscape; a landscape that to his dismay contained an easel and painting that now appeared, even from this distance, to be more water and a lot less colour.

CHAPTER

FIVE

THE shock of hearing the Chechen's voice on the phone rather than Amelia's had concentrated Savva's mind. The indecision that had trapped him for days evaporated; what he felt most now was anger – anger at a fate which had decreed that his one chance at life's adventure should be wasted and that those who had chosen to leave him in limbo for so long should now threaten his friend. But why? What was behind the Russian move? Had some information surfaced in Moscow that had changed things, and if so . . . what next?

Two things needed his attention straight away, the first was the question of Amelia's safety and the second was a source of information. Who would have some idea of the games being played? Savva scrolled a list of names through his mind. Names from the present and from the past. His networks, discreetly built in the émigré communities, must hold some – what was it that old Heimo used to call them ... Heimo Susijarvi – scandal merchants. Savva's brain raced, pieces falling into place. The crafty old Finn had also come to Australia at the end of the war and of all the names that came to mind, it was Heimo who stood out as the one person who might just be able to offer some assistance.

Having been shunted in and out of Karelia by the Russians and then having settled a short way out of Helsinki, Heimo was disgusted to find that under the peace treaty the Russians were given a fifty-year lease to the Porkkala Peninsula. Enough was enough, so he managed to get himself on a ship to Australia. The surprising thing about Heimo Susijarvi was that he held no grudge against the Russians who had so disrupted his life. It was all part of a great game and all he wanted to do was continue to play.

In the early days in Melbourne, Heimo had been active in the refugee community as a trader of information. As a Finn he posed no threat to anyone and so he could move across boundaries that usually kept outsiders at bay. There was nothing of the dour Finnish stereotype in Heimo; he talked, joked, and the only Finnish attribute he seemed to have in common with his countrymen was his ability to drink. He sat on many of the refugee committees and always had a bottle of vodka and a sympathetic ear for anyone with a story to tell. He collected the talkers; the scandal merchants as he called them. In the Melbourne cafes in the 1950s it was a common sight, late at night, to find Heimo deep in conversation with Greek businessmen, Corsican stonemasons, Russian–Jewish silversmiths, Croatian activists, or even members of the older Chinese community. Everyone knew him and everyone liked him.

Somewhere in Heimo Susijarvi's background was training in military intelligence – "a contradiction in terms" Heimo always said – and he valued information above all else. It was, he also said, the source of power. Within a few years of arriving in Australia he began to work for ASIO, the fledgling Australian Security Intelligence Organisation which had started operations in the year that Savva had arrived in the country.

Savva had been setting up his own networks at the same time, so it was inevitable that he and Heimo should meet, and when they did, they found they had a lot in common. For the first few years they would see each other every week, starting off with coffee and chess, then as the night wore on Heimo would start refilling their cups with vodka. The chess pieces would sit still and the talking would start. Heimo would talk quite openly about the "Gnomes of Melbourne" but never about his own role in the organisation, and at times Savva felt that if anyone in

Australia had ever come close to suspecting him, it was Heimo Susijarvi.

To Heimo, ASIO was a kindergarten secret service compared to the sophistication of the Finns, Russians and Germans that he had dealt with in his homeland, and he never took it too seriously. "The old boy is playing at young men's games," he would say of ASIO's head, Sir Charles Spry. But Heimo continued to dutifully move around the émigré community, listening and reporting back to the old Victorian mansion in Queens Road, which initially housed ASIO's Melbourne headquarters. He could drink anyone under the table and it was this ability that stood him in such good grace with his masters. While for Heimo it was all a game, the Gnomes thought highly enough of the intelligence he brought them that when they moved from Melbourne to Canberra he accepted a post in counter-intelligence and with it a comfortable house in Rivett – and that, thought Savva Vasilyevich, is where I will find him.

For a change, everything fell into place with ease. The bus to Canberra was on time and Savva felt some relief at being on the move again. A strategy was beginning to form in his mind, but it depended on how his approach to Heimo Susijarvi was received. He felt some trepidation at arriving back in Canberra, but he decided that the Russians were most likely betting on him going directly to Melbourne. He could do nothing yet about the problem of Amelia, in fact, it would be stupid to take the bait the Russians were dangling in front of him, so he pushed it to the back of his mind.

It was early evening by the time the bus pulled into Canberra, and after placing his bags in a luggage locker, Savva searched for the Rivett address in the local phonebook. To his relief Susijarvi was listed. He jotted down the address off Hindmarsh Drive and flagged a taxi.

As they drove through Woden, Savva asked the driver to stop outside a bottleshop. There was no Koskenkorva but he did find a bottle of Finlandia and even though it was not ice cold, he knew it would be welcome. Savva asked the driver to cruise the street slowly as he pretended to look for the house. He had actually seen it on the right as they drove into the street, but he wanted to be sure that nobody had double guessed him. The street looked quiet and sleepy so he paid off the taxi at the far end and walked back.

A modest late-model Japanese car was in the drive, although seeing the locked garage Savva guessed that there was something more sedate inside. A small pine sign to the right of the door proclaimed that the house was named *Viipuri*. Savva rang the bell and waited. It was not Heimo Susijarvi who opened the door but a slim woman with short dark hair.

"Oh, you must want to see my father," she said. "Who shall I say is here?"

Savva hesitated. "Um, tell him it's an old friend from Melbourne . . . I would rather like to surprise him."

"OK." The woman glanced down at the bottle in Savva's hand. "By the way, the doctor says he's supposed to be taking things easy at the moment."

"Of course. It needs to go into the freezer for a few hours anyway."

"Some chance of that, I don't think." Her eyes flashed, but with amusement, not anger. "Come in, you can surprise the old man in person. I'm Aino Richards."

She led the way into a large comfortable lounge room lit by a bright reading lamp over a paper-strewn desk at the far end. Her father rose from his place at the writing desk and turned as they entered. He was a huge man whose one-time strength had given way to an overall thickening in the arms and chest, and his frame now also supported an enormous belly. His cheeks were florid and his glasses appeared to Savva to be even thicker than he remembered, but his hair was the same bleached blond it had always been; just as full and just as untidy.

For a moment the elderly man seemed bemused and squinted in their direction as his eyes adjusted to the dimmer light, but then with recognition came a broad smile.

"You old bastard!" he bellowed, extending his hand. His accent after all his time in Australia was as thick as ever. "Now I know there's no justice, you should have been dead years ago!"

"No," replied Savva. "No, there is no justice."

"Aino! Get some glasses! This is Leon. We came to Australia at around the same time. Leon, this used

43

to be my daughter before she went off and married a poofter doctor."

Savva proffered the bottle. "I'm afraid it's not cold."

Aino was pleased to see her father's delight and despite her earlier warning, took the bottle with a smile. "I'm sure there will be a cold one in the freezer. I'll get the glasses, but I won't join you, I was expected home hours ago."

"She's very good, my girl, comes over every Saturday and puts a big stew in the crock pot." He indicated for Savva to take a seat. "Trouble is, she insists on making a salad as well. Bloody rabbit food! Never did like the stuff. Grew up on bread, meat, potatoes and porridge; bit late to change now."

He eased himself into his chair and sat for a moment, beaming.

"I know you won't have just dropped in out of the blue for old time's sake, but you will eat with me first . . . then we can talk?"

It was the acknowledgment Savva needed. "Of course. You might even bring out the chessboard, that is if you think your brain is still up to it!"

"My brain has a lot less to worry about these days, and that, my friend, leaves more room for cunning, not that I recall you ever winning a game against me in the past. I am sure it was you who dreamed up my favourite handicap?"

"You can play left handed?"

"That's it. It will be my pleasure!"

Aino returned with a frosted bottle of Kosken-korva and two glasses. "Are you the culprit?" she asked Savva. "Every time he finds someone new to play against he brings out that corny old line and expects us all to laugh!"

"I must plead guilty, but it was a long time ago and I thought it might confuse him. It didn't work."

Savva took the glass from her as she composed her face in mock anger and turned to her father.

"Behind the frozen peas, two bottles? I thought you were behaving yourself!"

Both men stood and, as they had done in earlier years, held the glasses at arm's length in a ritual toast.

"*Kippis!*" saluted Heimo, and with a rock steady hand brought the full glass slowly to his lips, then tossed it back in a single gulp.

"*Kippis!*" repeated Savva in Finnish (the only other word of the language he knew was "*sauna*"), and mirrored the older man's actions, feeling the cold fire burn its way down his throat.

Heimo's daughter collected her coat, said farewell and left. The two men sat in silence, listening to her car back out the drive.

"I think," said Heimo, after a time, "that we should have another, just to ease the shock of the first."

For a while the old men talked of Melbourne. Their conversation was threaded with silences; spaces into which the memories could emerge. Eventually Heimo stood up and, wiping the last of the melting ice from the bottle, refilled their glasses to the brim.

"And so," he said, looking straight into Savva's eyes, "What did you really come to see me about?"

Savva tossed the vodka back, using the pause to collect his thoughts.

"How old are you, Heimo?"

"Sixty-eight. Why? Going to offer me a job?"

"Well, maybe I am, in a roundabout way. I take it you've retired from the Gnomes?"

Heimo looked at him, then ambled back to his seat, bottle in hand.

"Yes, a couple of years ago, but they still drag me in from time to time to look at faces in badly focused photographs. You know, it beats me that after all this time they still can't find any bugger who can take a good photo."

"In the early days in Melbourne, you never asked me why I came to Australia. In all those years we always talked about other people, never ourselves. Did you ever wonder about me?"

Savva could feel the older man's eyes staring at him, and for a moment he thought he had made a mistake. Heimo laughed and poured himself another drink.

"Well, I thought you probably worked in the same game as me, just a different team. Israel's maybe . . . but I did a bit of a check and it seems you didn't belong to anyone, so I figured you must be clean. Pity really, had some vague notion of recruiting you, as I remember."

"I would have been flattered," Savva smiled, "but I did have employment; rather long-term employment as it turns out, and now I'm having a few problems."

Heimo laughed and pushed himself out of his chair.

"Come on, I have just the thing for you. There's an old Finnish saying, that if vodka or the sauna can't fix your problems, then the devil take you. We've had the first and the second's been heating for the last hour." He raised a finger to his mouth in a gesture for silence. "I know an accountant who can sort out your superannuation, no problem!"

He led the way out of the house into the Canberra night which was now chilly and drizzling, with mist descending into the tree tops. The back garden was obviously Heimo's pride and joy with a carefully planted clump of silver birches partly obscuring the sauna, the exterior of which was clad in treated pine. Over one end a tangled jasmine displayed a few late flowers. Peeping through the jasmine was a shower nozzle and beneath it a square of old bricks had been set into the grass.

Heimo glanced at the focus of Savva's attention.

"Well, I couldn't afford an ice-covered lake, so the shower's the next best thing. Illegal, of course. Bloody council told me it had to have a regulation drain. I told them it was for watering the lawn. Overhead irrigation."

Savva shuddered. "Only for summer use, I hope." The thought of a freezing cold shower on a night like this was enough to cut through the vodka glow.

"Damn water gets too warm in summer. Much better on a night like this. You'll see."

They entered beneath the jasmine that arched over the door. Behind four canvas-seated chairs and a small table that occupied the middle of the room was a row of hooks holding an assortment of towelling robes and bath towels. A door to the right led to the sauna.

Heimo tossed a towel to Savva and they undressed in silence. The man has aged, Savva thought as he watched Heimo place his spectacles on the top of a small refrigerator by the door. The heavy folds of skin on his breasts hung down like an old woman's bosom, and without his glasses his thick jowls were more apparent. Though apart from the signs of serious drinking in his cheeks, his skin looked a healthy pink.

"Come on," Heimo grunted, swinging the sauna door outward, "this will sort the men from the boys."

The wave of heat was accompanied by the scent of the timber walls. Illumination was provided by a low-powered globe set in behind pine slats, and it took a moment for Savva's eyes to adjust to the dim light. There were two levels of benches and Heimo had seated himself on the top level next to a wooden water bucket and ladle. At his feet was a tin bucket, also filled with water in which a birch switch was soaking.

"Welcome to my sauna, Leon." There was a native pride in the old man's voice. "One hundred degrees centigrade is just warm enough to keep my paranoia about microphones at bay."

"And anyone with a drop of sense." But, Savva reluctantly admitted to himself, it was not as bad as he had anticipated. The combination of heat and high humidity soon had him sweating profusely. They sat in silence for a while, then Heimo turned to him, his face glowing from the heat.

"So, you have been having problems with your employers?"

Savva hesitated. Sweat had started to run from his brow into his eyes, stinging them with the salt.

"Leon," Heimo continued, "I have a particularly old-fashioned code of honour that puts friendship above everything else . . . and in here you can tell me you plan to assassinate the Prime Minister and you have my word that apart from suggesting that it would be a fucking stupid thing to do, I will keep it to myself." He reached down and produced an old plastic jug and after dipping it in the tin bucket poured cold water over his head, then refilled it and offered it to Savva.

The contrast between his skin temperature and that of the water felt extreme but invigorating, so Savva repeated the exercise, washing the sweat from his face. Finally he looked at his old friend.

"Heimo . . . I'm not Jewish, I was never a refugee and my name's not Leon. It's Savva Vasilyevich Golitsyn. I was sent to Australia by what became the KGB."

For a moment Heimo stared at him, then his head rocked back and he laughed until his body began to shake. Savva felt a rush of anger and bewilderment at the old man's obvious delight at the revelation but before he could speak, Heimo had taken the ladle and expertly tossed a scoop of water onto the sauna stones. It vaporised with a loud *hiss*. Savva cringed and quickly covered his face as the steam began to condense on his already over-hot skin.

"Come!" bellowed Heimo, stepping down from the bench and pushing open the door. "Time for a break and a beer." He led the way out and quickly shut the door behind them.

Savva went to sit down, but a firm hand on his shoulder stopped him. He turned quickly; unsure now of the wisdom of having spoken freely for the first time. Heimo was grinning from ear to ear.

"First the cold shower, then the beer."

The water felt like needles, and he lasted under the shower only long enough to spin around once and grab for the towel that Heimo was offering. The warmth of the sauna was obviously deep in his flesh for as he sat down Savva saw that his skin was steaming and pink. He draped his towel loosely over his lap and picked up one of the cans of beer that Heimo had taken from the small fridge.

"I'm sorry," Heimo said. "It was wrong of me to laugh like that . . . It's just that I have been so bored since I retired and I actually felt a rush of adrenaline for a moment. You can miss it, you know. Cheers *tovarich*!" He raised his beer in salute. "So what happened, Savva Vasilyevich? The comrades have ordered you home, and you don't want to go?"

"No, Heimo," he sighed wearily, "the bastards don't want to know me."

They had been in and out of the sauna three times and consumed all the beer in the fridge by the time Savva had completed his story. For his part, Heimo had not said a word other than the occasional "And then?" to urge him on. They dressed in silence and returned to the house and the pot of stew that Aino had prepared.

"There are a few questions," Heimo said after they had eaten. "A few questions and then we will decide how we play this game."

"So you will help?" It was more a statement of relief than a question.

"Help?" Heimo snorted. "You would have to fight me off with a stick!"

He rose and put on a CD at almost full volume, then he retrieved the vodka bottle from its small pool of water on the coffee table. "Who are the bad guys in this scenario? The Russians; and they just happen to be my speciality."

Colonel Victor Ivanovich Danilov followed his instructions to the letter. He ordered Pavel, his driver, to turn the car around and take him, not via the main roads but back through the woods of the *dacha* estate, to rejoin the sealed roads at Profsoyunaya Street. Then, ignoring the smaller than usual demonstration in Manege Square, they made their way directly to the White House. It was a busy time of day and the comings and goings around the parliamentary corridors were a perfect cover. Once through the throng of Presidium members he headed for the basement and along the labyrinth of passages, arriving at a huge steel door. Two plain clothes men stared at him for a moment then opened the door and nodded him in. Danilov made his way through a large hall to the next corridor and into the room at the end.

There were three of them: Andrei Primakov sat at the desk as though he was carved from stone, while the other two stood impassively beside the door. Primakov was a good-looking man in his fifties who usually exuded an air of innocence and compliance that both charmed and disarmed at the same time. Today there was no sign of it. He was tense and pale. Someone's kicked him in the balls, was the thought that crossed Danilov's mind. He glanced at the other two. Neither was in uniform but they were Army. It was written all over them. No introductions took place. After a time Primakov looked up and handed him a file.

"Read it here and give it to my men before you leave. The man described is in Australia, has been for years. We are bringing him home and I want you to make the arrangements."

Primakov rose and loosened his tie.

"Oh, and I have added some other instructions for him in the envelope. I trust you will get this to him and impress upon him the importance of being tidy."

"You want me to go to Australia?"

Primakov had moved to the door but paused before opening it. He looked at Victor Danilov as though in pity but then smiled and shrugged.

"That shouldn't be necessary. The Chechen *pradavyet* in the embassy works for us. He can be instructed. Now I must get back to Parliament while we still have one."

As the door closed behind him one of the Army men moved to it and stood guard while the other sat on the arm of the chair. He removed a pack of genuine American cigarettes from his jacket and expertly flipped one to Danilov who accepted the light and gratefully inhaled the smoke, having yet again forgotten his doctor's advice.

It was strange, he thought as he opened the file, that they would bother bringing this old fool back. Better to arrange an accident and save themselves the trouble. He would have to be taken care of sooner or later anyway.

For a moment he looked at the face in the yellowed photo, wondering what kind of life had led to this. The young man looked thin but alert. It was a rural scene; autumn or spring, a little snow and bare trees. Whatever the weather he was hardly dressed for it. He wore a shirt and baggy trousers, but no coat, scarf or gloves. He was standing beside two other people but their heads had been clipped inexpertly from the print. Altogether, it was not going to be of much use. The man would be old and changed. He hoped the file was a little more up to date.

Something was wrong. It was the name. There had been a mistake. The name on the file read "Nikolai Nikolayevich Trinkovski", known as "Jack Zinner". The name Primakov mentioned on the phone was "Golitsyn". Danilov quickly opened the attached envelope and his expression changed. The beginnings of a smile strengthened into the real thing. He took the vacant chair and this time when he read, he did so slowly and carefully.

CHAPTER

SIX

WORDS gradually filtered into Savva's brain. He had fallen asleep waiting for Heimo to make coffee and something else to eat. They had demolished the stew a long time ago. It was late, very late and the combination of sauna, food and vodka had relaxed him to the point of oblivion. His head had been floating away . . . somewhere. But he surfaced and blinked like a mole in sunlight. He corrected what the Finn had been attempting to say.

"*You and I stopped at midnight on the steppe. No returning. No looking back.* It's Aleksandr Blok and your Russian is bloody dreadful!"

"Maybe, but the sentiment is right," Heimo said. "We can only go forward."

He replaced a CD that had been spinning endlessly on "repeat". The sound of woeful Finnish accordion music surrounded them as he sat and pushed a plate of bread rolls across the coffee table to Savva.

"Eat, they're *pulla*, Finnish rolls, they will soak up the vodka."

Savva sipped the coffee and struggled through a bread roll. Whatever else the microwave treatment had done, it had not cured the roll of a frozen heart. Heimo, used to his own kitchen's limitations, broke the bread and dunked it in his cup.

"But before we go forward we need to go over a few things." Heimo looked at Savva, then, deciding he was now fully awake, pressed on. "You went to the embassy. You told them you wanted to go home. Their claim that they had no record of you would only be a slight problem, if it were true. I don't believe them. It would be understandable if they were having trouble finding records. They would then have said, 'Come back tomorrow and we will see what we can find.' But they didn't. You are sure they were adamant about that?"

"Positive. I didn't exist as far as they were concerned."

"Then they are not telling the truth. For a start, I believe you. Second, it's all too quick. How did they know which synagogue you went to?"

Savva swallowed the last piece of his roll. "I told them, but –"

"But you didn't tell them about Amelia Lippmann."

"No."

Heimo took off his glasses and rubbed his eyes; a stalling gesture, thinking time, Savva remembered it from their Melbourne days. He anticipated the other man's next thought.

"And they wouldn't have found out about my relationship with her from the synagogue records. I was very discreet with Amelia . . . more for her sake really. I'm an older man, you know what the gossip can be like."

"Then," Heimo placed his glasses back and peered at him, "either they have been keeping very good track of you for a long time, or we have missed something. They probably ransacked the synagogue as a message to you, banking on the guess that you would ring your friend. Both messages got through so we are not dealing with bureaucratic bungling, missing files, or anything like that. And they don't go to this sort of trouble for no reason. What have you been involved with that makes you so important?"

"Nothing."

It was true. Years of waiting. Years of watching from the sidelines. It didn't seem to make sense. If he had done something, anything – but he hadn't and there was a growing feeling in his stomach; a sickness, at the thought that he was overlooking something simple that would make it all fit together.

"Nothing," he repeated.

"Then sleep in the spare room tonight and forget about it for a while. In the morning I'll get onto the scandal merchants."

"In Melbourne?"

"No." The Finn laughed. "No, no ... the Melbourne scandal merchants were kindergarten; here we have the best, all graduates."

The morning had retreated to make way for the afternoon before Savva awoke to the smell of stewed coffee. The house was empty but sitting beside the coffee pot and its bitter remains was a note informing him that Heimo had been up and out since early morning. He sniffed at the coffee before consigning it to the drain and, feeling like an intruder, padded his way around the house looking for the shower. The house was like a shrine to Heimo's home country; Finnish bric-a-brac was everywhere. It didn't take a linguist to translate the needlepoint above the phone – in any language it would have to be "Home, sweet home".

The bathroom was lined with pine and in the shower recess were the obligatory tar soap and shampoo. They were brand new. The Imperial Leather soap was the one being used and the open shampoo and conditioner boasted only "Scandinavian herbs and essences"; not a trace of tar was even hinted at.

By the time he had made fresh coffee and tricked the microwave into properly defrosting one of the frozen rolls, Savva was feeling much better. He had, surprisingly, no sign of a hangover despite the empty vodka bottle sitting on the sink. The thought of betrayal crossed his mind but it faded as he recalled Heimo's reaction to his story. No, he was safe, at least for the moment. The worst thing was that he didn't really know what it was he was safe from.

A car turned into the drive and he heard the garage door close. Heimo came in looking tired but satisfied.

"I have been doing some, what do they call it these days, 'networking'? And I had a stroke of luck. Thank God there is still a little *glasnost* left," he said, enjoying the moment. He poured himself some coffee with the air of a magician about to pull a rabbit from a hat. Without pausing, he swept up the sugar bowl and a spoon and headed for the lounge room. The accordion music of the night before was recycled and they sat again around the coffee table.

"Do you know who Koshlykov was?"

Heimo stirred his coffee slowly. The name was familiar to Savva but it took a moment or two for it to surface.

"Wasn't he the KGB man at the embassy in the early eighties?"

"Lev Sergeevich. Trained at the old Yasenevo, speaks Swedish and English so was a natural for the

Third Department of the First Chief Directorate. Bright man, from what I remember he graduated from the Moscow State Institute for Public Relations. He was the Canberra Resident for about six or seven years. It turns out he is in town, not for anything illegal that I know of, just some sort of travel perk he has worked for himself. The new Russia has opened up a lot of opportunities. Anyway, we met at the gallery for a chat."

The old Finn drained his coffee with a look of smug satisfaction.

"He knew all about you. In fact, he said you were the talk of the embassy. The official verdict is that you are a migrant loony who has lost his marbles."

"But?"

"But why would they be talking openly about something like this? Simple. They truly don't take it seriously. And the second 'but' is why wreck the synagogue and wait at Amelia's house for you to telephone?"

Savva nodded. "It doesn't make sense."

"From the embassy's point of view it does," Heimo replied, "if they didn't do it."

Savva was lost. It certainly didn't make sense to him and he was beginning to become irritated by Heimo's flippancy.

"No! It doesn't make any sense at all to me. I recognised the voice of the young *pradavyet.*"

Heimo heaved himself from the chair and turned the music off, ejected the CD and took another from an outlandish pink CD tower. This time it was Sibelius.

"The *pradavyet*," said Heimo, returning to his seat, "was, as you told me, a Chechen. How many Chechens have you heard of that made it big in the old KGB or especially, in the new MBR? And, given the latest troubles in Chechenya, his career is probably on the same par as real estate in Grozny. What kind of future do you think he has to look forward to?"

"I have no idea," Savva said. "Remember, I've effectively been an Australian for decades."

"Chechens, Kalmyks, Ingushi, Tartars, none of them get past first base. Even the Balts; the Estonians, Latvians and Lithuanians, when they were part of the old union, had a hard job proving their loyalty." Heimo paused and smiled. "But the Finns? Well, who do you think designed the original Yasenevo head-quarters?"

"The *pradavyet*?" Savva interrupted. "What about him?"

"Imran Talebov. He took some leave, quite suddenly it seems. According to my friends he's in Perth. An affair of the heart, was what they called it. He visits there quite often."

"But he was in Melbourne."

"He covered his tracks well. It would seem that his masters aren't his masters. It may be more difficult to find out who he's really working for."

The music faded away into a misty tone poem, bleak and cold. As if to echo the feeling, Savva

Vasilyevich noticed that outside the sky was covered in drizzle.

The *pradavyet* had been extremely lucky. He had waited for several hours outside Amelia Lippmann's house wondering what to do next. The day after his visit to the synagogue he had rested. It had not been a fruitless night as it turned out, because, although the records showed little about Leon Silbert, the note from the secretary about his connection with Amelia Lippmann had been all he needed. And to top it off, his trashing of the building had made the papers in the way he intended.

His luck had continued first thing on Friday morning. He had watched as the tall blond woman walked to her car. Then he timed his move to coincide with her backing from the drive, and as she had turned to look over her shoulder at the oncoming traffic, he tapped on the window.

The surprise gave him the advantage. The *pradavyet* flashed his Federal Police credentials at her as she began to wind down the window and was rewarded with an uncomprehending look.

"Sorry to disturb you, Mrs Lippmann. I believe you know a Mr Leon Silbert?"

"Yes. Why, what's happened?"

He kept the advantage; took his time, tucked the ID away and leant down to the pale face in the car.

"Oh no, Mrs Lippmann, nothing's wrong. It's just a routine inquiry. Mr Silbert has sold his house and there are a few questions I need to ask him. I wonder, when would it be convenient to have a chat to you? It doesn't have to be now, it's not urgent." He kept his voice friendly, reassuring.

"Sold his house? He didn't tell me that."

"I suspect there is quite a lot he hasn't told you, Mrs Lippmann."

"Look, could we talk on Monday? It's just that I've had a hell of a week, and I'm taking the day off to have a long weekend on the Mornington Peninsula."

"No problem at all. I'll give you a ring on Monday evening and arrange a time for Tuesday. Sorry to bother you."

Amelia, still looking pale and shaken, had simply nodded and reversed out onto the road. As he ambled back to his car, he smiled to himself.

"Have a nice weekend, Mrs Lippmann."

For a few minutes he had sat in the car and watched the traffic, then he drove into her driveway. The open approach was always so much less suspicious. The gate to the side of the house was unlocked and with the relative security of a high fence to his back, it had taken him less than a minute to ease open a window catch and climb in. So when Savva had rung the following day, he was waiting. Within two hours he had been at the airport and on his way to Perth for the rest of his short holiday.

CHAPTER

SEVEN

S AVVA was desperate to go to Melbourne to see
Amelia but he held himself back. There was
nothing to be gained by walking into what
might be a trap, and he certainly had no idea yet of
what the rules of the game were, let alone the
motivation of the Chechen *pradavyet* who seemed to
be playing a solo role.

Several times on the Sunday he had rung Amelia's
house but there was no answer, and according to a
friend of Heimo's, who was kind enough to do a
drive past, there was no car in the driveway. Amelia
would have to wait. In the meantime, Savva and
Heimo had collected his luggage from the locker at

the bus depot and returned to the house in Rivett to go over and over the few options that they could come up with.

Only one thing was clear, and that was Savva's determination to return to Russia. He could, of course, simply purchase a ticket to Moscow or St Petersburg using his Australian passport, hoping that the name Leon Silbert had not been fed into the computers at all Russian entry points. That seemed the most risky strategy, and if he did make it into Russia, what then? Savva felt confident that with his financial assets he could buy himself a new identity and blend into the landscape.

Heimo would have none of it. He was a cautious man and he also had a distinct advantage over Savva. He had been to Moscow and knew how much things had changed even in the last few years, let alone the decades that Savva had been away. There was something, too, about Savva's reception at the embassy that stunk to high heaven. A *pradavyet* didn't act without orders from somewhere and if he was not part of the regular security establishment, where were his orders coming from? Imran Talebov was an enigma.

For a while the two men hunched over a game of chess while teasing out the problems confronting Savva. After several hours they had decided against going in through one of the Baltic states. It had been Heimo's idea originally to try Estonia because of his familiarity with the language, but again they came up against the Russian border and the possibility that Savva/Leon was listed as unwelcome in the country. Latvia and Lithuania were even more difficult and so, in the end, an illegal entry seemed the only possibility.

It was after a sauna on Monday evening, as Heimo fished at the back of the freezer for another bottle of vodka, that the idea came to him.

"*Voi perkele satana!* Of course! You go back the way you came out!"

He slammed the bottle down on the table, then left the room. Savva was startled. He had never seen his friend so excited.

"Through Finland? Is that what you mean?" Savva took one of the small shot glasses, filled it and followed Heimo who had vanished into his bedroom. For a moment he thought the old Finn had gone slightly crazy for he was taking book after book from shelves beside his bed and, holding them by the spine, was shaking them. Eventually he was rewarded as a torn piece of a newspaper fluttered to the floor.

"I have a memory like a bear trap!" he exclaimed. "Have a look." He took the proffered glass of vodka and swallowed it in a single mouthful. "I knew it was there somewhere!"

Savva bent down and retrieved the yellowed scrap from the carpet. It was a faded cartoon from what, by the Cyrillic script, was obviously a Russian newspaper. To the left of the picture was a train with Finnish flags flying over the steam engine. To the right was a Russian bottle shop with a window full of vodka bottles. Between the train and the shop a line of Finns were turning into pigs.

"Helsinki–Leningrad, as it was in those days; every weekend! Not a problem!" Heimo was exultant. "Every weekend a trainload of Finns makes the trip to buy cheap vodka. It's simple, easy; you become a Finn . . . and best of all *mun poika . . .*" He lapsed into Finnish for the second time that evening. "Best of all my boy! I can come with you."

"Sure Heimo, and between now and then I'll just apply for a change of citizenship and learn the language." Savva Vasilyevich returned to the lounge room and sat looking at the bottle of vodka.

"Don't be an idiot, Leon . . . sorry, Savva. I can fix a passport for you and there's no need for language. You can be dumb!" Heimo stood beaming from the doorway. "I can use *viittomakieli*, sign language."

"Sign language? You're crazy! Nobody in their right mind would believe us."

"And why not? Your lack of speech would be on your passport as a distinguishing feature. We Finns are known for our silence . . . yours would be the same, but more so!"

The older man's confidence and laughter was infectious and Savva found himself reaching for the vodka. He drank, then refilled both glasses.

"Well, Heimo, I may not be able to talk but I'll have some signs for you that will be clear in any language!" He smiled at his friend and sat back in the chair, feeling the alcohol work its way through his system. "I suppose it might work. The security in Petersburg wouldn't be very tight for the Finns and one getting lost would probably be pretty normal. They would expect him to turn up in a couple of days after he sobered up. Yes, it could work."

"Do you know your way about the city?"

Savva was quiet for a moment thinking back through the years to his time there. Probably it had changed a lot. My outdated Russian will stand out as well, he thought, but I can pass myself off as some sort of dissident returned from a labour camp. That would explain why I was out of touch, may even give me a sympathetic edge if I need it.

"Do you know the city?" repeated Heimo.

"Yes . . . well sort of. As I told you, I spent some of my time there in the *dom vashen*. I suppose I could find my way around if it hasn't changed too much or been pulled down."

Heimo poured a third vodka for them and taking a notebook from the pocket of his jacket, started thumbing through it.

"I'll organise some passport photos to be shot here. No point in taking risks even at this stage, and I'll get the place swept in the morning, just in case."

"Swept? Here? But you're retired. I thought you were even a bit paranoid the other night, you know, only talking in the sauna or while you had music playing. That sort of thing went out of fashion years ago."

"You think so? Wait a moment, I'll show you something." He went to the study and returned with two small professional bugs in his hand. "The grey one is Israeli and the other . . . well, the Yarralumla cowboys say it's from China."

"But?"

"I would say it was made in Taiwan, and I would bet any money that it was one of ours planted just to make sure that the old man was playing by the rules and not inviting mad Russians around for a little on the side."

Savva put the bugs down on the table. "But that was before you retired, right?"

Heimo shrugged. "Well I still get the place swept from time to time, though I'm sure Maxy, he's my friendly non-aligned sweeper, I'm sure Maxy thinks I'm mad." He sipped the last of the vodka in his glass and put it back on the table with a contented sigh. "I've employed Maxy for years, in a private capacity, even when I was with the Gnomes . . . to keep them honest. They would send a department sweeper once a month and then Maxy would come the next day and remove their bug and put it in the spare room. That way they would hear a bit of noise occasionally but nothing of consequence. Well, apart from the nights Aino had her boyfriends stay over that is, and then we would replace it in its original position before the department sweeper came again. They never worked out why my house was so quiet!"

He laughed, suddenly remembering something. "Years ago when Sirpa was still alive and Aino was a teenager, oh it must have been just after we moved

69

here. Yes, the first year. We had a cleaning lady come in once a week to give Sirpa a hand; she was pretty sick, even then . . ." He paused, his smile fading for a moment with the pain of the memory. Then the grin returned. "It was one of the days we had the builder and his mate working on the sauna; couple of rough lads. The younger one had hair down to his bum in a pigtail . . . anyway, the cleaning lady let the department sweeper in and he's tip-toeing around the house like a bloody fairy in a suit, headphones on and magic wand waving in front going 'beep . . . beep . . . beep'."

"Well, the lads had never seen anything like this, and they are following him around trying to work out what the hell he's doing, and the cleaning lady is following them trying to get them off her clean floor. Now, Aino is in the kitchen with her boyfriend of the week and I come out of the bathroom wrapped in a towel and see this poor ghostbuster, blind as a mole to what's going on behind him. Suddenly he sees Aino and lover-boy in the kitchen and attempts to be subtle and back out without being noticed, when he trips over the builder's mate and falls on top of him. Laugh? I nearly wet myself! The department sent someone else the following month and I never saw the idiot again!"

Heimo collapsed into laughter, reached for the bottle but changed his mind.

"Enough is enough. Tomorrow I'll organise the passport; tonight I'll sleep. Why don't you give your

Melbourne friend a ring? I'm sure she'll be home now."

Heimo wandered off to the bathroom; hands out in front like antennae and every now and then saying, "Beep . . . beep . . . beep."

Savva watched him go, then went to the phone in the kitchen. He dialled and to his relief it was answered after the second ring.

"Hello, Amelia."

"You bastard!" Her voice down the phone was harder and colder than he had ever heard it before.

"You've got a nerve. Did you think you could pay me off? You didn't tell me you had sold your house. One day everything is sweetness and light and then this? What the hell do you think you're playing at?" She didn't pause for an answer. "Of course, I would never have known about the house if the man from the Federal Police hadn't mentioned it. Now tell me where the hell you are so I can send your bloody money back to you."

"Federal Police?" Savva felt a cold shiver go up his spine. No, he thought, it couldn't be. There was no possible way that the Federal Police could be involved. He took a breath and calmed his heart down.

"Amelia, I can explain about the other things. Please just give me –"

But she wasn't about to start listening now. "Do you know what I've been through over the last few days? Do you know what it feels like being dumped

71

so bloody quickly? No explanation . . . no nothing, Leon! I couldn't reach you at home, you had sold the place. Why, Leon? After all, don't I have a right to know . . . or have you been fooling me all along? How many other young widows have you been screwing? Now you've moved in with one, I suppose. Well I hope you will be fucking happy!"

The phone clicked, but Savva could imagine the force with which it went down. He waited for a moment and rang again. It rang until it rang out. He went back to the lounge, poured himself a final vodka and sat looking at the faded old cartoon, trying to imagine himself turning into a pig. It shouldn't be too hard, he thought, I'm halfway there already, and as for being dumb, that was looking more attractive by the second.

CHAPTER

EIGHT

IMRAN TALEBOV devoted most of Sunday to the beach. He liked the sun. His naturally dark skin deepened very quickly, and though it was the coldest time of the year in Perth, he spent every spare moment out on the North Cottesloe beach. Not working on my tan, he smiled to himself, but my alibi. He had few calls on his time. His girlfriend, who thought he was a Polish importer, only saw him occasionally but after a couple of satisfying hours in his room at the Radisson, she enjoyed accompanying him to the beach or the North Cott Cafe.

It was here that his contact found him. Imran and his girlfriend were picking their way through the remains of a salad when the man walked in and sat at a table on the opposite side of the cafe. Imran glanced at him as the man took out a mobile phone and made a call. A moment later one of the young waiters came to get him. The phone call, as expected, was for him.

When he returned, he apologised to his girlfriend and, giving her the key to his room, suggested, with a grin, that she go back and wait for him while he attended to business. She smiled and left.

Talebov paid for their meal and sauntered out and down the steps onto the beach. It was a perfect winter's day. Languid swells broke over the few brave swimmers, then onto the sand. Out to sea past the freighters waiting in Gage Road to dock in Fremantle, Rottnest Island could just be made out; a strip on the horizon.

"Imran! Good to see you again, man. Howzit?" There was no disguising the accent, it was pure Johannesburg.

"Just fine. Good to be out of Canberra at this time of the year. Shall we walk for a while?"

Talebov glanced around. Nobody appeared to be watching. Even if they were, so what, all they would see were a couple of old friends strolling along the beach.

Half an hour later he was back in the hotel explaining to his girlfriend that something had come up and he had to fly back east. There was still some time though, he explained to her as he took off his clothes, and without any preamble, entered her.

Later he saw her off in a cab and took the next one himself. He was not leaving until the morning and in the meantime there was work to be done.

Tuesday morning Heimo was up and had them both out of the house at an hour that Savva felt was far too early. Heimo's demand for security precautions was also annoying Savva but he swallowed his objections and indulged his friend. They drove the old Rover 90 to a phone box in an adjoining suburb from where Heimo contacted Maxy, who apparently leapt at the opportunity to practise his craft, even if it promised to be a futile exercise. The next call was to another tame expert, this time a photographer, who agreed to come within the hour.

They stopped at the corner shop to pick up the papers and some milk and bread and found Aino swearing at her car. She saw Heimo and came over.

"Bloody battery! Sorry Dad, but this is the second time this month. Everyone jokes about how doctors earn so much money, but I can tell you, I can't afford to shell out on a new battery every couple of weeks. I have a bloody good mind to –" She paused mid-sentence as she realised there was somebody else in her father's car. "Oh hello, Mr Silbert. I'm glad to see Dad hasn't drunk you to death yet!"

"Hello, Aino," he said, grinning. "No, I'm surviving."

"Leave the car, *kulta*. I'll give you a lift home and Mark can come and pick it up later."

"Not bloody likely!" she snapped. "He was supposed to make sure it was fixed last time. So I called from the shop and he's on his way now in a taxi with a spare battery. I'll wait and make sure he does it properly. And if it's not the battery . . . well I figure it's the alternator. I think I can replace it, but I'll ring you later if I need a hand. Thanks for the offer, though."

"You're a real dragon at times, Aino! I can't begin to think where you inherited that from." Heimo turned back to Savva with mischief written all over his face. "You should see the way she treats her husband!" He laughed and went off to do the shopping.

"My husband," said Aino, "may be a good GP, but he is the world's biggest wimp when it comes to cars. He couldn't change a tyre before he met me. Mind you, I soon showed him."

Savva could well believe it. The young woman leaning against her disabled car looked not only very sure of herself, but extremely fit. He vaguely remembered her father saying that she had been a top-class athlete of some sort. A javelin thrower, was that it? Her short cropped hair was jet black, which Savva had always thought unusual for a Finn, but her mother, Sirpa, had also been dark haired. Heimo had once explained that Finns were naturally dark and that it was only the centuries of domination by the Swedes that had introduced the blond gene.

Savva got out of the car and walked around to join her, leaning on the door, soaking up the meagre ration of sunlight.

"The first time I heard about you," he said, "you were a rebellious teenager who wanted to become a tour guide in Africa."

"I never got there." She laughed. "The nearest I came to it was working on one of the Free Mandela committees."

"So what did you do?"

"I went to the ANU and did two years of chemistry, then met this hopeless but lovable husband of mine. We actually met in Finland. I was visiting the relatives and he was a backpacker I gave a lift to. Typical Mark! It was winter, I was cross-country skiing and came across him on the side of the road waiting for a bus that wasn't scheduled to arrive until a weekday. He tried to say something to me in Finnish out of a phrase book. I let him go on for a while, then asked him if he spoke English. You should have seen his face when he heard my accent! I explained that it was Saturday and unless he wanted to freeze to death he could follow me back to my car. I skied and he floundered!"

"So you married him? Wasn't that a bit extreme?" chuckled Savva, warming to her. "Couldn't you have just given him a lift and left it at that?"

"What? And ruin a great dinner-party story? You know what it's like when you're sitting round and people say 'And where did you two meet?' Knocks them dead every time. If there are also some people we know at the table you can hear a collective groan as soon as the question is asked. They must have heard it a million times."

"Do you go back to Finland very often?"

"Not as often as I'd like. I try to get there every winter when I can, but Mark's work has made it more difficult."

"Why winter? I would have thought you would be too used to the Australian warmth to like that much."

"Ah, but I have this secret passion for biathlon. They have these great events where you ski over a twenty-kilometre course and stop four times for target shooting. I'm a bit old to be really competitive, but there are lots of other women doing it these days and we always have a fantastic time together . . . but, as I said, Mark's work . . ."

Heimo returned with what looked like enough supplies for a month.

"I hate shopping. I buy everything in sight so that I don't have to come back for a while." Heimo said as he loaded the bags into the back of the Rover. "Will you be right with your car? I don't want to abandon you."

"I'll be fine. If not I might borrow yours later."

Aino waved them off and went back to wait for the battery.

They turned into Heimo's street to find a car parked in the drive and an emaciated elderly man equipped with a bag and tripod camped on the doorstep. Heimo parked the Rover in the street, then led the photographer into the house, leaving Savva Vasilyevich to struggle with the shopping bags.

The photographer was a thin, old man with grey hair and sunken eyes; his skin was pale and stretched, giving him the appearance of a negative, more at home in the darkroom than the real world. But, thought Savva, he was an old-school professional. He hadn't asked for introductions or said anything other than "Still now" for the entire time. God knows where Heimo had dragged him up from.

In Savva's opinion, the man seemed to be taking an inordinate number of photographs.

"You never know when we might need them," Heimo said when Savva complained that he was fed up with posing. "And as for posing, you had better get used to it, for this new you is a role we may have to play for weeks on end."

At the end of the session the photographer quietly packed up his equipment, nodded at Heimo and left.

The instructions given to Imran Talebov on the beach in Western Australia had acted like an injection of a powerful stimulant. His loyalty had never been in doubt, but his superiors in Moscow had organised his attachment to the embassy in Canberra, and as far as the *pradavyet* was concerned, that was only one step above Siberia. Now though, he had a chance to show them his true worth. He was also a man who worked best running on adrenaline. At such times his mind sharpened, his nerves became rock steady and his resolve strengthened.

There was, he thought, something exhilarating about the breadth of the organisation's contacts. The small boy that still lurked inside him thrilled at the thought of what he was about to unleash. Certainly he remained only a tiny cog in the greater machine, but he would be noticed. The South African contact had been very precise. The "when" and the "where" of his next few moves had been plotted by strategists who were working on a much larger matrix, and Imran was not about to let them down.

Late Sunday evening he took possession of the plastic explosive. Early Monday morning he picked up the parts of the stripped-down rifle and telescopic sight and, as a back-up, a SIG Sauer P230 handgun and custom-made silencer. He changed his return flight and took the next plane to Sydney; the weapons and explosives shielded and unchecked in his diplomatic bag.

In Sydney he called on a man who was not expecting a visitor. The man was very frightened. Like Savva Golitsyn, he had been in the country a long time. Unlike Savva, he had not been thinking of going home quite yet. Monday evening that all changed. He looked in amazement at the new Russian passport and the blank space waiting for his photograph. The equipment and method of inserting and embossing the photograph with the official stamp was extremely simple, but he asked Imran to go over it several times.

Imran watched the man's hands shake as he held the passport. I hope, he thought, that the people in Moscow know what they are doing. After all, although according to his dossier this man had once been a very effective killer, it was a long time since he had been trained. The man slumped down into a chair; his head in his hands. Eventually Jack Zinner realised it would not all suddenly go away.

"A real passport," he said to nobody in particular. "And in my real name. Amazing!"

The *pradavyet* beamed and clapped him on the back. "Yes, it's all true Nikolai Nikolayevich, you are finally going home."

"Just like that?"

Imran saw the doubt creep back into the man's face. Time for the sting in the tail, he thought.

"There is one last job we would ask you to do." He switched to English. "I have an airline ticket for you to Canberra, and some other equipment and instructions."

As Nikolai Nikolayevich Trinkovski watched the *pradavyet* leave he thought, not for the last time, that he would rather the man had never come; being "Jack Zinner" had been somehow easier.

Maxy the "sweeper" didn't make it round to Rivett until late on Tuesday afternoon. He was nothing like Savva's image of an electronics expert; in fact, he came across as an eccentric. He must have been about Heimo's age, in his late sixties, and in spite of the cold and damp mist that had again settled on Canberra, he was wearing baggy shorts and a T-shirt. His one concession to the climate was a duffle coat which looked as though it had first seen service in the CND demonstrations of the 1960s.

Unlike the silence of the photographer, Maxy was garrulous in the extreme. Nothing seemed to stop him talking, not even the deadly looking cheroot that was clenched, unlit, between yellowed teeth. It appeared to be a permanent fixture.

But silence did come when he put his equipment to work. He pulled on a pair of battered headphones, swung his little magic box over his shoulder and plugged in what looked like a homemade TV antenna. With great thoroughness he worked his way from the front door, detoured into the kitchen, toilet, bathroom, bedrooms and finally into the lounge. For a while he hovered around Heimo's desk, removed the batteries from a small radio, shrugged and moved on. The two men watching saw him stop the moment he found the bug.

Maxy's body stiffened and what seemed like a perpetual stoop vanished. He quietly placed his equipment on the coffee table and went to the stereo. The Sibelius CD was still in the player and within moments the Karelia Suite was filling the room.

"I'll make some coffee," Heimo said, nodding at Maxy.

"Yeah! Great idea!" He paused and looked at Savva, gesturing for him to start talking. "You'd like coffee wouldn't you, er, Tom?" He grinned broadly at his own cleverness at inventing a name on the spot.

"Of course. I haven't had a cup all day."

"So how was the trip to Adelaide?" asked Heimo. "I haven't been there in years."

Neither have I, thought Savva, but that didn't stop him. For the next five minutes he recalled everything he could about the last Grand Prix that had been held there before it moved to Victoria. While the two of them chattered on, Maxy began to examine the curtain over the window to the street. The curtain was in two sections, meeting in the middle of a large central pane of glass. At either end of it were windows that opened only as far as a flyscreen.

Silently, Maxý pointed to the screen. At some time fairly recently it had been levered open, and then the light aluminium frame had been pushed back into place. Maxy gently opened the curtain while gesturing to them to keep talking.

The phone rang.

For a second everyone stiffened.

"Hang on," Heimo said, "I'll just get the phone."

He walked to the kitchen as Maxy backed away from the curtain and sat on the couch.

"So you like Adelaide then?" But he continued before Savva had time to answer, "Yeah, she's a great place. I like to get away from the city though, you know, up to the hills. Jeez they got some great nosheries in the hills. Me and the missus spent a month on holiday there and I reckon we ate out every second night and never went back to the same place twice. Never a crook one, though. One place did this thing with flowers, zucchini flowers, yeah, that was them. Anyway, they fried them in a real thin batter and you ate them just like that. Turned me nose up when I saw them. Missus wouldn't even try them. But good? Bloody oath, they were the best bloody tucker I've had in ages. You know, I tried four or five times to do them at home . . . never got it right. Silly really, growin' those flowers for bloody weeks and then stuffin' it up in five minutes in the pan."

Heimo came back into the room.

"Well," Maxy went on, "I reckon you oughta show me this sauna thing of yours." He tongued the cheroot from one side of his mouth to the other in a fluid movement, then rose and led the men out to the back of the house where he paused to turn on the shower beside the sauna.

"You've got a little nasty in your curtain, Heimo." His voice was quiet and serious now. "It looks like any one of a dozen Asian numbers. It's pinned into the fold in the curtain and has its little transmitting tail about five centimetres down the fold. Very professional little number. Custom made, same colour as your curtains. Point is, what do you want to do with it?" He didn't wait for an answer. "If we remove it, the offending party will be wise that we are wise to him. If we leave it, you have to play silly buggers in your own house, so what do you want?"

Heimo thought for a moment.

"I think I would like to have a sauna . . . look, could we do what we did in the old days?"

"Move it to the spare room?" Maxy thought for a moment. "Yeah, why not?" He turned to Savva. "You dossin' down there?"

Savva nodded.

"Well, all right. A bit of noise would be a good thing, just don't talk in your sleep. OK, the spare room it is. You blokes might as well go ahead and get your sweatbox heated up and so on because this is going to take a while, and I'd rather do it without any other noises around. The little bugger is actually sewn in somehow so I'll need to be a bit careful. I'll let you know when I've got it done."

Heimo turned on the sauna and also a small heater in the change room. While they waited for the sauna to warm up they sat around the heater and worked their way through the possible candidates who might want to listen in to Heimo's conversations and what those conversations might have been. Not knowing how long the bug had been there was the biggest stumbling block. One thing was certain though, and that was that it had been placed in position well before Savva had arrived, so it had nothing to do with their present plans. Though it could complicate them.

Eventually, after they had drunk the remaining beers in the fridge, the sauna was ready. Savva had not realised just how stressed he had been by the events of the last few days until he felt the tension begin to melt away in the sauna. As his body went into defence mode, his muscles relaxed and with every shot of water on the stones he felt less able to concentrate on the problems surrounding him. He gave in to the relaxation and nearly an hour later, as they were getting dressed, he had to admit to himself that he had not felt so good in years.

Maxy popped his head out of the back door.

"Sorry I took so long, Heimo. Bit of a bugger to unstitch!" he called. "I'm shooting through now. Catch you later."

He waved and disappeared through the house.

Somewhere in the next minute Savva Vasilyevich lost track of time.

The explosion in the street silhouetted the house with a sheet of flame. Then came the noise. Savva had never seen Heimo move so fast. The old man was around the side of the house and through the front gate before Savva realised what had happened. When he reached the front yard he stopped. The Rover, which had been left out on the street, was now stopped about six metres down the road; a burning frame, distorted like some macabre pyrotechnic sculpture. Whoever had been seated behind where the wheel had been, was now only a ghastly dark spot. What parts of the body that had not been blown apart in the explosion were melted into the seat.

Savva instantly assumed that Maxy was dead. But then he saw him, unlit cheroot still in place, crouched beside the bumper of his car, clutching his bag of instruments. For a moment Savva thought that Heimo had not seen Maxy.

"Maxy's OK," he called, but realised that was not what had stopped Heimo.

"It's Aino."

In the light of the burning car Savva could see the tears running down the old man's cheeks. His glasses were now in his hands in what looked like an attempt to render himself blind to the scene in front of him. He was struggling to get the words out.

"It was her on the phone. They couldn't get her car going and she rang to see if she could borrow mine. She had her own set of keys. I said to just pick it up."

There was a dreadful stillness, then as the neighbours began to gather around something in Heimo snapped.

"Maxy! Take my friend away." He turned to Savva. "I'll contact you through Maxy. Quick, get going before the police come."

Savva, feeling totally inadequate, gave Heimo a quick pat on the shoulder and ran after Maxy who was already starting up his car. He got in the old Renault and as they drove off, into his mind was burned the image of Heimo sinking down to sit in the gutter.

"Who was in the car?" Maxy asked. "The old man's daughter?"

"Yes." Savva could hardly speak. A cold wave of nausea engulfed him and his mind and vision felt all wrong. He gulped in a huge lung full of air. "Aino Richards . . . she came to borrow the car."

"Poor bastard," mumbled Maxy as he swung off the highway into a suburban street. "All those years playing the game and not so much as a brick through his window. Retired . . . and now this." He turned into a quiet side street and U-turned back the way they had come before switching off the lights and motor.

"I think it was intended for me," Savva said. "It doesn't make sense otherwise."

Maxy just looked ahead, both hands firmly gripping the wheel.

"I mean," he continued, "it certainly wasn't Aino they were after and I am sure Heimo was well out of it."

For a while they sat in silence, then Maxy switched on the engine.

"No little dickybirds on our tail. Safe to go." He drove back to the motorway. "Time to get you into a hot bath and then bed I think, mate. You've had a bit of a shock."

"Yes, I feel bloody lousy."

"Only natural." Maxy glanced across at him. "What am I goin' to call you? Might be good to have a name if we have to spend a bit of time together."

"What was it back at the house? Tom? That will do."

"OK, Tom it is."

Savva smiled at Maxy. "Seems a bit silly all this stuff –"

"Not silly, mate," Maxy interrupted. "Just like that fuckin' bomb wasn't silly."

For a long while after the last of the Federal Police had left, Heimo lay motionless on his bed. Outside he could still hear the forensic crew searching through the wreckage and every now and then the bedroom blinds were illuminated by the flash from the photographer's camera.

The old man didn't feel angry, sad or bitter; he didn't feel anything. In shock, his mind had taken itself into some inner emptiness. It was a space vaguely remembered from the death of his wife, Sirpa, but from which he knew he must rouse himself. In a moment he must get up, he thought, and ring his son-in-law. The police had agreed that he should be the one to tell him.

"Better than hearing it from a stranger," was the comment.

Seated in a corner of the bedroom, the ASIO agent watched the Finn force himself up from the bed and walk towards the phone. Heimo paused and, without looking at the man, took an open bottle and with shaking hands poured and drank a shot of vodka. His blurred eyes sought the phone and he stared at it as he willed himself to make the call.

"Shall I dial the number for you, sir?"

The young agent had come quietly to stand beside him.

Heimo shook his head and, as the man moved away, picked up the phone and slowly began to punch in the numbers.

But it wasn't his son-in-law who answered.

There were a lot of phone calls that night. Nikolai Nikolayevich Trinkovski rang the Russian Embassy from an airport phone just before his late flight back to Sydney was called.

A smiling Imran Talebov made a call from a very secure phone to a *dacha* outside Moscow. He was well pleased with the praise he received.

Later that night there was a rather drunken phone call to Maxy's house. Maxy listened patiently for several minutes and then spoke gently into the phone.

"Listen, old friend. One o'clock in the morning is a bloody stupid time to ring anyone, but it is even more stupid to expect me to wake Tom and invite him to a funeral." He paused, then continued, "I think we might go for a ride out to the forest tomorrow. Could be a good day for mushrooms. Why don't you join us?"

"I can't begin to say how sorry I am."

Savva watched Heimo's drawn face as he spoke.

"I had no idea they would go this far. I had no idea . . . no, I have no idea why. I would never have come . . ."

He glanced over at Maxy who was fussing around his car taking as long as he could to fetch some beer and glasses.

"I'll get Maxy to drop me at the airport and I'll be –"

"No!" Heimo's voice was hard and abrupt. "No! You bloody well stay here and we'll sort it out. You and I may not have been on the same team before, but we bloody well are now. We've been playing this game all our lives and so far we've been the lucky ones."

"Lucky? How can you say that after last night?"

Heimo's face turned down towards the forest floor as though hunting for the answer amidst the pine needles.

"No," he said quietly. "Last night was not lucky. I still can't forgive myself for that. When I rang to tell Mark what had happened and Aino answered the phone I was happy. For a moment it didn't matter that it was Mark, her husband, who was dead. All that mattered was that my daughter was alive." There were tears coursing down his cheeks and it was several minutes before he spoke again.

"If it had been Aino, I don't think I could have gone on. But now, well, I want revenge, not just for Mark but for the moments when I thought she was dead. That's why you must go along with me."

It was Savva's turn to feel helpless. "But . . ." he began, "what about Aino, she would never agree –"

"It was her idea."

"What?"

Heimo sat down on an old log.

"Listen. I talked to her for hours this morning. I told her things, you know, things I shouldn't have. She had some idea about my work, of course, but not everything. Then she said that Mark's death was hers to avenge, not mine. It was hers, and that if helping you was possible, then she wanted it this way. All she asked was that I check with you."

Maxy came over with the beer and for a few minutes the three men sat in silence.

"What about Mark's family, his friends?" The thought bothered Savva. If they missed any detail, the whole idea could go horribly wrong.

"His parents are dead," Heimo replied. "We'll put it around that he has gone to some conference in Europe and figure out how to break it to his friends later. When this business is sorted out we'll have a memorial service."

"You sure about this?"

"Certain."

A man, woman and two children, rugged up and all wearing gumboots, trudged towards them. As they passed they upended their basket to show the lack of mushrooms.

"They went that way," Maxy joked, pointing deeper into the pines.

The family smiled and walked on.

"Well?" Heimo asked after a time. "Shall we do it?"

Savva stared into his beer.

"Yes." His voice was almost a whisper. "Yes, let's do it."

Heimo stood up with a broad smile on his face.

"Maxy, I need your help. I have a funeral to arrange. My friend here would like to be buried on . . ." he turned back to Savva, "when would suit you? Would Sunday be all right? That will give me time to announce it in the paper for a couple of days."

"Yes." Savva smiled. "Sunday will be fine."

CHAPTER

NINE

IN the Russian Embassy, the *pradavyet* tossed the copy of the *Canberra Times* aside with smug satisfaction. He flipped open his diary and jotted down "10.30 am, Sunday". Leon Silbert's funeral was going to have an observer. He found it hard to keep his mind on the routine work. All he could think of were the rewards he could expect for services rendered.

In a matter of weeks he would find himself transferred back to Moscow and the real action. Too much was happening at home while he rotted in this shithole of a town. Fortunes and reputations were being made in Russia. Sure, the people were starving,

State enterprises were going bust, but a man with connections could make it there now, and Talebov knew he had the connections.

There was a bigger game as well and the longer he remained on the periphery, the less well positioned he was. Not that he would ever get one of the top jobs; no, the Russians had them all sewn up for themselves, bastards! But behind the scenes there was room for real power and if he played his cards right . . . The best possible outcome would be a return to Khartoum. He had only been involved in the initial setting up of the operation there, but if it came to fruition then what was happening in Russia was small change.

Enough of work, he thought as he pushed his chair back and rang for a driver.

"Take me down to Civic, Oleg. I deserve a coffee break with something better than the shit they serve here."

Yes, thought the driver, coffee and a whore. Some of these bastards never change.

Neither of the men in the Russian car thought to check for a tail. After all, who tailed anyone any more?

Maxy chewed his cheroot and smiled to himself as he allowed a car to slip between him and the Russian driver.

"Bloody amateurs," he said out loud to himself. "Couldn't spot the bloody tail on a kangaroo!"

In Civic, Maxy pulled into a loading zone and had plenty of time to shoot a roll of film before Talebov dismissed the driver and strolled over to a sheltered outdoor cafe. The Chechen was obviously staying for a while so Maxy drove around the block looking for a parking space. On a building to his left was a display that alternately showed the decreasing world area of rainforest and the increasing population and, although Maxy was not a man usually given to violent thoughts, as he watched the population index tick over he had a momentary reflection that included the Chechen decreasing the human race by a single digit.

Over the next couple of hours, Maxy sipped at coffee and mineral water while he watched his target do the same. Once Talebov went inside to the counter and picked up a couple of magazines, then later made a phone call, checked the time and set off on foot away from the centre.

He must be a regular, thought Maxy, as he watched the man disappear inside the brothel. He didn't have to look the number up before dialling and there had been no hesitation in finding the building. Nor had he even bothered to check around before entering.

Three quarters of an hour later, when Talebov emerged onto the street, Maxy was parked opposite and, with a clear view of the embassy car approaching, was able to watch his target slip into the passenger seat. Again there was no sense of a need for security.

"Just a little too sure of himself," was Maxy's final summation to Heimo. "Makes him an easy target."

"He may well be," Heimo said, "but he'll be even more so after the funeral. So let's just be certain we get it right."

Savva Vasilyevich stood up and reached for the vodka.

"I suspect Talebov will never be an easy target, no matter how relaxed he is."

Heimo smiled but did not comment.

The three men had been going over the plans for the funeral for more than an hour when Aino arrived. She was pale and drawn but holding herself rigidly straight. Savva hadn't seen her since Mark's death and after half an hour alone with her father she came into the living room. For a moment the two of them looked at each other; Savva uncertain what to say; Aino likewise.

As the tears began to flow down her immobile face, he moved to her and took her in his arms, as though she was his daughter, and held her until the sobbing started and her body let out the pain she had been holding in so tightly.

"I'm so sorry," was all he could say.

After a time she pushed herself back at arm's length but kept his hands firmly clasped in hers.

"Leon, don't blame yourself, that won't do any good."

Savva turned his head, unable to look at her, tears flowing down his cheeks for the first time in years.

"But the funeral . . . ?"

Her fingers held him tighter. "We must do it. There is no other way. Dad told you it was my idea. It is, and I mean it. Mark being killed like that is bad enough. Another death, possibly yours or . . . yours and Dad's would be . . ."

His face came up to meet her eyes. They were blazing with the intensity of the unspoken thoughts. She was right, too. It could so easily have been both him and Heimo in the car. This is what a daughter is, he thought. This is Heimo's blood speaking. There was no need to reply now. He simply pulled her gently back into his arms and hugged her again before releasing her.

Sunday dawned icy cold but clear. Not a single cloud dotted the winter sky and by 10.30 the temperature had risen to 8 degrees. Although there was no hint of a breeze the mourners at the cemetery huddled close to each other; black clothing and downcast faces. Around them rose a cloud of steam from their breath.

The rabbi's voice, as he began to chant the *Kaddish*, carried on the clear air to the carpark where Savva sat concealed, in the rear of Maxy's Renault. He stiffened as he heard a car approach, and then relaxed as he saw it was a late-arriving media crew. The Saturday edition of the *Canberra Times* had carried the first official release about the bombing and now the electronic media were in a rush to get footage to go with the story. It wasn't every day that a Jewish-Australian was incinerated in a car bombing, and the TV news editors saw a chance of getting international coverage for their story considering the number of terrorist bombings overseas in the previous months.

It was also not every day, thought Savva, that a man was able to be present at his own funeral in a condition where viewing was possible.

He watched Heimo in his dark suit supporting Aino, whose thick black veil did nothing to conceal the sobbing that was so obviously wracking her body, and, standing behind them, the small group of mourners that ASIO had hurriedly assembled. The negotiations with the security organisation had been very one-sided. Heimo had refused to give any assistance unless they played it out his way. It was a certain bet that they were carrying on their own investigations regardless, but they had pulled strings and opened doors for Heimo.

The Finn had personally cleared the way with the *Canberra Times* editor in order to keep the front page ready for the Saturday story. And the editor was only too happy to oblige. She had carried the story of the explosion earlier in the week, and although she had gone along with the official line that it was simply a tragic accident and that the victim's name was being withheld until relatives were contacted, she had felt at the time that there was much more to it than that. She had not often been wrong.

As it was Sunday, there was quite a bit of traffic coming in and out of the cemetery but none of the visitors was the man Savva expected. It was beginning to look as though the bait, so well laid, was not going to be taken. Then Savva saw him. Strolling through the trees on the hill above the grave, was the *pradavyet*. He was carrying a small bunch of flowers and was making a rather convincing show of stooping and checking headstones as he wandered past. He looked for all the world like a man in search of some long-dead relative's resting place.

Savva knew that this was the turning point. There could be no other explanation for Talebov's arrival at the funeral than his complicity in the bombing. This was all the proof Savva needed. So, he had a decision to make. He could remain in the shadows and to the rest of the world he would be dead. Building another life would not be difficult. On the other hand, if he wanted to find out why he had become a "non-person", and the target of an assassination attempt, he had to rise from the dead. The choice was his and the time for the decision was close at hand. He fished in his pocket for his dark glasses, put them on and sank further back in the car's shadows. There would be an opportunity to confront the Chechen, but it was not here and not now.

A couple of cars drove slowly between them. The Chechen was standing on the hill, a casual observer of the funeral below. Then, turning away as if disinterested, he drifted out of sight behind tombstones and trees. At exactly the same moment, Savva noticed a woman emerging from a taxi at the far end of the carpark. He sat forward with a start. Even at this distance there was no mistaking her. It was Amelia Lippmann. What in God's name was she doing here?

He panicked. Without thinking, he got out of the car and started towards her. It was a mistake. It was not Amelia who saw him, but Talebov. He had emerged from behind some trees at the foot of the hill and was now standing directly opposite Savva on the other side of the road. There was a momentary pause, a beat, then the Chechen straightened, the blood draining from his face. For an instant the two men looked at each other. Savva brought his fear under control, slowly removed his dark glasses and stared hard at the man who, for some as yet undiscovered reason, wanted him dead.

Suddenly something else took the Chechen's attention and, breaking eye contact, he turned and walked quickly away. Savva was confused. What had changed the moment? He looked in the direction that the *pradavyet* had headed and felt his stomach drop. To Savva's amazement, Talebov was walking over to Amelia, who, still in the process of paying the taxi driver, had her back to them. The Chechen came up behind her and, as she turned there was a flash of recognition in her face. The pair shook hands and started talking.

Savva's head spun with confusion. He felt the sweat break out on his forehead. How did she know Talebov? How did she know about the accident? The initial reports appeared in a couple of the papers outside Canberra, but none had a name for the body. The funeral notice had only been in the local paper and there was no way that anyone uninvolved could have linked the two. The first time his name had been connected to the accident was yesterday morning, in the *Canberra Times*.

Amelia still had not seen him, so he quickly climbed back into the old Renault. Maxy was now behind the wheel, chewing on a cheroot.

"You look like you seen your own ghost, mate," quipped Maxy.

"Just drive!"

"OK." He started the car. "Did the bastard show?"

"Yes. He's just over the other side of the road, talking to that woman who got out of the taxi."

"Then get down on the seat and we'll make a dignified exit."

It was all wrong, Savva thought, she shouldn't be there. How could she know? Someone must have made a point of telling her and apart from Heimo Susijarvi, who else knew? The obvious answer was the man who had greeted her. Savva had not told the Third Secretary about her. So, the *pradavyet*, Imran Talebov, was the only real possibility, but again the question was why? What had he to gain from it?

As the car left the cemetery grounds Savva forced himself to sit up.

"Sorry Maxy, I was feeling a bit queasy." He opened the rear window and drew the cold air down into his lungs. "Talebov showed up on cue. Carrying flowers and pretending to look for a grave."

"I thought you were supposed to stay in the car?"

"I blew it, Maxy."

"He saw you?"

"Oh yes," Savva said, beginning to feel a little better. "Yes, he saw me all right and then he saw someone else he recognised and did a very abrupt about turn."

"Who was the other party?" Maxy glanced in the rear-view mirror. "God, you look dreadful. Are you sure you're OK?"

"I'm just a bit tired, I think." Savva paused. "The other person was a woman I have been having a relationship with. The Chechen went over to her and greeted her as though they knew each other."

"I see." Maxy spat his cheroot accurately through the side vent.

They drove in silence. As agreed before the funeral, they were all to meet back at Heimo's house. Maxy parked in the garage so they could enter the house shielded from the gaze of prying eyes. Once inside, Maxy went to the kitchen to make tea and Savva excused himself, explaining that he wanted to lie down for a little while.

Although the nausea had gone he was still feeling pains in his chest and the last thing he wanted, he told himself as he shut the door and lay down, was a heart attack. That would have to wait. First he had to clear his head.

He let his breathing settle, then went over the events. It was not as baffling as he had first thought. The only person who could have told Amelia about the bombing was Talebov. In doing so the *pradavyet* was letting Savva know that he was behind it. But what was behind his greeting her? They must have met when he was in Melbourne. That could only mean one thing. She had let him wait in the house on the day Savva had tried to ring her and the Chechen had answered. She had not been in danger at all. She had been in collusion with Talebov.

The whole point of the funeral exercise had been to lull the Chechen into a false sense of security so that later Savva would have the advantage of surprise. It had backfired. The pain in Savva's chest was subsiding and he began to drift off to sleep. The last thing he remembered was some part of his mind telling him that he was far too old for all of this, and he should be celebrating a well-earned retirement in a *dacha* outside Moscow, or better still, somewhere on the Black Sea.

CHAPTER

TEN

IMRAN TALEBOV was concerned that he might not live long enough to retire anywhere. Having reported to Danilov that Golitsyn was dead, he was now in a spot of trouble. He was also unsure if he had done the right thing in informing the woman in Melbourne that her friend had died. He had done it to tidy up the loose ends. She had been expecting the Federal Police officer to contact her when she returned from the weekend away, and the last thing he wanted was for her to ring the office of the Federal Police in Melbourne and ask for a non-existent person.

She had been shocked by the news and understood that there was now no need for them to meet, but had not given any indication that she intended to go to the funeral.

He had nothing scheduled to do after returning from the cemetery but he nevertheless went straight to his office and spent the next couple of hours deliberating on what would be the best course of action. In the end, he decided there was only one way forward and that was to complete the job before word got to Moscow. As things stood, he could still be pretty certain of being recalled to Russia, but the outcome there would now be very different from that which he had planned. In the circles in which he moved, they employed an old-fashioned method of compulsory retirement. A bullet in the neck was the only redundancy package on offer.

Talebov told the Third Secretary that he needed to take a week off and return to Perth to clear up some minor details. There was no problem. The Third Secretary had no idea of what Talebov's real role in the embassy was, though he assumed it was MBR, and although the man was junior to him, and a Chechen, he certainly was not about to interfere in whatever it was he was involved in. A week would be fine.

The next call was to "Jack Zinner" in Sydney, though it was not the call the man had anticipated. There was no congratulations and no "please collect your airline ticket". Instead he was coldly informed of his failure to kill the target and warned in no uncertain terms that although he was to be given a chance to complete the task, a second failure would be fatal – in every sense of the word.

If Nikolai Nikolayevich shuddered at the thought of how difficult it would be to kill the target now that he was on his guard, then the final instructions from Talebov sent a chill through his whole body.

"And I want the others taken care of. All of them."

The sound of Trinkovski's breathing conveyed his uncertainty, so Talebov let him wait and then repeated quietly, "All of them. The Finn Susijarvi, his daughter and Savva Golitsyn. I want no mistakes. Do you understand?"

"No mistakes." Trinkovski hoped he sounded convincing. "And my ticket?"

"When the job is done ring me in Perth at the Radisson. I'll be in room 703 and your ticket will be waiting."

"Where?"

"In Perth. Book yourself Sydney–Canberra and then Canberra–Perth."

"But if –"

"There are no alternatives, and I want it done this week."

The line went dead. Trinkovski held onto the phone for several minutes. He was feeling decidedly unwell. By the time he had pulled himself together to call the airlines for his flight to Canberra, the *pradavyet* had already booked his flight to Perth. There was no way Talebov was going to be in town if things got messy, and he had to find out how much he could rely on his South African contact if he needed to cover his own back. If Trinkovski failed then he had nobody else he could use, and if there was one thing he wanted to avoid at all costs, it was getting his own hands dirty.

Savva Vasilyevich Golitsyn dreamed he was Leon Silbert again. It was a comforting dream with a glimpse of the Yarra in spring, of trams and football crowds. As he woke he fought a feeling that harkened back to his childhood. He did not want to go to school. He did not want to get up. Somehow, if he could stay in bed everything would be better.

He realised he was crying, but not the tears of a scared schoolboy. It was the futility of everything. His life, which so far had amounted to nothing, was decaying around him and like a transmittable disease was spreading out and touching those close to him. It was touching people he cared for. Amelia, Heimo, Aino – people who had played no part in the deception he had created.

Thinking about the devastation he had brought them, he knew he would rather have decided to stay in Australia. Maybe, he thought, it's not too late. Maybe he could rebuild a life as Leon; after all, he had the finance to do it and what about his relationship with Amelia? No. The hurt he had caused her was unforgivable. There was no going back there.

He checked his watch to find that he had slept much longer than he expected. It was six in the evening. Wearily he forced himself out of bed and, throwing a jumper over his crumpled shirt, headed towards the kitchen in search of food.

The scene that greeted him there caught him completely unawares. At one end of the table was a collection of empty bottles and at the other Heimo and Aino were carving a giant pizza. Maxy was at the sink pouring hot water onto coffee grounds in the large glass pot and searching in the sink for the plunger.

"Ah! We are five for dinner!" Heimo was drunk and obviously couldn't count.

"This . . ." Aino's voice was a little huskier than usual as she greeted Savva. "This, my elderly mate, is a wake. Now don't tell me the Irish are stupid. This is the best thing that has happened all day!"

"Coffee?" Maxy called over his shoulder as he prepared to push down the plunger.

"No!" bellowed Heimo; his command far too loud for the small kitchen. "Let it brew, you idiot! There is no place even in an old man's life for a premature plunger!"

Savva laughed. These were good people; friends. "Yes, Maxy. I'd love a coffee and maybe a vodka. It seems I have some catching up to do."

"So do I." The voice behind him was very quiet.

He turned to find Amelia standing beside the door.

"Hello, Savva Golitsyn."

"Hello, Amelia."

He looked at her for a moment. The others were watching intently, trying to gauge the feelings, aware they were watching a turning point.

Somewhere in the next few seconds Savva realised that it was the first time Amelia had ever said his real name. But there was something he needed to know.

"The man you shook hands with at the funeral?"

Amelia flashed a smile at Heimo. "Yes, we've talked about my relationship to him."

"And . . . ?"

"And I'm very disappointed that you didn't trust me. He was the Federal Policeman who approached me in Melbourne to find out what had happened to you. Mr Susijarvi has explained who he really is."

Heimo handed Savva a small shot of vodka and waved the bottle in Amelia's direction. "More, Mrs Lippmann?"

"It's Amelia . . . and yes, thank you. I'm sure one more won't hurt."

Savva, still not fully awake, sat at the table and drank. Heimo had been right; there were five for dinner.

By the time Savva had consumed several vodkas and a couple of slices of pizza he was feeling decidedly better and ready to hear about the rest of the funeral. None of the others had noticed the *pradavyet* speaking with Amelia, but after the service Aino had introduced herself to the woman, interested in who she was and why she was there. When Amelia had explained that she was a close friend of the dead man, it had taken Aino a few seconds to realise she was talking about Savva, not Mark. She excused herself quickly and told her equally curious father who Amelia was. Heimo had then gone to Amelia and insisted, gently, that she should come back to Rivett with them.

Once they had arrived at the house there had been some awkward moments as they attempted to convince her that Savva was, in fact, alive. In the end they quietly opened the door to the bedroom and let her see for herself. Her reaction had been a mixture of relief and anger – relief that he was alive, but anger at having been taken in yet again. Heimo had done his best to make her feel welcome and gave her a brief explanation of who Savva/Leon was but insisted that she wait until Savva was awake before he continued.

By the time the pizza, coffee and vodka had all gone, she was impatient to hear more. As Savva retold his story to Aino, Amelia and Maxy, Heimo pottered about cleaning up the kitchen. From time to time he threw in a comment but for the most part let Savva do the talking.

Maxy and Aino had heard much of it before, but for Amelia it was all new and she found it devastating. How little I knew of this man, she thought, as he fell silent.

"Why should I trust that what you say is true? Hasn't your whole life been built on lies? Isn't this another one?" Her anger burst forth; the words razoring through the tension in the room. "I mean, Leon, Savva . . . whoever you are, was I just part of your disguise; your cover? And what happens now?" The anger struck out again and though she realised she was shouting, she had no desire to control it. "Do I just forget all this happened, go back to Melbourne and pretend you never existed? Am I supposed to be happy that you've risen from the dead?"

She faltered and turned to Aino. "I'm sorry, I'm so confused, I keep forgetting that you've lost your husband . . . but you, at least, had someone real you can grieve for. What have I got?"

She turned once more on Savva, who sat, head bowed, knowing there was absolutely nothing he could say.

"I've got a fabrication. I feel used, Leon . . . I feel . . ." She threw her head back and sobbed loudly, her hands clawing at her face as though trying to scratch out the hurt or bury it beneath some pain more physical and immediate.

Aino rose from her seat and, gesturing for Maxy to make room for her, crouched beside Amelia's chair and held her in her arms. After what seemed to Savva like a long time, the sobbing subsided. Aino kept holding her with one arm while she softly stroked the hair from Amelia's damp face.

"Why, Leon? Why did you choose me?"

The power of her voice was replaced by a sadness that touched him deeper than the anger had.

"Because I loved you."

Amelia looked up, hesitant, vulnerable, unwilling to believe something that might still hurt her.

"And now? What happens now?"

Savva Vasilyevich felt self-conscious, aware that the four of them were watching and that he had to decide about much more than simply his relationship with Amelia.

"I want to see it through. I have to find out why I was not welcomed back to Russia, but I . . ." he paused, unsure for a moment and then felt his chest tighten as he knew what his words would be. "When I've done that, then I want to stay here."

"I should think so," Aino said, sounding like a den mother who had just witnessed the resolution of a kids' squabble.

"Good! Then we must decide what our next move is." Heimo's face was beaming.

"No, it's my job. You have all done enough and I won't need any help from now on."

Heimo looked at Savva, the smile vanishing. "That would have to be the most bloody stupid thing you've ever said. We are in this as well. We have a stake in it, too."

"And," Maxy said, "seeing I'm involved, how about some more coffee?"

"I think I would like to go back to the motel." Amelia's face was still pale; tears only just held back. "Thanks for your kindness." She stood up and turned to Savva. "And if you would like to come with me . . . then . . ."

Savva just nodded and rose wearily to his feet. The world felt out of kilter. The day had been too long, too disjointed and though part of him welcomed her invitation, there was another part that wanted nothing more than to be alone, asleep, avoiding whatever was happening. "I'll just get some things from my room."

He sat on the bed, forcing himself to breathe deeply. The depression would pass, he told himself several times, but this thought did not relieve his black mood and his tiredness of spirit seemed a palpable presence.

There was a gentle knock on the door and Heimo came in carrying an old beach bag.

"Don't bother with your luggage. Take this for your things tonight and we'll have another crack at sorting everything out in a couple of days."

"Thanks."

Heimo put the bag down on the bed beside Savva. The Russian looked beaten . . . much older and somehow shrunken.

"Savva –"

"I know, I know. I have to pull myself out of this."

Heimo sat down next to him, his face florid with vodka.

"You don't have to do a fucking thing! Give Aino and me a couple of days to sort things out here and we will come with you, at least as far as Helsinki. We have to organise a locum to take care of Mark's patients straight away. After that we'll give you a hand."

Savva wanted to protest but he simply nodded and began to gather some fresh clothes, pyjamas and his shaving bag.

"You should also take one of these." The Finn held open the beach bag, and Savva looked inside.

"No, I don't think so."

"Savva, this isn't a training exercise." The voice beside him was harder now. "We've offered them a bait and when they come for it we can't afford not to be ready."

"I have never –" Savva began.

"Neither have I, well, at least not for over half a lifetime."

"Where did you . . . No, forget that, I don't want to know."

He gingerly removed the smaller of the two pistols and handed it to Heimo.

"I'll take the Browning, it must be almost as old as I am."

"And as hard to handle." A smile flashed over Heimo's face as he tucked the Smith and Wesson into his pocket. "It's nine millimetre and there's a spare magazine in the side pocket of the bag. Use both hands if you have to fire it. They don't work like in the movies."

Savva tucked his pyjamas over the pistol and threw his shaving bag on top.

"Will you be all right?" he asked Heimo.

"Me? I have this." The Finn patted his pocket. "And don't forget, my daughter is a champion shot. She has a bigger armoury than the rest of us put together, and hers is legitimate. Aino's asked if she can stay with me for a few days, and if we go to Finland she wants to come along. I told her we might go for six months or more but she was happy about that, she has friends there and she could use a change of scenery."

"She is remarkably composed, Heimo, are you sure she is OK?"

"She's Finnish. She'll hold it in until she's alone. Grief is like snow melting, it doesn't happen overnight." He turned to the door. "Come, Maxy is going to drive you to Amelia's hotel and wait while she checks out and then take you on to the Argyle Apartments."

"What's wrong with her hotel?"

"She booked in under her own name. I've asked Maxy to book you into the Argyle as Professor and Mrs Clements." He fished a battered wallet from the back pocket of his trousers. "Leave your wallet and ID with your luggage. This has a credit card and . . ." He flipped open the wallet and with a theatrical flourish produced a business card. "You are Professor of Politics, specialising in Peace Studies, retired, from Monash."

"And I can actually use the credit card?"

"Well, you'll need to sign the back first . . . but it will be paid from an account that has had a couple of thousand dollars in it for over ten years now. I set it up once as a bit of insurance in case I ever needed it . . . pity to waste it after all this time."

"I rather like being a professor," Savva said as he zipped his own wallet into the side of his suitcase and pushed it back under the bed. "Thank you, Heimo, there's no need for money, I have more than enough, but for everything else. I don't know how I will ever repay you and Aino . . ."

But the old man was already out the door.

The professor didn't get to unpack his pyjamas that night.

When Mrs Clements took him in her arms as the door of their apartment closed behind them, his body responded. It appeared that Mrs Clements was pleased to see her husband after some time apart and, clothes shed, they fell to the bed, and after a time her body opened to him and he came home.

There were moments, he thought, when sex was not about passion, but comfort. She had held him like a mother, and when his body had jerked in orgasm, she had cried softly, "It's all right, I have you . . . I have you."

Later, when he was drifting in and out of sleep, he heard her say, "I thought I had lost you. I thought I wanted to hunt you down and kill you . . ."

He propped his elbow up on the pillow, resting his head on his hand, he watched her as she spoke. Her eyes were open, staring into the dark, tears rolling down her cheeks.

"I thought how much I wanted to hurt you, and when I heard you were dead, I stopped feeling. It was strange. The hate went away, but there was no love. No, nothing, not even emptiness. And when that old man told me that you were alive and that his son-in-law had been killed, I hated you again. I wanted you to be in that coffin. But then you came through the door and you looked so old, so vulnerable, I wondered how you could have done this to yourself."

For a while the words stopped, but she didn't sleep.

"Amelia –"

"No. I don't want answers. I just needed to say it."

Savva let his head down onto the pillow.

"You know what else I wonder?" Her voice had a smile in it.

"What?"

"How is it that you have such a young body beneath that old face."

Her giggle muffled in his chest as she rolled towards him and her mouth began to nibble at the base of his penis. He hardened and reached down into her wetness, but she pushed his hand away, only relenting and letting it rest when it found her breasts. Slowly she took him deep into her mouth and, despite his protests, didn't release him till he came pulsing into her.

She collapsed back, laughing. "I've never done that before. A girl could get lock-jaw!"

"Silly, I was fighting to hang on because I thought you were going to want me to . . . you know. You could have told me."

Amelia sat up with a look of mock horror.

"My mother told me that nice girls don't talk with their mouths full."

They looked at each other for a moment and then kissed slowly.

"I feel like a young woman with a new lover. I always found Leon interesting, but there is something exciting about this Mr Golitsyn, and Professor Clements – maybe I should have lots of lovers." She laughed. "And you could be all of them."

"I'm Savva Vasilyevich," he announced as he padded over to fetch a glass of water. "Though I might have to be Leon to get back into Australia. The complications of trying to change back to Savva might be a bit too much for the authorities to go along with."

Amelia fell silent, watching as he returned and offered her a glass. "Will you really go?"

"Yes. I couldn't be happy here if I didn't follow this through. Maybe, before Mark was killed, but now I owe it to Heimo and Aino."

"And to yourself." It was a statement.

"I suppose so. Yes."

His hand reached out and found hers and when he awoke several hours later he was surprised to find he was still holding it.

CHAPTER

ELEVEN

THE man from ASIO took the tapes and locked them in his desk drawer. Monday would be soon enough to hand them over to his supervisor. They would sit for a week before someone got round to transcribing them anyway. First he needed to pay the mortgage. It had been a while since he had learnt anything worth cashing in but this time he felt he was on a winner.

He dialled the mobile number and heard the familiar voice.

"I have a name and location of the party you were interested in. The name is Professor Clements and the party is staying with a woman at the Argyle

Apartments. The party appears to be armed with a nine mil' Browning. The other parties are talking of visiting Helsinki."

The phone went dead without a reply being spoken. The ASIO man was not concerned; that had been the response on the previous occasions. The mortgage money always arrived.

Stupid old bastard, that Finn, he thought. Moving the bug and then getting pissed and forgetting about it. Oh well, their loss.

Monday dawned crisp and clear. Amelia and Savva had a late breakfast, then headed out to the airport so that Amelia could catch her midday plane. Savva made sure he was visible to anyone who might have been interested as he waved her off. All very normal.

Back at the Argyle he phoned Heimo and let him know that Amelia had returned to Melbourne without incident. Heimo and Maxy were organising the passports and papers they would need for the trip, and Aino was busy finding a locum to replace her husband. Savva turned down the offer of a late afternoon sauna and vodka, pleading, truthfully enough, that he was exhausted.

An afternoon sleep put an end to the day and it was only hunger that drove him from the apartment. He walked briskly to Civic where he was pleasantly surprised to find a few shops still open. After a wander around he decided on bread, butter, cold ham. As an afterthought he bought a bottle of beer, then headed back.

Deep in thought, he nearly didn't see the man outside his apartment. He stopped just in time and watched as the man stood listening to the night sounds. Savva checked his own position; no, the man wouldn't be able to see him. For a moment he studied the man. He was thin and tall, imbued with a characteristic sureness that comes from being well briefed and well armed. Maybe Eastern European. Not as young as Savva would have expected, but then an older man was either a very good hitman or a part-timer. The man seemed relaxed standing outside the front door; to anyone passing by he looked as though he had simply stepped out to enjoy the night air.

Savva breathed deeply to calm himself, then quietly turned and retraced his steps to the front of the apartment complex from where a side path took him to the back door. Letting himself in quietly, he was relieved to find that he had left the television on. The noise and flicker must have convinced the man that he was inside. Savva left the back door unlocked and, whistling loudly, gathered up a towel from the bedroom and, checking that the Browning was loaded, went into the bathroom.

After turning the lights on and adjusting the dimmer downwards, Savva strode past the toilet door to the shower recess and turned the hot tap on full. Confident that in the dim light and the rising steam no one could see into the shower, he went into the toilet, placed the towel on the lowered toilet seat and sat and waited.

If this man was any good at all, the front door lock should prove no test. If he was an amateur, then the back door was open. All Savva had to do was wait in the dark with the toilet door ajar.

To keep his mind still and his hands from trembling, Savva concentrated on his breath, counting each inhalation until he had reached one hundred. He had just started back at one when he saw the man step into the bathroom. For a moment the man looked at the shower and began to raise the silenced revolver which he appeared to grip steadily with both hands.

The shower recess was about three paces from the door, and as the intruder took another step forward Savva stood and took aim. The noise of the shot seemed enormous in the enclosed space of the toilet, causing Savva to flinch as he pushed open the door and prepared to shoot again. There was no need for a second shot.

The impact had blown the man forward, and he had fallen into the shower where the torrent of hot water was already washing the blood from a ghastly wound at the base of his skull. Savva had a flash of an old Hitchcock movie. Like *Psycho*, he thought, except in colour.

Trembling, he turned the shower off and knelt down beside the body. The man was even older than he had looked when he had been standing outside.

Nearer my age, thought Savva grimly, wondering what sort of life had led the man to this awful moment. Quickly he went through the man's pockets and removed a wallet, papers and a room key from the Canberra Holiday Inn. He replaced them with Professor Clements' wallet, minus the credit card, and gathering up his bag, let himself out the now wide open back door. Bloody amateur, he thought as he walked towards the Holiday Inn.

A group of agricultural scientists were checking in for a conference beginning the following day, so Savva had no problem ambling past the desk into the elevator. He pushed the button for the third floor and, as the doors closed, fished out the wallet he had taken from the dead man. As he expected, it was the working wallet of a professional. All it contained was a driver's licence and a credit card in the name of one Jack Zinner, from Sydney. For a moment he studied the photograph on the licence and the issuing date. It was three years old and seemed genuine, which meant that the man had either been in Australia for a while or had very good connections. The only other thing that the photo told him was that Jack Zinner wasn't particularly photogenic.

As the lift opened Savva paused and checked the numbers on the wall in front of him. The room was just to the right. Outside the door he stopped and patted the gun in his pocket. The odds were good that Zinner had been working alone, but it paid to be cautious. This was not the kind of contest that gave consolation prizes; there was no second place. He knocked gently and stood back.

Behind him the lift door shut, causing him to momentarily stiffen, but he forced himself to relax and slipped the key into the lock and opened the door.

Savva panicked as he attempted to turn the lights on, then he realised that the switch was one of those power-saving devices which needed the key tag inserted before it would activate.

Slow down, slow down, he thought to himself, take it easy.

The room looked as though it hadn't been slept in. After looking for several minutes he finally found a bag in the back of the wardrobe tucked up on a shelf behind the spare pillows. He carried it to the bed and unzipped it. One by one he took the contents out and laid them on the bedcover. At first he didn't know what to do. He just looked until his brain caught up and took over. He reached for the phone.

Half an hour later there was a quiet knock at the door and he rose and let in Heimo and Maxy. He had obviously caught them before the sauna as they were both sober.

They were like an old, well-oiled machine. Maxy moved into action, checking the bathroom, the windows and kitchen, while Heimo fumbled in his pockets for his glasses before pulling a chair up to the bed, turning on the bedside lamp and picking up the passport. He flicked through it, held it up to the light, then turned it over several times, rubbing the cover.

"And this . . ." Savva handed Heimo the embossing tool.

"Genuine?" His eyebrows raised quizzically.

"I think so."

"And the owner?"

In the pause, Savva felt, rather than saw Maxy turn his attention back to them.

"Dead."

"How do you know that?"

"I shot him."

Behind them Maxy whistled.

"Where?"

"In the head . . . or you mean . . . ?"

"Yes." Heimo grinned. "Where's the body, Rambo?"

"In the Argyle Apartments . . ." Savva paused, trying to recollect the scene accurately. "He's in the shower with his gun still in his hands. I went through his pockets and took this." He tossed the wallet onto the bed. "And I put Clements' ID in his jacket."

"Jack Zinner." Heimo peered at the driver's licence. "Or Nikolai Nikolayevich Trinkovski. Which do you think is real?"

"Trinkovski. Unless he was something more dubious than a hitman, I'd say that Zinner was the legend and Trinkovski was the ID he was returning to in Russia. It stinks of Talebov. This man was from out of town, someone was feeding him very good information. I trailed my coat a bit at the airport when I dropped Amelia off but I think this man didn't just find me, he knew where to look. How, I don't know."

Heimo shifted his weight. "It's my blunder. I forgot all about that bug we took out of the living room and put in the spare bedroom. I talked about Clements and the Argyle in there, remember?"

"Shit. And who's listening?"

"Well, I don't think it's the Russians. My guess would be ASIO, but with a leak to Talebov. He hears the information and flies a man in. By the look of this stuff I'd say he was on the promise of a return to the motherland."

Heimo stood up and glanced around the room. "I don't suppose Mr Zinner is going to mind if we help ourselves to the mini-bar."

"Don't you think we should check out?" Savva was beginning to feel the adrenaline wear off.

"Not till I've had a drink. I was hoping that this was the man who killed Mark, but it doesn't look like it. Still, Trinkovski; it gives us another name to follow up."

For a moment they sat nursing their drinks while Maxy, having given the room the all-clear, started going through Trinkovski's bag.

"It seems pretty straightforward," said Savva quietly, "I put one of my photos in the passport, emboss it and become Trinkovski. That way I can simply purchase a ticket to Moscow and fade away into the crowds until I find a way to dig into why

Savva Vasilyevich Golitsyn has become a non-person." He held out his glass as Heimo twisted the top off a miniature scotch. "Problem with that course is that it leaves me being someone I know nothing about and doesn't get us any nearer nailing Talebov."

"You might be able to combine both, mate," Maxy said. "Have a sticky at this." He handed over an airline ticket.

The Qantas business-class ticket, Sydney to Canberra, was for that morning and showed an onward connection to Perth for the following day.

"Very kind of Mr Zinner to book your flight." Heimo squinted at the ticket. "He's a Qantas Club member, how handy." He reached for the phone.

"Yes, good evening, it's Jack Zinner, member number triple-oh, eight-seven, eight-nine. Couple of things. Can I just confirm I'm on Canberra–Perth tomorrow? Fine, via Melbourne, no problem. Now, the other thing. I'm not sure if my travel agent gave my membership number for the last couple of flights I booked. Could you just check when you have me down as flying last?" He gestured quickly to Savva for a pen. "Yes, today and before that on . . . last Tuesday morning, Sydney–Canberra, and returning Wednesday morning. Yes, that's in order. Thanks for your help." Heimo placed the phone back, his face white. "You nailed the bastard, Savva."

"You think so?"

The Finn rose and poured himself another drink. "Has to be. He arrives the same day Mark died and flew back the next morning. Same pattern as this time . . . only difference was this time he fucked up."

"I might break a long-standing rule and have a beer on the strength of that," said Maxy, helping himself to a Fosters from the fridge. "But I should remind you blokes that we have some housekeeping to do before you all go jetting off around the country."

Heimo nodded. "There's nothing we can do about Zinner's body. And anyway, it'll take a while for them to work out what a retired Professor of Peace Studies is doing being dead in a Canberra motel with a gun in his hands. Which reminds me, did you leave him financial?"

Savva grinned and passed over the credit card he had taken from Clements' wallet. "Dead men don't need Visa."

"Very thoughtful of you," Heimo replied. "Saves me a couple of grand and will confuse things for a while. Though with a gun in his hand they are hardly going to expect robbery. I just hope that ASIO doesn't get efficient in the next couple of days. The tape of the bug is bound to surface sooner or later."

Maxy tossed back the last of the beer. "I wouldn't hold yer breath waitin' for that to happen. The Feds will be all over the shop before ASIO even thinks of sticking its snout in. But I think we should pay Mr Zinner's bill and move on." He looked to Heimo for confirmation. "And I've got the photos ready, so we can do the Russian passport tonight, no sweat."

He dug in his pocket and casually, as though it were an afterthought, handed a folded yellow Post-It Note to Savva. "I reckon you can probably read this. Beats me. You guys missed it. It was on the back page of the ticket."

Savva peered at the note under the light of the bedside lamp. The Cyrillic script was clear and unambiguous. The meaning of "the Finn, the daughter and Golitsyn" left little to the imagination. The fascinating part for Savva, though, was the scribble underneath. He read it out. "Room 703 Radisson Perth. Phone T."

"Talebov?" Heimo asked.

"I would bet on it."

"And," chuckled the Finn, "if you don't phone T, then T is going to get very jumpy."

"You mean, all the better for calling in on?" asked Savva.

"Exactly."

"Is that all it says?" Heimo took the note from him. "What's this at the top?"

"Just a shopping list," yawned Savva. "Nothing to bother about."

Down in the foyer they checked Jack Zinner out, explaining that old friends had turned up and offered accommodation. The night manager had obviously not laid eyes on Mr Zinner before and was more than happy to accept extra cash to cover the mini-bar expenses. The amount they left would have bought the entire bar, but who was he to complain?

CHAPTER

TWELVE

ONDAY was not the best day of Imran
Talebov's life. For most of it he sat in his
room waiting for the phone to ring. He
didn't want to call his South African contact until he
had confirmation that the mess in Canberra had been
dealt with. There was also no point in ringing
Danilov in Moscow. Not yet. For a while he tried
reading a spy novel he'd picked up at the airport. He
managed to reach the point at the end of the second
chapter, where the fate of the free world hung in the
balance and only the hero could put things right, and
gave up. The implausible plot and the superhuman
endurance of the hero was too much for him. It was

all action. Real life was different. Real life was ninety per cent about waiting. So he waited.

On Tuesday evening, feeling in the need of a little distraction, he rang his girlfriend to let her know that her Polish importer was back in town. The answering machine greeted him and told him that she was in Margaret River for a few days holiday, but please leave a message after the beep. He hung up.

For a while he switched channels on the television, catching the various news broadcasts but there was nothing. So he slept. It was a way of passing the time.

Tuesday was a good day for Savva Vasilyevich. He made his plane with time to spare and in a relaxed frame of mind, knowing that he could use the long flight to put his thoughts in order. The Russian passport now carried his photograph and was tucked away in his luggage. He could, at any time, simply become Trinkovski.

He and Heimo had spent hours going over the possibilities while Maxy had completed the work on the passport, but in the end they decided to keep everything open ended. Talebov was waiting for a phone call. That wouldn't happen. Sooner or later, though, the body would be found and the media would pick up the story. At this point they could expect Talebov to relax and that would be the moment to strike. He would still be unsure why Trinkovski hadn't contacted him but the last person he would expect to confront him would be Savva. Not that Savva was keen on confrontation. The idea of simply walking up to room 703 at the Radisson and shooting the Chechen didn't hold much appeal. Savva had no regrets about shooting Trinkovski but was in no hurry to make a habit of such things.

"There are other ways," Aino had said. She had taken over the role of coffee maker while her father went through the options with Savva. But she had been following the conversation intently. Her drive for revenge was not far below the surface as she suggested that shooting was too good an end for the bastard. Her husband's surgery had a drug cabinet full of possibilities. But Heimo had dismissed the idea on the grounds that drugs were too difficult to administer without first subduing and restraining the intended recipient.

The conversation had then gone on to the longer term plan of Savva's return to Russia. Even though he now had the passport and could go direct, Heimo and Aino were sticking to their plan of spending at least six months in Finland. They could do with the holiday and were a lot closer in the event that Savva needed some assistance. Heimo gave Savva a contact number in Helsinki.

"It's the reception desk at the Kalastajatorppa, a hotel on the road out to Lehtisaari."

"The Kala . . . what?"

"Kalastajatorppa. It means 'fisherman's hut', but don't be fooled by the name. It is, in fact, a very large hotel. If you ring and ask to leave a message for me and give a contact number, even if I'm not there, someone will get back to you."

Savva did not ask why Heimo still had such links in Finland, but it did cross his mind.

"Think of it as insurance," the Finn said. He then gave Savva the address in Moscow for his Russian contact, Koshlykov. Maybe Lev Sergeevich Koshlykov could be prevailed on to run a check and see what had happened to Savva's file. It was a risk worth taking and although the Russian had helped Heimo out recently, the feeling was that the Finn's credit was good enough to call in another favour.

By the time Savva was ready to relax the cabin lights had been dimmed for the in-flight movie. It appeared to be about a talking pig trying to take on the persona of a sheepdog. It felt somehow appropriate to the moment. Savva Vasilyevich was asleep long before it ended.

He woke up well before the flight landed in Perth. He walked to the exit and, for a moment, thought he must be still asleep and dreaming. Standing at the head of the economy-class passengers, waiting to disembark, was Aino Richards. He looked at her; something was different. She nodded to him.

In the arrival hall he watched her approach. It was the dramatic brown lipstick, teased-up hair and a skirt much shorter than anything he had seen on her before. This was more a woman on the make than a grieving widow. As she came closer she gestured for him to follow her. Perplexed he trailed after her to luggage collection where, following an interminable wait, they picked up their bags and went out to the cab rank.

She did not speak a word as they waited in the queue but when they finally reached the front she opened the rear door of the cab for him, put their small bags on the seat, then slipped into the frontseat, beside the driver.

"The Kimberley Hotel, please."

The driver grunted and moved off.

"I rang ahead and booked rooms for us, Dad."

Savva, with the feeling that he had just been hijacked, could only nod, and they made the journey in silence.

At The Kimberley, Aino paid the driver and emerged from the cab to be greeted by a man whom she addressed as Gavin. Gavin, it appeared, was the proprietor. He was also extremely pleased to see her again and what a pleasure it was to meet her father and how was her husband and how much he hoped that Mark would have another conference in Perth soon so that he could welcome him as well. The rooms were, as before, on the fourth floor and would they please accept the bottle of Evans & Tate that he had left with the complimentary basket of fruit? Savva felt out of breath just listening.

They had adjoining rooms overlooking the river and, as he stepped outside, Savva realised they also shared a balcony. There was a gentle knock and before he could reach it the door opened and Aino came in with the bottle of wine.

"I think we had better have a drink and a chat, don't you, Dad?" Her expression was serious for about three seconds, then she collapsed into laughter. "You should have seen your face on the plane! I thought you were going to pass out on me!"

"That thought occurred to me, too. I'd been sleeping and thought I was having a nightmare."

"Thanks a lot!"

"I didn't mean it like that." He handed her the bottle opener from the mini-bar. "I have a fair idea why you're here. Does Heimo know?"

"I didn't want to upset him."

"You think this won't?"

Aino concentrated on getting the corkscrew involved with the cork for a moment then looked straight into Savva's eyes.

"He thinks I'm in Melbourne with an old school friend. If he rings, she's agreed to cover for me."

"And what exactly is it that you intend to do?"

Aino shrugged her shoulders and then stood, placed the wine bottle between her legs and pulled the cork.

"Savva, Talebov knows you. He'd recognise you at a hundred paces. Me, he's never seen, especially like this. As far as we know, the nearest he came to seeing me was at the funeral and then I was behind a veil. I can get to him –"

"And? And what then?" It was going to take a lot more than this to convince Savva. He had no doubt that he was dealing with a very capable woman and that she was fired by a huge commitment, but she had no training. She had no idea of the type of man she was up against.

"I went through Mark's surgery and grabbed enough tranquillisers and muscle relaxants to dope an entire Melbourne Cup field."

She was certainly confident.

"But we are dealing with a trained killer, not a race horse."

"Savva, I may have been a married woman for the last few years but I think I can still charm a man with a hell of a lot more certainty than I could a horse." She raised her glass to him in silent acknowledgment of a pact that he hadn't yet agreed to.

He sipped the wine realising that he was, in fact, better off with her by his side than going in alone. Maybe she could at least have a nose around the hotel and check on Talebov's movements.

He found himself raising his own glass. Damn her, he thought, but if she's charmed me . . . well, maybe she can do the same to the Chechen.

"I can describe him to you, I suppose."

"No need." She tossed a packet of photos on the table. "These are the shots of Talebov that Maxy took in Civic. I'd recognise him half pissed."

"I hope it won't come to that."

"Let's hope." Aino flopped back into a chair. "But let's drink up, just for practice."

Wednesday's newspapers carried a short item, tucked away in the middle pages, but it was not small enough to escape the attention of Imran Talebov. By the time he had read it several times, he was in a decidedly better mood. It appeared that some retired academic had been caught up in a criminal fracas that had resulted in his being shot in the back of the head at close range. The unusual allegation of criminal involvement was arrived at when it was disclosed by a police spokesperson that the retired Professor of Peace Studies had been in possession of an unlicenced SIG Sauer P230.

Talebov thought that the gun was a fine touch. It would certainly muddy the waters for a while. Trinkovski had obviously shot Golitsyn with it, then placed it in the dead man's hand, knowing there was no way that the police could ever trace it. Had he left the gun that the ASIO informer had said Savva was carrying, it might have been traced back to the Finn and the dead man's identity may well have been discovered. No, this was a good professional job. And so he said in his triumphant phone call to Moscow. For their part, the people in Moscow were also impressed and promised that Trinkovski would be suitably rewarded on his long-overdue return home. They also hinted that Talebov could expect good things. Did he remember his trip to Khartoum?

Well, the links he had established were paying dividends, and he should prepare himself for another visit to Sudan.

The next call Talebov made was to his South African contact who was also duly impressed, though the mention of a continuation of the project in Sudan was of far greater interest. The eradication of Golitsyn had simply been a bit of housekeeping, whereas the Sudanese project was the main game. Pull that off and . . . well, they could all retire early and healthy with enough assets to set up a lifestyle anywhere they fancied and with enough time to become thoroughly accustomed to it.

The only small detail that still worried Talebov was Trinkovski's failure to telephone. Stupid bastard's probably wiped himself out celebrating, he thought. There was no hurry now anyway. So he relaxed and tried his girlfriend's number again. The answering machine let him know that she was still down south. Talebov was not unduly disappointed. There were, he mused, many other fish in the sea and it was not an area where he had a record of failure.

The newspaper was also read with grim interest in The Kimberley Hotel. It seemed everything was falling into place and so, after breakfast, Aino and Savva hired a car and drove first to Cottesloe and then along the coast road to the Radisson. For a while they sat in the carpark and watched the people walking in and out. It seemed highly unlikely that

Talebov was going to make an appearance so, while Savva waited in the car, Aino took a stroll past the shopping arcade to the foyer and through the ground floor of the hotel.

When she returned she was carrying a new scarf and grinning broadly.

"Been shopping?"

"Trying myself out. The guy in the shop would have invited me to dinner if I'd stayed another minute. He tells me that most people come down to the piano bar next to the foyer. I checked it, and it's perfect. You can nurse a drink and watch all the entrances."

"When?"

"Tonight. A lonely woman on a Wednesday night, shouldn't be too much competition."

"With you there I don't think the competition would have a chance any night of the week."

It was out before Savva could self-censor. For the first time in years Savva Vasilyevich found he was blushing. The kiss on the cheek that followed did not help matters.

CHAPTER

THIRTEEN

APART from a lone barman, the piano bar was deserted when Aino arrived at seven-thirty, so she did a couple of circuits of the shops and one side trip to locate the toilets. In the washroom she put down her shoulder bag and checked herself in the mirror. The hours she had allotted to shopping and having her hair done that afternoon had been well spent, and although she had changed outfits three times before she left The Kimberley, she was now more than pleased with the result.

The woman who confronted her in the mirror looked about thirty years of age and very single. Her make-up was minimal and her hair swept back so as not to compete with her high cheekbones or her lips' subtle glisten. She unzipped the side of her ankle-length skirt and retucked the simple white cotton blouse. She undid another button so that when she leant forward an astute observer would glimpse enough cleavage to confirm the suspicion that she was not wearing a bra. She looked elegant but uncomplicated; a woman dressed for an after-dinner stroll along the beach before having a nightcap and heading for bed.

Then, remembering her promise to Savva, she opened her bag and took out the scarf that she had purchased on her scouting trip that morning. It was perfect. Its colours matched the aqua and rust of her skirt. She tied it loosely around her neck. Now she not only looked a little more demure, but it would give her an item to remove at an opportune time. There was no point in exhibiting everything at once. She had a moment of panic when she thought she had left her mobile phone in the car or worse, back at The Kimberley. Fortunately, it had simply slipped to the bottom of the bag. She repositioned it in a side pocket. Earlier, she and Savva set it up so that all she had to do to contact him in the car was press "recall". She closed the bag and hoisted it onto her shoulder. She was ready.

Back in the piano bar, a tape of Chopin nocturnes was working its magic on the potted palms and lone barman. Fuck, thought Aino, I'm going to look like a bloody shag on a rock. Then to her relief she spotted a couple tucked away in an alcove to one side. They were attempting to negotiate two straws through a single huge cocktail creation replete with flags and umbrellas. At first glance it looked like a sea that had undergone some environmental disaster involving coloured dyes and a container load of tropical fruit. But, she giggled to herself, the world can relax, for by the look of the number of flags staked into the iceberg, the United Nations had the situation in hand. The barman approached her.

"What's that thing called?" She nodded in the direction of the cocktail.

The barman must have only just graduated from the local Hospitality Industry training course. He was not old enough to have graduated from anything else. He was also, Aino noted, extremely embarrassed.

"Um . . . it's called a 'Group Grope'." He was blinking furiously and the flush in his cheeks was doing nothing for his pimples. A gold name plate informed the world that he had been born "Brian".

"I think I'll pass on that. Could I have a glass of water with a slice of lemon?"

The barman nodded, relieved to be able to turn away. "I'll bring it to your table."

There are some people who can never do a thing simply, thought Aino when her drink arrived with the slice of lemon transformed into a swan supported by two miniature corks; a cross between a bird and an outrigger canoe. Maybe, though, the fault lay with the Hospitality Industry training courses; run by the same people who used to be attracted to window dressing. Aino reached out and touched the barman's arm.

"Is there an alternative to the Chopin?"

For a moment he looked bemused. But they had trained him well and with a broad and now confident smile he pulled himself up to his full height.

"We haven't any at the moment, but we've got some ordered."

"How long have you been working here, Brian?"

"Three weeks. I graduated at the end of last year, but this is the first real job I've had."

Aino rewarded him with a friendly grin, then beckoned him closer.

"I want you to do me a favour, Brian."

"Certainly, ma'am."

"I may have a friend joining me. Now, if I do, and I end up ordering a gin and tonic, could you make it very, very weak?"

Brian had obviously received a high pass in customer relations.

"You could order a half."

"No. I'll order a full, or even a double. But I want only a tiny drop of gin." Her mind was only just keeping ahead of her voice. "I'm taking some medication that can't really mix with alcohol, you see, and I really don't want my friend to know. You understand." It was plain to her that he did not, but she sensed what his confusion was. "Charge us for a full or a double. Money isn't the problem."

"Right."

"By the way, the swan is beautiful."

Brian beamed again.

"I can make lemon umbrellas as well."

I'm sure you can, she thought, as he returned behind the bar and started furiously polishing wine glasses, the colour in his cheeks only slowly receding. Nearby she heard a loud slurping noise, then muted giggles. The "Group Grope" was obviously going down well. Aino drank slowly and attempted to settle herself down. She was painfully aware that she was maintaining a very firm grip on a mixture of emotions. Despite the fact that her grief was a driving force, she was extremely scared and she was reacting the same way she always did when she felt fear. Her mind was making a joke of everything. It was as though the more serious the situation, the more frivolous the thoughts. Being aware was one thing. Doing something about it was another thing again. She pulled the corks and toothpicks out of her drink and sank the swan.

By eight-thirty several other couples had sauntered in and the Chopin had been replaced by a Morricone tape that she vaguely remembered from some SBS movie. Mentally creating subtitles for each occupied table, she drifted off into directing her own movie until she was abruptly brought back to the real world by a voice beside her.

"Can I join you?"

The *pradavyet* was better looking in the flesh than Maxy's photos suggested, and he had also gone to a bit of trouble to look the part. An expensive blazer was held over his shoulder by a crooked finger. His polo shirt was stylish, monogram-free and the jeans were just worn enough to give him an air of studied casualness. The dark hair had recently emerged from a shower and been simply slicked back. The look was open and fresh.

Aino let her gaze settle back to his face.

"Sure. I've run out of small talk with Brian."

"Brian?" A dark eyebrow raised itself.

"The barman. He does strange things to lemons."

The jacket went over the back of the chair opposite. "Can I get you something fresh? You've been nursing that for a while."

Damn, she thought, just how long had he been watching her? "Why not." She smiled up at him. "I'll have a g'n't."

"A gee 'n' tea?" Then he saw the dismay on her face and smiled. "Sorry. English is my second language and I mostly order beer or vodka."

"A gin and tonic." She laughed. "It's a tropical cure-all. Tonic for the malaria and gin for the boredom."

"Right, now I remember, the tonic has quinine in it, yes?" He turned on his heel and strolled over to the bar.

Inside she felt nothing but turmoil. Come on girl, you can do it, she repeated a couple of times and then forced herself to take a deep, heart-slowing breath. He certainly scrubbed up well. Forty-ish, maybe a well-preserved fifty. Hard to tell. Nothing in the demeanour suggested the evil her imagination had prepared her for. No stereotype here; no Jack Kevorkian, no Hannibal Lecter, no Temple Brooks Gault. She pulled her mind back to the task in hand. Her stomach churned as she reminded herself that this man had ordered her husband's death.

"Half or full?" Talebov was calling from the bar. Behind him, gin bottle poised, Brian winked at her.

"Hell, why not? Make it a full."

Be careful, she told herself. This man's charming.

The tray that arrived was another Brian creation. An oriental umbrella draped itself over the edge of a glass in which a corked lemon dolphin swam in a sea of tonic bubbles and ice cubes. Beside it, a plate of nuts sported a sprig of parsley and a tall glass of beer was nestled up against a small shot glass that, she guessed, must contain vodka. To one side, two paper napkins had been folded into approximations of the Sydney Opera House and on the other a small glass held toothpicks that had been ingeniously induced into wearing tiny cellophane tutus. The overall effect was a disaster.

Talebov sat and raised the shot glass to her.

"Here's to the defeat of boredom and malaria."

"Cheers," she giggled, before removing the umbrella and taking a sip. Her tongue searched the tonic and was rewarded with the merest hint of gin. Malaria was obviously not going to be a problem and, given the present circumstances, she certainly didn't need the alcohol.

"So, if English is second, what's first?"

The drained shot glass was placed back on the table. He remained silent for a moment, his eyes openly appraising.

"Take a guess." He raised the beer to his lips and took a small sip then grinned. "I'll give you a clue. It's not Swahili."

"French?" The face opposite was impassive. "No, wait . . . Italian or Spanish?"

"Spanish?" An eyebrow raised again.

Versatile, she thought, that was the other eyebrow. Behind him there was a groan from the alcove of the "Group Grope". It was living up to its name. The couple had moved to the same side of the table and were deeply involved in checking out each other's throats with their tongues. The cocktail creation was abandoned; melting away to slush.

"The hair. And your complexion. I thought, well, I thought it might be Mediterranean. I give up."

He shook his head with mock sadness.

"Russian. Not very fashionable I'm afraid."

"I don't know. Have you seen *A Fish Called Wanda*?" The response was again a blank face. "It's a film . . . never mind. And is there a name that goes with this Russian?"

"Nikolai. My friends call me Nick."

"Suzi . . . my friends don't call me enough."

"I don't believe that for a moment." He flashed a smile at her. "I mean, I bet you came here just to get away from the phone."

"If only it were true. But enough of me. I'll get another round and we'll swap life histories. Isn't that what one does in situations like this?" Without giving him time to respond, she signalled to Brian and indicated she wanted the same again. Aino avoided the obvious pleasure in the Chechen's eyes by turning her attention to untying her scarf and flicking it over the back of her chair. Things were warming up nicely, she thought.

For Savva Vasilyevich things were far from warm. Sitting in the car he had plenty of time to be thankful that he had put on both singlet and bulky jumper. His only break had been almost an hour ago when he made the first of the scheduled trips around the foyer and back. He had been rewarded by the sight of Aino talking to a young barman. There had been no sign of the Chechen. Outside, the night had actually been warmer than he had begun to imagine and so, with some pleasure, he prepared for his second sortie.

He pulled a coat over the jumper to achieve the increase in bulk that he wanted. The irony of his scoffing at this "spy stuff" didn't escape him as he jammed on a silly looking hat and walked slowly back towards the hotel. A lifetime of being ready to do this, the very thing he had been trained for, had gone by and suddenly it was necessary if he was bent on retirement.

The night staff gave the old man checking his watch no more than a cursory glance. He was obviously waiting for someone. Savva did the circuit and paused beside a display rack that held brochures extolling the many one- and two-day trips available for those with the time and money to spare. He could also go further afield to some place called Monkey Mia and swim with the dolphins. He read the brochure slowly, then glanced into the piano bar as he walked back towards the entrance.

There was no change in his pace but he felt his pulse rate rise as his mind deciphered what he had seen. He recognised the *pradavyet* even from behind. And the scarf? Yes, the scarf was over the back of the chair as arranged. No problem. Everything on track. He marvelled at her composure. Only a Finn could even contemplate what she was planning, her hatred temporarily transformed into an icy resolve. He caught a momentary glimpse of her face, but it was enough to tell him that she had a better than even chance of making the next step. She had looked flushed and happy; her attention fully on Talebov. There was something else. Yes, the glasses. Several glasses on the table, small and large meant that the Chechen was relaxed and drinking. Savva smiled grimly to himself. This might just work. He went back to the car and took off the coat and hat. Damn it, he thought, why is it suddenly so warm? He took the jumper off as well and settled down to wait for phase two.

By half past ten, Suzi and Nick had finished swapping fictitious histories and moved on to politics. Talebov was impressed by this woman's grasp of the domestic political scene. Most of the Australians he had come across even on the diplomatic cocktail circuit were apathetic in the extreme. Here, though, was a woman who could talk about everything, from the gaps between policy and implementation, to the hidden agendas and the powerbrokers behind the scenes. She was also, he conceded, very attractive. She did not seem to be playing sexual games with him, but every now and then she would lean forward and reveal her cleavage. Each time it had appeared accidental. Each time he was aware of what a potent effect it had on him.

For her part, Aino was totally aware of the effect she was having. Throughout the evening she had managed to keep a part of her awareness detached and on guard. She also knew that it was time to move on to the next phase. A vague worry was that she hadn't seen Savva checking on her. She hoped her back-up was in place because once she made the move, things could go dreadfully wrong, very fast.

"Nick." She leaned forward and picked up his empty shot glass. "Could I try one of these?"

"A vodka?" His eyes glanced down at her breasts.

"I should go home soon, so just one for the road."

Talebov moved quickly to the bar and returned with two icy shots of vodka.

"To you, Nick," Aino toasted. "And thanks for turning a boring evening into something special." She felt his eyes on her as she tossed back the drink. He was looking for her reaction to the vodka so she obliged by gasping for breath and doubling forward. Come on, you bastard, she said to herself, make your move. Now!

The Chechen held his glass up and looking over it, he said quietly, "The night doesn't have to be over yet, Suzi."

She took the scarf from the back of the chair and threaded it between her thumb and forefinger, then pulled it through, like a slow-motion replay of a magician about to produce a dove. For a couple of seconds she kept her eyes down, letting him wait. She was very aware that he still hadn't moved. The glass was still held out, the offer very open.

"Nick." She looked up and smiled gently. "That's a very tempting offer and maybe another night. But I'm rather tired and . . ."

Talebov shrugged casually and downed the vodka. "Another night? I'm here for a couple more nights and," he added conspiratorially, "I have a bottle of much better vodka in my room."

"That is almost irresistible. I think you are a very wicked man!" Aino laughed.

"Can I give you a lift?" He was on his feet, reaching for his jacket.

"Are you certain it's no trouble?" The concerned look on her face was just right. Inside she was punching the air and giving herself high-fives. Yes! Yes! They had not been able to discover whether

Imran Talebov had hired a car or somehow had one at his disposal. It had been the one flaw in the plan and although a shared taxi was a possibility, it was definitely plan "B".

"No trouble."

Aino moved to his side and kissed him on the cheek. Then stepped back as if struck by a sudden thought. This was the moment she had to take control. She beamed, looking him up and down as though it was the first time all evening she had had a sexual urge.

"Nick, I've just had a wonderful idea!" She paused and took a deep breath as though plucking up the courage to say something risqué. "You know what I'd like to do? I want a swim! If you're going to take me home, it's on the way. Great beach and the water's not too cold even at this time of year. We'll have the ocean to ourselves."

"I don't have swimming trunks . . ."

She put her finger to his lips and whispered, "Nick, it's a nude beach."

"And the water's not too cold?" His hesitation was all bluff with his flashing eyes glaring advertisements for his desire.

"Don't tell me that a Russian is scared of the cold. I thought you were all brave men who went swimming in a hole in the ice on New Year's Day. I saw that on TV a few months ago."

Talebov held up his hands in mock resignation. Surrender, capitulation. The smile went from ear to ear.

Assuming the dominant role was proving easy.

"Sit!" Aino pushed him back into the chair.

"What?"

"Sit. I'm going to get us a little surprise. I don't want my Russian catching a cold." Laughing, she dug into her bag and produced a small hip flask. "I," she declared with great authority, "am going to get us a lifesaver. If you behave yourself and come swimming with me, I shall let you share my vodka." Aino kissed him on the forehead, then made her way to the bar and informed Brian that she wanted vodka.

Talebov was having trouble containing his delight. He really didn't have the time to invest in another night of wining and dining. But a quick swim to sharpen the senses, a little more vodka to mellow the pleasure ... And this woman! She was something, he thought, as he watched her leaning over the bar while the barman filled the flask from a drink measure. Much easier to be with than most of the Australian women he'd seduced. She was not in awe of him, of his foreignness. This was more a meeting of equals and he was going to enjoy himself. He rubbed his hand on his groin, aware of the stiffness he was just managing to keep in check. And, he thought, I doubt she'll be disappointed.

The first reminder that something could still go wrong came straight away. Aino said she would rather walk down to the carpark to collect the car but he insisted that it should be brought round the front by the doorman. She didn't push it, hoping that Savva would guess what was happening. It still worried her that she hadn't seen him, but her attention had been elsewhere.

The electricity between them was palpable. They had already committed themselves to a mating dance and words were no longer needed. His hand on her shoulder. His hand gently stroking down her neck and down further, lingering between her shoulder blades, letting her know that he knew she wasn't wearing a bra. The trembling that her body produced was natural. There was no need for acting now. There is a fine line between sex and danger, she acknowledged to herself, and she was walking it willingly. Her fingers scratched him through his shirt and were repaid with a low growl from his throat. All this, Aino forced her attention back to the task in hand . . . all this, and we're still waiting for his bloody car.

In the car, she directed him along the coast road towards Swanbourne Beach and then sat back and marshalled her thoughts. There had been no sign of Savva or their car as they had pulled away from the hotel and Aino knew that she had to go on alone. She was trembling, scared. She removed his searching hand from where it had pushed her skirt up to her thigh.

"First, we swim."

Aware of her trembling, Talebov drove slowly, savouring the power he felt. There was something delicious in watching a woman melt. He could feel his erection cramped within his trousers. He imagined how wet she must be in expectation. Even though she is trembling, she is strong, he mused. Her removing his hand was exciting. Compliance was fine but nothing was better than a mental struggle and . . .

"Turn here." Again her voice had that ring of command. He turned slowly and parked.

"Now . . ." Talebov began.

But she was out of the car. "Now we swim."

The beach was deserted.

Carrying her sandals in her hand, Aino was very conscious of her vulnerability. There was no one she could call out to for help and no sign of Savva. She was sure he would now have no idea of where she was. Behind her she could hear Talebov; he was extremely aroused. Any doubts Aino might have had about that had been dispelled as he emerged from the car. He had made no attempt to hide his arousal and neither had he flaunted it. It was a given; part of the equation.

"This," Aino declared, drawing a line in the sand, "is the girls' change room. Boys on that side."

Sitting on the sand, Talebov untied his shoes, removed his socks and then lay back, relishing the pleasure of watching Aino undress.

This is a striptease, she thought as she unbuttoned her blouse. So, make it a good one. She let her blouse open, but left it on as she unstrapped her watch and, leaning over put it in her bag. Straightening up she unzipped the skirt and let it fall to the sand. Stepping out of it she paused and then, locking eyes with the Chechen, slowly removed her underpants.

This was almost too much for Talebov. He stood, quickly divested himself of all his clothes and moved to take her in his arms. For a moment he felt her tense up and then, as he pressed his hardness against her stomach he felt her relax and her tongue move towards his mouth. The shudder that went through Aino was a dreadful mixture of emotions. There was shock at how turned on she was and the horror of being in this position at all. But she knew that there was no turning back. If she was to go through with this, she had to have him so turned on that nothing else mattered.

To the Chechen, the shudder he felt go through her body was simply another stimulus to his desire. He removed her blouse. With one hand he pulled her tighter to him and let the other quickly brush over her breast and down between her legs. Aino shuddered again as his fingers expertly parted her pubic hair and slipped inside her. Dreadfully conscious of her own wetness, she allowed her hand to come down to his penis. It was inflamed and hard as steel. Gasping for breath, she pushed his hand away and, turning, slipped out of his grasp and ran down the beach.

Without looking back she plunged beneath the first breaker and screamed out all her pent up feelings. It was dark and cold beneath the water but she took her time to surface. Above all, she knew she had to remain in control. His strength came as no surprise. It was her own weakness that was frightening.

Unlike her wild plunge, Talebov's entry to the water was slow and considered. He stood at its edge watching the slim form first plunge in and out of the breakers, then head along the beach with a steady and powerful stroke. Swimming had never been a pleasure to the Chechen, but swimming in pursuit of this woman was a different story. He waded slowly out until a curling wave took away his breath and his erection.

Several times he tried to grab her in the water, certain that proximity would bring his shrunken penis back to life, but each time she laughed and slipped from him like a salmon from a net. In the end he floated, tilting his head back to stare at the Southern Cross flashing high above them. For a fleeting moment he entertained the notion that this was not only a beautiful part of the world, but more astonishingly, that he could somehow, in another existence, have enjoyed a normal life in such a place.

A voice brought him back to the business in hand. Aino, naked and bathed in moonlight was standing on the shore calling him. He needed no second invitation and was quickly out of the water and following her up the beach. Ahead of him, he saw her take the hip flask from the bag and, throwing her head back, gulp down a large amount of vodka.

As he reached her, she wiped her lips with one hand and passed him the hip flask with the other.

"I saved you a little. A girl could get a taste for that." Her flesh was covered in goose bumps and he could clearly see that her nipples were now taut and hard.

She let him look, adjusting her stance to part her legs a fraction more.

"In *A Fish Called Wanda*, the film I mentioned, this woman gets very turned on by her lover talking to her in Russian." Aino moved close to Talebov and let her fingers wander up his wrinkled and shrunken cock, before stepping back. "I would like that very much. I would like you to drink that, and then fuck me in Russian."

She holds her drink well, he thought. The hip flask was half empty already and she was just as feisty as ever. She wanted to be fucked in Russian, then who was he to argue? He tipped his head back and, realising that she was still testing him, drained the rest of the vodka from the flask and tossed it onto the sand.

He felt the alcohol coursing through him, knocking the edge off his chill. There was going to be no trouble with the equipment. He grabbed for her, but she evaded him. So that was how she wanted to play it. He was happy to oblige. They ducked and weaved around each other and then she leapt to the side and ran up a small dune and flopped down on her back.

"Lick me!" It was an order. The *pradavyet* was used to obeying orders. He obeyed this one and was rewarded with the moans of a woman well pleasured.

"Now my turn." Her voice was rasping, laboured.

Her strong athlete's arms rolled him onto his back and she had him, first in her hand and then, as his vigour was restored, she took him in her mouth, tongue teasing, flicking and then slowly, agonisingly, deliciously, sucking. There comes a point, thought the Russian, that you either abandon yourself to this or intervene with some good old-fashioned fucking. That time had come. He raised his hands to lift her head from his penis but, strangely, it felt heavier than anything he could remember. Talebov tried to sit up . . . and failed. He was aware but immobile. In a moment of panic he realised he could move . . . nothing. The woman stood up and peered into his face.

"Can't you keep it up, Mr Russian?" She was laughing. "History should have taught you something, remember the Winter War? Never fuck with the Finns. You're a slow learner, Imran Talebov."

Drugged, he thought, then thought he heard her talking to someone on a mobile phone. He thought no more for a long time. Orpheus and the Finns had just conquered Russia. It may have happened before, but never on a beach in Western Australia.

Savva Vasilyevich was struck with panic. Twice more he had checked on Aino and each time seen her in intense conversation with the Chechen, the scarf remaining in place as an indication that everything was fine. Then nothing. No Talebov and no Aino. The barman was not much use. He gabbled something about ginless gin and tonics and then vodka in the hip flask. Well, at least that had been expected. But where the hell were they? The possibilities really came down to two. Either she was in his room, or they had gone to Swanbourne Beach as planned.

He sat tight. Then the phone rang and the wait was over. He lunged for it and was relieved to hear Aino's voice.

"I have a naked Russian here who doesn't seem to be able to dress himself. Can you give me a hand?"

The drive to Swanbourne seemed to take forever but he eventually found the turn off and pulled in beside Talebov's car. There was no one else around, so he took the toolbag he had picked from the boot and headed for the ocean.

Down on the beach Aino had been busy. She was dressed and had already managed to get most of the clothes on the unconscious Talebov, who was lying on his back, his breathing slow and irregular.

"The dose rate seems to have been fine." It was an observation rather than a question. They had ended up guessing how much of the soluble muscle relaxant to use. The problem being that too much would have resulted in breathing failure, and that would have rendered the final part of their plan obsolete.

"Seems so. The barman was fantastic. He half filled the flask exactly as I asked and I had no trouble fooling that bastard into thinking I had drunk half before him. Sucked in!" She was on a high with a huge dose of adrenaline.

"So now?"

"Do the fence. I'll tape up Talebov. But hurry, I can't keep going for much longer."

From inside the bag, Savva produced the pliers and a roll of gaffer tape. The former he pocketed and the latter he tossed to Aino. She was clearly near breaking point. The energy she had derived from anger was at an end and he could see that what she needed to do now, more than anything in the world, was to curl up somewhere and grieve. He shuddered at the thought of what this whole experience had done to her.

"See you in a minute." He touched her gently on the shoulder, then vanished over the low dunes.

By the time Savva returned, Aino had the *pradavyet* gagged and his feet taped securely together. She had closed Savva's tool bag and attached it to Talebov's belt. All seemed ready, so they began the long slow job of dragging the body up and over the dunes to the hole in the fence that Savva had just cut. A few metres away, a sign warned that the public were forbidden to enter, as the property was restricted to Defence Department Personnel and live ammunition was used on the firing range. Not tonight, thought Savva. Not tonight.

CHAPTER

FOURTEEN

WEDNESDAY morning was fine and cool. A gentle breeze had to work hard to do more than disturb the red flags at the end of the firing range at Campbell Barracks. Ideal conditions for the first target practice for the new recruits. Captain Hawkins watched Sergeant Simon Adams explaining the basics. The new men were particularly keen to do well. The Special Air Service Regiment was a prize worth working for and having been accepted into the SAS was no guarantee of staying there. Hawkins looked at his watch. Where the hell was the butt detail? He called the sergeant over and discovered that the twenty-four men who were supposed to be down in the butts had been delayed by a traffic accident. Half an hour was the estimate. Well, there was no point in throwing the day's schedule out. Check the butts are clear, and get on with it.

Private D'Hage was particularly keen. His entry into the SAS was line ball. One dip and he was out. He settled himself down and aimed at the full-size plywood figures at the end of the range. The sergeant picked up the radio-phone and called the butts. No one answered. All was clear.

"Five rounds, independent fire!"

The order came, and Private D'Hage aimed and managed to get all his shots in a neat cluster in the chest.

At the in-camera enquiry that followed a few days later it was never determined who was the first to notice the problem. Captain Hawkins and Sergeant Adams both appeared to have reacted at the same time. Adams was, of course, much closer and so was able to bellow at D'Hage to cease firing. For a moment there was confusion. Gradually, the new intake got to their feet and stared in disbelief. No one had made a rule that said that plywood targets must not bleed, because it had never occurred to anyone that it would ever happen.

The enquiry determined that the man, whoever he was, had been alive at the time the first of the five shots entered his stomach. He was alive and, given that someone had cut small slits in the plywood in front of his eyes, it was clear that he had watched the events. Sometime during the night, a person or persons unknown had dragged the man from the dunes and tied him to the back of the target with strips of barbed wire. The barbed wire proved to be that which had been taken from the fence. Very efficient. The forensic experts would, in time, determine what substance the man had been subdued with. On the other hand, the linguists who translated the Cyrillic script scrawled on the bottom of the target, were baffled. They had never heard of the *Istrebiteli*. Unfortunately, that didn't stop a leaked report reaching the newspapers, and some hours later the news filtered through to an old man in the Ukraine.

Private D'Hage was exonerated in a special closed court hearing. But he left the force a few months later and never touched a rifle for the rest of his life.

The same day as the "execution" of the *pradavyet*, Imran Talebov, a man let himself into a room 703 at the Radisson and removed an airline ticket. It wasn't really theft as it did have the intruder's name on it.

The following day Nikolai Nikolayevich Trinkovski cleared Emigration and Customs and boarded a flight to London with a connecting flight to Moscow.

The reason for travel on the emigration card simply read: "Going home."

PART
II

CHAPTER

FIFTEEN

COLONEL VICTOR IVANOVICH DANILOV was smoking again. There were some suggestions from his superiors that he had not been performing. There were suggestions from his wife that he had. Anna Petrovna was still on at him about leaving his wife and she, too, had started to make comments about his performance. All in all, he considered, it was not the right time to give up cigarettes. His doctor continued to disagree. Screw their mothers, he thought and reached for a packet.

The flight from London was already over an hour late, and although that was not unusual, Danilov was in a foul mood. The fact that he had been asked to act as escort to this jerk was demeaning. Hell, they could have sent the driver by himself, or told the fucker to take a cab. They were going to kill him anyway, so why bother? He broke three matches before managing to light the cigarette. Nothing worked well any more. He inhaled and glanced up again at the arrivals board.

Moscow Airport was presenting its normal face to the world. It was total chaos. When the flight he was after eventually made it upon the board, it proceeded to change gate numbers and ETA several times. Victor Ivanovich decided to stop straining his neck watching the board and have a coffee, but that turned out to be the wrong decision. It tasted like reconstituted bear shit.

Danilov had been at work at the Special Projects Research Institute since early in the morning and his stomach now reminded him that what he actually needed was food. The early starts had been going on for a month now and were not balanced by going home any earlier. Not that home was much of an option since his wife had found out about Anna Petrovna Florensky. There was, of course, no directive that commanded him to be at his desk at first light but, with the stuff-ups and tensions at the Institute lately, it certainly did not hurt to be seen to be hard at it.

It was not just that he needed the job, everyone needed a job, but more than anything he needed the perks and the contacts. Without them this was no kind of life. The *dacha*, the booze, the hard currency and American cigarettes took the edge off an otherwise bleak existence and kept him going. It had not always been this bad and with a bit of work and a lot of luck, maybe the good old days could be resurrected.

According to the arrivals board the flight from London was still an hour away so Victor Ivanovich wandered through a sea of stranded travellers to the tea, lemonade and *piroshki* sellers on the pavement. The smell of the little mince-filled pastries would have put most people's digestive systems on red alert but Danilov was too hungry to care. The sight of the three *piroshki* being fished from the battered old stove by a grubby kid who should have been at school was, if anything, even worse, but he paid an exorbitant amount and wandered off to find a bench. Hunger triumphs over common sense, he thought, as he juggled the greasy bundles from one hand to the other in an attempt to avoid first-degree burns. The coarse paper napkin disintegrated under the onslaught of hot fat, and he let it fall to join the mounds of detritus in the gutter.

Andrei Primakov was a man used to issuing orders. Orders that were obeyed. Some people wondered what gave him the right to do so. After all, he was only a government adviser. It was true that in the parliamentary halls there were those who paused to hear his voice. It was also true that he controlled the dispersal of frightening amounts of government funds, but essentially he was a servant of the State. Those who wondered about Primakov were few in number, for he was a man of subtlety. His orders often came from other mouths. Those who had gone as far as voicing their concerns about him paid dearly. They were now dead. But Primakov killed none of them. It is probably true to say that he had never, in his fifty-two years, held a gun. He had no need. In just the same way that often his orders came from other mouths, so too did other fingers do the work of squeezing a trigger or gripping a knife.

Maybe it is not surprising that a man who was so used to issuing commands lived in dread of receiving them. The phone call had taken him from the security of familiar surroundings to streets he seldom travelled. The driver was not his driver and had indicated, in the first few sullen minutes, that he had an aversion to conversation.

Eventually, the driver seemed assured that no one was following them and slipped onto the ring road and out towards Sheremetyevo Airport where Victor Danilov was still awaiting a plane from London. But the driver had no interest in planes and continued out towards Klin, then turned off near Solnechnogorsk. By this time, Primakov was becoming extremely concerned for his own safety. This was the kind of ride he ordered for others, and it was always one-way. In his mind he hunted for the mistake he must have made but could come up with nothing. In any case, there was little he could do to avoid what lay ahead.

The car stopped outside a small mean cottage on the outskirts of a rather nondescript village. This was not a Russia he had seen before or desired to see again. The people who lived here may just as well have inhabited a different galaxy as far as he was concerned. Although feeling physically sick he was very aware of details that disturbed him; the driver was wearing a pistol under his jacket and driving a car with no number plates. It didn't augur well.

He entered a room that was bare of all furnishings save a small table and chair. The windows had been thrown open in an attempt to capture any breeze careless enough to venture in their direction. Behind the desk sat the man who had phoned. It was too dark for Andrei Primakov to see the old man's face, and he had no desire to do so. They had met once before and although the outcome had been very favourable for Primakov, resulting in his elevation to his current position, he had, even then, no desire to meet the man again.

"Be healthy."

His greeting vanished into the shadows. There was a long silence during which he felt the old man studying him.

"Be healthy. You have taken care of our little Australian problem."

It was a statement; the man's voice quiet but not feeble. At least now he knew what was on the agenda. Maybe this was not going to be as bad as he had feared. Yet the old man travelled infrequently and he would not have come to Russia for some trivial reason. Maybe, thought Primakov, he has more important things to do and is simply filling in time by making contact with me. But as he thought it, he knew he was wrong.

"Yes," he replied. "Golitsyn is dead."

"There are no loose ends?" This time it was a question but behind it lay a threat.

"None."

"And the man we gave you to do the job?"

"He returned to Moscow this afternoon. I will have him disposed of when I return."

"You will treat him like a hero." The old man didn't raise his voice.

"I thought you –"

"He will be treated with great respect. We may have need of his expertise."

"But he's an old man and . . ."

The words were out before he realised what he had said. Primakov's heart sank. He had never knowingly angered this man and was not intending to do so.

"Not as old as I am, Andrei Petrovich. I hope you aspire to such an age."

The use of his patronymic was a mixed signal, at the same time intimate and formal.

"I meant no disrespect, but he has few talents not already available in our small team."

There was silence, as though the old man had lost his train of thought. Primakov had a feeling that there were other men in the cottage. There would have to be. And where was the old man's transport? Had he flown in? Was there a helicopter somewhere close at hand?

"We have far better men –" Primakov attempted to continue.

"He speaks good English."

"So does Imran Talebov, and I plan to reward him by bringing him home."

The old man chuckled. "Talebov stays in Australia."

"But why?"

"He's dead. No, I don't know who yet, but if the intelligence I have is correct, then it was old enemies or those wishing to be seen that way. The *Istrebiteli* signed their name beside his body."

"But they no longer exist –"

"Enough, Primakov. Put this man into the Institute on analysis, or something. Make certain that the major project material is filtered to him; enough to give him a feel for the area. We may need him. If not, then we kill him later. In the Institute he's safe. Find him an apartment and make it secure."

"I will take charge of it myself."

And that was it. The next thing he knew he was back in the car with the taciturn driver and heading for Moscow. Things were not as bad as he had thought. He unwound the window and lit a cigarette.

He felt the driver's eyes on him. Go fuck your mother, thought Primakov. He had come through one of his worst nightmares; having to be alone with the old Ukrainian. Nothing could stop him now, and he could go back to being the one who gave the orders. A sudden thought brought him out of his buoyant mood. He leant forward and tapped on the glass partition.

"Get a move on. Take me to the Institute, not to the Parliament." He hoped that Danilov would not get sick of waiting and carry out his orders before he arrived. He had told Danilov that they were to get rid of Trinkovski. But had he asked to see him first? He felt himself break out in a cold sweat. I hope I asked him to wait, thought Primakov. Otherwise, not only would Trinkovski be dead but so would Danilov and there was every reason to suspect his own death would not be far behind. He needed to get to the Institute very fast indeed.

The arrivals board in the European Arrivals Building at Sheremetyevo Airport was contradicted by the public address system. The plane had landed. As Danilov ambled towards the arrivals lounge he fished in his pocket for the piece of card with the name "N. Trinkovski" scrawled across it in large letters. The only photograph he had seen of Trinkovski was forty years out of date, so he rated his chances of recognising him as extremely low.

The passengers looked as though they had just come off a flight from hell. Drained, exhausted faces searching the crowd for people they wanted to meet, or didn't. If the flight was bad, thought Danilov, then *Gospodin* Trinkovski, wait for the reception. Killing people didn't worry him one way or the other usually, but this man had kept him waiting and was indirectly responsible for the pain in his gut which felt as though his digestive system was engaged in a losing battle against the remains of the *piroshki*.

He held the card above his head. Yes, he would enjoy taking this man down to the sub-basement at the Institute and ushering him into the soundproof room where he could find out what hell was really about. Danilov felt the eyes on him before he saw Trinkovski and turned to greet him. The man had been on the far side of the crowd, masked by the other passengers. The face was gaunt, but with dark eyes, that held his. This man had an inner strength and determination. Mind you, he would have needed that strength to have survived for so long in Australia, thought Danilov, as he tossed the card onto the ground and extended both hands to grasp Trinkovski's.

"Welcome back to Russia. I'm Colonel Victor Danilov."

"Thank you, Comrade Colonel. It has been a long time but somehow the flight seemed longer." Although tired, his onyx eyes flashed with a sense of humour.

"Ah, but one such flight in forty years is not a bad average." Danilov released Trinkovski's hand and lowered his voice in mock conspiracy. "But these days I am simply Colonel Danilov. The word 'comrade' has become a casualty of the new order, alas. And you who have worked so long and hard for the motherland have been reduced to plain 'Mr'. Still, we have other ways of rewarding such a long-suffering servant of the State."

"I'm sure that given a little time I can adjust, Colonel."

"Victor Ivanovich. Please, you must call me Victor, Nikolai Nikolayevich. Come, you have luggage?"

"One bag."

"So few souvenirs? No matter, we can avoid the formalities. Position opens doors, that much is still the same."

He turned and led the way down the stairs and, after flashing his security clearance, through a swing door to the rear of luggage collection. If the terminal had been chaotic then this was like a scene from some surrealist nightmare. The area reverberated to the whine and scream of jet engines and reeked of Av-gas exhaust fumes. Warning lamps rotated in grimy glass of various colours, illuminating then concealing, casting shadows down a smoking tunnel from which a small pair of yellow eyes approached. They belonged to a dented tractor pulling a line of over-flowing luggage carts. From out of the shadows a group of dark faces emerged and stood, smoking, looking at the luggage.

"Get on with it you, lazy sons-of-bitches!" barked Danilov.

The handlers appeared to be from one of the Asian Republics now lost to Russia. They ignored the uniformed Colonel. Or couldn't hear him.

"Can you see your bag?" There was an urgency in Danilov's voice. "Just point it out."

The handlers paired up and swung each bag between them and then released it to crash onto the metal rollers that carried the bags to the conveyor belt and into the terminal. They could not afford to travel. They could not afford the dutyfree booze and perfumes. So? So, if we can't have it, why should you shits? It was egalitarian. It was the new order. Had Danilov and Trinkovski not been there, some bags may not even have made it as far as the conveyor belt.

"It's that one."

"Grab it." The colonel turned away and started to abuse one of the handlers.

Trinkovski couldn't hear what was being said, but he saw that it was effective. Danilov returned with a man who, after pocketing some money, picked up the bag and fell in behind them.

Outside, an old Chaika was parked in a no-parking area; the driver asleep, his cap pulled over his eyes.

"Volodya!" Danilov slapped an open palm on the nearside window. "There are plenty more waiting for your job, you lazy bastard!"

The driver shrugged and started the engine. As they banged the doors shut his eyes went up to the rear-view mirror in an unspoken question.

"To the Institute, Volodya, and take the scenic route. Our guest has not seen the splendours of Moscow for forty years."

The driver nodded and slipped out into the traffic.

"Relax and enjoy, Nikolai Nikolayevich. We have a small welcome for you at the Institute, then you can have a well-earned rest." Colonel Victor Danilov lit a *Novostj* and stretched out. Yes, he thought, we'll give you a rest . . . a very long one.

CHAPTER

SIXTEEN

SAVVA VASILYEVICH GOLITSYN looked out on the Moscow evening through glazed eyes. A debilitating weariness had overwhelmed his body shortly after taking off from Perth when he had acknowledged that he had really done it. He had walked through Customs with absolutely no problems; the Trinkovski passport was examined and not found wanting.

Although he was so tired, sleep wouldn't come; his head racing backwards and forwards through the decades. The days in Melbourne, the acquaintances, friends, people he had slipped into calling his colleagues. Heimo Susijarvi, Aino ... She had vanished, back into her grief. He knew he would not have made it this far without her. Sometime, when this is all over, he told himself, I will repay these people. The faces of his friends flicked in and out of his mind and behind them, Amelia. Always Amelia Lippmann. Her voice and face saddened him and took him down into inner realms that he feared to acknowledge. All his life he had shielded himself from the young boy who cried inside. The boy who didn't remember his parents; whose fantasy of a mother had never been allowed to surface. Yet, here, high above the Indian Ocean, his need to know her rose and brought him closer to fear than he had ever been.

The small brave boy who had survived the orphanage was suddenly scared. Somewhere, deep inside, was a pain so primal that he shied away from the memories. He became, instead, the young man in his uncle's care and, later, he explored the mixture of pride and fear that had accompanied him into the training that had set him on the path to Australia. Somewhere, between sadness and fear, he slept and awoke to find himself in the cloying steaminess of Bangkok.

The transit time was four hours. It felt like a hundred. For a while he wandered the airport halls which seemed, at the late hour of his internal clock, endless. The restaurant was the only place with any spare seats so, after holding off as long as possible Savva gave in and wandered over to the counter. He had no Thai *baht* in his pocket but found that for five

Australian dollars he could purchase a pre-packed salad sandwich and a coffee. Neither added anything to his despondent state of mind. The sandwich had discovered some way of drying out; no small feat given that any air that could enter the moulded plastic container was very humid. And the coffee appeared to turn grey when the Long-Life milk was added.

Why was it, Savva mused, that those milk containers were so small? Another five millilitres and they would not only make the coffee drinkable, but would also probably increase the profitability of dairy farmers. His solution to a perennial Australian rural problem, however, did nothing to improve the taste, so he went up to the counter and eventually managed to get another container of milk. It cost him a dollar coin. At this rate the dairy farmers would become millionaires.

Eventually they boarded again and headed towards the Arab Emirates and the final change of aircraft before Moscow. How he needed a vodka. He attracted the attention of an aisle-cruising flight attendant and, knowing that they wouldn't have Finlandia straight from the freezer, ordered a vodka on the rocks; plenty of rocks. He raised the glass to himself and the choices he had made that had brought him to this moment. His choices – had they truly been that? Or had they been a gravitation to a re-creation of the patterns set in place at childhood. His intellect scoffed at such an idea. Where in all of this lay the place of "free will"? Then he knew. His decision to leave a country he had grown to love and call home was his breaking of the template. He might not have much time left, but bugger it all, what time there was, was his. Inside the small boy smiled. Outside, the man toasted himself and slowly drained the vodka.

Primakov didn't wait for the driver to open the door. As soon as they pulled up in front of the Institute, he was out of the car and up the front steps. Good, there was no sign of Danilov's car. He pressed his ID card up against the scanner and, as he heard the click of the locking mechanism, pushed the door. There was a chance that the idiot had sent the car away with the driver. He strode to the lift and looked up at the indicator. Fuck it all, it was down in the basement. Shit! That meant someone was down there. He didn't bother to go to the security desk to see who was logged into the building, but took to the stairs at a run.

As he pushed the bottom fire-door open he saw that all the lights were on. He rushed along the passage that led to the sub-basement.

"Danilov!" he screamed. "Son of a bitch! Are you down there?"

"It's only me, sir."

He spun round. It took him a moment to recall the woman's name. She had been with the Institute since the beginning; an expert on the European Union.

"Zoya Maximovna. Have you seen Colonel Danilov?"

"Perhaps you should try Anna Petrovna's flat?" The smile was less than subtle.

"He was on his way here from the airport –"

"I have been working for the last two hours. I would have heard the lift or the door to the stairs."

"Thank you." He brushed past her and down the stairs to the soundproof room. It was shut and sealed from the outside. "Good," he said to nobody in particular, then turned and made his way wearily up the stairs. Beside the research desk he stopped and put his hand on Zoya Bogdanov's shoulder.

"You should not work so hard, Zoya Maximovna, Brussels will still be there in the morning. I cancelled the nuclear strike for tonight."

The woman turned, a smile on her tired face. She nodded, touched his hand in gratitude and turned back to her books.

Just then Primakov heard the lift. As the doors opened he recognised the look on Danilov's face. It showed he had been through a shit of a day and he was about to take it out on the sod standing at his side.

"Ah! Comrade Colonel!" Primakov knew how jumpy Danilov got at being addressed as "Comrade". "And this must be our returning hero: Trinkovski. Or should I say Jack Zinner? A remarkable effort. A great contribution!"

"I was just taking *Gospodin* Trinkovski downstairs," interjected Danilov, putting emphasis on the old Russian *Gospodin*, a title usually reserved for foreigners.

"No, no. Not good enough. I'll tell you what, Victor Ivanovich. I don't think you had anything important on tonight, so while I take Nikolai Nikolayevich up to the office for a welcome home drink, why don't you arrange the best hotel room you can find and take care of all the arrangements. Check it out personally and call back for Comrade Trinkovski in a couple of hours." The tone brooked no argument. Danilov turned on his heel and opened the lift door for a bemused Trinkovski.

"Oh . . . and Victor Ivanovich, take the bag with you. Save having to carry it later."

The door shut and *Gospodin* Nikolai Nikolayevich Trinkovski began his move up in the world, quite literally.

Though it was still late summer some of the leaves in the forest around the *dacha* were beginning to turn russet and gold and the night air seemed to creep in with a whisper of winter on its breath. For Savva the whisper was welcome. It had been a lifetime since he had experienced anything colder than a Melbourne winter. Mind you, he smiled to himself, that had seemed pretty miserable at the time. He stopped and looked at the trunk of a silver birch in front of him. I wonder, and a broad grin spread across his face, I wonder how Collingwood will go this year? He imagined trying to explain to someone like Danilov why the black and white of the birch reminded him of Collingwood. Or explaining Aussie Rules football to Primakov. He laughed out loud; the sound eaten up by the *les* – the forest that was preparing for winter.

He knew the *dacha* was a way of keeping him under observation but it was welcome, nevertheless. He needed time and space in which to ground himself. The prevailing sensation of the past few weeks had been one of disorientation. He had only seen Primakov on a couple of occasions since that first night, and then only briefly. Victor Danilov, on the other hand, appeared to have been designated as his minder; a role he obviously found distasteful. It was not that he did not facilitate the necessary arrangements, but that he did so with a contemptuous lack of enthusiasm bordering on hostility. Somehow, Savva noted, Danilov's position had been undermined, as though he had been replaced as class favourite.

The Hotel Ukraine, where Savva had stayed for the first two weeks, was comfortable enough and he had been free to do as he pleased while an apartment was found. By the beginning of the second week Danilov was all set to install him in a tiny flat near Kiev Station in Dorogomilov Street, but Primakov had turned up just in time to pronounce it, "Only fit for *blini*-cooking peasants; the *borshch* and sausage brigade." He had driven off again immediately, leaving Danilov white with anger, fumbling for another cigarette.

The following day they had been summoned to look at an apartment on Berezhkovskaya Embankment and had arrived to find Primakov smugly waiting outside. The building had been constructed for some of Stalin's favoured bureaucrats and, though he and they were long gone, it was still imposing. Primakov had handed over a key and suggested that Nikolai Nikolayevich should take a look around. If it was suitable then let Danilov know and Victor Ivanovich would make all the arrangements for furnishing it, to Nikolai's taste, of course. With that he had driven off and left Savva amused and Victor Ivanovich apoplectic.

Danilov had stayed in the car while Savva took a look around the fourth-floor apartment which turned out to be far better than he had expected. Savva had whiled away a good few minutes just taking in the view, before ambling slowly down the stairs to the car and tossing the key to Danilov. It would be fine.

When it became obvious that the repainting and furnishing was going to take at least a month, the decision was made to install Savva in the *dacha* at Arkhangelskoe. Danilov had been glad to be free of *Gospodin* Trinkovski for a while, but he realised that until the apartment was completed, he and Anna Petrovna would not have use of the *dacha*. His mood did not improve, but the speed at which he pushed the work on the apartment did.

Savva smiled as he walked back towards the wood smoke rising from the *dacha*. He was hungry and knew that the housekeeper would have prepared the dish he had requested. She opened the door for him as he approached and came out to greet him. She was a plump, older woman, not one of the *russkaya krasavitsa* – the Russian beauties – but of friendly disposition and a great cook.

"I'm all done for tonight, Nikolai Nikolayevich. The food is on the table."

"Thank you, Vavara Semyonovna. I will see you tomorrow."

She bade him goodnight and took herself off through the forest to the units that housed the staff from the surrounding *dachas*. Savva watched her go, then went inside. On the table sat a crock full of steaming *borshch* and sausages, and waiting on the other side of the vodka bottle were Sverdlovsk rolls covered with icing sugar for dessert. Scratch a Golitsyn and you'll find a peasant, he thought, as he raised a glass to his reflection in the window. Be healthy!

His life, he considered as he lay in bed, was very much like the *les* outside. Beautiful and calm at the moment, but showing signs of autumn and only too well aware that winter was approaching. He rolled over, contented. This would not go on for ever but he was damn sure he would enjoy it while he could.

CHAPTER

SEVENTEEN

Just under a month later, Savva took possession of the apartment. Having left all the decisions on its decoration to Danilov, he expected the worst and instead was pleasantly surprised by what he found. It had been repainted in soft mushroom tones with the colour picked up and reinforced by darker Marimekko curtains. Like the curtain material, the other furnishings were also Finnish, including a kitchen setting that was a reproduction of an Alvar Aalto design. It was superb. He had seen the style twice before; once at an exhibition at the Melbourne Museum and again in a Finnish design brochure in Heimo Susijarvi's home. He picked up a beautiful

Iittala Glassworks shot glass and headed for the freezer compartment of the refrigerator.

A bottle of *limonnaya* lay in waiting.

As he was about to break the seal on the bottle, the phone rang. For a moment he was nonplussed. It was less then twenty minutes since Danilov had dropped him at the door and declined to come in, claiming to have seen enough of the apartment in the past month to last him a lifetime. The ringing stopped, then, after a short pause, started again. Savva did not remember seeing the phone in the entrance hall or the dining room so, apart from the balcony, that only left the bedroom.

The ringing was coming from a brand new Nokia phone on a small writing desk set back into a window alcove. Savva strode past the bed and picked it up.

"*Molodyets!* You found the phone, Nikolai Nikolayevich."

"I don't need congratulations, Andrei Petrovich. It was exactly where you had it installed." The smug tone was having the same effect on Savva as it did on Danilov. "But I'm sure you're not ringing to see if the phone works."

There was silence on the line for a moment, then a low chuckle. "You know something? You have been away so long you have developed a foreign sense of humour, Comrade Australian!"

Savva held the phone away from his ear until Primakov's laugh subsided.

"But tell me, Nikolai Nikolayevich. The apartment? Has that peasant Danilov done a good job?"

"The apartment is fine."

"Did I interrupt something, Comrade Australian? You are entertaining maybe? Some young beauty with a big set of *siski*?"

By the sound of things, Primakov had been drinking. Savva glanced at his watch – ten to six. It was still too early for anyone but an habitual drinker to be sloshed. On the other hand, he might just be in a playful mood. Savva decide the best way forward was to play along and, he had to admit, he found himself warming to the man despite the smugness.

"No, Comrade Primakov. Not even an old beauty with no *siski*. It was something far more important."

"And what would that be?"

"I found the bottle of lemon-flavoured holy water in the freezer and I was about to deflower it, when some maniac decided to ring a phone I was not even aware that I possessed."

Again he held the laughter at arm's length.

"Do you think this lemon-flavoured beauty would share her favours?"

"With a little pepper and sausage, I think she would take on all of Dynamo and their reserve bench. Mind you, she might feel better if she had a girlfriend."

"I'll pick the girlfriend up on the way over. Thirty minutes."

The phone went dead.

A good session would certainly remind him that he was back in Russia. Savva laughed. It will be a little different from a binge in a Fitzroy pub or a wine bar in Lygon Street. Ah! That was something! His mind raced around the world. That was really something. Sunday morning in St Kilda. A walk along the main street with Amelia at his side, the faces and languages from a dozen nations on the footpath. And those shops! The cake shops with their almost obscene concoctions of glazed fruit and chocolate and cream. And the coffee at Leo's . . . Stop it! He clamped down on the thoughts. I wanted to be here and now I am. I need to . . . But in truth he realised that he did not know what he needed to do. Just below the surface was a longing that he had been repressing since his return to Moscow. It would fade in time but at the moment it flared and burned into him.

The part of the mind that reasons clicked into action, letting him know that it was understandable to feel this way. After all, his entire adult life he had lived in Australia. A part of him was Australian, as Australian as John Smith, Nicko Theophanous or Heimo Susijarvi. He even thought and dreamed in English for God's sake! At that moment he wanted Australianness; whatever it was. He wanted things he had never allowed himself before: six packs and beaches, a trip to the Dandenongs, a walk on a beach followed by an iced coffee. The very things he had turned away from, thinking of them as kitsch, for the tourists, he now wanted. Fuck it all, he would give anything to be able to go to the MCG and watch a cricket match, and that was really saying something because he hated cricket.

This was an important moment for Savva Vasilyevich Golitsyn; he renewed his resolve to return. He was to remember this time, sitting at a desk in a strange apartment, looking through an early autumn shower at the lights reflecting on the Moscow river. He was to remember it because life, although it does not always deliver what you want, often gives you what you need. He realised then that unless he acted, he would get neither.

"*Blyadoslovye*!" roared Primakov, slamming his glass down onto the table. "Bullshit! It's incomprehensible! Is there no rule that tells you when to double it? To repeat it?"

"None!" Savva could hardly see the glass to refill it. The tears of laughter rolled down his cheeks. But he steadied the bottle with both hands and spilled very little.

"No. Wait. Let me get this straight, people understand if you only say it once?"

Savva leaned forward conspiratorially. "Ah! Only with one of them. All the others you have to say twice. I know it sounds crazy, but it's true."

"Which one? Which one can you say once, or twice?"

"Wagga Wagga. You can just say Wagga if you like. But Woy Woy, Grong Grong, Gumly Gumly,

Bungle Bungle, you have to repeat. As I said, they're Aboriginal names."

"Wagga Wagga. Vodka Vodka ... You know what that means?" A light had come on in Primakov's bloodshot eyes. "That United Nations mongrel, Bhutros Bhutros, is an Aboriginal. We should get our UN ambassador to denounce him as an Australian spy!" He staggered to his feet. "I tell you a secret, Nikolai. I have a peasant's thirst but a bourgeois bladder." He belched loudly and wandered off to the bathroom.

Savva took his glass and poured it down the sink before refilling it with water and returning to the table. Emptying the first bottle of *limonnaya* had not been too difficult; he had paced himself and eaten as much bread, gherkin and cold sausage as he could. True to his word, Primakov had brought the food, another *limonnaya* and a bottle of pepper vodka. The second bottle of *limonnaya* had been a little more of a problem for Savva as Primakov had insisted that they alternate between it and the pepper vodka. Then nature had come to the rescue in the form of Primakov's frequent trips to the toilet.

"Tell me," said Savva, as Primakov sat again, "how is it that I have not been debriefed? I expected to spend the first few weeks –"

"Debriefed!" Primakov's laugh cut him off. "Listen, Comrade Spy. These are the 1990s. The Cold War is over, we are all friends now. If we want to find out anything about Australia we can read it in the papers, or watch it on television. This isn't the era of the spy, this is the era of *biznes*, of *biznesmen*." The sneer in his voice that accompanied the Russian words which had become synonymous with crooked entrepreneurs was not subtle. "I'll tell you a State secret, Nikolai Nikolayevich. Last year our banks shipped forty billion in US hundred-dollar bills into Russia. Forty billion! Think about it. That's worth more than all the *rubles* in circulation. And is that forty billion being spent helping the workers? Is it rebuilding our economy, our hospitals, our defence forces? No. It's for *biznes*. For the fuck-their-mothers *biznesmen*!" He drained his glass and refilled it.

"Can nothing be done?"

It was a gamble and Savva knew it. Push too hard and Primakov might clam up or wonder what lay behind the questions. Then again, Savva might wait a long time for another opportunity like this.

"Ah, there are some things one shouldn't talk about even in such enlightened times." Primakov pointed at the ceiling in a gesture that indicated that the apartment was not free of listening devices. "Fortunately, Nikolai Nikolayevich, I am in a position to withhold the tapes of such things."

"Of course," Savva laughed. "I would expect no less of my esteemed colleague." Deciding to push a little further, he continued, "After all, it was you who installed them! I appreciate the furnishings in the apartment, but the taste is too refined to have come from Victor Ivanovich."

"Danilov couldn't redecorate a country shithouse!"

"But such an accomplished job of interior decorating does not come without a price." Savva made a show of draining his glass. "I just thought you should know that I share your taste in subtlety, Andrei Petrovich."

Primakov busied himself cutting another slice of sausage and chewing it slowly as he regarded Savva. Then, as though he had come to some decision, he refilled the glasses. "Come, drink with me, comrade."

The pepper vodka burned like fire down Savva's throat. The *limonnaya* he could tolerate, even enjoy, but this? Primakov grinned at the pained expression on his drinking companion's face and the water streaming from his eyes. "You know what I call this stuff? Wild lilac water!" Seeing that Savva had no idea what he was talking about, he pulled him closer. "You have been away too long. Such innocence. Wild lilac is what we call CN gas, tear gas . . . no, never mind." He released Savva's shoulder, picked up the pepper vodka and got to his feet, beckoning Savva to follow him into the living room.

"I need padding under me. Those Finnish chairs may look great but my arse needs comfort." He collapsed back onto the settee and heaved his legs up onto the coffee table. "That's better. Now some music, Nikolai Nikolayevich." He indicated a very compact Japanese sound system. "Maybe I should have called in at the Arbat Restaurant and brought along a couple of good, honest, working girls?"

"Another night, Andrei Petrovich. I am having enough trouble working out how to press buttons on this bloody machine. I think that between your wild lilac water and my lemon friend, I would have had a little problem."

"That's treason!" Primakov roared. "You think our *russkaya krasavitsa* don't know how to raise the dead? As I said before, you've been away too long. Most of the men they work with are in a worse state than either of us, comrade."

"But," said Savva, "I am an old man and at my age, you know what vodka does? It whets the appetite but drowns the man."

A burst of rock music blared out from the tiny speakers. Turning the dial he found some traditional folk music. He raised a quizzical eyebrow to Primakov who smiled and nodded. Savva turned the volume down slightly, then pulled a chair up to the coffee table. As he did so Primakov took his feet off the table and leaned forward. Suddenly he no longer seemed to be as affected by the alcohol.

"You asked if anything can be done?" His voice was quieter now, serious. "These are strange times indeed. But, as our Chinese comrades are always keen to point out, the other side of the coin of chaos is opportunity." His eyes flashed up to make certain that he had Savva's attention. "In the past, we would have looked for a surgical cure –"

"October 1993? It didn't work for Khasbulatov and Rutskoi. Or August 1991 for Yanayev and his committee."

"Or General Kornilov seventy-four years earlier? No, a coup is no longer an option and neither is the democratic process. We need strong leadership. Our people have always needed that. But not imposed."

"You're talking of the people rising?"

"The Russian people have always banded together when the threat has come from outside."

"The Great Patriotic War." Primakov was right. When the Wehrmacht had launched Operation Barbarossa in the early hours of 22 June 1941, it not only signalled the greatest invasion in military history, it also signalled a call for unity to which the Russians had responded. All this, Savva had studied over the years, but what it had to do with wherever Primakov's mind was heading, he was not sure.

"Exactly! Any fool can see that we were unified then, we were unified when the capitalist Americans were the enemy, but now? Now the enemy is within. A cancer called greed. A cancer called apathy. Harder to beat than the Americans. What brought us undone was money. The West outbid us in the Cold War. Don't you see? We spent and spent but couldn't match them and we won't make the same mistake again." Primakov's eyes were flashing. "So we need an external threat and we need preparations for a response."

Savva shrugged and sat back. Was this vodka talking, the new voice of Russian impotence, or a bit of both? He imagined that he could have heard the same outpouring in any Moscow bar on any night of the week. Not that it wasn't understandable. The collapse of the Soviet Union and the old ways being swept aside so suddenly had been cathartic enough for him, observing from afar. How much stronger it must have been, must still be, for those who lived through it.

"Come on, Andrei Petrovich. The theory's fine, but I'll bet you a river of vodka that it won't happen. Sure, we have always rallied under external threat, but the American people were just as tired of the arms race as we were, and there is no way they will threaten us again."

Primakov drained his glass, then pushed it away as if to say, enough is enough. He gazed through Savva for a moment and then focused.

"Nikolai Nikolayevich, I'm not talking about the Americans. The Muslims. Think about it. What are we surrounded by? How many of the old republics are drifting deeper and deeper into the arms of Islam? Chechens, Abkhazians, Azerbaijanis, Uzbekistan, Kazakhstan . . . and behind them, backing them up, fuck knows what countries. Think about it!"

"And, if this is chaos, where is the window of opportunity?" Savva had to agree that there was a grim streak of reality running through the man's analysis. "And who can take advantage of it?"

"I am starting to really like you." Primakov ignored Savva's questions. "I think we should talk some more. Now I must go wake that pig-fucking driver of mine and leave you to test your new bed." He crossed to the window, flung it open and paying no heed to the fact that it was four in the morning, roared at his driver to wake up and start the fucking car. At the door he turned. "Did Danilov mention that you're invited to the Institute on Monday? He has a little job you might be interested in."

Savva wondered, as he headed for the bedroom, if Danilov had been told about the Monday meeting, let alone the idea of some job.

On Saturday, Savva decided it was time to dig a little deeper. He was no longer concerned that Primakov might suspect him of being anyone other than Trinkovski, but knowledge was power and at the moment he had very little of either. The fact that neither Primakov nor Danilov had seen through him was probably an indication that they had no access to the old files. But somewhere someone must. The obvious, indeed the only contact he had was Heimo's friend, Koshlykov. Savva saw no point in taking the risk of using the phone in the apartment, so he decided to make his way out onto the streets.

Outside the apartment, he became a tourist. For a while he wandered along the Embankment, unable to pick out a tail. There were plenty of people on the street and cars cruising slowly, mainly driven by private citizens looking to pick up a little extra cash acting as taxis. Most of the cars seemed to be held together with a combination of wire and good luck; old Zhiguli 8s, an Audi, and a limping Moskvitch or two. Any one of them could have been a tail. In the end it was a matter of percentages. Logic told him that they couldn't all be following him so he waited until one was almost past him and waved it down.

The question of money came up before the driver would even attempt to crash the car into gear, but, after negotiating a ridiculously high price, Savva sat back as the old Volga spluttered and farted its way toward the Zoo. They stopped by an icecream kiosk outside the Zoo as did three other private taxis; all disgorged passengers. He sat on a bench and enjoyed the sun. Enough of the paranoia, he decided eventually, and walked to a phone. Savva fished in his pocket, only to find that he needed to turn around and head back to the icecream kiosk. The taxi fare had cleaned him out, leaving him with nothing but Australian dollars.

"Got any change?" He spoke English and laid a small pile of Australian notes on the counter. It was a long shot but one that paid off. The notes vanished and he found himself holding an already melting icecream. Anyone watching would have thought it quite normal.

"*Angliski?*" The man had his back to Savva and was furiously punching an ancient calculator.

"Aussie . . . Australian," Savva replied, and was rewarded with a shrug of the shoulders.

"You wait."

This was probably the extent of the man's English. He smiled, revealing a row of teeth that looked as though they had been repaired in a steel foundry. With his black hair and darker skin he was not Russian. The eyes were oriental. Maybe Tartar?

Savva attempted to look casually around as he fought a losing battle with the dripping icecream. It tasted foul. The flavours and colouring looked and tasted as though they were a creative use of industrial effluent. He had missed the young boy when he ran out of the back of the kiosk, but saw him returning. The boy handed a soiled envelope to Metal Mouth and received a coin in exchange. The man nodded discretely to Savva.

"*Sem'sot rublei.*"

There was no discussion even though Savva, without the benefit of a calculator, could work out that he had been robbed blind. He looked at the wad of tattered notes. They wouldn't help much.

"Telephone?" He mimed dialling.

"Ah! *Telefon. Da.*" The man handed a couple of coins to Savva and gave a return performance of mime as though he was explaining to a child who had never seen a payphone before.

Savva turned to find that a small crowd had gathered to watch the exchange. So much for subtlety, so much for tradecraft. There was no point in attempting to hide what he was doing now, so he turned back to the moneychanger.

"Thanks, mate, *spasibo.*"

The man shrugged. He was already involved in trying to sell icecreams to the crowd.

It took a while to find a phone that was in working order. He dialled the number and waited. After a time a man's voice answered. Savva realised he hadn't thought this through. The last thing he wanted to do was compromise this man.

"A friend of mine said you might be able to get some theatre tickets?"

There was a pause. Savva could feel the tension in the voice.

"I think you have the wrong number."

"My friend said he mentioned my name to you on your recent trip."

There was another pause.

"Could you repay me with his favourite vodka?" the man said.

This time the hesitation was on Savva's end, but only for a moment.

"I don't know if I can find Koskenkorva in Moscow."

"I would love to help but I'm going to be . . ." The voice hesitated for an instant, then continued, "in the capital of the Czech Republic at seven this evening. It's a private function. You're welcome to attend, though."

The phone clicked and went dead.

Savva spent an hour wandering around the Zoo working out what his next move should be. He needed more information, but he could think of no way of gathering it without attracting attention.

A good walk would help, he decided, so he strolled through the streets until he crossed the bridge and arrived at the Hotel Ukraine. Inside, he found a table and called over one of the waiters he recognised from his short stay there. He ordered a beer and inquired if there was such a thing as a list of theatres and restaurants. The information stands in the foyer were, he had noticed, empty as usual. The waiter took more money than was reasonable and said he would do what he could. Ten minutes later he returned with the beer and two information cards. He offered not even a *kopeck* in change.

Savva scanned the theatres but couldn't find one named Prague. He turned his attention to the restaurant lists and was rewarded almost immediately. There it was; the Prague Restaurant in Arbat Street.

"Are you finished with those?" The waiter must have found another customer for his tattered information cards. "Or, is there something else I can do?" He obviously thought Savva had more money than sense.

"Yes," Savva said, taking out one of his traveller's cheques. "What kind of vodka do you have?"

There was a look of mild surprise on the young man's face. Drugs, guns, boys, girls, icons, he had been asked for them all. Vodka was a valuable commodity, but you could order it at the bar. This man was truly mad. But, traveller's cheques? The blackmarket loved them.

"Vodka? Kuban, Russkaya, Starka, lemon, pepper. Whatever you want. How many bottles?" Maybe it was a bulk order, but he could already see his cut diminishing.

"Just one." Savva paused to watch the waiter's face hit rock bottom. "But I want Koskenkorva. It's Finnish. I thought, maybe some of your guests . . ." He shrugged and gestured towards the crowded bar in the next room. The waiter's eyes didn't leave the cheque that Savva was about to sign.

"Maybe you would prefer it blank?"

The US fifty-dollar cheque vanished along with the two information sheets. In very quick time the waiter was back with another beer. Savva hadn't ordered another, so he guessed it was a token of the establishment's pleasure at his patronage. The new Russia was in some ways so much like the old one. Only the currency had changed.

Even at this hour of the day, the militia at the entrance to the hotel were doing a roaring trade. Savva watched as they offered a light to an endless stream of young women who smoked and chatted with them before being allowed in. He couldn't pick the moment when they slipped the militiamen the money, but the men's pockets were filling fast. Most of the girls seemed too young to be servicing the tourists like this, but, as one woman swung her hips past his table, he could see that her youth was an illusion propped up on one side by cosmetics, on the other by desire. He smiled at her but shook his head.

"Your parcel, darling." The woman displayed a set of ragged teeth.

An old GUM store bag was placed beside his chair. He didn't bother looking. If it was right, it was right, if not . . . well, there was nothing more he could do. He pushed his chair back and went to find a taxi.

CHAPTER

EIGHTEEN

THE ringing of the phone startled him out his afternoon nap. His dreams had been of absurd car chases in which he had attempted to avoid being caught by a derelict Chaika. The old car had broken down just before reaching him and when the Trabant he was driving managed to get a block or so away, it too broke down. Mechanics worked feverishly to get the cars back on the road, but as soon as one fault was repaired, another developed. He and the other driver would chat amicably during the repair stops and only become mortal enemies once they were both back on the road. If it had been a movie, it would have been a collaboration between Jacques Tati and Roman Polanski. He woke, half expecting his hands to be covered in grease.

"Nikolai, I trust you are recovering?" It was Primakov.

"I'm only just beginning to think that living might be an option. And you?"

"Memories of good company are the best cure."

"Then we'll both survive."

"Good. I must return to my desk. I just needed reassurance that I hadn't damaged you. I don't indulge frequently, but when I do . . ."

"If that is now the standard debriefing, Andrei Petrovich, then I look forward to more."

"I am sure we can arrange that. Oh, by the way, I am impressed by the way you have grasped the new economic realities. Icecream kiosks invariably give a better exchange rate than the banks."

Savva thought he heard a soft chuckle before the line went dead. In a way it was comforting to know the rules by which this game was being played. It would have been stupid to imagine that he was not being watched, but Primakov's tone suggested it was just a formality. He was being courted or evaluated, he was not sure which. One thing was very clear – he would have to take more care when it mattered. Let them think he was an old fool attempting to play the game with out-dated tradecraft but . . . The thought trailed off as Savva realised that he had arrived at a pretty accurate description of the situation. He walked away to wash his hands. Somehow they still had a greasy feeling.

At about five o'clock, Savva, carrying the plastic GUM bag, wandered out onto the street and strolled south down the Embankment. Anyone observing him would have thought he was taking an early evening constitutional. Not once did he check over his shoulder, preferring rather to give his attention to the river or the buildings, and several times he paused to sit on a bench and take in the view.

He gazed over the river to a park and beyond it, to the Lenin Stadium. Quite a few people were walking along the other bank and as though recognising someone, he waved and then tapped his watch in an exaggerated gesture. Quickly turning on his heel, he increased his pace and made his way not on or back, but down a short street running away from the river. He then turned left and strode briskly along Kosigina Street to the red "M" sign that indicated the metro. Here he paused just long enough to take a wad of paper from his plastic bag, tear it into strips and push it deep into an already over-flowing rubbish bin. As he went through the metal turnstile he glanced over his shoulder and had the satisfaction of seeing a man fishing through the rubbish with one hand, while holding a two-way radio in the other.

Less than thirty seconds after Savva boarded the train, the doors shut and he began his journey towards the city centre. At the first stop a large crowd of people left the train, many of them wearing sporting clothes. Savva smiled to himself. No doubt the man he'd seen sorting the rubbish had let someone know that their subject had waved to somebody over the river, and they would be waiting to follow him as he emerged from the station. Good for them, but he didn't intend to leave the train before Marx Prospect, and that was still five stations away. He wondered if the man going through the rubbish would be pleased to find several pages from the Moscow phonebook and if he would be thorough enough to check the underlined entries. Savva hoped so because he wanted the message to get back to Primakov, whom he felt sure would appreciate the joke. Savva had underlined the names of four companies, all of which distributed vodka.

At Marx Prospect Station, Savva decided against leaving the metro and instead abandoned the orange indicators and headed for the blue ones that would lead him to a train heading back towards Kiev Station. After travelling past a couple of stops, he emerged at Smolenskaya and made the journey from there to Arbat Street on foot. He still had plenty of time before his rendezvous, so he stopped to watch the street musicians and hustlers on the Arbat pedestrian mall. At first he thought it was an ideal opportunity to see if he could pick out one of his minders, but he soon realised that there were simply too many people and gave up.

Just before seven o'clock he had reached the end of Arbat Street where he dumped the plastic bag and stood, bottle in hand, a little back from the crowd outside the Prague Restaurant. By twenty past seven he was ready to give up and go back to his apartment. People had been coming and going but there had been no sign of anyone even giving him or the bottle a second glance. Just then a waiter tapped him on the shoulder.

"I believe your friend is already inside. Maybe you would care to follow me?"

The man led him up to the third floor and indicated a private room. As Savva entered, the waiter closed the door quietly behind him.

Lev Sergeevich Koshlykov was alone, staring out onto Kalinin Prospect. Unsure of what to do, Savva waited by the door, reminding himself that this man was not the face of the new Russian security ministry, the MBR; he was the old KGB, through and through. Resident in Australia, Resident in Oslo and, God knows where else.

"Can you imagine what Canberra would have looked like if our great Soviet architects and builders had won the contract to build it, Savva Vasilyevich?"

It was not the question that shocked Savva, it was the use of his real name. His first instinct was to turn and leave, but reason told him that nothing he could do now would change anything. He stood his ground.

"Maybe the setting would have inspired them to produce something a little better than those boxes out there, Lev Sergeevich."

Koshlykov turned, smiling. He was older than Savva had imagined, but there was a strong spark in his eyes that lay somewhere between strength and humour.

"So, we have both done our homework and I see you have found Koskenkorva. You are a resourceful man. It's a pity you were not placed where we could have used your talents a little more than we did." He indicated a chair. "Sit! We have much to talk about and very little time. I have ordered some food. You drink if you want to. I am, unfortunately, under doctor's orders."

"I drank more than was wise last night. If I may join you in mineral water?"

The older man filled two glasses and handed one to Savva.

"I heard an abbreviated version from our mutual friend but I need to hear the story from you."

The only interruption during the next hour was the arrival of the food and two more bottles of mineral water. When Savva had finished speaking, Koshlykov pushed himself up from the table and, after opening a window, lit a cigarette.

"When Susijarvi told me your name, it didn't mean a thing and, of course, when the embassy did a search, they found nothing. After I returned from Australia I pulled in a few old favours from places where records go back further than memories. I had been shown a list of illegals and sleepers before I went to Australia for the first time in 1977 and I recently managed to retrieve that list. You were on it, as was the other man you mentioned, Trinkovski. But that list doesn't match with any of the later lists, or, in fact, the earlier ones. Somehow the records have been sanitised, but obviously not quite as thoroughly as certain people might hope."

"But why? To what end?"

"The same end as always, power." Koshlykov flicked the remainder of his cigarette out over Kalinin Prospect and turned back to Savva. "The interesting thing about the sanitising is that not all of the agents vanished as you and Trinkovski did. Only two others. The rest – and there were more than you would imagine, and I must say, more than we could ever have needed – the rest were left undisturbed in the files and under MBR control. You and Trinkovski, however, had been effectively poached."

"And still never used –"

"Trinkovski was. Otherwise you wouldn't be here."

"I still don't understand how or why." Savva felt a surge of anger rise up through him. A pawn in internal KGB/MBR politics?

"The answer is right in front of you. Who's controlling you, or I should say, thinks they're controlling Trinkovski, now?"

"Primakov?"

"Exactly. He has always been the power behind the Special Projects Research Institute. I don't have anything I can prove, and worse, I am no longer in much of a position to know who to prove it to. I have grave doubts about the effectiveness of the MBR. But I have a very good idea of how this has happened. My biggest concern is that I am not quite sure where it's headed. I've been digging pretty deep and may have disturbed some things that would have been better left alone."

Feeling suddenly chilled, Savva rose and closed the window.

"Tell me about the Special Projects Research Institute," he said.

"Its predecessor was the KGB's Information Analysis Administration. It was started in 1990 under Valeri Lebedev. It not only processed all incoming information for every organ of government, but its role of dissemination put it in a unique position of power."

"Meaning it could give what it wanted to whoever it wanted?"

"And with its special bias. Everyone relied on it for analysis and recommendations. The crisis that came to a head on 18 August 1991 had its beginnings in the IAA. You obviously followed the events."

"Yes," Savva said. "It would have been hard to avoid them, even in Australia. Gorbachev isolated by the conspirators in his *dacha* at Foros; chaos in Moscow."

"Not all chaos. There were those who saw the coup faltering and used the events to cover their actions. From what I can piece together, the KGB ordered the destruction of all the IAA files on the afternoon of the 23rd. But it was already too late. A team of men had moved at around 3 pm on the 21st and by seven that evening, the work was done."

"All the files destroyed?"

"A mountain of ashes, certainly, but all destroyed? No trace of the files has ever surfaced, but someone knew about you and Trinkovski. What does that suggest to you?"

"And no investigation?"

"By whom?" Koshlykov shook his head. "No. No investigation. You must remember that the KGB was in transition. The new MBR had only been set up in January 1991 and at the time of the coup attempt it was an organisation in name only. It had just twenty positions and that included secretaries and typists. At that time it needed all the help it could get and it came in the form of a bureaucrat, Andrei Petrovich Primakov. He proposed a semi-private organisation to be known as the Special Projects Research Institute. Somehow he had influence. He certainly managed to tap into the much needed funds."

"So he was given the go ahead?"

"Yes. It took him about three months to find and take over the buildings near Vnukova Airport 2. He hand picked every member of staff and installed the director."

"Where did the staff come from? No, don't tell me. The old KGB?"

"Of course. There was an oversupply of applicants from both the old Central and the Union branches. Most of them were ex-Fifth Administration who had shifted to the Third after the Fifth was restructured. They had worked against dissidents, you know the types."

"You mean they were 'patriots'?"

"Exactly! Men and women of vision. Though not necessarily the vision shared by the rest of the emerging Russia."

"So how does Primakov run the Institute from his position as a parliamentary secretary?"

"Discreet lines of communication, and, of course, I would assume he has certain files that allow him to keep people in line."

"You are saying that what he has created is, in effect, another version of the Information Analysis Administration, but this time he is accountable to no one?" Savva had listen with a growing sense of both trepidation and anger. Now he could no longer keep silent. He took one of the old man's cigarettes and lit it.

"And," Koshlykov continued, "he hires only hard liners who think that the Soviet Union was betrayed and sold out. They supply information analysis to various government departments, but I'm willing to bet that this is only a secondary function. Who knows what the main one is and how many agents like you and Trinkovski they have, still thinking they are working for the Russian Government."

If even only half of what Koshlykov thought was true, it was enough to fill Savva with dismay. "Why haven't you gone to the authorities?"

"What authorities? Who do you trust? I've served my country well and for a long time, and now I want to get to know my grandchildren. You too. You must want these things. Why should we get ourselves killed now? I fear what I may have disturbed, digging even this far. I won't do more . . . and you? You should find a way to leave this country and go back to Australia. I understand you have friends waiting in Helsinki."

The two men sat in silence for a moment. The thought of Heimo and Aino in Finland offered such an easy route out to Savva but it was an option he was still not ready to contemplate. He realised that behind the old man's reference to Helsinki was an offer of assistance; perhaps the only thing the man felt safe enough to hint at. Slowly he shook his head.

"No, thank you, Lev Sergeevich, but I must see this through."

Koshlykov shrugged, rose and put on his coat. He looked even older and more frail now. He picked up the bottle of Koskenkorva, looked at it briefly, and then placed it in front of Savva.

"A foreigner can come here and live all his life and never become a Russian. But a foreigner goes there and in two years he's become an Australian. It's a fine country, Australia. You would fit back in. It's a rare place. Take the vodka back to Heimo and drink my health, Savva Vasilyevich, I'm going to go and watch my grandchildren grow up."

For a long time Savva sat alone, digesting what he had heard. It was clear he could either cut and run or stay and dig a little deeper. Whichever of the options he took he would have to do it alone. If Lev Sergeevich could find no one to trust, then what chance had he? Somewhere in the next half hour Savva's anger was transformed and though his fear had not subsided, his mind had been made up. At the first opportunity he would get out. The game that was being played was for younger men and women. They could have it. His aim had been to go home and retire, but somewhere on that journey everything had gone wrong. He was about to start working for a very suspect organisation and along the way the word "home" had come to mean Australia.

CHAPTER

NINETEEN

ON a grey Moscow Monday morning, Savva Golitsyn started work at the Special Projects Research Institute, though as far as the Institute staff knew he was a man named Nikolai Trinkovski. It would also be true to say that he did not actually start work until the afternoon, the morning having been taken up with the issuing of security clearances. By one o'clock, Savva was in a cramped but private office on the third floor. The room was only just big enough for a desk and two chairs, although a nineteenth-century romantic artist's vision of the Taiga had been hung on the wall in an attempt to give a feeling of depth. Either that,

218

thought Savva, or in an attempt to depress me. The effect certainly did nothing to atone for the lack of a window.

The surprising thing about the office, though, was the equipment. A brand new Japanese IBM clone sat on the desk next to a printer and, even more remarkable, a high-speed modem. A Nokia handset, identical to the one in his apartment, was the only other object to grace the desk.

Danilov's greeting had been perfunctory in the extreme. Since then, Savva had been handed from one person to another, and so it was a relief to close the door and sit for a while. He turned on the computer and watched it go through its preliminary routines. The Windows application popped up on his screen with a request for his password before it would let him into what, Savva assumed, was the Institute's network. A password? Checking his laminated photo-ID and his swipe card he found nothing. A further search of the desk drawers told him only that the desk had been factory assembled and inspected by "#238".

From his jacket pocket he took out the Trinkovski passport and tried entering the birth date. Nothing. He tried the passport number, again nothing. After several more futile attempts he gave up and went in search of coffee. At the end of the corridor, he had been informed, he would find a small staff kitchenette. There were only two chairs behind a small table and a man was seated in one with his feet up on the other, engrossed in a paperback. The coffee looked old and stale and as Savva could see neither milk or sugar, he turned to the seated man.

"Is there sugar?"

For a moment the man looked up at Savva.

"Go fuck your mother," he snarled, closed his book and walked out of the room.

As he watched the man leave, Savva realised that he had seen him before. That time his nose hadn't been deep in a book but, rather more unpleasantly, he had been up to his elbows in a rubbish bin retrieving some useless pages from a phonebook. Obviously his superiors had not been overly impressed. A sudden thought struck Savva and, leaving the coffee on the bench, he hurried back to his office. With a sinking feeling in the pit of his stomach he typed in "Koskenkorva". To his dismay the screen cleared and he was presented with an internal communications screen that informed him he had two unread e-mails.

He realised that his system had been set up not by just any technician, but someone acting directly for Primakov. The meaning of the designated password was all too clear; he had failed in his attempts to throw Primakov's watchers off his trail. Worse though, was the thought that he had compromised Koshlykov.

He had been a fool to think he could still play this game. Primakov was not only a good tactician, but also appeared to enjoy the psychological cut and thrust. The fact that he had not simply arrested Savva gave at least some credence to Koshlykov's theory that Primakov was an espionage entrepreneur, playing outside the system for his own ends. It was a depressing conclusion. Although no one would wish for the return of the Cold War, at least then, most of those involved had the justification of duty or patriotism. Certainly there had been the avaricious and the opportunists, but an overwhelming number must have been "good" men and women. Now it was all about capitalising on the disintegration of a nation. Everyone was out to grab a slice of the pie, a piece of the action.

With resignation rather than fear, Savva clicked the cursor on the e-mail icon. As he had expected the first one was from Primakov, but it was with bewilderment and a growing sense of relief that he scrolled down the screen.

Comrade Australian, greetings!

Enough! I capitulate. Even if I had the temerity to ask my men to check up on you again, I doubt that they would agree. It was edifying to watch them outwitted by an old fox, but as I said, enough is enough. You will understand that I had to confirm your abilities for myself.

To business. This system is as secure as any we can devise. The log-on procedure initialises an encryption process that safeguards your files. Don't be worried about the network status. It is separate from the Institute system and linked by the modem on a dedicated line to my terminal.

The other file I have sent you is some background on a major area of interest and is relevant to the discussion we had the other evening. Please familiarise yourself with its contents and do a daily update from the suggested Internet newsgroups. They are not reliably sourced information, but they will give you an idea of how others see this part of the world. No need to e-mail the updates. File them under date and I can read them when I have time.

Friday night I will make amends. I have telephoned the suppliers you indicated and have a case of their product being delivered. I look forward to sampling it with you. Seven-thirty at the Ritza (about a block from the Rossiya Hotel in Razina Street).

Like a bloody roller-coaster ride, that's what it feels like, grinned Savva. One moment I think I'm about to be shot, the next I'm a new-found drinking buddy. Oh well. He clicked on the second icon and watched as a compressed file started to unzip. He read for almost two hours before he shut the system down, his brain on overload. Needing a break to let all the information sink in, he walked past the kitchenette, down the stairs, signed out of the building and went in search of real coffee.

Primakov was no longer anxious. His report over the secure line to the Ukraine had been well received. The old man had obviously been running a parallel check on Trinkovski, but the results were the same as before they activated him in Australia. He was a cautious but gifted operator and not in need of anything but the normal security precautions. Better still was the reaction to Trinkovski's first week's work. He had combed the networks to come up with information relevant to the subject areas and had shown himself to be a much more gifted analyst than his training so long ago would indicate. It merely went to prove that all those years in Australia had not been wasted, as was so often the case with agents left to themselves. This man had researched almost every area of armed conflict around the world, and quickly identified those where some opportunity presented itself for either commercial or political exploitation. It had been a remarkable performance.

"And our one area of special interest? How did Trinkovski rate it?" The old man's voice snapped Primakov out of his self-congratulatory reverie.

"It was the only one he dismissed without hesitation. Oh, he gave reasons, and they were all the right ones."

"Which confirms that we have chosen well. If all the analysis suggests there is no possibility of any gain, then it's the last area any of our opponents will think of looking."

"Exactly."

"Move him into it. I have the third shipment ready and I am simply waiting for the transport schedule to be agreed to. I would like him on site by the time it arrives."

"When will it reach its destination?"

"At the outside? Three months, four months."

Primakov decided to broach his one lingering doubt about Trinkovski.

"Is there any word on what happened to Talebov?"

The old man paused, as though unsure how much he should disclose.

"Relax. I'm certain it wasn't our new comrade. The latest information is that it was a very creative woman. I suspect she was pregnant to him because he was drugged, before he was killed, by a muscle relaxant normally used for preventing miscarriage. Nice touch. Anyway, forget Talebov. Everything is on track, Andrei Petrovich. You have done well."

It was the first time in the decade they had known each other that the old Ukrainian had ever paid him such a compliment. A very satisfied Andrei Primakov hung up the phone.

The old man was glad that his choice of Trinkovski was working out so well. He was far more comfortable with the older men. Primakov was good, too, but as for most of them? Well, they did not have the wisdom of the old hands. His experiences, years before, in the Kremlin had taught him that old wolves may be slower, but they were invariably more reliable.

Friday had been dull and misty, and by the time Savva arrived in Razina Street it was raining steadily. It was a most unlikely choice of restaurant. Savva

224

had, in fact, been able to smell it before seeing it. He picked up the sharp cheese smell of *khachapuri* and his youthful memory proved accurate. The Ritza was a squalid little *kachapurnaya* – a Georgian-style fast-food cafe.

Inside the smoke-choked cafe, a counter and stools ran down one wall and a single row of small round tables and chairs were lined up along the other. In the middle was a space barely large enough for the waiters to move. To make matters worse, the remnants of what had once been linoleum were wet and slippery, perhaps as a result of extremely clumsy waiters, the patrons' lack of table manners, or the water tracked in from the street by the customers. Savva guessed it was a combination of all three.

Peering through the smoke, he saw no sign of Primakov, not that he could really imagine the man in this setting. The place looked as though it failed to meet even the rudimentary Moscow health standards and must have owed its existence to large payments into the coffers of the Chechen Mafia, most of whom appeared to be occupying the tables. The patrons, engrossed in cards or chess, paid him no heed as he carefully made his way down the aisle. The fact that most of them were drinking and smoking, rather than eating, did little to convince Savva of the culinary prowess of the establishment.

"Niki! Nikolai!"

It was Primakov's voice and it appeared to be coming from the kitchen. Savva shuffled past a waiter carrying a tray full of beers and found his host beckoning him to follow him through a cheap curtain of glass beads strung on nylon. The kitchen looked no bigger than a toilet; its size diminished by the presence of a large *babushka* who flashed a toothless grin at Savva as he passed. In front of him, Andrei Primakov was beaming, holding open a door to a back room.

"Welcome to my favourite den of crime and corruption! Don't be put off by the crowd. I have taken care of everything, Maria and Tomaz will cook us up a feast."

In complete contrast to the rest of the cafe, the room was not only clean, but well furnished with a sideboard and a large maple dining table. There were two bottles of vodka on the table and a half empty bottle of *Zhigulovsky* beer.

"I've brought you a present, Andrei Petrovich," Savva said, taking the bottle of Koskenkorva from his overcoat pocket. "You have no idea how much trouble I had getting it!"

"Only partly true. But I know you paid too much. After that . . . who knows? So how was your first week? That pig Danilov hasn't been bothering you?"

"No sign of him, well, not unless you count the warm welcome he gave me for about ten seconds on Monday. No, it's been fine. Interesting." It was true. He had been enjoying the research.

"Don't worry about Danilov. He does a good enough job of running the Institute, but you and I, well we have better things to do." He saw the question on Savva's face, but shook his head. "No. We eat and drink first, then I'll explain my little proposition."

At the end of the meal, Tomaz joined them for compliments and a quick vodka. He was a veteran of Afghanistan, where he had been fortunate to have left only the lower half of his left leg. He rolled his trousers up and proudly displayed the most unusual prosthesis Savva had ever seen. It was carved from a single block of wood and had been fashioned to look like the twisted branches of a tree, woven loosely together. If it were not for the fact it had a wooden foot at the end, it would have been a superb piece of folk art. The food had been far better than the exterior of the Ritza had suggested, and so they drank a toast to Tomaz and his wife. The Georgian then left them with the promise they would be alone until Primakov called for his special dessert.

"Special dessert?" queried Savva.

"Wait and see," Primakov replied, reaching for the Koskenkorva. "Come, let's find out what the Finns have got to teach us."

"Well, I can assure you that temperance won't be one of them." The combination of food and vodka had already created a warm glow in Savva; it had been a long time since he had relaxed and enjoyed an evening as much.

Primakov had chatted on and off through the meal and Savva had the feeling that there was the potential here for a genuine friendship. Often, he thought, good men get caught up in ugly worlds. Primakov claimed to have had no special advantages in life, other than his intelligence and an ability to negotiate with people – skills which had found their natural home in his parliamentary work. He had spoken openly of the horse-trading that went on between the factions and his enjoyment of the process. Of his involvement in the Institute, he said little, other than that he was on a committee to oversee its efficient functioning. If the parliamentary work was about process, Savva guessed, then the Institute was about content.

"It is not advisable, Nikolai Nikolayevich, to talk of certain things in specific terms, so forgive me if I stretch a metaphor. Let me paint a scenario." Primakov pulled his chair closer. "What would you do if you had all your valuables in a bank and then found that, not only was the bank charging you interest, but it was letting your enemies into the vault to help themselves?"

"I'd change banks."

"And how would you know that the next bank wasn't doing the same thing?"

Let him play this at his own speed, thought Savva, he's obviously leading somewhere. "I'd keep a better eye on it."

"Yes. A discreet bank that your enemies didn't know about, but also with your own people on the inside."

"Right."

"The situation for us in Russia is, unfortunately, worse. Our branches in the Soviet Union have been taken from us and the bank we are left with is being plundered by the West."

"But you're not talking, literally, of banks?"

"I'm talking of . . . certain military assets."

This, thought Savva, is where the world gets suddenly ugly.

Primakov paused and sipped his vodka, looking for a reaction. Savva gave none. Primakov continued.

"A few important people have set up their own bank where no one would even begin to look for it. The Institute has been facilitating the transfer of a few assets and started trading with them. Small amounts, with clients who can only survive if all parties are discreet. The problem is that even a small and lucrative business is subject to takeovers. It hasn't happened yet, but it is inevitable that sooner or later someone will attempt it. Our people in this 'bank' are, for the most part, technicians, the tellers and accountants if you like. We need you to do an audit."

It took every bit of will-power Savva possessed to stop his hand from shaking as he filled the glasses.

"It would seem to me, Andrei Petrovich, that you would be far better off with a senior specialist in this area. Someone who commands respect, not an old and rather jaded amateur."

"The job description comes with only three criteria: English speaking, skilled observer and an analyst trusted by my committee. You fulfil all three and you have another asset that is invaluable. You have been out of circulation so long that the bank will not even suspect an audit. More importantly, neither will the customers. You may remember a previous conversation we had concerning those who surround us. Well, they are the customers."

"It makes no sense," Savva said, thinking back to the discussion about the Islamic republics, "to trade our assets with those who would threaten us with them . . ." and then he saw it. It was so simple, he suspected he was wrong, but he continued anyway, riding the hunch. "Of course, it would mean that you would have an exact tally of those assets and maybe even control."

The delight on Primakov's face was obvious.

"Fuck it all, I knew you were good! We need a threat to unify the people, and we minimise the danger by controlling the source of that threat and provide ourselves with an excuse to eliminate the threat once that unity is achieved."

Savva's hunch had been right. There were many other questions he wanted to ask, but he knew that the answers would be provided if he accepted the assignment. He needed only two more answers now.

"I take it that those who run this bank don't know who the real owners are?"

"No. They think it's been set up by a group of private Russian entrepreneurs."

"And where exactly is it located?"

"Nikolai, think!" Primakov laughed. "You found it this week."

Savva quickly went through the countries and conflicts he had analysed during the course of his work, but none of them was quite right.

"The place you eliminated because it showed no potential?"

The logic was stunning. It was a forgotten country involved in decades of forgotten turmoil, its leaders were involved in an attempt to forge a network of Islamic states to counter the West.

"I know very little about it. It's not my area of expertise . . ."

Right country, wrong person was the response his mind threw up. But his words were saying, "Yes. Maybe with some briefing . . ."

Primakov tossed back his head and laughed. "Some briefing? Nikolai Nikolayevich, when I've finished with you, you will know more about Sudan than the GRU and KGB ever did. Here! A toast!" He quickly refilled the glasses. "To the auditor, Jack Zinner!"

"Jack Zinner?"

"Of course, who is going to suspect a long-term migrant Australian? No one has ever heard of you and we can construct a legend that will be impregnable. Trust me!"

There was a knock at the door and Tomaz's wife, Maria, brought in a tray with coffee. She placed it on the table and left without a word.

For a while they alternated between coffee and vodka. Drinking in silence, each lost in their own thoughts; Savva recreating the conversation in his mind, raising objections . . . squashing them. For his part, Primakov was pleased. He knew he had the right man for job. And if not? Well he had, as always, a fall-back plan. He hoped it would never come to that because he realised that, in Trinkovski, he had chanced upon one of the few people in their game with whom he could talk and drink, confident of being understood. Many of the others were brilliant in their fields, but fuck, who would want to drink with them?

"Do you understand the world?" asked Savva, after a while.

"I gave up. Look at us, we had a philosophy. Philosophy may attempt to understand the world . . . what really matters is to change it."

"But surely to change it one must understand what it is."

"No. You could spend lifetimes trying to understand. People have. But that's a way of putting off . . . of procrastinating. Listen . . ." Primakov's speech was thicker now, the vodka talking. "The common theme, at least in our country, is that change comes from the masses. That is simplistic. First, they have to be motivated and unified. For that you need an individual and the individual has to have an idea that the people can grasp."

"But this individual . . . haven't we come full circle, is his idea not his philosophy?"

232

Primakov slammed his empty glass down in mock frustration. "No, it is just an idea."

"Of what?"

"An idea that can change the world. But if he doesn't act quickly, the philosophers will have him by the nuts and procrastinate their way from arsehole to kingdom come. Idea! Action!"

"You think you can do that?"

"What? Change the world? No."

"Then what?" Savva had a funny feeling that he had lost the thread. Somehow he didn't care. He was drunk and full of good food.

"I can have an idea –" Primakov was still on track, or thought he was.

"At your age?"

"Yes. Why not? And what about you, Nikolai?"

"Maybe at my age that is all I can have."

"What?"

"An idea that I can change the world."

There was a feeling that they had managed to reach some conclusion. Primakov slapped Savva on the back and slumped in his chair. Savva had the fleeting impression that maybe they had arrived at different conclusions, but the thought was swept away as Primakov rose to his feet and bellowed out the door.

"Tomaz! Tomaz! Time for our dessert!"

The two girls who Tomaz ushered in were not the usual working women that one saw outside the tourist hotels or down on the river bank at Luzhniki, by the Lenin Central Stadium. They reeked of money and none of it was *rubles*. Theirs was a foreign currency world that allowed them to dress as though they had just stepped off a plane from New York or Berlin. Savva wondered how they had survived the walk through the cafe. He also wondered if he would make it through the rest of the evening, or more immediately, even out of his chair.

CHAPTER

TWENTY

SOMEWHERE in the weeks that followed, Savva Golitsyn felt himself changing. It was not something that happened at any well-defined point, but rather a slow realisation that he was different. The years of marking time in Australia had produced a particular mind set; an attitude of "wait and see". Now he felt energised. He studied all day at the Institute, then walked the streets, digesting the information.

He had always been a walker, but this was something more; long hours that took him all over Moscow. He didn't see the streets. He was barely aware of the people or traffic and, when the first winds of winter started sweeping the pavements with rain or snow, he simply donned a warmer coat and kept walking. When he found himself outside a sports complex one evening, he added swimming to his routine.

It was on a cold Sunday, hurrying back from an afternoon swim, that contact was made. Lost in the swirling descent of great snowflakes, he had almost walked straight into the couple. He, tall and blond, she, wrapped in a full-length fur, head in a woollen scarf.

"Excuse me? Do you speak English?"

The man touched Savva's arm. His accent was thick, Finnish. Savva stopped and nodded. He pounded his gloved hands against his arms in a gesture of cold and impatience. The last thing he wanted to do was arouse any suspicions. Talking to foreigners was not recommended in his line of work.

"Yes. I speak English."

"My friend and I are visiting and we were wondering if you knew a good restaurant?"

"No. I'm sorry, I don't usually eat in this district. You could ask at any hotel."

Savva began to push past the couple when the woman put her hand out to block his way.

"I have heard that the Prague Restaurant is very good."

It took every ounce of self-control Savva possessed not to put his arms around her.

"I will show you which metro to take. After that I am afraid I must go home."

He steadied himself and walked in front of them towards the station.

"We think you should come home with us." Aino's voice was quiet but clear. The falling snow seemed to have muffled the city sounds and Savva had the feeling that the three of them were drifting aimlessly behind a curtain of white.

"I cannot. But tell your father I am fine."

"We have a Finnish passport for you. We have tickets from here to St Petersburg and then on to Helsinki."

The man had dropped back. A professional, he was checking the shops casually. He shrugged at the glance Savva shot him. It appeared they were not being followed.

"Heimo says the people you are involved with are extremely dangerous . . ."

He took her arm more firmly than was required. With his other hand he pointed to the metro sign now much closer. He was just a friendly Muscovite helping out a tourist.

"Tell Heimo they believe I'm Trinkovski. Tell him that I am going to Sudan. I have a chance to find out about the illegal sale of arms. I will contact him when I can through that hotel . . . the Fisherman's Hut?"

"Kalastajatorppa . . ."

"Yes."

"You won't come with us?"

"No. Not yet."

"Amelia said you would say that."

"Amelia is in . . . ?"

"No. We talk on the phone. She also has a fax now on that number if you need to contact her." Aino paused and opened a small bag she was carrying. As she did so she nearly overbalanced as her feet slid on some ice. When Savva steadied her she pressed something into his hand.

They were outside the metro.

"Can we meet again?"

Savva shook his head.

"Just follow the metro," he said to the tourists and turning, trudged back into the snow. It was a long walk home. Once there, he discovered he was carrying a small laminated photograph of Amelia. On the back in Cyrillic script was the single word "love".

The preparations for his departure had taken several weeks longer than either he or Primakov would have wished, but it was a very well briefed and physically fit man that Primakov, with genuine affection, hugged goodbye at Vnukova 2 Airport.

"A sensible *lastochka* migrates away from this climate," were Primakov's final words. Somehow, although he liked the image, Savva realised he felt nothing like a swallow. A sheep in wolf's clothing. A sitting duck on a wild-goose chase maybe . . . but a swallow?

PART
III

CHAPTER

TWENTY-ONE

IT was an icy Moscow that Savva left behind on 3 January, maybe, he thought, for the last time. For, although he had thrown himself into the role he'd been given, he knew he could only play the part for a limited time. He still had no names to go on, but it had become blindingly obvious that the men behind Primakov were setting themselves up for a major roll of the dice. Knowing that they would probably only ever have one chance, they intended to make sure they would win. Their wisdom in avoiding a military coup meant that they were potentially both more dangerous and harder to stop. The only indication of their strategy Primakov had divulged was the creation of a major external threat to Russia. A threat serious enough for the people to demand the return of the hardliners who now waited in the shadows.

Savva felt that, somehow, what was taking place in Sudan was a critical part of the equation. He knew he was no young Rambo ready to save the world, he smiled at the thought, but if he could get proof of the thrust of their strategy, he could, at the very least, pass that information on to those equipped to deal with it. And then? He would be free to retire for the second time. As for the danger? What he was doing right now was probably the most dangerous thing he had ever done; he was flying Aeroflot.

There were many hours of travelling and two changes of aircraft ahead of him before he touched down in Khartoum. He welcomed this time as a chance to review the huge amount of information he had ingested over the last three months. Savva glanced at the passenger in the seat beside him. The young Englishman looked as though his farewell party had been a great success and lasted several days. His gait had been less than steady as he boarded the plane and he had tripped over Savva while finding his seat. Reeking of alcohol, he was asleep before take off and it appeared as though chatting would be the last thing on his mind if he awoke before London. Savva returned to his mental review of the past few months.

The briefing and preparation had been in two phases. The first concerned the logistics of the

242

operation in Sudan, while the second phase was a crash course in Sudanese history and politics followed by a deeper analysis of Sudan's recent moves to establish an Islamic Brotherhood. The idea behind the term "Islamic" was to draw in a wider group than simply a pan-Arab movement and, given the resurgence of fundamentalism worldwide, it was certainly a timely move. Savva was fascinated by the man who appeared to be both the architect and driving force behind the Brotherhood. Hassan El Turabi was also the head of the ruling party in Sudan, the National Islamic Front. While on paper, General Omar Bashir was the head of government, Turabi was, without doubt, the power behind the throne.

Watching the few interviews the man had given to foreign journalists, Savva was impressed by Turabi's mind and personality. He came across as a reasonable and pragmatic Islamic scholar with a remarkable intellect. His command of English was formidable and spoken with a slight accent that at times hinted at training in England, rather than the United States. Bashir was a very different character; straight out of the mould that had produced tin-pot dictators many times in countries around the world. A dangerous puppet? Savva wondered how much of the damage Bashir had inflicted on the Sudanese people was at his own behest and how much came from the iron fist of the softly spoken Turabi.

There were apparent chinks in Turabi's armour, not the least of which was his rivalry with his deputy,

Ali Osman Mohammed Taha. The radical wing of the NIF belonged to Taha, and his differences with Turabi were not about objectives but about means. Whereas Turabi was the diplomat and cautious tactician, Taha presented as an unsubtle man who openly supported the training and export of terrorists. Savva had to acknowledge that the factional squabble could well be a smoke-screen, employed by Turabi to confuse the outside world and lead to him being seen as the reasonable dove amongst the hawks.

The other big question that Savva's research had raised, but failed to answer, was the French connection, which began to emerge in late 1992 and early 1993. A decision had been made to court the French and, not only were invitations to visit Sudan issued to French journalists and scientists, but French was made a compulsory school subject in several provinces. At first it looked as though this was simply another attempt to break the political isolation that had come about when the USA had added Sudan's name to the list of countries supporting terrorism. This was the price they paid for advocating the Iraqi cause during the Gulf War. The deeper Savva dug, however, the more convinced he was that this was part of a much larger game-plan.

The collaboration between Khartoum and Paris went too deep to be explained away as an exchange of cultural pleasantries. With total disregard to Sudan's pariah status, the *Direction Générale de la*

Sécurité Extérieure (DGSE), the French secret service, had hosted four Sudanese security service delegations in Paris in the short time between October 1993 and January 1994. As if the flurry of activity had not been extraordinary enough, Savva was astonished to discover that the cast of characters had included DGSE Colonel Jean-Claude Marchand, who had emerged from a thirteen-year posting in the Central African Republic to assume control of the Sudan desk in 1993. His companion at the secret talks was the head of counter-intelligence, General Phillippe Rondot. Savva was not surprised to discover that the cast members were firmly allied with the right-wing Gaullist clique in the Ministry of Defence.

He took a little longer to find the names of the Sudanese participants, but when he did, he spent many hours studying them. The first name to emerge was that of General Hachim Abu Said, the head of all four Sudanese security services, but it was the second man who merited most attention. Only two photographs of El Fatih Irwa were available and both of them were old. One photograph had been taken during a strange episode known as Operation Moses, which had involved the evacuation of Ethiopian Jews to Israel. It showed a slightly stern but open-faced man, standing beside the door of an ancient DC3. It was a poorly taken picture. The second was worse. An indistinct scene shot with a telephoto lens showed El Fatih Irwa in army fatigues, crouched beside a fire in what looked like a clearing in some jungle. The man with whom he was obviously in earnest conversation, was a much younger looking Jean-Claude Marchand.

El Fatih Irwa gave a strong clue to some of the other motives behind the French connection. He was not only the Sudanese presidential adviser on security, but also the man bequeathed the task of recapturing Southern Sudan from the Sudanese People's Liberation Army, the SPLA.

Savva's thoughts were interrupted by the arrival of some indifferent airline food. After eating, he drifted off to sleep, only to be woken, what felt like minutes later, by the young man in the next seat making a dash for the toilet. He returned looking better but smelling worse. For the rest of the flight he chain-smoked and stared morosely at a tattered photo of a girlfriend who, by the look of her, was going to have no trouble finding a replacement for her departed lover.

The flight was half an hour late landing, and the connection to Nairobi was already boarding as Savva reached the gate lounge. The positive side of the late arrival was an upgrade to business class on the British Airways 747. Almost as good as Qantas, Savva thought, as a very handsome young flight attendant led him, in a swirl of expensive dutyfree aftershave, to the forward cabin. For a good five minutes it seemed to Savva that he would have peace and quiet all the way to Africa, but, glancing over his shoulder in an attempt to will the cabin crew to "arm the doors and cross check", his heart sank as a slim, bespectacled parody of an academic made his way forward.

By the time they were airborne, Savva had resigned himself to a very long flight. It was moments like these that he wished he had mastered the art of the sarcastic put down or the abrupt dismissal. He searched his repertoire for a suitable phrase but nothing occurred to him. He sighed and accepted the business card that had been thrust into his hand even before the man had removed his coat and sat down. Reading it immediately was out of the question, as he attempted to keep track of a conversation, the general thrust of which seemed to be an attack on the lack of a coordinated European Union policy on a varietal approach to potato production.

The arrival of a flight attendant bearing complimentary champagne gave him pause enough to read the business card. Savva discovered that he was sitting next to a plant physiologist from the International Potato Institute, located in Lima, Peru. That was bad enough. He could almost imagine himself surviving on a diet of potato statistics all the way to Nairobi . . . but how, in the name of God, did you keep a straight face with a man whose parents had either been insane or malicious enough to christen him Jesus Maria when his family name was Christos? That he had been christened seemed inevitable, but how in hell had he escaped the priesthood, to become a potato . . . whatever?

Jesus Maria Christos was indeed a religious fanatic and, although Savva could have enjoyed a lengthy discussion about Orthodoxy versus the Catholic Church, or even, given his newly found expertise, a discussion of Islamic fundamentalism, the object of his travelling companion's religious ardour was, unfortunately, the potato. Savva tried going onto automatic pilot but to no avail. Almost like a schoolmaster, Christos would ask questions to make sure that his captive was paying attention and fully understood the important role that the taro and yam played in the cosmic scheme of things.

Unwilling to fail, Savva gave in and paid attention.

"Take tomatoes . . ." How on earth had he got on to them? "Take the pumpkin. Then, ask yourself, how is it they are domesticated and the potato isn't?"

Savva had a mental image of pet pumpkins being walked on leashes while feral potatoes flashed their wild eyes at them from the roadside. It was all too silly.

"I've never thought about it," he confessed truthfully.

"Outside the cave, the women planted every seed of anything edible. They didn't know about seasons or anything but, with a little water, a percentage of those early seeds came up. Ten per cent. Why? Because all plant seeds have a suicide gene and about ten per cent are programmed to come up as soon as there is water. Yes?"

"I'm sure you're right . . . but –"

"The other ninety per cent of seeds would have failed to germinate. Then, because the women only harvested those that had come up, the ten per cent, the ones with the suicide gene, they had domesticated them. They had a found a primitive method of selective breeding –"

"Wait a moment." Savva had a dreadful feeling that he might be getting involved. "If the ones with the suicide gene actually germinate, why are they called that? Surely the purpose of suicide is to die?" There! He had him!

Christos' smile revealed a perfect set of teeth; they had all germinated.

"Exactly! I tell you Jack, you should have been a horticulturist! Of course they come up. But, they come up when the women want them to. If the women were not there to tend to them, they would come up and die. That was nature's way of making sure that they didn't all come up and choke each other." His expression of glee was that which was reserved by God for the faces of true potato fanatics. He leaned over and tugged Savva closer. "Let me tell you a secret. I've cracked it! I have manage to isolate suicide gene in potatoes! Can you imagine what that means?"

For all that the enthusiasm and the rapid disintegration of his grammar was infectious, Savva had to admit to himself that he hadn't a clue what Christos was talking about. Being a man sensitive to the sensibilities of others, however, he decided to bluff.

"You mean –"

"Yes! You have it! If I can isolate the gene, I can breed for it and then, instead of having to save half the crop to plant the next one, all the potatoes can be eaten and the seed . . . that tiny little seed, can be planted to produce more potatoes. In some agricultural economies that could make the difference between starvation and survival. Especially if we can crossbreed some of the local stock to produce disease and drought-resistant varieties."

"Jesus! That's fantastic." The profanity was lost on his fellow passenger, but enough to attract the attention of the flight attendant.

"A vodka for my friend and for me!" The man scuttled off. "You know that this is the stuff Nobel prizes are made of?" Savva confided. "At the very least, you are going to be the true king of the potato."

Christos produced another one of those smiles that sends photographers into paroxysms of filter fitting. "You think so?"

Fortunately the attendant returned with two small tumblers of vodka. Savva took his and proposed a toast.

"*Bitvy sei Vy . . . Tsezar!* Of this battle you are . . . Caesar!" It sounded grand in English or Russian. Pity it's not original, he thought, as the potato expert struggled with the interaction between throat and vodka.

Christos excused himself to visit the toilet. Savva fished the ice out of the vodka and drained it. He signalled for another and was granted almost five minutes in which to drink in complete silence and contemplate where the hell the quote he had used as a toast had come from. He hated the untidiness of things that popped up into consciousness without invitation and, worse, without bearing labels showing origin.

With the return of the potato man came a very sobering thought. They were due to land in Nairobi at nine in the evening, local time, and Savva had a sudden flash of them entering the New Stanley Hotel, where he was booked to stay overnight, only to find that rooms were scarce and he and the potato man were asked, "Do you mind sharing?" He banished the thought and turned off his reading light.

"You going to have a sleep?" Christos asked, taking off his glasses.

Savva grunted a reply.

Just as he was dozing off, he remembered. It was a poem by Tsvetayeva ... Marina. Um, can't remember the name ...

He awoke twice before Nairobi. Both times, Jesus was sleeping like a baby.

The potato man was myopically searching in the seat pocket for his glasses as Savva left the plane. He didn't risk telling him that they were in his shirt pocket. He would find them soon enough. After collecting his bags and wandering through a very relaxed Customs inspection, Savva boarded the complimentary bus. The atmosphere, the smells, the people all assailed his senses and Savva found, to his delight, that he was thrilled to be in Africa.

The view from the bus window, as it sped into town, was of the half built and the half fallen down. But it was Africa and it was new. The exhilaration was reminiscent of childhood excursions from the orphanage. After the isolation and depravation, each new face and street was a mental feast. Presented with too much to consume on the spot, he had developed the facility for storing away the images. Later, in the dormitory, while others fought or played games he would open up his mental scrapbook and examine each image. Here, thousands of miles and a lifetime later, he realised he was examining an image of his earliest memories of image collection.

The New Stanley was, to all intents and purposes, the old Stanley with televisions in the rooms. He dumped his bags on the bed and went to look for food. The outdoor brasserie had shut down its spit roast, but he managed to talk his way into a hamburger and chips. Drinking a South African Amstel instead of coffee, he idly wondered if it was possible to catch suicide genes by eating chips. Enough, he told himself. But his mind took a long time to slow down.

At eleven the following evening, he arrived at the airport alert and refreshed, to find a very different crowd checking in for the Sudan Air flight to

Khartoum. The queues contained fewer African faces and more people of various Arab stock. Some of the women were veiled, others, in total contrast, were draped with ostentatious amounts of gold jewellery, looking out of place and over-dressed. There were few other Europeans on the flight; he counted two men and a woman. The frail young woman, dressed in the habit of some religious order, looked as though she had been too long in Africa. The men could not have been more dissimilar. One had the appearance of a Boer farmer who was only just managing to hold back from voicing his disgust at having to stand in the same queue as the rest of the passengers. The other was as bronzed as the South African, but open and intrigued by everything that was going on around him. A slightly plump and balding man in his forties, he was dressed in a uniform that Savva had seen many times before. The jeans were faded Levis, the scuffed boots, and probably the shirt, were R. M. Williams and the hat, dangling from his hand, was an Akubra. Much as it would have delighted him, Savva held back from changing queues in order to talk with this man.

There seemed to be more than the usual amount of scrutiny of passports, tickets and Kenyan Government tax stamps, and by the expected departure time, Savva had still not reached the front of his line. A couple of Indian businessmen behind him were complaining quite loudly, until someone quietly told them that as the plane was going on to

Cairo extra security was needed because of the tensions between Egypt and Sudan. In Moscow, Savva had been following the border clashes and incidents along the Red Sea coast. It had been an uneasy relationship for years, but recently the Egyptians had captured a hit squad that they claimed trained in Sudan for the purpose of assassinating Egyptian leaders. It was probably true.

When he finally made it to the counter, it was mayhem. The Sudanese Security staff were being abused by everyone except the Sudanese passengers and, at the same time, were involved in a shouting match with airport security for stepping on their turf. The airport controllers were on the two-way radios, asking why bay twenty-three had not been vacated as they had an aircraft waiting to slot in there. The counter staff were being harassed by a supervisor who needed them to check in a planeload of people on their way to Addis, some of whom had almost no chance of making the only connection to Sanar, in Yemen, in a week. And who would be responsible for accommodating them for that time?

"Jack Zinner?" The security man took the Australian passport and checked it against a sheet of paper on his clipboard. Obviously everything was in order. The passport came back and Savva was ushered through a swing door to a bus waiting to transport passengers to the Sudan Air Airbus. The fact that the Airbus was French did not escape Savva's notice.

"Sudden Death Airlines." One of the Indian businessmen had moved into the bus beside him. "That's what they call them."

"Comforting."

"Mind you, these newer planes mean that they may have to rely on pilot error to keep up their average."

"You travel Sudan Air a lot?"

"Not if I can help it, but on rush trips to Cairo I sometimes have to take what's going."

Savva nodded his commiserations. "And how long have they had the Airbus?" He was racking his brain to remember the details of a Sudanese cabinet-level trade mission that had gone to France in early 1994. He couldn't recall the names but he seemed to recollect that they had quietly visited the oil company Total, the civil engineers *Grands Travaux de Lyon* and the Airbus aircraft consortium.

"I've had the textile plant in Cairo since 1990 and I don't think I scored a Sudan Air Airbus flight until . . ." he frowned, attempting to pin down the date, ". . . must have been late 1992. I think they had two or three then. I read that they ordered four more last year."

"But I thought the International Monetary Fund had some sort of ban on business with Sudan?"

"Bugger them!" The Indian man's companion chipped in with a laugh. "The IMF's loss is our gain. Unless you prefer to travel on converted Antinovs?"

"That bad, huh?"

"I reckon the engineers who did the converting had graduated with a major in water pumps or tractors."

Savva joined in the laughter as the bus disgorged them at the steps of the Airbus. They embarked under the watchful gaze of two guards with machine pistols.

Khartoum International Airport is not the most welcoming of places at the best of times. The middle of the night is not the best of times.

Although there were separate counters for Sudanese nationals and foreigners, Savva watched with growing frustration as only the counter for Sudanese was opened. The motives of the Customs officers were transparent as they quickly processed the Sudanese passengers. If they could obtain visas to travel, then who knows what connections they might have? Better to be courteous with them. The foreigners, however, were a different matter. They could wait.

Eventually, only the small group of non-Sudanese remained. An officer called them to attention. First in Arabic, then in passable English.

"We need you to cooperate with the Customs and Immigration officers. Please follow their instructions. I inform you that should there be any irregularities, you will be deported. The aircraft you arrived on is being held waiting for that eventuality. Should you be unlawful, you will be placed on that plane and held responsible for its late arrival at its next destination."

They were then instructed to step over to the counter assigned to aliens. At the head of the queue were what looked like a couple of extremely wealthy Saudis. The man waited impassively, the only sign of his frustration being the clicking of a set of large amber prayer beads. His wife stood several steps behind, accompanied, another few steps back, by an Indonesian maid who had charge of an overloaded luggage trolley.

Next in line was the Australian whom Savva had noticed in Nairobi. His only luggage, a backpack, was being used as a seat. The man looked exhausted. The other passengers were a group of African businessmen; Ugandans, was Savva's guess, though how they had obtained visas was questionable given the troubles between the two countries. Maybe they were Kenyan.

The Saudi party was soon on its way and Savva's heart lifted; perhaps it was not going to drag on until dawn. But then the Australian was turned away from the counter and sent off to a side room. The African businessmen were treated in a similar fashion. Savva stepped forward and slid his passport across the desk.

"Have you filled out a currency declaration form?"

"No one mentioned . . ." Savva began, knowing it was pointless.

"Over there." The man indicated. "You should hurry before it closes. Your flight was very late and we are not here at your convenience."

There was no point in disputing the obvious, so Savva picked up his bag and followed the Australian and the Africans. The Currency Declaration Office was just being unlocked as Savva arrived. The elderly man who opened the sliding glass window spoke no English and the form was entirely in Arabic. Fortunately, the Australian seemed to be familiar with the process and, after emptying his pockets and counting the foreign notes, he entered the amount on the paper and signed it. The form was stamped and a duplicate handed to him.

"Don't lose this one," he said quietly to Savva. "The bastards won't let you out of the country without it."

After acquiring the stamped form, Savva made his way back to the now almost deserted immigration hall. Outside, the plane had departed, the security lighting had been turned off and the runway was in darkness. Only two staff remained and, after a thorough examination of his papers, Savva found himself heading for the exit. Hopefully his contact would be waiting outside.

"Mr Zinner." It was the English-speaking officer, looking somewhat flustered. "General Sinada apologises for his inability to meet you in person at this hour, but a car is waiting."

"Fine." Savva nodded.

"Let me take your bag, sir." The change in attitude was remarkable. "Had the General informed us of your arrival in advance, we would have dispensed with all this . . ." He gestured at the empty hall, hoping that Savva understood the implication.

"I'm sure you would have," said Savva pointedly. Let the bastard squirm.

On the bonnet of a black Mercedes, a card game had been in progress for some hours. Drink cans and cigarette packets littered the ground between the feet of the uniformed driver and two other men dressed in traditional white *jelabirs*. They were engrossed in the game and appeared to be playing, not for money, but for sips from an old Pepsi bottle containing a clear liquid.

The airport security officer stopped at the top of the steps leading down to the carpark and called to the driver. There was a flurry of activity during which the Pepsi bottle vanished.

"Guava flavoured *araki*," confided the security officer. "Twenty lashes if they're caught breaking *Sharia*."

"Oh yes," replied Savva wearily. Any fool could have guessed what was in the bottle; only a bigger fool would give himself away by saying what flavour it was. No wonder this man was on night duty.

The car pulled up in front of the building and the young private was quickly up the steps to take Savva's suitcase.

"We have been very efficient and friendly for your arrival," called the security officer hopefully as Savva made his way down the steps.

"I shall mention it to the General," he lied and slid into the back of the Mercedes.

Fortunately, the driver either knew no English or was too busy chewing mints in an attempt to disguise the smell of the *araki*, for he was silent for the entire trip. They travelled well below the speed limit, a wise decision given the number of potholes in the road and that all street lighting had been turned off. There must be a power shortage, Savva thought, remembering the shut down at the airport. It was as though there was an order in force which went along the lines of, "Would the last one to leave the country please turn off the lights".

Even though Savva had spent hours with Khartoum street maps he was too tired to follow the journey, but at one point he recognised the border of the Sunt Forest and guessed correctly that they would soon turn towards the Blue Nile. They slowed at the next roundabout and took the first left exit. Savva now knew exactly where they were heading. He heaved a sigh of relief. The Hilton was just what Mr Zinner needed.

CHAPTER

TWENTY-TWO

A SHORT distance from the Hilton, Lieutenant-General Faisal Mohammad Sinada was having a very busy morning. He had been woken with the news that Jack Zinner had checked in and was expected to sleep until midday prayers, if not longer. That suited Sinada. He had arrived at the Friendship Hall at dawn and the meetings had started immediately. Delegates from over eighty countries were in Khartoum for the Islamist Conference and, though the Lieutenant-General had no time for the vitriolic speeches that were the staple fare at the main podium, he was very interested in the subtle nuances expressed by the men who came to the small side room in which he was working. These were not the men who made speeches. These were the men who made a difference.

He found it amusing to see the number of Western diplomats who were strolling near the cinema or the National Museum entrance. They were there not because of their interest in culture, but rather in the vain hope of catching a glimpse of some of the visitors who arrived behind the deep tints and armour plate of the limousines. They would have little satisfaction. Sinada's last guest had come in the staff entrance with a tray of croissants on his shoulder. Others were already in the hall, having drifted in as anonymous secretaries or lowly functionaries.

The small television monitor beside the desk was the Lieutenant-General's only contact with the official conference program. At the moment it showed the American Nation of Islam representative, Akbar Mohammad, addressing the floor. The translator's whispers expressed no hint of contempt as he informed the delegates that, "The Nation of Islam is the Hizbollah of America!" There was faint applause and the camera shifted from the grinning Akbar Mohammad in his blue jeans and trainers to the flowing robes of Sheikh Naim Qassem of Hizbollah. The Sheikh was looking somewhat bemused. Sinada turned the volume down and his attention back to the matters at hand.

His previous visitor had been a hard man to placate. Most of the unofficial delegates were here because of what he could offer, not to complain about it. The head of the Palestinian intelligence service, Amin al-Hindi, was the exception. While he was only too happy to have access to the secret training camps, he was less than impressed to have come across extremists in the self-rule areas who, under interrogation, admitted to having been trained in the same facilities. Sinada had endured the tirade without comment and, after agreeing to look into the conflict of interest, played his trump card. He casually mentioned that there was the slight possibility that a new source of top quality armaments would soon be available. The result was the same as for all his other guests. He added al-Hindi's name to the list of future clients.

In his position as deputy chief of staff for logistics in the Sudanese Army, Sinada had been present at the military cooperation talks with a Russian delegation a couple of years earlier. It had been an interesting series of meetings held at Port Sudan, the headquarters for the Sudanese Air Defence and Marine forces. Although Sudan had not been a client state of the Soviet Union since 1971, the Russians needed new markets for military hardware. Some business had been concluded but it was a relatively small amount due to the same problem on both sides: hard currency. The Russians desperately wanted it. The Sudanese had none. They could barely afford to keep the lights on in Khartoum, let alone buy the arms they needed.

What had proved more beneficial was the quiet approach made after the talks had ended. An unimportant member of the Russian delegation had asked Sinada to meet him privately back in Khartoum. On a quiet balcony of the Acropole Hotel, the man had made an extraordinary proposition. What it had boiled down to was a joint venture. If the Sudanese could provide a suitable secure location, then it might be possible that the interests the Russian represented could ship certain armaments, along with technical expertise, for storage and future sale to third parties. "A rather exclusive arms supermarket" had been the phrase the man had jokingly used. The profits would be shared and, of course, should the Sudanese wish to take their profits in kind . . . then discounts were assured.

The need for security had determined the pace of progress on the venture, but now, over two and a half years since that April meeting, it was a reality. Two shipments were already in the "supermarket", a third was due in Port Sudan any day now and the Russian's "supermarket manager" was asleep in the Hilton Hotel.

Sinada glanced at the list of clients. It was impressive and included Moslem groups from Africa, Europe and Asia: Islamic Jihad, Hamas, two of the Algerian groups, an-Nahda and the FIS, Hizbollah, the Chechen Separatists, the Taliban forces, Tajiks and a new Bosnian group. All of them claimed to have the funds and were keen to submit shopping lists. And there were more to come.

Sending this man Zinner had seemed a strange choice by the Russians, but stranger still had been the man who made the original offer. He was a Chechen. Long ago, Sinada had run every check he could on Imran Talebov and come up with nothing. The trace on Jack Zinner had been a little more fruitful. According to Sinada's contact in the Ukraine, Zinner had apparently been a long-term illegal in Australia and was travelling on an Australian passport. The Ukrainian contact had vouched for him and that was that. He glanced down at his schedule. The Front Islamique du Salut representative would be shown in at any moment, then there was just the Egyptian Gamaat Islamya and the strange little man from Jihad Eritrea. When that was over he looked forward to greeting Mr Jack Zinner with the good news that the supermarket's opening sale was shaping up to be a sellout.

The Khartoum Hilton is located at the confluence of the Blue Nile and the White Nile, where it sits well back from the traffic on Nile Avenue and about a kilometre west of the Friendship Hall. It was after midday prayers when Savva Golitsyn awoke and, after showering, made his way down to reception. A message informed him that the Lieutenant-General would be unable to meet him during the afternoon, but if Mr Zinner would care to take a taxi to the Friendship Hall at about five o'clock, they could perhaps enjoy an early supper together.

It took Savva less than five minutes to walk from the Hilton down to the banks of the Blue Nile. He found a bench on the river side of Nile Avenue and sat for a long time. "The Nile!" Savva said the words out loud with a feeling of immense, childlike glee. Looking out across the water, he found it easy to envisage the Mahdi or General Gordon sitting in this exact spot.

The river at this particular point in its long journey would have been more aptly called the very brown and muddy Nile, and Savva wondered just how many days travelling upstream it would be before the word "blue" became applicable. If you could work out a way to avoid the various dams and cataracts, that, mused Savva, would be the trip of a lifetime.

He had plenty of time before his appointment with Lieutenant-General Faisal Mohammad Sinada and, as the afternoon sun was still very warm, even under the trees on the riverbank walkway, Savva headed for the Mograin Family Gardens and a cold drink.

It was strange not to be able to order a beer in such a place. He imagined himself with a group of friends – Amelia, Heimo, Aino and Maxy – winding down after a day of sightseeing, having a refreshing ale and a vodka or two. Maxy would have probably headed down the bank to throw in a line and catch supper. Maybe that was permitted under the present regime, but the alcohol, well, it would have to wait until the revolution. Around him a few adults sat at umbrella-shaded tables and sipped Pepsi or Sprite while they kept a watch on their children playing in a shallow wading pool. Savva bought an iced tea and a slice of date cake from a kiosk and moved away from the families to a table with a view down-river.

It was a picture-book setting. In front of him, across the Nile, he could see all the way over the Murada *Suq*, past the old city walls to the Khalifa's house and there, shining gold in the afternoon sun, was the conical roof of the Mahdi's tomb. Savva's research back in Moscow took the gloss off the view. He found it impossible to forget that, down south, the bodies of the Dinka and Nuer floated in the same river. Fighting for their independence, they are victims of the Mahdi's successors. Savva tossed the remains of the dry and tasteless date cake to a scavenging bird. He got to his feet, aware that he needed to make a move. As he put the disposable teacup into a bin he glanced back at the distant roof of the tomb, but the image was no longer romantic.

It was five minutes to five when Savva wandered up the steps of the Khartoum Friendship Hall. A crowd of people were streaming out of the main entrance, and a fleet of taxis and limousines queued as they awaited their passengers.

It must be an international meeting of some sort, he thought, as he shouldered against a tide of bodies.

The vast and grand foyer had obviously been constructed in more prosperous times but no matter what the present economic climate was, the cool marble and the air-conditioning were a welcome relief from the dry heat of the city.

The foyer was almost empty now except for a group of cleaners who had started work on the two red carpets that crossed the entrance. One strip led from the central door across the floor and up three steps to the main auditorium. The other vanished up a flight of stairs at either end. Above the stairs was a black marble balcony and it was there that Savva saw his host.

Lieutenant-General Sinada was an extremely good-looking man with a strong sense of self-assurance. He strolled down the staircase with a casual air of ownership. This was a man who was very aware of his own power.

"Mr Zinner! Welcome to Sudan." His face was open, smiling and he extended his hand in greeting. "My apologies for being unable to attend you at the airport."

"Not a problem, General." The handshake was firm. Out of the shadows, Sinada's skin colour was lighter than Savva had expected, contrasted with the dark moustache and eyebrows. He was taller than Savva and solidly built.

"Your hotel is suitable? Good. Tomorrow we'll drive out to the site and your accommodation. Not as fine as the Hilton, of course, but you will like it, *In'shallah*."

I will have to like it, whether Allah wills it or not, thought Savva. He knew that he would be living at the storage site, but he did not like the idea. In Khartoum he could possibly evade the constant presence of security guards, but it would be more difficult out at the site.

"I'm looking forward to it, General."

"Please, Mr Zinner, my friends call me Faisal. You and I can dispense with the formalities. We are going to do great business together but hopefully we can also . . . What is it you say in English? All work and no play . . ."

". . . makes Jack a dull boy? Fine by me, Faisal. My two friends both call me Jack, you're welcome to join them."

"Good! Now, I have no more work today so we can go and try some good Sudanese cooking. You like fish?"

"Sure."

"The restaurant is very old Sudanese, but the fish is good. Afterwards, we can visit a friend's house for another Sudanese specialty which . . ." Sinada shrugged, spreading his hands in mock resignation, ". . . the government, in its wisdom, has seen fit to ban. But we Sudanese are irrepressible."

It did not take Savva long to realise that he needed to be very careful with this man. He was attractive and charming with a well-developed camouflage of nonchalance. His disdain for the conventions of *Sharia* was that which often accompanied the breaking of rules by those whose job it was to police them. Savva had seen in it in the

KGB and, he smiled to himself, in the Victorian Police Force in Australia.

The evening, though, was very enjoyable. The restaurant turned out to be not much more than an open-air cafe; one of a string of them on the banks of the Nile just past the Murada *Suq* on the Omdurman side of the river. The *Suq* was long closed and only an inordinate amount of rubbish remained to indicate that there had been a market there at all.

The car deposited them then departed. Sinada's driver was an almost neckless brute of a man who looked as though he spent his off-duty hours in the notorious ghost houses torturing political prisoners. How easy it is to judge the ugly, Savva castigated himself. He was probably a devout Moslem with a loving family. Who knows? The driver appeared to be on remote control for he and Sinada did not exchange a single word all evening. Yet, every time he was needed, the car would glide forward from the shadows and out he would spring to open the doors for his passengers.

The conversation over dinner had stayed well clear of politics, religion and the business at hand, with Sinada content to play the part of tourist guide. Every detail of the meal was explained although, as both men knew, grilled fish is grilled fish. The only item on the table that was not explained was the tall lidded pitcher. Savva noticed that there were several other tables occupied by military officers, including one entertaining the Saudi he had seen at the airport.

There was no sign of the man's wife. The pitchers were present only on the tables at which the military men were seated. Sinada shared the contents of the pitcher between them, pouring it into ceramic tumblers. The taste, though surprising in the circumstances, was very welcome. It was beer. Savva thought back to Sinada's remark about the Sudanese. Maybe it was only the ruling elite who could afford to be irrepressible.

Several tables were occupied by women, all young, all in Western clothes. Savva quickly realised that more than one *Sharia* precept was being broken here. Several times the women eyed their table but, receiving no encouragement, sipped their tea and turned their attentions to better prospects. As Savva and Sinada chattered over coffee, Savva noticed the Saudi businessman was now accompanied by one of the young women. Cultural exchanges were obviously planned.

After the meal, they strolled along the riverbank until the car, ignoring the right-hand rule, pulled across the traffic and stopped beside them. Instead of heading back across the bridge to Khartoum, the driver turned across the oncoming traffic again and joined the lane heading into Omdurman. There was no point in Savva attempting to keep track of where they were now. Once they had left El Khalifa Square behind, they headed towards the main *Suq*, but then started to wind their way through roads that had neither lighting nor names. Herds of goats slept beside small camp fires on every vacant lot. Two camels ambled in the opposite direction.

Another square, and rather than driving around the potholed road, the driver cut across the centre, through makeshift dwellings of tin and plastic. This was a far cry from the wide avenues of Khartoum and the people here were not the "irrepressible" Sudanese. Several of the people they caught in the headlights were obviously southerners. Tall proud Dinka trapped in poverty, servitude and *jelabirs;* the Islamic clothing looking sadly wrong on their gaunt frames. The tallest race on earth brought low.

Savva felt a perceptible increase in tension in the car as they slowed right down and crawled along a series of walled streets. They stopped, did a three-point turn and slowly retraced their route. Outside a high, rusted iron gate, Sinada tapped the driver on the shoulder and slid from the car, gesturing to Savva to do the same, without waiting for the usual door-opening courtesies. The car lowered its lights and purred off down the street.

It was an eerie feeling. There was absolute silence and stillness. Not a breath of air moved down these streets and neither, it appeared, did people. Where was the sound of children, the noise of a stereo? Nothing. Although he could not see them, Savva had the feeling that security police were not too far away and that for some reason the area was being very well protected.

Sinada knocked lightly on the big gate and almost immediately a small section of it opened.

He stepped through and beckoned Savva to follow. They ignored the man who had opened the gate and walked down a small pathway between two mudbrick buildings. Behind them, Savva heard several bolts sliding back into place. The narrow alley opened up onto a courtyard. From a doorway on the other side stepped a man in jeans and a Madonna T-shirt. It was one of Madonna's older but better known poses in which she was wearing a huge conical breast plate. The shape reminded Savva, for a fleeting moment, of the roof of the Mahdi's tomb. It was an association he felt should be kept to himself. Sinada had removed his beret and was indulging in a bout of hugging and back slapping. He then turned to Savva.

"Jack! This is my cousin, Ali."

"Hi, Jack!" The accent bore all the hallmarks of a North American college education.

"Pleased to meet you, Ali."

"Jack has only just arrived in Khartoum for the first time, so I've been showing him the sights."

There was a false hilarity about it all. Something wasn't being said.

"Come and have a seat; I'll organise some drinks." There was a split-second pause. "I take it you have nothing against a little drink?" The question was spoken to Savva but Ali was looking to Sinada for the reply. Savva decided it was time to break the tension, so he spoke before Sinada could open his mouth.

"Ali, there is nothing I would like more than some local *araki*. It has a great reputation, specially the guava flavoured *araki*."

The two men exploded into laughter, and Sinada slapped Savva on the back.

"You Australian bastard! One day, and already we've turned you into a Sudanese. Mind you, we may have to do a little more work on the skin colour."

Ali cocked an eye at Savva. "Australian, I didn't recognise the accent?"

"And I didn't recognise yours. What is it? Omdurman, with a trace of . . . Texas State?"

"Ohio. And yours? Sydney, with a trace of Moscow?"

"Ali!"

Sinada let forth a sharp burst of Arabic then turned to Savva.

"The trouble with Ali is that his irrepressible Sudanese nature is unfortunately blended with intelligence and a false belief that he is invulnerable. But we will get him back over the river one of these days."

He gestured towards the house and a slightly contrite Ali disappeared inside, to return almost straight away with what looked like an old wine bottle filled with something that had never been near a grape. They sat around a table and drank. It was a serious business and there was not much talking until after a young, undernourished Dinka boy appeared with a tray covered by a beautifully woven *tabac*. The child set it down on the table and removed the *tabac* to reveal four or five trays of cakes and biscuits. He returned minutes later with coffee which he poured, then he moved a little way away and squatted on the ground, waiting.

"Forgive my hasty tongue," Ali said. "It has caused much grief for my family and it seems it's not yet tamed."

"My cousin came back from America with a few Western attitudes which resulted in him upsetting the authorities. Had it not been for well-connected friends, he would still be in Kober prison." Sinada pulled his chair closer to the table and lowered his voice. "But he is working for us at the site. He oversees the unloading of the freight from the rail line and its transport to the secure area. He is proving his worth and in time will be able to move his family out of here."

"And what did you study in Ohio?" asked Savva. He was not particularly interested, his mind was elsewhere, but he did not miss the quick glance that shot between the other two men before Ali answered.

"Physics."

Savva wondered what the man could have done to end up in Kober. It was not, as they say in criminal circles, the prison of choice. Something else was wrong as well. The compound had no feeling of being a home. The doors off the small court in which they sat felt more like offices and there was no sign of the rest of Ali's so-called family.

The cousins began speaking quietly in Arabic, and so Savva sipped his coffee and turned his attention back to the Dinka boy. He was probably fourteen or fifteen and could not have been in the north for long. Savva had no idea at what age the Dinka performed initiation rites, but it was a fair bet that it was not long after reaching puberty. The boy squatting on his heels in the dust had tribal scarring on his forehead and there was no way that ritual had been performed in Khartoum. In the research files back in Moscow there had been only a passing mention of the Dinka, as the largest tribal grouping in the south. There had also been reports of the children captured during the fighting in the south being transported to a settlement just outside of Omdurman and being sold in, what was effectively, the only fully functioning slave market in the world. Having grown up without his own parents, Savva felt sympathy for the young boy who was in a far worse situation. For his part, the boy just squatted and waited.

Sinada, aware that his guest had drifted off, brought the proceedings to an end and they were quietly and quickly out the gate and into the car. On the return journey, Savva committed every twist and turn to memory. He might never need to come back here, but he now felt that it would at least be possible.

Sinada dropped Savva at his hotel and, after bidding him a good night's rest, arranged to pick him up at eight the next morning for the trip out to the site.

Savva was glad to be out of the car and away from Lieutenant-General Sinada. It was difficult to pin down but his sense of unease refused to abate. Perhaps the awkwardness was simply a cultural difference, but Savva could not rid his mind of a nagging worry that again he was only a bit-part player in a much bigger drama. The problem was always the same – the other actors had seen the entire script. Savva felt as though he only ever had a few pages and that he should either quit now or somehow get a copy of the full drama.

He was too restless to sleep yet, so after waiting in the foyer for a few minutes, he turned round and walked outside. It was a warm, clear night and he strolled down to a bench beside the river. In front of him the Nile flowed towards Egypt, leaving a sickle moon in its wake.

The next morning, Jack Zinner booked out of the Khartoum Hilton and set off for his new home. The Lieutenant-General sent his driver to collect him, as he himself had apparently gone ahead to make sure that everything was in order. This was something of a relief for Savva, as it left him free to concentrate on the route they took. His assumption that it would have to be on the main rail link between Port Sudan and the capital proved to be correct.

After driving about forty or fifty kilometres north they came to the end of the sealed road. Past the town of El Geili they turned right and after crossing the railway line and an oil pipeline, they began a gentle climb to higher ground. About five kilometres out, they were stopped at a security checkpoint and a couple of kilometres further on they came to a boom gate manned by a detachment of soldiers who went through the car and Savva's luggage with great thoroughness. Savva wasn't sure whether this was standard procedure or just Sinada's way of showing him how efficient the set-up was.

As he waited outside the car, Savva could see just how seriously security was taken. Spanning from the boom gate in both directions was a four-metre high razor-wire fence. As an added precaution, signs attached to it depicted, very graphically, the kind of voltage that would go through anyone foolhardy enough to touch it. The land on either side had been cleared of all scrub and another sign warned that landmines were liberally dotted about. A tin-roofed mudbrick guardhouse was set well back from the gate and boasted a small but efficient looking machine-gun positioned to its right. Two armed sentries watched from a guard tower fifty metres away, and at least six more men were stationed at the gate. Communications must have been by radio, for Savva could see no sign of phone lines, but perhaps they emerged from the ground in the same way the electricity supply did. Someone had gone to a lot of trouble to ensure that a visitor was either invited or dead.

The driver opened the car door, indicating that they were free to continue and the boom gate rose to let them pass. He drove up the hill for another few hundred metres and then, as they came to a crest, he cut the engine and indicated that Savva should get out again. For a moment Savva was unsure of why, but the driver was walking away to the side of the road, so he followed. Then he understood. This was the scenic route, the backdoor entrance. Below them, the land fell away into a crescent-shaped depression. A group of buildings backed onto the hill in a semicircle and it appeared some of them were actually built into the hillside some fifty metres below where they stood.

By far the most impressive aspect of the layout was the rail line. The Sudanese must have been very confident about the profitability of this venture to build a branch line from the main trunk that was probably some fifteen kilometres away, in El Geili to the west. The line came across the plain below them and only turned as it entered the open side of the crescent. Then it vanished into a line of three warehouses.

The driver tapped Savva on the shoulder and pointed to the fence that followed the ridges down on both sides. For a moment Savva did not know what he was supposed to be looking at. Then he saw the gun emplacements. Dug into the hillside, and overlooking the rail line from either side, were two concrete bunkers which appeared as though they could deal with anything that came within ten kilometres of the site in any direction but the rear of the hill. Savva had no doubt that there would be something in place there as well.

He gave a thumbs-up sign to the grinning driver and they returned to the car. It was all very impressive, if you closed your mind to the possibilities of an air strike. A couple of well-armed aircraft from almost any country in the world could probably obliterate the place in less than fifteen minutes. Oh well, he smiled to himself, you can't have everything. Maybe it was all about show. Maybe it was a way of impressing the buyers who would soon be invited to come and inspect the goods on sale.

They wound down the hill to the centre of the complex. A smiling Lieutenant-General Sinada strode forward and personally opened the door.

"Jack! Welcome!" He was all old-buddy handshakes and back slapping. "Hope you enjoyed the scenic route. You don't have to go that way every time, but the first time I thought you might like to see the view, yes?"

"Fantastic. It looks very secure." Savva returned the beams and retrieved his slightly crushed hand. "Faisal, you didn't tell me about the rail link. How the hell did you get the money for that?"

The question was rewarded with a modest shrug and eyes raised to heaven. *El humdulillah!* Allah had obviously come to the party. Savva noticed that a young soldier had taken his bag from the car and was heading toward one of the buildings built into the hill.

"Come. I'll show you your quarters." Sinada fell into step beside him. "So, let me explain. The containers come from Port Sudan. At El Geili they are shunted off to a siding and immediately picked up by our diesels and brought here. In the first warehouse the container numbers are identified and unloaded. The goods are then checked against the inventories you will provide us with and then stored in the other two warehouses. The samples are kept separately in those buildings." He indicated the first of the smaller units built into the rock to their left. "And over there." He pointed to a larger, L-shaped complex set apart from the others. "That is the sales office. We will assemble a display in there to fit the requirements of a particular client."

"And to safeguard against them seeing other items?"

"Of course. And we'll include a variety of merchandise from other sources so as not to arouse too much interest in our chief suppliers." There was a smugness in his tone that implied the idea had been his. Savva ignored it, knowing that it had been one of the basic conditions of on-sale that the end user was not made aware of the extent of the operation. There was no way of stopping the various clients exchanging notes but the nature of the business usually precluded it. From the Russian end, too, he knew that much of the merchandise was of mixed origin, having originally been manufactured in the armament factories of the old Eastern Block, from Czechoslovakia to the Baltic Republics.

They reached a low-set concrete-block building in front of which someone had attempted to plant a few shrubs to give the appearance of a garden. The stepping-stone path that led to the door looked as though it might be very useful if it ever rained in such an arid area. Savva imagined that at the first hint of precipitation most of the site would be turned to mud.

The garden and the stepping-stones gave the impression of a cottage but, thought Savva, only an impression, and only just. The front door was opened by a young captain who was introduced by Sinada simply as Sadiq. He could speak English, and it was his task to make sure that Mr Zinner's every wish was catered to. Nothing would be too much trouble. He would even drive him into El Geili if he was in need of diversion. The fact that he would also keep tabs on Mr Zinner was so glaringly obvious that no one deigned to mention it.

By way of a welcome, they sat in the air-conditioned front room and had a cold drink, which Sinada explained was called *kakade*. He pointed outside to the garden. A small shrub, about half a metre high, was giving every indication of wilting. That was *kakade* and it apparently produced the red flowers that, when dried, made the slightly bitter, though refreshing drink. It reminded Savva of Ribena without the sugar, and he rather liked it.

"By the way, your airfreight arrived last week. It's in the study." Sinada indicated one of two doors to the rear of the room.

Savva's general impression of the house was one of claustrophobia and the effect was heightened when they entered the study. It, and presumably the kitchen, had been cut into the rock and although cool, it felt oppressively solid. There was no window at the side and while the rear rock wall had been whitewashed in an attempt to lighten the atmosphere, the attempt was a failure. A small wooden desk, a chair, a filing cabinet and a telephone were all the room contained.

"A dedicated secure line, as requested." Sinada picked up the handset to check the phone was connected. "And operational." He replaced the phone and turned to Savva. "Well, I'll let you get settled in and maybe you'll join me in the mess for lunch. It would be good to introduce you to the team."

"The mess? What time?"

"Sadiq will show you the way at . . ." he glanced at his watch, "say, twelve-thirty?"

"Fine. Thanks, Faisal. This all looks perfect." The lie slid from his lips with so little effort he surprised himself.

The couple of hours until lunch went very quickly. Sadiq, having completed his kitchen duties, took himself out the front where he sat on a bench and read a magazine. For his part, Savva prowled around the house looking for a room in which he felt comfortable, but did not find one. He eventually went back into the study and after checking the seals, unpacked his computer and printer. The two cartons had arrived intact and bore no trace of having been opened.

Connecting the leads and testing the system took a little time, but when it was done, he powered up the computer and wrote a single line on the screen. From his pocket he took a disc and ran the encryption program. The single line became gibberish. As the file was so small he did not bother compressing it. He simply plugged the modem lead into the telephone socket and selected the macro he had installed back in Moscow. It took a while for the connection to be made, but when it was, the gibberish was gone.

In a secure room in the basement of the Russian Parliament, a screen flashed up an icon that signalled an incoming message. The man on duty clicked on the icon but what came up on the screen was unintelligible. He dialled a number and let the man who answered know that contact appeared to have been made. A little while later, Andrei Primakov entered the room and slipped a disc into "A" drive. The decryption was instantaneous.

A single line appeared on the screen: "Your *lastochka* has landed."

Primakov smiled broadly and typed congratulations.

"*Molodyets!*"

He did not bother encrypting it. Primakov took the disc from the drive and tucked it back in his pocket. He was a happy man. His "swallow" had landed; migrated, all the way to Africa. Now the action could finally start. He clicked on the "send" icon and watched the screen go blank.

Lunch at the mess was a very ordinary affair. Lieutenant-General Sinada went into full official mode and made a few crisp comments welcoming Mr Zinner and hoping that now the groundwork was complete and another shipment due any day, they would work together as a team. It was an important operation and would, *In'shallah*, make a valuable contribution to the prosperity of both their countries. Seventeen off-duty guards and the five Russian technicians applauded.

Sinada excused himself and left Mr Zinner and the Russians chatting over coffee. The Russians made no pretence of accepting or perpetuating Mr Zinner's Australian cover story, although as a concession they started referring to him as "Jakski".

Savva had gone through their files before leaving and there was very little he didn't already know about his fellow countrymen. Vladimir Bunakov looked after the safe storage of their merchandise. He had been head of technical stores at the Zvezda

Design Bureau at Tomilino, outside Moscow. It was always debatable as to where his priorities lay. Some had said that he was more concerned for the articles he stored than the safety of those who stored them. In the end, what mattered was that he knew his job. After some of the solid and liquid rocket fuels he had had command of, this was a breeze, or so he claimed over lunch.

Yuri Sobolev and Ivan Teterin were two very hard men whose only gentleness was reserved for the stripping and cleaning of their beloved weapons. They had a reputation for being able to strip and reassemble anything. The details of their previous service had been kept under wraps but Savva gleaned enough during the meal to place them in either OMON special units or a *Spetsnaz* division.

"So, you are Australian?" Sobolev asked.

"Yes, from Melbourne."

"I nearly killed two Australians."

"You have been there?" Savva asked, unsure if he was being fed a line.

"No. It was in Red Square."

"What? A car accident?"

"He shot them!" Teterin interjected. "During the 1993 coup."

"Our unit was defending a position and a warning shot ricocheting off the paving stones hit this Australian woman in the foot. I saw her fall and then her companion, an Indian, ran out to her."

286

"What were they doing in Red Square during the fighting?" Savva was intrigued now that he sensed the men were speaking the truth.

"Fucking Intourist! They had picked a busload of them up from some legal conference and sightseeing was on the schedule, so they had to go sightseeing; coup or no coup."

"But this woman recovered?"

"From what I heard, they took her to some nearby hospital and did reconstructive surgery on her foot," Sobolev said. "But eventually the Australian Embassy airlifted her to St Thomas's in London. Silly bastards. She would have been better off in Moscow."

"Why?"

"Our doctors had learned plenty from fixing up our boys from Afghanistan."

Sobolev was probably right, thought Savva. The other interesting thing about the story was that it explained why Sobolev and Teterin were here in Sudan. They had obviously backed the wrong faction. They seemed content enough with their work maintaining the ordinance that came on site. The fact that they would also be called on to provide demonstrations was an added bonus.

Oleg Filatov's presence in the team was easier to explain. He had been one of the financial advisers to the ill-fated Valentin Pavlov before the 1991 coup attempt. It was Filatov who had fed Pavlov the constant diet of figures he used to sustain his arguments in favour of a restructure of the gigantic Soviet military–industrial complex. What he did on site was less illustrious and hopefully more practical. He set prices and took charge of the circuitous money trail that was employed to return what they hoped would be vast amounts of foreign currency to their Russian masters. He was a reclusive and rather unlikeable man whom the other Russians all referred to as "the Banker".

The final member of the team was the ballistics expert everyone called "Veevee". He was in charge of everything from hand-held rocket launchers to the more expensive and deadlier SAMs, the surface-to-air missiles. Veevee was, in fact, Valentin Viktorovich Mikhailov. Savva had not paid much attention to his file, but the name rang a bell. Valentin Mikhailov under the name of Sadovnikov had been the second KGB Resident sent to Australia years ago. He asked Veevee if he was related and received a very curt denial. Savva let it go. As they left the mess, Bunakov whispered in his ear, "He's the son of ex-minister Mikhailov."

Savva kicked himself for not picking it up. Of course it made sense. He remembered that Valentin Mikhailov's file mentioned that the ballistics expert had spent several years in the closed city of Arzamas–16, east of Moscow. Arzamas–16 was a nuclear weapons research establishment and Veevee's father was Victor Mikhailov, the former nuclear energy minister.

CHAPTER

TWENTY-THREE

THE next shipment was not due for four days so Savva used this time to familiarise himself with the El Geili site and to answer a string of questions from Primakov about security. Eventually he knew the place backwards and had Primakov placated. The inventory of the next shipment was soon dealt with; a copy to the banker and storeman, then discussions with the others about storage requirements.

On the day the shipment was scheduled to arrive, Savva rose early and asked Sadiq to drive him into town to check out the security arrangements. It was the first time he had been off-site since arriving and he felt his spirits lift as they drove out of the hot dry hills back towards the Nile. This time they did not go over the hill but took the direct route that paralleled the rail line all the way to the town and then to the junction slightly north of El Geili.

It was a beautiful place to await such a deadly cargo. The Nile foamed its way over the spectacular Sabaluka Cataract, and on the far bank Savva managed to catch the occasional glimpse of a variety of animals in the Sabaluka Game Reserve. The driver, as efficient as ever, had brought everything Savva asked for. First the binoculars to watch the animals, then a chilled thermos of the *kakade* he had grown to appreciate. Many things may be certain in Sudan but the arrival time of a train is not one of them. All Savva's efforts to pin down the time had been met with shrugged shoulders or shaken heads, so he was prepared for a long wait.

He swung the binoculars around to the rail junction. An attempt had been made to give it the appearance of a small, country station. A diesel sat quietly at the end of the siding, its two engineers boiling something over an open fire. Further along, a large wooden hut had been dumped none too gently beside the main track and a brand new sign read – Savva checked again, his reading of the Arabic script had improved only slightly from zero ability to . . .

"What does the sign say, Sadiq?" He passed the binoculars to the driver.

"*Shimal El Geili* – El Geili North. Are you happy with the men?"

Savva took the glasses again and did a slow sweep of the area. Sinada's cousin, Ali, was squatting in the shade of the station hut with a group of about a dozen men, all dressed in overalls.

"Yes. They look like workmen all over the world. Just as well. It might arouse some suspicion if they did anything."

Sadiq shaded his eyes from the sun and squinted at Savva, unsure if he was being serious. The cultural gap created by Savva's attempts at humour had become a chasm.

"Relax, Sadiq. It's fine." Savva smiled. "Now, give me another one of those dreadful cigarettes of yours. We can stop at the store on the way back to the site and I'll buy you a carton."

He took the cigarette and the proffered box of matches. It still made him feel slightly ill, but he had fallen into the habit of smoking whenever he was bored and, over the last couple of days, that had been too often.

The train did not pull in to North El Geili until just before noon, by which time the temperature was in the high thirties. Two powerful diesels slowed as they approached the siding with their huge load of almost fifty containers. The first twenty or so were of no interest to Savva. He had the binoculars firmly focused on the tail of the train, looking for the dull grey colour that had been chosen as the mark of their cargo.

At last his wait in the heat was rewarded. The cargo had arrived. Ali's men swung into action as soon as the train finally came to a standstill; the string of wagons were uncoupled and the two diesels moved off to continue their journey to Khartoum. Once the last of the train's wagons was out of the way, the lone diesel started its engine and prepared to shunt out of the siding where it had been waiting. Soldiers moved ahead of it and manually switched the lines to allow the engine onto the main line. It was soon coupled up and, pushing the wagons in front of it, headed off on the tracks to the site.

Savva heaved a sigh of relief and settled back for the air-conditioned ride to a late lunch in the mess.

After eating a little, Savva wandered over to the chain of warehouses to inspect the progress. Each container was unloaded separately under Bunakov's watchful eyes. Sobolev, Teterin and Mikhailov had command of small squads of soldiers who assisted in loading pallets and directing a team of forklift operators to the various destinations. Thousands of West German and Czech pistols, having been given the once-over by Sobolev and Teterin, were sent to the small-arms bunker. Landmines, hand-grenades and tear-gas canisters went to another. Savva nodded his approval to Bunakov and carried on up the full length of the train, past the eighteen wagons to where a moody Oleg Filatov was sitting on the steps to the diesel engine's cabin. He appeared to be off in a world of his own. A copy of the latest inventory sat on his knee. He looked up as Savva approached.

"I hope that fuckwit Faisal has got his shit together. He'd better have some clients with more money than sense."

"Why, Oleg? Hungry to turn this stuff into cash?"

"Of course. But have you taken a good look at that shit? Most of it's older than my grandmother and just as useful." It was an exaggeration, but with an element of truth. The cargo was a pretty mixed bag.

"The people Sinada has lined up would buy homemade Molotov cocktails if it was all they could get. And I believe him when he says they have the money. Don't worry, Oleg, we'll sell this lot and much more."

The man was still looking gloomy as Savva headed back to his quarters.

They all need to have a break from here, he thought. Well, after the shipment was stored he would try to talk Sinada into taking the men off-site, to somewhere where they could have a quiet drink or two.

Savva decided it was time for a small rest, a euphemism really, he acknowledged to himself, for he had begun to deal with both the heat and the boredom by indulging in the luxury of a regular afternoon sleep. He went inside and dismissed Sadiq who had developed the bad habit of settling himself in the lounge and reading and re-reading the English language magazines that Sinada had bought for Mr Zinner.

When he was alone, Savva realised that he couldn't settle. Something was nagging at him and he didn't know what it was. He lay on the bed for a while, but it made no difference. Something was wrong. Slowly he reviewed the images in his head. The warehouse? Then it came to him. The diesel engine had been at the head of the wagons. It should not, no, could not, have been. He closed his eyes and replayed the scene beside the Sabaluka Cataract. The engine was at the rear, pushing, and yet there was no other siding, no way that it could get to the front.

Then another inconsistency dawned on him. He had not consciously counted the wagons but on the main trunk his image was of twenty-one wagons. In the warehouse there were eighteen. He sat up and castigated himself. I'm getting too old, he thought as he hurried into the study and switched on the computer. Fishing the encryption disc from his pocket, he inserted it and opened up the original inventory document. As he scanned down it he realised that he was on the wrong track. Eighteen was the number on the consignment sheet.

He switched off the computer and pocketed the disc. Eighteen wagons had left Russia and made the journey down the Baltic and halfway round the world to the Red Sea. Eighteen had been unloaded at Port Sudan and eighteen were in the warehouse. He made some tea and tried to read but when, after a couple of hours, the feeling of unease had not dissipated, he went to the front door and roused Sadiq from his sleep on the bench.

"Come. We're going into El Geili. I promised you a carton of cigarettes this morning and we came straight back without them. Make up a flask of tea, Sadiq, and we can sit by the Nile and have a smoke. It'll be a hell of a lot cooler than this shithole!"

"To El Geili?" Sadiq's uncertainty was written large in his face.

"El Geili, Sadiq. It's a little town over there . . ." The sarcasm was lost on his driver who simply shrugged and went to get the tea.

"I'll be back in five minutes," Savva called out, and headed across the site towards the warehouse.

His feeling had been correct. When he had walked through the warehouses earlier he had seen no sign of the man who was supposed to be supervising the unloading. And neither had anyone else. No one had seen Ali, well not since that morning, in El Geili. One of the soldiers suggested he couldn't be far away as his utility was parked just outside the first warehouse.

Savva looked into the cab of the ute, but apart from the fact that it was locked there was nothing to suggest anything unusual. A packet of cigarettes and a box of matches lay on the passenger seat. A small duffle bag had been tossed on the floor. Savva turned his head to read the airline tags. They were nothing. Sudan Air, Ktm–Ny and Ny–Ktm. Khartoum return to Ny . . . who knew where the hell that was? Who cared? More interesting was the open glove box. Under a pair of pliers was what looked like a tattered copy of a hard-porn magazine. The part of the man he could see was white and a large caption proclaimed mysteriously "*Bonne bouche!*". Savva felt that it didn't really matter that he spoke no French.

As he walked back to the house, Savva acknowledged that he was not making much sense of the situation. A train at the wrong end of a string of wagons and a vague memory of there having been twenty-one. And now a glimpse of what might have been Ali's misdemeanour. Ahead of him Valentin Mikhailov came out of the mess hall.

"Hey! Veevee. Have you seen Ali?" Savva called.

"No. Why, should I have?"

It was too defensive. Mikhailov must have realised that he had been a bit abrupt so he stopped and turned to face Savva.

"He went back to Khartoum with Sinada."

"And left his car here?" Savva said quietly. "That doesn't make much sense."

"I have to work with these black mother fuckers!" Mikhailov spat. "I don't have to fucking nursemaid them!"

Savva watched as Mikhailov strode away. Very jumpy! There was, he thought, an undercurrent running through the entire operation and again he had the feeling he was drifting into a backwater while elsewhere the main river was running strong.

As Savva reached the car, Sadiq sprang out and opened the door. He had not only made a flask of tea, he had also changed out of his uniform and was in jeans and T-shirt. He was all smiles.

"So, we have a night on the town, Sadiq?"

"Yes, sir! And I will get a little treat for us from my friend."

"And which friend would that be?"

"It is probably better that Mr Jakski does not ask." He used the nickname the other Russians had given him. It had obviously spread through the camp.

Savva smiled and relaxed into his seat. Sadiq was right, he did not need to know who his friend was, but he hoped the friend gave Sadiq enough *araki* for both of them. There was much about the Sudanese regime that he abhorred but the people themselves, what was it Sinada had called them? Irrepressible, that was it. That was what he admired. As they approached El Geili, Savva casually mentioned that he would like to see the Sabaluka in the light of the half moon. Sadiq, of course, had no objection.

The siding was absolutely deserted. Savva spent a few minutes gazing into the cataract. It was a truly beautiful sight, but he was in no mood for the wonders of nature. As soon as they arrived he had seen what he expected. There was no second diesel engine parked where it had been parked this morning. After a time, they turned around and drove into town.

When they arrived, El Geili looked as though it was closed for the night – no street lights and no traffic. This turned out to be an illusion. As they pulled up outside the main store and turned the car lights off, Savva became aware of a myriad of little fires. People were crouched around them, sitting on woven mats, squatting in the dust or perched on old fruit boxes. A silence had greeted them as they got out of the car, but once the locals saw Sadiq, they started talking again. A low hum of conversation filled the dusty street.

A young boy with a cane hoop raced in front of the two men, and a group of small dark faces in the shadows revealed themselves as laughter exposed their teeth. Sadiq knocked on the door of the shop and it was opened by an extremely overweight old woman. Her face, crisscrossed by wrinkles, broke into a broad grin as she recognised Sadiq and gave every indication that any friend of Sadiq's was a friend of hers. Having purchased the promised carton of cigarettes, they turned to leave but the woman was having none of it. She made a great show of giving Savva a very warm bottle of Fanta. Despite his efforts to pay her for it, he was bundled out of the shop.

"You must be the first person to buy a whole carton," explained Sadiq as he broke it open and popped a couple of packets in his jeans pockets. "Sometimes rich people like me buy a packet or two, but usually she sells the cigarettes . . . er . . . one by one."

"Individually?"

"Ah! That's the word. Individual cigarettes." He tossed the remainder of the carton onto the car seat and carefully locked the doors.

For the next hour they wandered from group to group along the main road. Everyone seemed to know Sadiq and everyone had a drink for him. After Sadiq explained that "Mr Jakski" was a trusted friend, he was also offered a drink. The *araki* varied in rawness and flavour, but never in strength. It would make great Molotov cocktails, Savva thought as he accepted a rather dirty mug. It would also, he realised, sterilise any stray bacteria that might lurk in the various containers he had drunk from.

Eventually, Sadiq settled in for a session with a group that included a couple of very attractive young women who were quick to come and sit with him. Savva gave Sadiq a knowing smile and excused himself to look for a toilet.

"Try the station, Mr Jakski." He pointed into the darkness.

Sadiq had probably meant that he should just piss anywhere. But Savva, possessed of his own irrepressible nature, managed, within ten minutes, to navigate his way in the darkness to El Geili's main railway station.

A elderly man, in what Savva took to be a Railways Department uniform, greeted him first in Arabic and then, to Savva's pleasure, in reasonable English.

"Good evening Mister." The man appeared to bow from the waist, it was almost Shakespearean. "Sadness to inform you that train is closed. Coming back at . . . oh-six hundred yesterday."

Savva bit his tongue. The English accent was from another era, the construction from another planet.

"Sorry to disturb." This was rewarded by a vacant smile. "I don't want to catch a train," Savva explained. "I want to know if a small army train went today."

"Next train yesterday, kind sir."

"No." Savva tried mime. "Small train. Today. Three wagons?"

"Today? Not yesterday?" The smile had remained constant but now a tinge of concern was hovering at the corner of the man's mouth. "Come!"

The old man tugged at Savva's sleeve and gestured for him to follow him into the office. The oil lamp gave very little light and Savva had doubts about the old man's eyesight. He took the liberty of turning the wick up just enough to increase the illumination but without endangering the national debt. Off in a darkened corner, the railwayman was mumbling something to himself, but just as Savva was losing patience, he returned with a very large book. He spread it out beside the lamp then hunted in a drawer until he found a dimpled rubber finger stall. He huffed and puffed but finally fitted it onto his finger and then, much to Savva's delight, he licked it. All the preparation rituals completed, he opened the volume to reveal page after page of hand written records of the comings and goings of trains.

It was in times like these that Savva regretted not being able to read Arabic. However, he could read the dates.

"Gentleman, please see. Train yesterday will arrive early morning." He stabbed his rubber-encased finger at the left-hand page. But Savva's attention was firmly on the other. There were only four entries. Beside each were times. The first had 0620 in the right-hand margin. The second: 1205. Then in pencil rather than ink was an entry marked 1325. The final entry was 1650. Savva glanced at the expected arrivals for the next day. There were only three; the times exactly the same as the three ink entries on the following page. It had to be! The missing diesel had gone through El Geili at twenty-five past one.

"So one ticket? For early train yesterday?"

"No, thank you. Maybe another yesterday." Savva smiled and as an afterthought took the warm bottle of Fanta from his pocket and gave it to the man.

It was with mixed feelings that he walked back to the main street in search of Sadiq. He was pleased that his hunch had proved to be right, but being right in this circumstance seemed a long way from understanding.

The camp-fire conversations had warmed up a little and the *araki* continued to circulate. Sadiq, however, had vanished into the dark with one of the young women. Waiting for him, Savva sat on a tea-seller's mat and returned her smiles as she served him some sweet hot tea out of a chipped but clean glass. For a moment he imagined that there was no military regime in Khartoum and no arms depot up in the hills. This was what northern Sudan must have been like since time out of mind. A warm balmy evening, hot sweet tea and good company. It had a lot going for it.

The incident with the train was not repeated with either of the next two shipments, so Savva put his suspicions on hold. It was, of course, conceivable that the extra wagons had been mistakenly taken out to the site and then returned ... any number of scenarios could be contemplated. Everyone he quizzed about the incident shrugged and claimed to know nothing about it. He had several e-mail discussions with Primakov about it but he, too, dismissed it. Savva let it slide.

Four months went by without incident, and Savva relaxed into the routine of the El Geili site. Sinada rarely appeared, claiming that he was convinced the joint venture was able to carry on without him and that the legitimate business of the Sudanese Army required his presence. His cousin Ali turned up again and, when Savva questioned him about his disappearance, claimed an affair of the heart. Given what he had seen in the glove box of Ali's utility, Savva believed the affair part of the excuse, but doubted very much that the heart was the organ involved.

Three very successful sales had been made. Two to well-financed radical Islamic groups and one to a Latin American delegation. Each time the displays and demonstrations set up by Bunakov, Sobolev and Teterin had been faultless. In their expert care, even some of the more dubious Bulgarian machine-guns had fired off belt after belt without jamming.

At the conclusion of each negotiation Vladimir Bunakov organised some very circuitous delivery routes, and as soon as he got the nod from Oleg Filatov he despatched the merchandise. Nothing left the site until Filatov was happy that the money was in the bank and, as the amount being transferred back to Russia grew, so did Filatov's self-esteem. Savva guessed he had had more than his career ruined by earlier events in Russia and had retreated into himself. The new Filatov was never outwardly ebullient, but he had been the one who suggested that they take a couple of days off after each sale to relax in Khartoum.

Savva had developed a very pleasant routine for his time away from El Geili. On the first trip he had discovered the Acropole Hotel on Zubeir Pasher Street. He had arrived outside it by accident on one of his rambling evening walks and it had taken him a couple of minutes to work out why the name seemed familiar. Then he remembered that it had been the name on the book of matches that he had pocketed from Imran Talebov's desk at the embassy in Canberra. The memory caused him to hestitate before entering the hotel, as he had no idea of Talebov's relationship with the owners. In the end he decided to put aside his paranoia as unreasonable.

The facade of the hotel had been white but not for some years. Time, sun, dust and the sandstorms, the *haboobs* that hit the city each year between April and September, had all added their marks, but the general effect was pleasing.

Walking inside, he followed a flight of stairs up and around to a wide lobby that housed a reception area, a tiny branch of the Bank of Sudan and behind a scattering of lounge chairs and coffee tables, the manager's office. The decor – the ceiling fans and the potted palms – transported Savva back to the way he felt life must have been forty or more years ago. He liked it. After booking in, he wandered out onto the balcony and ordered a glass of iced tea. He had seen cleaner hotels, and in most hotels the staff were required to stay awake on duty, but Savva knew he did not like most hotels. Too often he had sat in a bar looking at an array of clocks showing the time in various world capitals and felt he could have been in any of them.

On his subsequent trips to the city he stayed at the Acropole and was now greeted like an old friend. The Greek owner Lex, and his wife Elena, were two of Khartoum's great survivors. They had held onto the hotel during famine and flood and through two coups and various regimes. During the Eritrean War of Independence, the hotel had become a de facto head-quarters for the Eritrean resistance. Lex boasted that not only had he been the first person in Khartoum to have a fax machine, but that at times it had been the only link to the outside world. Despite the fact that he was quietly critical of President Bashir and the National Islamic Front, he was tolerated and did good business at the lower end of the hotel market.

Early on, Elena had taken a shine to Savva. He put her age at fifty-something but on a good day she would tie her red hair back in a pony tail and don a pair of jeans. On those days, Lex would nudge Savva and ask who the thirty-year-old was. The three of them became firm friends.

The Russians from the El Geili site all came to look forward to the now regular free time in Khartoum. That is, everyone except Mikhailov. He did his work on the various sales that involved his ballistics expertise, but he withdrew further and further from the others, even to the point of going off on his own for breaks far more frequently than was warranted. After his third absence from the camp, Savva started to worry. He and Primakov had established an almost daily routine of exchanging encrypted e-mails and it was during these electronic conversations that Savva mentioned Mikhailov's habit of disappearing, occasionally for up to a week at a time. Primakov suggested that Savva, mostly for his own peace of mind, should take a closer look at how Mikhailov filled his free days.

After each sale, the team would travel together into Khartoum, then split up. Sometimes the men would simply book into a hotel; other times they would all go their own separate ways. Ivan Teterin and Yuri Sobolev usually went together to either Suakin or Arous near Port Sudan where they had developed a passion for scuba diving. Bunakov headed for the low life. With an unerring instinct, he seemed capable of discovering every distiller of *araki* in Khartoum. His return to the site was usually followed by a couple of days recovering from self-inflicted excesses. The "Banker", Oleg Filatov, was more of a loner and, apart from an occasional movie, seemed content to swim lap after lap of a hotel pool or hang around the banks, keeping an eye on the international money markets.

Valentin Mikhailov was the real outsider. The only person he managed to strike up a friendship with was Sinada's cousin Ali and, on the trips into the city, he often stayed with him over the river in Omdurman. When they were in Khartoum after the conclusion of the third arms deal, Savva bumped into Ali in Abdul Moneim Square south of the city centre, and Ali asked him to give his regards to Valentin. This was a troubling development, for, only the morning before, Mikhailov had excused himself from the rest of the group with the claim that he was off to spend the time with Ali.

Lying on his bed back at the Acropole, Savva reviewed the situation. Somehow he was going to have to confront Mikhailov, but with what? Having an affair with Ali? No, Savva grinned, that didn't fit. Ali had a sense of style and no matter how you contorted the definition of style, it could never be made to fit Mikhailov. Anyway, he was certainly not with Ali on this trip. So where was he and what was he doing? In the end Savva filed the Mikhailov problem into the temporarily "too hard basket".

He had a much more pressing question. Savva had been aware for a long time that he was marking time. The original desire that had prompted his involvement in all these events had been to go home. During the last year the goal had shifted. No longer was home a definable place. Maybe, he thought, it is a condition, a state of mind.

Savva had let events take control and had relegated himself to the role of passenger. No, that was not quite true. The acquisition of his file by the people who were behind Primakov had been beyond his control. A decision was starting to form in his mind, but, unready to confront it, Savva opted instead to cut short his time in Khartoum and go back to El Geili. There was something more going on than the sale of arms, and he needed proof, or at least a solid indication of what it was; something to bargain with, if necessary. If he was going to jump ship he wanted to make certain he had a life raft.

Savva realised he was dripping with sweat. The temperature had been climbing over the last few days and it felt like a storm was on the way. The problem with Khartoum, he thought, was that the storms usually meant a *haboob*, with flying sand and dust, rather than refreshing rain.

For a moment he considered having a shower, but experience had taught him that such an exercise at the Acropole could often prove counter-productive. The first few times he had attempted it, he had been frustrated by engineering. The baths were big, but there was never enough water to wet the plug. A notice above an instant water heater proudly proclaimed that the device was the most modern and energy saving in the world. It was probably true. They saved water by never allowing any to escape from the shower head. Every now and then a strange gurgling noise in the intestines of the device would be followed by a groan, a hiss and an ejaculation of a small amount of water and steam from an overflow pipe. This display was invariably followed by the illumination of a red pilot light. Under it, small print announced that the "Heating phase is engaged and luxury of a piping hot shower is only minutes away." It was a lie.

Savva opted to splash water from the sink over himself. Then he lay down on the bed and allowed the ceiling fan to do the cooling. There was an air-conditioning unit on the wall opposite the door, but he had long since grown tired of its emphysemic wheezing and its annoying incontinence; it leaked condensation onto the marble floor, making it a slippery death trap.

At dusk, Savva went along to the reception desk where Mohammad, a huge, white robed figure, was on duty.

"Any chance of finding a taxi for me, Mohammad?"

It was one of the rules of Khartoum, everybody had a brother, cousin, uncle ... who would, for a price ... Fifteen minutes later, one of Mohammad's relatives called for Savva, and the payment in advance meant that no questions were asked. He had transport for the entire evening.

Savva took almost an hour to retrace the route he had travelled in Omdurman with Sinada on his second night in Khartoum, but eventually he found what he was looking for. He selected a spot two streets away from Ali's house and instructed the driver to return in two hours. As they had driven by, Savva had noticed a vacant lot on the corner of a small lane that ran to Ali's place and a couple of old car bodies on the lot that would provide reasonable cover.

The silence and tension that had been in the air on his previous visit was noticeably absent. Children played on the streets, a donkey cart trotted along in the dust and goats foraged amongst the rubbish. The first car body was too far back on the vacant lot to be useful. The second not only afforded a view across to the iron gate, but was also blessed with a reasonably intact seat on the passenger side.

The first hour provided Savva with only a battle with tiredness. His fight to stay awake was unexpectedly aided at one point by the intrusion of a goat's nose through the window, but apart from that, nothing.

Savva became aware that something was happening when the neighbourhood suddenly went quiet. The moon was much fuller than it had been on the previous occasion and he was able to see the security team move into place. A dozen armed men emerged from the compound and vanished into the shadows. Fortunately, none of them came anywhere near the vacant lot where Savva was now very wide awake.

Nothing happened for about fifteen minutes, but when he saw the three black Mercedes drive out of a street to his right, he knew that his luck had changed. As they pulled up outside the gate, Ali was clearly visible in the headlights. Sinada, in full uniform, jumped from the front of the first car and opened the rear door. There was no mistaking the men who got out. Their photographs had been part of the files Savva had studied in Moscow. The head of the Sudanese security organisations, General Hachim Abu Said, was accompanied by the Sudanese President's security adviser, El Fatih Irwa.

The six passengers in the other cars were all Europeans but there was nothing about them that gave any indication of nationality. Many times Savva had felt that another game was being played from which he was excluded. Now there was no doubt, but he was just as far from understanding what it was. The cars began to back away, but then one of the Europeans signalled for them to stop and began to walk towards the rear car. As he did, Savva saw his face in the full beam of the headlights. The man was dressed in casual slacks and an open-necked shirt. It was the French DGSE officer, Colonel Jean-Claude Marchand. He opened the rear door and took a folder from the seat, before returning to the others who were now filing through the small door in the iron gate.

On the way back to the Acropole, Savva attempted to fit the jigsaw piece into the puzzle. He could not connect the French to the El Geili operation, but it began to dawn on him that the link could be with Ali and Mikhailov. Only one possible connection came to mind and that was too dreadful to contemplate. Savva needed more information and the only place that it was now safe to request it from was Moscow.

CHAPTER

TWENTY-FOUR

A WEEK later, on a fine, clear but cool day in Moscow, Andrei Primakov made his way down to the basement of the Parliament building to send a reply to Nikolai Trinkovski's request for some rather strange information. It had been easy to find and, given the superb way the operation in Sudan was running, he was not about to upset Nikolai by suggesting that he might be getting a little paranoid. Primakov knew enough about the stresses and strains that buffeted an agent in the field, and anything that he could do to assist was worthwhile in this case. Trinkovski had not been his choice for the mission, but with the death of Imran

Talebov, there was no one else with the background and the command of English. It was a gamble that had paid off handsomely.

In the computer room he loaded the file, encrypted and then compressed it. Within seconds it was gone. He watched the empty screen wondering if Nikolai was waiting for it. What the hell was the time in Khartoum anyway? It would be great to get the old man back to Moscow and go on a bender together. He had really enjoyed Trinkovski's company, but he knew it would be many months before he could find a way of bringing him home. Primakov was just about to leave when a "message-waiting" icon popped up on the monitor. He double clicked on it and started to read. Five minutes later he was grabbing his coat and hat and yelling for his driver. The day had suddenly turned very nasty.

The El Geili site was being sand-blasted for the third day by a *haboob*. The sandstorm had shut everything down. There was a total ban on even opening a door to any of the storage areas. Bunakov had been adamant – until the storm abated everything stayed closed. Yuri Sobolev and Teterin had backed his judgement. Although it was the stinging sand particles that made it unbearable for anyone stupid enough to venture outdoors, it was the fine dust particles that were the real enemy. They would play havoc with the armaments.

The Russians sat around in the mess playing cards, dreaming of beer and vodka. The Sudanese soldiers were, to a man, in a foul mood. The necessity of guard duty did not disappear during a storm, but it certainly was not something to look forward to. Morale was low, and a couple of times, tempers had flared over trivialities. The only person who welcomed the *haboob* was Savva. His time since returning early from Khartoum had been not only busy, but productive.

The notion he had entertained in Khartoum of jumping ship had hardened into a resolve to find an escape route, but between conception and execution of such a plan lay a huge gulf. His situation was such that simply booking an air ticket and flying out of the country was impossible. The road he was on was not blessed with exit signs. For a few days he went over the various options and, in the end, he came back to the same conclusion – getting out was not going to be easy. Instead of worrying about this, he turned his attention to preparing the items he would need for a departure. He put together a very basic travel kit, all of which fitted into a small shoulder bag, and he started taking it everywhere with him. If the circumstances presented themselves, he was ready.

Another task was also awaiting the right circumstances and, a couple of days after his return, an opportunity arose. The sandstorm hit at about lunchtime and, after the initial rush to close the place down, the men gathered in the mess to grumble and play cards. Once the games were underway, Savva excused himself and after putting a scarf over his face, made a dash through the eerie, false dusk caused by the waves of stinging swirling sand. Rather than going to his quarters, he headed for Valentin Mikhailov's small cabin. Savva had expected to carry out an exhaustive and probably fruitless search for some indication of what Mikhailov did with his free time. The answer, however, was waiting for him in the bedroom, in the form of a small travel bag on the floor beside the unmade bed.

Inside were some clothes, a couple of books and an airline ticket. Savva picked up the ticket and examined it. It was an Eastwest Airlines return ticket from Khartoum to Nyala leaving on Saturday. Three days away. The return portion was for eight days later. Even more interesting was the fact that there was no charge for the ticket. What appeared to be an official requisition number had been stamped on the reverse side of each copy of the ticket. Eastwest was, Savva knew, a privately owned airline whose major shareholder was reputed to be a senior government minister.

Placing the ticket back in the bag, he picked up the books. The first one was in Russian, a small scientific manual of some kind. Suddenly Savva realised what he was holding. He shut the book quickly and, with a now trembling hand, picked up the other. It took thirty seconds to confirm what his mind was refusing to accept. Numbed and angry, he replaced the books and rezipped the bag. The fact that it bore airline tags marked Ktm–Ny did not escape his attention, but the question of where was not as important as why. He let himself out of the cabin and into the maelstrom of sand. The sun was completely obliterated and the howling wind flung the sand into his uncovered face, but nothing reached him. He walked slowly back to his cabin and sat in front of the blank computer screen, wondering what to do with the information that was creating its own storm inside him. Finally he decided to make a cautious move. He switched the computer on and sent a single request for information to Andrei Primakov. There could only be two responses. Either he would get an answer, or someone would walk into his quarters and put a bullet through the back of his head.

In his worst nightmares, Andrei Primakov often saw himself dying in a situation not dissimilar to that in which he now found himself. The call to present himself at the *dacha* at Arkhangelskoe had been unexpected. Why now? There had been no doubting the tone of the command that the old Ukrainian had used. Why the *dacha*?

Outside the house was a very official looking ZIL. On the steps, two men in civilian clothes with machine pistols seemed disinterested in his arrival. All he got from one of them was an inclination of the head to indicate he should go inside. Slowly, he made his way up the steps and into the cold and darkened rooms. A light was on in the kitchen.

The old man, wrapped in a fur coat, was hunched over a couple of photographs. A bottle of vodka and a single glass were at his elbow. Leaning against the unlit wood stove was another of his bodyguards, also cradling a machine pistol. Primakov felt his stomach churn as the old man looked up and fixed him with his eyes.

"You know who this is?" He slid a photograph across the table.

Primakov fumbled, trying to get the photo off the table and into his hands. It appeared to be a studio portrait of a middle-aged man.

"No. I've never seen him before."

"No." The old man heaved a sigh. "I was certain you hadn't."

He slid another photograph along the table.

"And this one?"

The second photograph was of a different man and he was dead. It was obviously an autopsy photograph. The man had been shot in the head.

"No . . . I'm not sure. Maybe this one is Russian?"

"Oh, very good, Primakov." The sarcasm was naked and aggressive. "He was found in a Canberra motel."

A sense of relief flooded through Primakov. So this was what it was all about. Of course he knew the man's name.

"Sir, I would suggest that this is Savva Golitsyn."

The old man's gaze fixed on him again.

"Let me tell you how you fucked up, Primakov. The first photograph is of Professor Clements. He died of a heart attack in Melbourne some fifteen years ago. When the body that was found in the motel was described in the papers as being that of Professor Clements nobody took much notice, but just before the inquest, a relative phoned the Coroner's Office in Canberra and said that there had been a mistake, and that Clements had died some years before. In an attempt to identify the body, the morgue photo was published and several people came forward and said it was a Mr Jack Zinner. They described this Mr Zinner as being an Eastern European migrant who kept pretty much to himself. And you and I, Primakov, know why that was. He was Nikolai Trinkovski."

For a moment Primakov's mind went totally blank. He heaved in a breath and reached out for the back of a chair. He had to sit. The enormity of what the old man had said was only overshadowed by the knowledge that his premonition of death was not far from becoming a reality. He was conscious that the old man was far away at the end of a long white table and, through the mist of his fear which now clouded everything, he thought he saw him raise a hand holding a pistol. He gulped for air. Forcing himself to breathe, storing up the oxygen in his blood.

"So, you really did not know?" The hand held not a gun but a vodka glass.

"What can we do?" Primakov heard his voice coming from far away.

"Play him like a fish, until we find out who he's working for and then kill him. Give him a scare. Give him enough line to run, then let's see who he runs to." The old man downed the vodka and gestured to the bodyguard to give him a hand out of the chair. Primakov looked a mess. Maybe the Ukrainian should have shot him as he had intended. No matter, there was plenty of time for that, and if Primakov was not up to sorting out this fuck-up, well, he had others in Sudan who would do it for him. As he rose, he slid the vodka bottle down the table.

At the door the old man stopped.

"Had I not believed you, you would be dead now, Primakov." He did not turn around. "There is no second chance from here on." He started towards the door, then called over his shoulder, "You might like to have a chat to Danilov. He's upstairs."

After a time, Primakov reached for the bottle and gulped a mouthful of vodka. Slowly he felt the energy returning to his body. He was still alive. Suddenly he was very cold, shivering. He moved towards the door, then remembered that he had been instructed to explain to Danilov.

Wearily, he made his way up the staircase. Danilov was not in the upstairs sitting room. Primakov found him in the bedroom. He and Anna Petrovna were in bed together, naked. They had been shot where they lay. As he turned, he saw the body of the housekeeper propped up against the cupboard. Her throat had been cut.

Primakov's driver sat with the motor running to keep warm. He saw his boss come out of the house and down the steps, and so he clambered out into the cold to open the door. His boss did not make it to the car for several minutes, however. He was too busy vomiting.

CHAPTER

TWENTY-FIVE

To Savva's great relief the message he was expecting from Primakov was waiting for him. He quickly decrypted the file and read:

Greetings Comrade,

In answer to your request: the student known as Ali Abdel-Aziz Shiddu graduated with first class honours in nuclear physics from Ohio State University. There is no record of any disciplinary action by the university or criminal charges against him by American State or Federal authorities.

I toast your health each day in Koskenkorva!
Andrei.

For a long time Savva sat looking at the screen.

Eventually, he typed in a response for Primakov and let him know he would be at the Acropole in Khartoum for a few days following up on Mikhailov. He was about to sign off when he decided that it was time to indicate where things were heading. In a few simple sentences he described what he had found in Mikhailov's bedroom. When it came to the books he simply wrote:

> The first book was a scientific text concerning minimum critical mass experiments for producing low-level nuclear explosions and the second was a safety procedures manual for handling a binary nerve gas named *Novichok–6*. It was published by GSNIIOKT, the State Union Scientific Research Institute for Organic Chemistry and Technology, in Volsk–17 on the Volga. I want your word you knew nothing of our involvement in these areas.
>
> Nikolai.

For the rest of the evening, Savva tried to think of other ways of dealing with what he had stumbled into. Finally he gave up and spent his time committing to memory every contact number that he might need in the coming days. Outside, the storm lashed at the site as though it wanted to bury it beneath the sand. Around midnight there was a lull. How long it lasted Savva could not tell, because when he awoke the *haboob* was back at full strength, blasting the windows and hiding the dawn.

In the morning the computer had no answers for him. It was time to make his move, so he struggled through the storm to the mess and informed Bunakov that he should take over control of the site as he had to go to Khartoum for a few days to sort out a problem with the next shipment. Then he let Sadiq know he should pack some clothes as he could expect a few days off in the capital while "Jakski" attended to business.

"You want to drive in the *haboob*?"

"No, Sadiq, I want you to drive. Don't look so concerned. We can go very slowly and when we get there, you can have three days off to spend with your family."

"Fine, Jakski, we drive slow." The look of concern had been replaced with a grin that suggested he had no intention of spending the time anywhere near his family.

The trip to Khartoum was even slower than expected. The road was free of traffic but at times visibility was down to only a few metres, and drifts of sand often covered the surface. As they neared Khartoum, the storm eased and by the time Sadiq dropped him outside the Acropole, Savva stepped out into bright sunshine.

Walking up the steps, he was greeted by Lex.

"Back so soon? I will have to make a permanent booking."

"Only overnight."

"Tell Mohammad to put you in Room Four and anything else you need, let me know."

"There are a couple of things. Maybe we can have a talk when you have a moment?" Savva knew that he was stepping into dangerous territory. A man like Lex did not survive in Khartoum without compromise, and although he was quietly critical of the government, it was never clear where his loyalties would lie if he was put to the test.

"I'm just going around the corner to the airline office to pick up some tickets for a couple of guests, so why don't you put your bag in your room and meet me in, say, half an hour?"

"That would be good." Savva paused, and then took the plunge. "Could you see if you can get me on a flight to Nyala tomorrow?"

"Certainly. Coming back when?"

Savva looked him straight in the eye. His instinct told him that Lex would not be a problem. His instinct could be wrong.

"One way, Lex."

The Greek would be a formidable opponent in a poker game, thought Savva. There was not a flicker in the man's eyes; instead he put a hand on Savva's shoulder and smiled.

"I think we should have a chat now. Those other tickets can wait for a while."

Lex turned and led the way back up the staircase and headed for the reception desk.

"Mohammad, check that Room Four is ready for Mr Zinner. He can fill in the registration later."

"Good to have you back, Mr Jack!" Mohammad said, and smiled broadly.

"Good to be back, Mohammad."

"I'll be in the office for a while. I don't want to be disturbed, OK?"

"Sure thing, Mr Lex."

"Sit down, Jack." Lex shut the office door and pulled down the blind before sitting, not in his usual place behind the desk, but in the lounge chair next to Savva. "I used to have an English missionary staying here for a few months each year and whenever he ran into problems he would come in and mumble something at me. For a long time I thought he was complaining about the food and I couldn't make head or tail of what he was saying. Another guest eventually explained to me that he was saying 'trouble at mill'. You look like you might say the same thing."

"I have a question first. How easy is it to get across the border into either Chad or the Central African Republic?"

The Greek stared at Savva for a moment and then went round the desk and fished out a packet of American Camel cigarettes from a drawer. He lit one and passed them to Savva.

"I take it you are not talking of an official exit point?"

Savva shook his head.

"You do have a problem." He walked to the window and stared down into the street. "I wouldn't try Chad or the CAR, not unless you have friends to meet you. The surveillance on both sides has been stepped up to try to stop refugees crossing. The

French have done some sort of deal with both governments and installed some very sophisticated deterrents." He turned and crossed to a map of Sudan hanging on the wall behind the desk. "I don't know how you intend to travel, but that is a hell of a long way through very unfriendly desert."

"Are you saying it's impossible, Lex?"

"No. Just very difficult. The way I would go is south." He traced a line down the map with his finger. "Again, not easy, but there are two routes. Either one of the bush tracks south of Nyala, or down the dirt road going east to Babanusa and then south through Muglad. Both are very long and unpleasant choices."

"How long?" Savva folded the butt of the cigarette over itself and put it out. He was feeling sick enough without the nicotine.

"The track? Five hundred kilometres to Aweil in Bahr El Ghazal province. The road, well, probably eight hundred at least. You have other problems as well."

"Such as?"

"Jack, I do not mean any disrespect, but it is a young man's journey. At this time of year the rivers, especially the Bahr al Arab and the Lol, will be flooded. It's the wet season now and the *toic* is inundated."

"What is the '*toy-ch*'?"

"It's the name of the grasslands around the rivers. Each wet season they flood then dry out and produce grass for the cattle in the dry months. A huge area of Bahr El Ghazal is a basin – it fills up in the wet."

The two men sat in silence for a moment, eyes fixed on the map as though somehow an answer was going to present itself. Savva walked over to the window. Outside, the storm was breaking up; windblown sand was everywhere.

"You said your choice would be south. Why, if it's so difficult?"

"Because a lot of illegal traffic uses that route, especially the tracks. You could probably team up with a group going south. The army would not be a problem until you got to Aweil. If you took the dirt road you would have to skirt every town because there are usually roadblocks and security checks either side of them. If you could go far enough south, you would run into the Dinka people or the Nuer and, because English used to be taught in all the schools, you would probably be able to enlist some help."

"I'm sorry to involve you in this, Lex."

The Greek smiled and sat again.

"In what? All I have been doing is giving you a geography lesson."

"So, will you organise a ticket to Nyala for me?"

"I will do better. I will book you on a plane to Kutum."

"Kutum?" Savva was confused.

"It's a very small place on the edge of the desert just north of the Marra Plateau. You take a plane to

Nyala and your connection to Kutum is not until the next day. No problem. You stay in Nyala and no one is going to care if you miss the flight to Kutum. I'll book you back to Nyala and on to Khartoum a few days later. There is no point in advertising the one-way nature of your trip."

"How can I thank you?" He was relieved that, for at least a few minutes, someone else was doing the clear-headed thinking. This was a sensible way to proceed. The detour he was intending, however, was another matter.

"The best way to thank me is to never let anyone know how helpful the proprietor of the Acropole Hotel is to his guests. In this business it doesn't pay to advertise."

The laughter was genuine and seemed to defuse the tension of the last few minutes. Savva shook Lex's hand.

"Lex, the secret of your excellent service is safe with me. Oh, one other thing; can I use your computer for a few minutes?"

"Sure. I'll just go and tell Elena that you're here, then I'll head off to the airline. Lock the door when you're done."

The office computer had a rather slow, old fax–modem attached to it but it was better than nothing. The first number Savva dialled into gave him an instant result. He took the encryption disc from his pocket and within a couple of minutes the message from Primakov appeared before him.

You have my word. Do not leave Khartoum until we talk.

Wait around in Khartoum until you get someone to eliminate me? Not a chance. He sent no reply. It was going to take a lot more than a one line e-mail to convince him that Primakov was not somehow involved in whatever was going on in Nyala.

The second fax he did not encrypt.

Dear friend,

The holiday in Sudan has been wonderful. Some of the scenery reminds me of Mururoa, but without the sea. I'm sure you understand what I mean. It is interesting to notice that the same travel agents are making a quiet living here and working with some of my ex-countrymen. All very highly qualified. I would like to share some of my travel stories with you. I had hoped to visit Chad or the CAR, but I have visa problems. So I will try to find the time to go south. It would be good to meet a gnome who was a Collingwood supporter. Maybe they could look out for me. If I don't make it south, maybe someone could make a visit.

Pass my love on to Amelia.

Regards

S.

He addressed it to Heimo Susijarvi, c/- Kalasta-jatorppa, Helsinki, Finland. After three attempts to connect, the fax went through.

Sometime that night a gentle knocking on his door woke Savva from a troubled sleep. He was still fully dressed. Several times before he had dozed off he had considered abandoning his attempt to leave Sudan, at least for the meantime. Surely, he thought, other opportunities would present themselves. The bottom line, however, was that Primakov now knew he had uncovered a far more dangerous side of the operation, and there was no doubt that he would be moving to contain any damage that Savva might cause. The first step would be for Savva to be disposed of.

As the knocking was repeated, he got cautiously to his feet and went to the door.

"Yes, who is it?"

"Elena. There's an urgent phone call for you. A man is ringing back in five minutes."

Savva unlocked the door and opened it. Elena had obviously been woken by the call as she was in a dressing gown and slippers, looking like he felt, half asleep.

"Sorry you were woken."

"Oh you silly man, you've been sleeping in your clothes." She laughed at him then turned and led the way along the passage to the office.

"Wait in there, I'll go and make some tea."

She turned and headed off to the kitchen.

When she returned a few minutes later the phone still hadn't rung, so Elena poured the tea and sat down beside him. There was no conversation between them for a few minutes. Savva refused the offer of a cigarette, content to sip the tea and worry about the incoming call.

"Lex told me that you have a few problems at the moment." Elena's voice was very quiet. She avoided his glance, staring into the teacup. "I hope everything works out. I don't suppose you will come back again."

For a while longer they sat in silence. The phone still refusing to ring.

Then Savva was aware that she was talking again, almost as though it was to herself.

"Thirty years we've been here. Six months on, six months off. The other half of the year Lex's brother, Spiro, and his wife look after the place. So many times I have told myself that this was the final year and I would never come back, but each time I have. So many things have happened here. So many people have been ... Spiro says it is the worst city in the world and it brings out the best in people. I don't know. Some of the things that are happening now, especially to the children. The refugee camps outside of Omdurman would break your heart. Little kids from the south, some with their mothers, and living in such conditions. There is so much pressure on them to become Moslems and many of the children are taken to special schools where they are beaten if they don't learn the Koran ... and then there are young children sold as slaves . . ."

Her voice trailed off as Savva moved to put his arm around her shoulder. A lifeless butt between her fingers was all that remained of her unsmoked cigarette.

"But you and Lex have helped so many people during that time . . ."

He knew it was weak, but he was floundering, unsure of how to comfort her. He felt her breathe in and straighten her back as if with new resolve.

"It's just the night, the storms. I often get a bit depressed at this time of year." She turned and took his hands between hers. "Listen, Jack, I don't want to know what you do or who you do it for, but you are a good man. If you go south and you need help, find the Dinka. They are a generous people and if they know you are in trouble with the Arabs, as they call them, you'll be fine."

Savva was about to thank her when the phone startled them both. Elena rapidly gathered up the tea cups and gestured to Savva to pick up the phone.

"Hello?"

It was an extremely bad line and for a moment he could not understand what the voice at the other end was saying. Then he realised that it was someone speaking Russian. The "someone" was Andrei Primakov.

"Can you hear me?"

"Yes, but it's a bad line. Please speak up." Behind him, Elena took the tray and left, closing the door behind her.

"This is not a secure line, but I rang to let you know that I was not informed about the subject you raised in the e-mail."

"I received your reply. I need convincing," said Savva cautiously.

"We have been used, both of us. I have even less information than you do. Please, trust me. I have only a short time on this phone, so listen. They know who you are. Do you understand?"

It took a few seconds for that to sink in. Unsure of what he was hearing, Savva's mind raced – was this another move in the game or was Primakov being honest?

"Are you still there?"

"Yes," Savva replied. "I'm still here. What are you going to do about it?"

"For fuck's sake! I'm warning you! What else can I do. I am leaving here. Understand? I am going away. I don't know who you are working for, but can they help me?"

The man was too frightened to be attempting to trap him into divulging something. Savva hesitated at first, but there was nothing to give away as the truth was far simpler than Primakov suspected or would possibly believe.

"Listen. I am not working for anyone. But I will trust you. When you get to a safe location, ring a Finnish telephone exchange and ask for the number of the Fisherman's Hut in Helsinki. I can't pronounce the name of it in Finnish but the operator will know what you are talking about. When you get the number ring it and leave a message for Susijarvi." Savva spelt the name slowly for him. "Did you get that?"

"Yes."

"The message should say that you would like to play left-handed chess with him and you prefer to drink Koskenkorva. I know that sounds silly, but he will understand that you are a friend." Savva paused, then said quietly, "I hope you are a friend."

"If we get out of this I will repay you. I must go. Be careful because once I disappear they will be in a panic and try to close down everyone, and you are top of the list. I hope I see you again."

The phone went dead. Savva hung it up with a strange mixture of feelings. Primakov was an old-fashioned reactionary, hankering after the return of the hardliners, and yet with a perverse moral streak that forced him to back away from those who would deceive him. Savva's feeling that he had made the right decision in passing on Heimo as a contact remained with him. Anyway, he thought, as he absent-mindedly lit one of Elena's cigarettes, it's done. Both of us have entered on a course of no return. The peculiar image that came to him was of parachuting, something he had never done nor had he any desire to do. They were like untrained parachutists, about to jump from the aircraft hoping that somehow they would find the ripcord and manage to pull it, and that when the earth came up to meet them, they would somehow know what to do.

CHAPTER

TWENTY-SIX

A T six the next morning the Eastwest Airlines flight for Nyala took off. It was exactly on time. There had been no last minute complications. After making an illegal banking transaction by exchanging traveller's cheques for American dollars, which records would show he did not possess, Lex insisted on driving Savva to the airport. The Greek's contacts extended to a couple of airline employees whose pleasure, and profit, it was to assist Mr Zinner on boarding the antique Fokker Friendship away from the normal queues and procedures.

The flight was uneventful other than the sudden and unscheduled descent into El Obeid where someone, with even better connections or more money than Lex, was waiting to board. It turned out that his connections were of a spiritual nature. Within ten minutes the passengers had been shuffled around in order to give the *mullah* a front row seat, and the plane was airborne again.

Having a window seat, Savva was able to get a good view of Nyala as they began their descent. For as far as he could see in every direction, the countryside was dry and flat apart from a large group of hills to the northwest. The wet season did not appear to have made much difference in this region, although he did see a couple of small rivers near the hills as they dog-legged around to make their approach. The Fokker flew in very low over the city and afforded Savva some brief glimpses of a market and a minaret above a mosque.

The heat hit him as the door was swung back, so he waited in his seat while first the important passenger from El Obeid and then the less well connected disembarked. As he stepped outside it was as though he had just walked from a refrigerator into an oven. The heat reflecting off the tarmac was more intense than even the worst day he had experienced at El Geili. Any breeze that might have existed in such a place had fled south, which was just as well, he thought, a fan-forced oven would have been even more intolerable.

Ahead of him the passengers were being herded through a security checkpoint. A couple of heavily armed soldiers stood beneath the shade of a tattered umbrella while a third colleague inspected identification papers and travel documents. The passengers waited in the sun. The *mullah* had been exempt, of course, and Savva watched enviously as a large old Ford forced its way through the crowd inside the airport fence and engulfed the holy man in its tinted and air-conditioned comfort.

Savva guessed it was still too early for anyone to be looking for him, nevertheless he felt his stomach knot up as he stepped forward to hand in his papers. The special army pass that Sinada had furnished him with had always worked wonders before and this time it was, thankfully, no different.

"Welcome to Nyala, Mr Zinner. Please enjoy your stay."

He was in. The problem that arose now was very different. Up until this point he had been following a logical path. Go to Nyala and try to find out what Mikhailov and possibly Ali Shiddu were up to that took Mikhailov away from El Geili so often. All that was clear. But now he was flying blind. It was a bigger city than he had expected and he had no starting point. An old and much maligned piece of wisdom was the answer: when in doubt, ask a taxi driver.

Savva Vasilyevich Golitsyn was not the only one flying blind. Unfortunately, the difference between Savva and the others in the game was that they were far better resourced. Two separate pieces of information arriving at the same time had brought an elderly Ukrainian to near fury. To make matters worse, he was in a meeting with his closest collaborators when the news arrived. In an uncharacteristic explosion of anger he had thumped the table and stalked from the room. When he returned he had regained some of his normal composure, although none of the other men at the table had ever before heard such venom in his voice.

"That cunt Primakov has not been seen since yesterday, and Golitsyn made an excuse for leaving El Geili and has vanished into Khartoum."

"A coincidence . . ." It was a brave but foolish suggestion. It was ignored.

"Listen. We all have too much riding on this venture to throw it away because of two fucking traitors. I have ordered everyone at my disposal to hunt them down and kill them. Golitsyn is probably not stupid enough to attempt to board a flight out of Khartoum and our Sudanese partners have said they'll seal the country off, but I don't want to depend on a bunch of half-witted Arabs. Let me be very clear about this. Some of you have assets that you have never disclosed to me. I know about every fucking one of them, so if you want to leave this building alive, I suggest that you activate them immediately. As for Primakov, he's probably gone to ground somewhere. We can't waste time trying to dig him out, but the moment he surfaces, anywhere, I want him taken care of. Does anyone want to suggest a different approach?"

No one did.

The fourth taxi driver Savva approached was a young Sudanese boy who spoke enough English to make communication possible. After they pulled up on the roadside a kilometre away from the airport, Savva showed him both his army pass and enough American dollars to make absolutely certain that the driver was giving him his full attention.

"I want to drive past every foreign-owned business in Nyala. I am especially looking for any French companies."

The driver needed nothing more than a fistful of dollars to fill up the tank of the geriatric Toyota and they could be on their way. There was a queue outside the shop with the petrol pump, but this proved no problem. A group of teenagers, sheltering from the sun up against the shop entrance, were called over and after a brief exchange and a lot of furtive glances at the infidel in the passenger seat, they ran into the shop and emerged with the owner in tow. A few dollars changed hands and the next moment the queue was being rearranged. The teenagers shouted at the other drivers to reverse out of the way and the shop owner took to enforcing the move by hitting slower cars over the bonnet with a small cane. In less than five minutes they were at the head of a very angry line of motorists. The Toyota was filled up, not by the attendant, but by the owner himself. Meanwhile, the customers unable to be served inside had emerged to join the crowd and watch the action. The teenagers who had first been called over had assumed some kind of special status that only American dollars can bestow and had organised a group of younger boys. They were busily washing the entire car. Another handful of dollars changed hands and they were on their way. Glancing back, Savva caught a glimpse of the scuffles breaking out among the younger children as they fought for their share of the loot.

"I would rather not attract so much attention from now on, if you don't mind."

The driver threw him a nod and a smile.

"Of course. We will be mega cool."

Savva sighed and attempted to reposition his back around the springs that protruded from the seat. Mega cool? Oh well, at least he didn't have a baseball cap on backwards. Still, it was probably only a matter of time.

By eleven o'clock, Savva had seen more of Nyala than any tourist could reasonably expect to see in a week. Not that any reasonable tourist would come here, he thought grimly. They had found only a couple of foreign businesses; one sheet-metal factory that, according to the driver, was owned by Iranian brothers, and an Italian funded Christian school. It appeared to have about four pupils. Savva realised he was being taken for a ride both literally and figuratively.

His threat to get another driver brought instant results.

"I was saving the best for last, man."

I bet you were, thought Savva. They headed back past a now deserted *Suq* to a sidestreet near the centre of town. There, in all its whitewashed splendour, was a very new single-storey building proudly proclaiming itself to be the *Caisse Française du Crédit Agricole*.

"Keep driving," said Savva quietly.

When they were out of the centre Savva asked him to pull over. The young driver looked crestfallen, sensing that the golden goose was about to abandon him.

"Now, tell me, do you know why a French bank is in Nyala?"

The smile came back to the boy's face. This was not the end.

"Sure. For the . . ." he hunted for the word, ". . . for the roadworks."

"What roadworks?"

"Big roadworks." The boy pointed to the road in front of them. It certainly had not seen a road worker in years. "Up to Zalingei, maybe even to Al Geneina and Chad . . ."

"You mean the French are building a road all the way from here to the frontier with Chad?"

"Sudanese people are building." The boy's national pride came to the fore. "But French bosses and money."

"Show me."

The boy looked perplexed.

"Zalingei is over two hundred kilometres –"

"Just show me where the French construction company people live. Is that far?"

The boy was obviously relieved.

"Not far, about another twenty American dollars." He saw Savva reach for his wallet and added quickly, ". . . each way."

A few hours earlier, in Nairobi, a man sat back in his seat for a flight to Khartoum. It was just as well that the new diplomatic passport had been accepted as the real thing, for without diplomatic immunity his bags would have been subject to a thorough search and that would have caused a few problems. The Kenyan authorities would not have taken kindly to him carrying a hand-gun on board. There would be no trouble at the Khartoum end. Some army creep by the name of Sinada was going to take him through Customs. It was only a small pistol and a single clip of bullets, but then he only intended to fire a single shot. In his coat pocket was an enlarged identity photograph taken at the Special Projects Research Institute in Moscow. The back of the photograph had the man's name in both Russian and English characters: Nikolai Nikolayevich Trinkovski. The South African knew it to be wrong. The man was Savva Golitsyn and he had a score to settle with him. He was happy to carry out the assignment that his Ukrainian boss had ordered, of course, but he was going to be even happier getting rid of the man who had killed his colleague, Imran Talebov, in Perth.

The journey to the French road construction camp was much further than Savva had expected. Just outside Nyala they had been forced to pull over for a security check but a couple of dollars saw them through without a single question being asked.

They were almost at the base of the hills Savva had seen from the plane when the boy turned off the main road. So far, there had been no evidence of anyone having done even the most basic road maintenance on the fifty or so potholed kilometres they had travelled. They met only one other car but there had been several overloaded trucks heading to the *Suq* in Nyala. A lot of livestock, mostly scrawny goats but sometimes donkeys and a camel train, graced the verge of the road. Once they veered off the road to make way for a garishly painted bus that carried its passengers both inside and on the roof.

"Refugees from Chad," the boy explained.

Savva had the feeling that they should have been heading in the opposite direction, but he kept it to himself.

Off the main road a path cut through the low straggling scrub, and the thorn bushes had been cleared well back on either side to allow passage of some reasonably big vehicle. The tracks they followed attested to the weight of some of the trucks that had gone this way.

As Savva drew closer to the hills it became clear that they were higher than it had seemed when viewed from the Fokker window. They erupted spectacularly out of the dry plain and the presence of large areas of green vegetation on them suggested that somewhere, in amongst the rocky outcrops, there was a constant source of water. Savva was going to ask about the hills when the driver turned a corner and the taxi started to run alongside a fence protected by some nasty looking razor wire.

A few hundred metres further on they drove up a small rise and the camp was clearly visible to their right.

"Pull over under the tree," Savva instructed.

He took the binoculars from his bag and, resting them on the roof of the car, focused them on the nearest buildings. It appeared to be a particularly well-built complex for a roadworks site. Several pre-fabricated buildings clustered together near what Savva took to be three large water-storage tanks. To the left was a group of roadworking vehicles – graders, bulldozers and a couple of fully laden gravel trucks. He could just make out some workmen sitting in the shade of one of the trucks, and he was imme-diately reminded of the workmen at the rail siding beside the Sabaluka Cataract. These were soldiers.

Further left and he found he was looking at a water pipeline running down a spur jutting out from the hill behind. Turning the other way he scanned past the trucks and buildings and came to a halt on a group of, he counted carefully, twenty-one objects. If he had any doubts that this was where Mikhailov was spending his time, they now evaporated. At the rear of the camp, stacked three deep, were seven rows of containers. They were identical in colour to the ones they had received at El Geili. He swept further left and found nothing. Looking around the other way he thought he could make out something further back, between the containers and the buildings. Carefully he re-focused the binoculars. Under a camouflage canopy was a large truck tray. It was hard to make out because of the netting and the shadows, but it looked alarmingly like a carrier for at least three medium size missiles.

Lieutenant-General Faisal Mohammad Sinada took an instant dislike to the South African. Sinada had seen the type before. He was a mercenary like so many of the others who trained at the twenty or so secret training camps in the desert north of the city. They fought in African wars because they believed that the blacks and Arabs were incapable of winning, and after the fighting was over they moved on. The only markers of their passing were the bloated bodies and flies. Sinada straightened his beret and fixed his smile in place as he saw one of his captains bring the man to the Airport Security office. He rose to greet him.

"Welcome to Sudan –"

"Cut the shit, Sinada," the man snarled as he entered. "And tell this goon to fuck off, man."

Sinada gestured to the captain to leave and then tried again.

"Would you like some tea?"

"What have you got for me?" demanded the South African.

"Well, we have a man who may be able to tell us where Mr Zinner has gone."

"The bastard's name is Golitsyn, and what the fuck do you mean by 'may be able to tell us'? Either he can or he can't."

Sinada sighed; this was no way to begin a working relationship. There was also, he realised, no way of putting off the inevitable.

"Come, I'll show you." He got up from behind the desk and moved towards the door. "I must warn you that some of my men appear to have been a little over zealous."

"What the fuck does that mean?"

Sinada ignored the remark and quickly led the way along the corridor to where a soldier stood on guard outside an adjoining office. He gestured with his hand for the guard to open the door.

"See for yourself."

On the floor of the office lay the body of a very fat Sudanese man, his *jelabir* torn, no longer white, but covered in blood and dirt. The smile that Mohammad, the Acropole receptionist, usually wore was gone, as were most of his front teeth. He was still breathing but barely conscious.

The South African turned to Sinada, hardly able to contain his anger.

"What has he told you?"

"Nothing, so far."

"Well, he soon will. Get the fuck out of here, Sinada, and do something useful, man. Shoot the stupid bastards who did this, while I have a talk to him."

Twenty minutes later the South African was back in Sinada's office.

"The fucking Russian isn't trying to get out of your bloody country at all, man. He's gone to Nyala, and I hope I don't have to explain what the fuck that means. The shit hits the fan if he gets anywhere near Jebel Marra."

The look of shock on Sinada's face caught the South African's attention.

"Oh stop the bullshit! This isn't fucking kindergarten we have here. This is the big league. I know what the fuck goes on there and if you have any sense of self-preservation, man, you'll get me on a plane to there five minutes ago."

Five minutes ago? That couldn't be soon enough as far as Sinada was concerned. He picked up the phone and issued the order for a plane to be ready as soon as possible, knowing that none would be available until the morning.

"The plane will only be available at six tomorrow morning."

"What sort of fucking country you running here, Sinada?"

"We try . . ." He let it drop. "In the meantime my entire team is at your disposal."

"Good. You might want someone to take care of fat boy. I think he had a heart attack . . . oh and while they're at it, drop all this Moslem shit and tell them to get me a fucking beer."

TWENTY-SEVEN

S AVVA could see nothing more from the road, and he was beginning to feel exposed in his present position. In addition to this, he had the feeling that not enough food and too much heat were gradually sapping his energy. He turned to the young driver.

"Is there a road up the hill?"

"Yes. You want to go up Jebel Marra?"

"Jebel Marra?"

"That's the name of the hill. Very famous hill. Lot of Sudan holiday people. Nice cool forest. Also some cold drink, maybe?"

It sounded good.

They travelled on along the access road to the construction site and as they sped past the gate Savva noticed a sign in Arabic and French. He couldn't translate it but he did recognise the name of the civil engineers *Grands Travaux de Lyon*. It was the company that had been mentioned in his research in connection with a Sudanese Government visit to France.

About four kilometres further on they came to a crossroad that offered them the possibility of heading south to rejoin the main road or north to the foot of Jebel Marra. They turned north. The road became progressively worse as they approached the hills. It was hard to imagine any Sudanese wealthy enough to own a car subjecting the shock absorbers to the punishment of this road. The entire surface changed from dirt and sand to hard and jagged rock fragments, the smallest about the size of a clenched fist.

After almost twenty minutes they came to a roadside *Suq*. The driver did not need urging to stop; the sight of food and drink was enough. It was a tiny market, protected from the afternoon sun by woven straw mats tied up between the trees. The limited supply of food on offer ranged from lamb stew on couscous to goat stew on rice. It all looked to Savva's eye as though it had been made several weeks before. Hunger and thirst, however, came between him and his better judgement and to his surprise the taste of the lamb he settled for was fine. An enterprising merchant had somehow managed to transport several

350

large blocks of discoloured ice to the *Suq* and had a variety of drinks that were actually cool. Savva, who had never been a great cola drinker, managed to gulp down three delicious bottles of Pepsi.

When he had finished and was heading back to the car, Savva realised that he did not know the driver's name.

"Sam," the boy said.

Savva did not believe it for a minute, but if having a wad of low-denomination American dollars in his pocket made him feel like "Sam", that was fine by him.

It had seemed impossible that the road up Jebel Marra could get any worse, but it did. The size of the rocks covering it grew as they climbed. Soon they were reduced to a low gear crawl over a surface that would have tested a four-wheel drive. On either side of the road, the hillside had somehow been cultivated and sorghum stubble indicated that some crops had recently been harvested. Further on they came across fields of low shrubs planted in rows.

"Kar-kar-dee . . . *kakade*," Sam explained. "You dry flowers and make drink. Good for hot days. Good for eyesight."

"Good for eyesight?"

"Yes. Has vitamin see."

"Vitamin C?"

"Sure. See good."

Savva was not certain if Sam was attempting a joke.

The temperature dropped as they went higher and soon they were afforded a panoramic view of the vast expanse of land some two and a half thousand metres below them. They drove now through the dense green leafiness of the forest that Savva had noticed from down on the plains. A few minutes later they came to an unattended boom gate across the road, and so Sam swung the Toyota off into a parking area beside a battered jeep and a couple of old utilities. He clambered out of the car and beckoned for Savva to follow him.

"Come. I show you a beauty."

It had been Savva's aim to get a view down into the construction camp but they were now too far round the western face of the mountain. Having no other options, he made his way down a small walking path after the extremely nimble Sam.

"Look!" Sam had stopped between two trees and was pointing down to his right.

In front of him was an amazing sight. Two sharp rock spires jutted up to the sky and in the cleft between them tumbled a waterfall, the sides of its fall covered in mosses and ferns that clung defiantly to the cliff face. At the base of the waterfall the water boiled into a large circular pool in which a man was swimming. The air was cool and moist, almost a shock to Savva's system after the biting dryness of the plains. Sam had already scrambled down an embankment and was greeting a family of Sudanese who were enjoying a picnic in the shade of the surrounding rock walls. Savva couldn't possibly take the route his young driver had followed, and it took him a couple of minutes longer to find an easier path. He arrived on the slippery rocks at the water's edge as the man who had been swimming made his way out of the pool.

To the surprise of both Savva and the swimmer, they realised they had seen each other before. He was the Australian who had arrived on the flight into Khartoum several months earlier.

"G'day," the man said. "Still in Sudan? You must be a tiger for punishment!"

"Nice to see you again." Savva shook the man's wet hand. "Well, the same must be said of you perhaps?"

"Me?" The man laughed as he made his way carefully over the stones to where his towel lay draped over a log. "No way, mate. I've been home since the last trip."

He made room on the log for Savva to sit.

"Beaut little spot, eh?"

"Yeah." It was the first time he had relaxed into an Australian accent for a long time. "But why isn't everyone swimming?"

"No way. Not them. All the people around Dafur province are desert people. They have a strange relationship with water. Something to drink or irrigate with, I reckon, not something to play in."

The two men sat looking at the water for a while. Wherever the dampness touched, plants appeared to be bursting out of the soil. Even on the sheerest rock face a small shrub had somehow managed to establish a bonsai existence and from a gnarled and stunted trunk and branches, surprisingly broad leaves caught the spray and sucked in the moisture.

"Where do you come from?"

The Australian's voice startled Savva out of his botanic reverie.

"Melbourne. You?"

"That's bloody amazing! Melbourne!" There was an almost childlike delight on the man's face. "Can you imagine the odds against two Aussies meeting here? Bloody amazing! I'm Peter Lucas, by the way. From Fitzroy."

"Jack Zinner." For the second time in five minutes Savva found himself shaking the man's hand. "So what brings you to Sudan twice in the same year?"

"I work for an aid organisation and we have a couple of small projects in Dafur. I've just spent a couple of days at a place called Milabeda where we've been helping the local women set up a flour mill. I flew in with a Red Cross flight and was due out this morning, but there was some problem with the engine so I had a day spare, and here I am. What about you?"

"I've been working on a consultancy for a European transport company setting up a branch in Khartoum. Very boring. So I'm taking a break. The young kid over there drove me out from Nyala."

The Australian looked at him for a moment and then leaned closer, lowering his voice. "Fancy a beer?"

"A beer?"

"Yeah. Not Fosters, just Kenyan Tusker, but better than bloody raspberry cordial. Some just happened to fall into my bag. You know how it is. Look, I'll tell you what, why don't you stay the night here? Send your driver back and I'll give you a lift into town in the morning. I've got a big tent and enough grub for both of us."

"You sure it won't be any trouble?" Savva managed to hide his delight, not so much at the offer of a tent to sleep in, but the thought that he might be able to talk his way onto the Red Cross flight.

"Trouble? Beats the shit out of sitting here talking to myself all night!"

Five minutes and almost fifty dollars later, Savva had convinced Sam that he no longer needed a driver, but would be sure to find him when he arrived back in Nyala. Sam did not believe the lie, but neither did he care. In one day he had become rich beyond his dreams.

Fine particles of sand, lifted high into the desert atmosphere by the storms, turned the sky burnt orange. Nearer the horizon, pinks and apricots shifted and changed. Far away to the south, tall stacks of cumulus, huge pancakes, gold-topped but bleeding away through angry reds and oranges, were piled on deep green-stained lead, then vanished into darkness.

It was one of the most spectacular sunsets either of the men had ever witnessed. As darkness spread across the country its seeming emptiness was betrayed by bright pinpricks; small camp fires, villages and sometimes the lights of vehicles dipped and bobbed, sending their shafts of light into nothing. Soon a full moon, deeply soiled by the atmospheric dust, washed out the competition. As it rose it left the dust behind and reverted to the pale orb they were more familiar with.

"People would pay quids to see that, don't you reckon?"

Peter Lucas stood and stretched. They had sat after dinner on a rocky outcrop a few yards in front of the tent and, being the only campers, had made no effort to hide the beer. Peter gathered up the empty bottles and headed back towards the tent.

"I think I'll turn in."

"Okay. I might go for a stroll first. See how far I can get down the ridge over there," said Savva, eyeing the small circle of lights below. "I won't be long."

Behind him he heard the sound of the bottles being dropped in a rubbish bin. Other than that, nothing. The ridge was easy going and led slowly down several hundred metres, veering sharply to the left as it descended. As he had expected, he soon came to the razor-wire fence but what he did not expect was the well-made track around the perimeter.

He stopped for five minutes and listened. Below, in the construction site, he heard voices and some laughter. Behind him a night bird took flight, then again there was silence.

Taking the track outside the fence was easy, but somewhat exposed, as occasionally it passed from under the trees into full moonlight. The path was now no longer heading downward but taking him further and further around the side of the hill. Four or five hundred metres on, he reached a small clearing which he skirted, then came to a gate in the fence. It was padlocked. A few metres below him he saw some concrete-block buildings and beyond them, under the camouflage net, was the truck he had first seen from the road. There was a big difference with this angle of vision. He had no doubt that it was a missile carrier, but he was staggered to see that it was one of five.

There was simply no way that he could scale the fence or cut his way through. Even if he could, Savva realised that it would serve no useful purpose and would most likely result in him being apprehended. He committed the scene to memory, that was enough. He was about to turn when he heard the sound of a footstep. He froze and then, when he heard no further sound, slowly turned around.

"I was going to call you Nikolai but they tell me there is some doubt about that being your name. It's certainly not Jakski."

The man was standing in the darkness under the trees at the edge of the small clearing, but although

Savva couldn't see him distinctly, there was no disguising the American accent in the English.

"Expecting me were you, Ali?" His voice was calm and bore no relationship to the pounding panic in his heart.

Ali Abdel-Aziz Shiddu took a step forward into the moonlight. The light glinted off the barrel of the shotgun.

"Actually, we weren't expecting you for a couple of days yet but I figured you old guys are pretty smart. You would not have stayed alive so long if you were dumb. Also, they have offered a lot of hard currency for you, so I thought I might do a little hunting."

"Very clever of you, Ali. But they tell me that not even your American degree makes you employable." Get him talking, Savva thought desperately. Was that not his weakness? It was certainly the only avenue open. The younger man was far fitter than he had ever been, even at his best.

"What do you mean?"

"Oh, nothing really, just army gossip, you know what that's like. All nonsense."

"You tell me what the fuck you're talking about or I'll blow your head off and tell the army to go fuck their orders."

He's going to bite. Savva kept working on lowering his heart rate which was still thumping alarmingly. He was aware of beads of sweat trickling down his temples and knew that it was not a reaction to the warm night. This is how a heart attack starts, he thought with frightening clarity.

"They say you are just the token Sudanese. They don't need you –"

"That's bullshit! Those guys in there are out of the ark. The Russians have been locked away in their so-called secret cities for years. I did my research at the cutting edge, in America, not in Arzmas–16, Tomsk–7 or fucking Chelyabinsk–40. They are back in the SS–18 generation. Some of them didn't spend a day of their working lives doing anything other than devising safe ways of storing heptyl. This is the first time some of them have got anywhere near attack 'ems'."

"Attack what?"

"Army tactical missiles."

"They got a lot closer than you would have in your tame little American university. Just knowing the theory isn't worth anything."

Savva was breathing slower. His pulse was still high but the pain in the chest was subsiding. Ali was fired up as though it was true that his colleagues did not take him seriously. His pride was talking.

"You Russians wouldn't know what the hell I did. The university did research for all sorts of people – Bulova, Northrop, Varian, Westinghouse – you name it, and when one of the boys got stuck they would even talk about it in the canteen. What the Americans know about security you could put on the head of a pin. They think all the hi-tech equipment is security. It doesn't stop people talking."

"So what do you do, Ali? Make the coffee?"

"I'll tell you, a lot of what's happening here is because of me. Just getting weapons-grade material is one thing. Any bastard could have got the stuff your people brought out of Georgia, Azerbaijan and Armenia. Knowing what to do with it is the big question."

"And the little American graduate had the smart answer?"

"All you old men knew about was connected to the SS–18s, 24s and 25s. All old, all far too big. So I suggested the attack 'ems' approach. ATACMS. Think small, think sneaky. The ATACMS can reach up to 300 kilometres and, like your Scuds, they can be adapted to carry a warhead with just under a thousand cluster bomblets which can be spewed over a wide area. What I suggested was to change the payload. That's where our French friends came in. They had been working on smaller and smaller nuclear explosions. So we are marrying the two lines of research. Flexible, variable payload. Novichok gas if that's what the clients want ... or something with a low radiation component ... Elegant solutions, that's what I had to offer."

Before Savva could grasp what was happening there was sudden flash of movement and a cracking sound. The next thing he realised he was looking at Ali's body in the clearing and Peter Lucas standing beside it with a thick, but now broken, piece of dead wood.

"Quickly, get his shirt off." Peter was trembling, unable to move for the moment.

Savva grabbed at Ali's feet and dragged him back under the shadow of the trees. Even here there was too much moonlight.

"Don't bother. I've got this." Peter was at his side, a small pocket knife in his hand. "Get the gun," he whispered as he started to rip strips from Ali's shirt. The unconscious man was breathing but he was also bleeding profusely from a nasty wound on the back of the head.

The shotgun lay in full moonlight in the middle of the small clearing, but Savva just looked at it, frozen by some fear that even now it was all going to go wrong if he moved out of the shadows. Then he told himself he would have a far better chance with the gun in his hands than if he did not. The sound of his feet on the ground now seemed amplified and he could not imagine how anyone could not hear him. The weight of the gun surprised him but he closed his hand around it and made it back under the trees. He realised that he was in a state of shock, so he sat on the bank and forced his mind to come back under his control.

Peter was working with far greater efficiency and soon had Ali's arms and legs tied and a simple gag in his mouth. Together they dragged the man up the slope and propped him against a small tree.

"Come on, let's bugger off."

Peter saw the glazed look on the older man's face and recognised the symptoms. He gently took the gun from Savva's hand and pushed him forward.

"Let's go."

Walking through the trees would have slowed them down and probably created more noise, so they opted for the exposed but faster route along the fence line. They got back to the ridge without incident and Savva felt his fear diminishing as they began the climb up around the curve of the ridge to the camp site. The physical exertion required to climb the steep ridge seemed to have the effect of flushing his system of the excess adrenaline he had experienced over the last half hour. By the time they reached the tent Savva was exhausted but back in touch with himself.

"Peter –"

"No time for talking now . . . Just get the stuff and we'll piss off." In one sweeping movement he had ripped the tent, pegs and all, from the ground, and was jogging along the track to the jeep. Savva gathered up the rest of their belongings and followed him as fast as he could.

The jeep was parked, nose into a bush, on a small incline, so as soon as they were in, Peter released the handbrake and let the jeep roll backwards. There was just enough momentum to turn it around without starting the engine. Slowly they rolled forward and began the long rocky descent of Jebel Marra. The moon, now directly overhead, provided them with more than enough light, so they not only kept the motor off, but the lights as well.

Neither of them spoke during the entire thirty minutes it took to get down as far as the site of the deserted *Suq*. Even though he knew that there was no danger of them being followed, Savva could not stop himself occasionally glancing back over his shoulder.

As the road's surface improved, they lost the incline and had to start the jeep's engine, but they kept the lights off. They wouldn't have any problems with other vehicles. They had an excellent view down onto the plain and they had not seen one set of headlights on the main road back to Nyala.

"Keep going," Savva said as they approached the junction.

"What's down that way?"

"The main entrance to the complex." There was no way Savva wanted to drive by the front gate this time.

The two men lapsed back into silence for the next twenty kilometres. They were well away from the so-called construction site when Peter pulled over to the side of the road and switched off the engine. Behind them, Jebel Marra was a strangely beautiful sight, bathed in moonlight, and arising out of the dark plain. Peter opened the door and stepped out onto the sandy verge. Without a word he leaned back into the jeep and pulled the shotgun out from where he had stowed it behind the seat. He took a step back, then spun, and in a single movement threw the gun as far as he could into the night.

As he started the engine again, he turned to Savva.

"You going to tell me what the hell I've got myself mixed up in?"

A long way away, a perplexed night manager at the Kalastajatorppa was unsure what to do. Someone with no Finnish and very bad English had rung twice from St Petersburg demanding to leave a message for a person called Susijarvi. It turned out there was such a guest name on the computer file but he was not actually booked in. Maybe he was a regular. Twice he ran another search on the computer, but nothing came up. He was about to give up but there had been such urgency in the caller's voice that he decided it merited a little more effort. It was a long shot, but he might find something on the old card system they used as a back-up.

To his surprise he not only found a card but also a fax that had not been delivered. He picked up the card. On the back was a neatly printed request from the Finnish Foreign Ministry that any messages for Mr Susijarvi should be immediately phoned through to their offices at any time of the day or night. The night manager took the card and fax to the front desk and picked up the phone. Whoever had filed the fax had obviously not looked at the back of the card. Still, he thought, as he read the fax, it did not seem particularly urgent. Now, where had he put the telephone number of the caller from St Petersburg?

The story that Savva told Peter Lucas was the nearest to the truth that he had told anyone in a long time.

He borrowed Peter's pen knife, unpicked the inside of his travel bag and retrieved his Australian passport in the name of Leon Silbert. It felt strange holding it in his hand as though it was an old skin which, like a snake, he had long since discarded. Yet his survival required him to somehow crawl back inside it. I'm stumbling, he thought, stumbling along between the fantasies. And, in a bigger way, stumbling between the immensities of truth and lies, black and white and finally between earth and death. Peter's voice brought him back.

"I don't know why you blokes do this. Jesus, and I thought I lived an exciting life." He laughed. "What I don't understand is why Australia's involved. I thought this stuff was all Yanks and communists."

"It was by accident really. The Russians pulled some sleepers, some people, out of Australia, you know, people they weren't really using." Savva was improvising. "They decided that because of my background I could swap places with one of them and . . . well, here I am."

They drove in silence for a while until Peter asked the question they had both been struggling with.

"What do we do now?"

"We have to go through the security checkpoint just outside Nyala. Then I would like to get a ride on your plane to . . . where did you say?"

"Loki. That's Lokichokio. It's the Operation Lifeline Sudan base. OLS have been there for years ferrying food and medicine in to the southerners."

"Could you take me there? I have to get the information about what's happening at Jebel Marra out as quickly as possible."

"We both need to get out as quickly as possible. We're both dead meat if anyone catches us." He paused and then smiled. "Maybe they're not even looking yet."

"Peter, they're looking, at least for me."

Up ahead they saw the lights of the checkpoint. It seemed to be unusually bright and when they reached the roadblock they saw why. What looked like an official car was jacked up having a tyre changed. Someone had moved a small lighting generator from one of the huts out to the road to provide more illumination. On the edge of the lit area, Savva could make out a couple of elderly men in suits sipping tea.

A guard came up to the car while three others stood around fussing over the officials. The distraction seemed as though it might work in their favour.

"Let me do the talking," Peter said as he wound down the window.

The guard, however, had other ideas. No foreigners were going to breeze past this checkpoint while the Minister and his adviser were so close.

"Out!" He opened Peter's door to emphasise the order. He moved quickly around to Savva's side and did the same. Savva thought he heard Peter swear quietly.

The man made a point of marching them in front of the dignitaries and into a small hut.

"Passports!"

They handed them over. Savva's stomach knotted up again as he realised he had handed over the passport in the name of Leon Silbert. He glanced at Peter. He was white.

"What is your business?" The man was being louder than necessary in order to impress those outside.

"I work for Food Aid and I've just been to Milabeda where I picked up my friend. He is an agricultural scientist." It was a feasible bluff, he thought. There was something about the older man that gave him the air of an academic.

"Where is your letter of authority to travel?"

Peter stared at the man.

"You and I both know that I don't need one. I am helping to give aid to the people in your country."

Savva watched, holding his breath. The officer was thumbing through Peter's passport. When he did the same to his he would quickly see that there was no visa for Sudan.

"Are you criticising Sudan?" the man exploded. "You know we have very good plans for helping our own people."

Behind him, the door opened and one of the two men whose car was being repaired poked his head round the door. He spoke rapidly to the officer who shot to his feet before replying. Peter was visibly distressed and Savva imagined that he must look the same. He attempted to appear relaxed.

The man in the suit turned to them.

"Please have a seat."

He went to the door and called out to someone then held the door open for his companion. After exchanging a few words, a couple more chairs were produced and they sat down.

"Please. I am sorry about the inconvenience. I understand one of you is an agricultural scientist. I am the Minister for Agriculture and this is my chief scientific adviser. We would be very interested in what brings you to Sudan . . ." He picked up the Leon Silbert passport and opened it. "Mr Silbert."

"A real pleasure to meet you, Minister." Savva played it to the hilt. He stood and shook hands with both men and then sat. "I am interested in finding a location for my research and your country offers some splendid opportunities."

And what are they? He thought this was how a drowning person must feel when they come to that moment when they know they can no longer tread water.

"And what are they?" The Minister smiled invitingly. The adviser looked sceptical.

"The dry wadi beds." His schoolboy memory of Egyptians planting in the receding waters of the Nile flashed before him. "The wadi silt with a little natural fertiliser would be ideal."

"Excuse me." The adviser sat forward on his chair. "But what is your speciality? What is it we are discussing here?"

A good question. Savva felt the water reach his throat. Was this when everything flashed before you? Then it did. He saw a light, a halo . . . he saw Jesus.

"Sorry!" He beamed. "I work with the International Potato Institute in Lima. I'm a plant physiologist and my main area of study is suicide genes. I am looking for a site to set up a series of selective breeding programs in order to breed for the suicide gene. Let me explain. The domestication of certain plants was an unconscious step in mankind's early climb up the horticultural ladder. The potato . . ."

A little while later someone came to the door to let the Minister know that his car was ready. He was sent away with the order to make some tea for the guests. Peter Lucas was wide eyed, unable to believe what he was hearing. For the first time in a long while Savva felt in control, and though he was still aware that his visa-free passport was sitting on the Sudanese Minister for Agriculture's knee, he began to enjoy himself.

At the end, the Minister shook hands with Peter and putting his arm around Savva led him back to the jeep with the promise of every cooperation in what could turn out to be a mutually profitable research project. The agricultural adviser was also beaming. A happy minister was as important to his survival as a good harvest.

Passports in their pockets, the two waited until the Minister's car was ahead of them, then drove off in silence. Peter could hold it back no longer.

"Potatoes? Where the fuck did you get that bullshit from?"

Savva sighed. "If I told you, Peter, you would never believe me."

As they approached the airport Peter slowed down.

"Get in the back, under the tent. I'm going to try to get you to the plane."

Ahead of them the airport was in semi-darkness and it looked as though only a small number of security staff were on duty. A card game was in progress just outside the gate, and by the time they drew level with it Savva was well and truly buried. By the way the lone guard wandered over to the jeep, Peter knew that he was not going to have any problems. No alert had been issued here. Everything was normal and very relaxed.

The guard turned out to be the same one who had been on duty a couple of nights before when they had been prevented from flying because of the engine problem. He smiled in recognition.

"Oh, Mr Lucas, your pilot gone to hotel. He thought you not come until morning."

"Is the plane fixed?"

"Plane OK. He all set to go."

"Thanks. I'll put this junk in the plane then I'll be right out."

"OK, Mr Lucas."

Savva heard the guard's footsteps as he walked along the length of the jeep, then back towards the gate. As the jeep moved forward he pulled himself free of the tent and crouched, holding onto the side for support.

The plane was an old Twin Otter, repainted in white with a large red cross on the side. Under the cross were the letters ICRC. It had, by the look of the scratches and dents, led a very interesting life, thought Savva, as he moved back behind the netting into the luggage area. The tent followed.

"Keep under that. If you need a piss, there's a tiny loo but don't try to flush it."

The door shut and a few seconds later he heard the jeep putter off into the night. The space was not big. About the size of a coffin, was the thought that crossed his mind as he lay down, but soon, despite the heat and the cramped conditions, he was sound asleep.

CHAPTER

TWENTY-EIGHT

AT three in the morning, Ali Shiddu, having regained conciousness and somehow freed himself, stumbled down into the Jebel Marra camp and raised the alarm. He remembered his confrontation with Trinkovski but he had no recollection of being hit. An attempt to limit the damage by capturing the intruders was discussed by the Jebel Marra project leaders but rejected. Instead, they phoned Faisal Sinada in Khartoum. At 3.30 am Sinada phoned the South African and, after a very unpleasant conversation he phoned his counterpart in Nyala and instigated a full security alert. A photograph of Mr Trinkovski was faxed to all police stations and to the airport.

Two hours later, every road in and out of Nyala was closed. The card game at the gates of the airport vanished and by dawn the entire area was sealed tight. No one got in or out without a full security check.

The activity around the airport did not escape Savva's attention. At the sound of the first troop trucks arriving he made his way forward and, crouching well back from a passenger window, got a fairly good view of what was happening. It looked like a military coup. A machine-gun was mounted on an armoured car beside the main airport entrance, and half a dozen army trucks were disgorging soldiers onto the tarmac. The troops fanned out to all sides of the landing strip and Savva could hear the crackle of two-way radios as they confirmed that they were in position. It was not a morning for a quiet stroll.

Savva returned to the luggage compartment and pulled the tent back over himself. Peter had not told him what time they were scheduled to depart, but as the air temperature was rising fast, he hoped it was an early flight.

Following a premonition that they might run into problems at the airport, Peter had woken the Red Cross pilot early and they both skipped breakfast. But, apart from the pilot's foul mood, things went like clockwork. The security check was thorough, however as neither of them looked remotely like the fax-photo that was now taped to the wall of the checkpoint, and because they were representatives of the International Red Cross, they were cleared to enter the airport.

After opening the door and dumping their overnight bags inside, the pilot circled the aircraft removing the chocks and doing his pre-flight check. Peter scrambled in and took the pilot's bag to the cockpit, then went aft to the luggage hold.

"Keep quiet. I haven't told Walter that you're here. He's a bit of a stickler for Red Cross rules. I'll wait till take off." He clipped the net back in place and waited by the door for the pilot.

After about five minutes Peter's nerves got the better of him and he went down the steps and looked around. The pilot had gone. At the airport gate a large crowd were now backed-up, awaiting clearance. A refuelling truck was trundling up to a DC3 painted in military olive and brown, a couple of baggage handlers were getting a line of trolleys sorted out, but there was no pilot. He went up into the plane and sat. A noise outside startled him and he spun around, only to receive a clip over the head from the grinning pilot.

"You rush me out of the hotel without breakfast and now I nearly forgot to file our flight plan!" He laughed. "Come on. Get the door shut. If we don't get going now we'll be here all morning. There's a special flight from Khartoum due any minute and then the army are expecting some extras in. Looks like there is some kind of a flap on."

It seemed like a lifetime before Savva heard the engines whine into life, then an even longer time either sitting or taxiing. Finally he heard the change of pitch as the revs went up and the propellers bit into the hot dry air. He forced himself to breathe. The rocking and jolting stopped and they were flying. There was no gunfire. There was no last minute hitch. They were actually in the air! He stretched full length, forcing his feet hard against the aft bulkhead, his head into the netting, then relaxed. There was no doubting it, he thought, as excitement replaced the tension and fear, no doubt at all. He was going home.

A few minutes after they levelled out Peter unclipped the netting and gestured for him to come out. Steadying himself against a seat the younger man pulled him closer. He was not looking as pleased as Savva would have expected.

"I told Walter and he's . . . well, extremely angry would be a mild description."

"Why?" Savva shouted above the noise of the engines.

"He says he could lose his Red Cross job for this. They are bound by all these rules and it seems we've broken most of them."

"So what's he going to do?"

"Nothing." Peter smiled. "Walter wants to talk to you. Let him read you the riot act. He certainly isn't about to turn round and go back to Nyala."

They made their way up to the cockpit. Whatever insulation the plane may once have had against noise was long gone and so the pilot pointed to the spare headset. He was a good-looking, well-built man in his mid forties who was either prematurely bald or had for some unknown reason shaved his head. Savva decided it was the former. He did not look to be the kind of man who would do anything on a whim. Notwithstanding the fact that he had been dragged out of his hotel so abruptly by Peter, he still seemed to have been well prepared. His uniform was immaculate with even the shirt sleeves ironed with very crisp creases.

"Mr Silbert, I make this clear. You should not be on this flight as you are not appearing on my manifest. The ICRC is only able to operate in these sectors with the kind goodwill of the Sudanese Government and you put our entire humanitarian work at grave risk." He paused and looked at Savva. "Are you understanding me, Mr Silbert?"

The relief at being out of Nyala was still percolating through him, so Savva had to resist the temptation to say that the pilot's English was very good and he understood every word, but having heard stories of the Swiss–German sense of humour, he decided against it.

"I understand fully, sir. I will be only too happy to explain to any authorities that I stowed away onboard your flight. That is, as long as those authorities reside outside Sudan."

"Please take a seat in the back of the plane. I will inform you of what I decide before we reach Lokichokio."

Savva removed the headset and sat as instructed. Before catching up on some sleep, he leaned over and pulled the curtain across the window. He had not even the slightest desire to catch a last glimpse of the Northern Sudanese landscape. In fact, at this particular moment he did not care if he ever saw it again. The cabin door was hooked back and, from where he sat, he could see Peter deep in conversation with the pilot and although he could not hear what they were saying, once or twice he had the impression that they were laughing.

The South African was not laughing. He was very close to shooting someone. He had just come out of the security hut at Nyala airport where he had been involved in a shouting match with a very disgruntled Minister for Agriculture. The man had not only objected to the security arrangements which were delaying his flight, but had declared that the photograph they were displaying was certainly not that of a Russian spy but a very distinguished agricultural scientist. A heated exchange had followed as Sinada had stepped in and insisted on interrogating the Minister on every last detail of his meeting the previous night. It was at about this point that someone mentioned that the jeep in question was not only already at the airport, but that its occupants had taken off in a Twin Otter just fifteen minutes before the South African's flight had landed.

Sinada was still down in the security hut questioning the Minister as the South African burst through the door of the control tower and flight centre. Less than thirty seconds after looking at the flight plan he was screaming orders at some very bewildered air-traffic controllers. He took even less time to realise that he was yelling at the wrong people. He pounded down the stairs and pulled Sinada away from the now extremely anxious Minister for Agriculture.

"Those fuckers are on their way to some shithole in Kenya. Now you talk to whoever you need to, but get that fucking plane down on the nearest airstrip! Order it down now! They haven't a hope in hell of getting over the Kenyan border for a couple of hours yet, so force it down if you have to and if that doesn't work I want it blown out of the fucking sky!"

A gentle hand shaking his shoulder brought Savva out of his dreams of childhood terror. He was locked in a closet by a teacher and forgotten. A bell had rung. Children's voices had faded away and somewhere a large iron gate clanged shut. He awoke with a slight sense of chill but glad to find he had not been abandoned.

"We've got a problem." Peter's face was drawn and pale.

"The plane?" Savva had a flash of fear as he sensed that they were descending faster than was normal.

"No. The Sudanese military have ordered us to land at Rumbek. We're to the north of there now."

"Can't we ignore them? How far is it to Kenyan airspace?"

"No chance. And Walter won't do it anyway."

"Where's Rumbek?" The all too familiar feeling of panic was returning with a vengeance.

"About 800 ks southeast of Nyala in Bahr El Ghazal province. It's a garrison town. The government has held it for years but it's pretty much surrounded by Garang's SPLA, the Sudanese People's Liberation Army."

"What will the government do if we ignore them? They won't try to shoot us down?"

"Walter thinks they would go that far, but reckons they're more likely to have scrambled a few of their old MiGs and will probably force us down."

"No other options?"

"One. But it's a big risk. Walter says there's a dry-season strip just south of Rumbek, disused except for emergencies. But he's willing to try it and claim we had an engine problem. No one's going to believe it, but it would give you a head start."

"A head start, to where?"

"There's a little village called Akot just over thirty kilometres east which is in SPLA territory. Food Aid have a primary health-care worker stationed there. If you could make it to Akot you could hole up until a relief flight comes in."

"And you two?"

"We'll stay with the plane. That will at least keep some of them busy for a while."

"But –"

Peter shook his head. "No. It's decided. Anyway, we have to find this bloody strip first and at this time of the year it could be under water."

"But . . ." Savva realised he was talking to Peter's back.

At the cabin door Peter turned and forced a smile.

"In the case of emergencies no line of lights will come on . . . Just get the hell out." Then he added, as if it were an afterthought, "Walter says to strap yourself in tight."

The frame of the Twin Otter groaned in protest as Walter pushed the nose even further down. Torn between a realistic feeling of impotence and a desire at least to see how close the ground was, Savva reached for the curtain over the window. As he did, he was forced up out of his seat and then down again with a sickening jolt as they hit some turbulence, then suddenly started to climb again.

From the cockpit, Peter shouted something to him but with the engines screaming he could not make out what he was saying. For a moment or two the plane levelled out and the engines were throttled back. Peter tried again.

"There isn't much water on the strip, but there are some cattle. That's good."

That's good? How could an airstrip playing host to a herd of cattle be a good thing? Now he was not only feeling airsick for the first time in his life, but perplexed as well.

Savva fixed his eyes on the cockpit window. Every time the nose dipped a little he caught a glimpse of the tiny patch of flattened land that Walter called an airstrip. It was little more than a clearing in what looked like clumps of thick trees and dense grass. As they came closer he noticed that even the grass on the runway was tall. There was no way that anyone approaching from the air could tell what sort of condition the surface was in. The ground came closer and closer and Savva's hands gripped the seat, pulling, trying to will the nose up, convinced they were going to crash. Seconds from touchdown he heard the engine cut completely and for the last few metres they seemed to waft towards the ground.

The initial impact was not the sickening thump he expected. It was gentle and perfect. Then, just as his nerves were about to relax, the plane was lost in a plume of water and started to lurch sideways. First he was thrown forward by the sudden deceleration and then he was tossed from side to side as Walter fought to keep the plane on course. Another plume of water, then silence. They appeared to have stopped under some trees at the far end of the strip but it was hard to tell as the cockpit and all the cabin windows were splattered with mud.

Somewhere something was hissing, in protest at the treatment that had just been meted out.

"Come on, out quickly. Grab your stuff," Peter shouted, tossing the small bag to him.

"But we're OK, aren't we?"

"Come on, Mr Silbert." It was Walter. He had his flight bag in one hand and a first-aid box in the other. "We're better off outside, I think."

They watched as the steps disappeared into high grass. It was only as they clambered down that they saw that the bottom of the ladder was ankle deep in water. Savva looked at the pilot who was already halfway to the trees.

"Walter, that was one hell of a landing."

The pilot turned with a smile, then screamed, "Run! Run!"

Peter spun round on the bottom of the ladder as he saw what Walter was reacting to. He grabbed Savva and pulled him off the steps and into the water.

"To the trees. Go!" he yelled as he tugged Savva to his feet and, running beside him, propelled him away from something that, although Savva had not seen, he could now hear. Coming out of the east were three jet fighters. They were still a fair way off but closing fast and it was a better than even bet that they were Sudanese Airforce MiGs. They must have just spotted the plane on the ground, for the first of them was already completing a steep banking turn, preparing for a run over the strip.

In a matter of seconds they were on them and over. No weapon was fired but the three men flinched as the scream of the jets tore at their eardrums.

"Quickly. We must go further," shouted Walter, but this time Savva needed no urging. He threw himself forward before the others and was suddenly up to his waist in water. He was about to turn and climb back up the bank but saw that the other two had followed him.

The grass here was over their heads and as the sound of the jets again grew louder Peter, who was now leading the way, signalled them to get down. Lying in half a metre of water, they could see the MiGs high above them. For a few seconds the jets looked as though they were returning to their base, but they then turned in an almost lazy motion, appearing to be falling from high in the sky. They levelled out at an altitude of about a hundred metres, coming in flat and low. From each aircraft came the smallest of flashes followed immediately by a burst of cannon-fire.

There was no telling what damage the cannon rounds did, but it was of little consequence, for, as the noise reached a crescendo, there was a low bass crump followed by an explosion as the Twin Otter went up in a swirling ball of orange flames and jet black smoke. A couple of smaller explosions were heard, then nothing. Just a dark stain of smoke on the morning sky.

How long the three men lay in the water Savva was not sure. The MiGs made a couple of slower passes once to the south of the runway, once directly above them on the northern edge. Looking around, all Savva could see was grass and water. He tried to stand but he lost his balance and fell sideways, grasping at the stems of grass which did nothing to stop him toppling once again into the water.

"Over here."

It was the pilot's voice, but as Savva regained his balance and stood up he could see nothing but grass.

"Hang on, Walter, I'm standing on my bloody bag." It was Peter somewhere to Savva's right. "You OK, Leon?"

"I'm wet from head to foot and I can't see a bloody thing," he snapped. Something else was eating away at him and he decided that here in the elephant grass was as safe a place as any to make a change. "Look, do you two mind calling me Savva? I haven't been Leon for so long I have to think twice before answering to it."

"Savva? What sort of name is that?" Peter asked.

"It happens to be the name I was born with, and I'm sick and tired of being anything else." There was an anger in his voice that unsettled him, but the two men made no further comment.

"Stay there," called Walter. "I'll come to you."

The grasses parted and a slightly less immaculate Walter was standing in front of him. He was still clutching his flight bag and medical kit. A large part of his bald head was covered in mud and the neatly ironed white shirt had gained colour and lost its creases.

"Thank you for what you said about the landing. Very kind." His formality seemed strangely out of place.

384

He attempted to wipe the mud from his head, but merely achieved a more even distribution. "Now, all we have to do is find some high ground and walk east."

Again the grass parted and Peter joined them. He was in no better shape than the other two, but he sported a huge grin.

"Yeah, nice landing." He glanced at Savva. "You know what flashed through my head as I was half drowning myself, hiding from those planes? I thought, that's the last time I offer . . . Savva . . . a beer. Life hasn't been the same since."

"I'll buy you the next one," Savva promised. He turned to Walter. "I just lay there wondering why you thought it was a good thing there were cattle on the strip?"

"Oh, yes. Cattle is good. Cattle means that the Dinka are nearby and I think they would be better company than those who have ruined my plane."

"Ruined" seemed a bit of an understatement to Savva.

"So?" he asked. "Which way?"

Walter checked his watch then squinted up at the sun.

"Straight ahead." He pointed at a wall of tall grass, and started to force his way forward. The depth of the water remained constantly above their knees and the going was not easy. After a few minutes Walter stopped to catch his breath.

"Do you know what I was thinking about in the water? I was thinking, why is it I seem so tired and yet it is still only morning?" He checked his watch again. "Still only seven minutes to ten."

They took over two hours to reach higher ground, but when they did scramble up a rocky bank out of the long grass and water, the men found themselves on the remnants of road. It was a reasonable assumption, given that there were so few roads in the area, that fortune was on their side and that this was the road between Rumbek and Akot.

The joy at getting onto higher ground faded as they looked ahead. For several kilometres the road, built up from the *toic,* had been cleared of all vegetation. They were totally exposed.

"We need to get off here very quickly." Walter cast a sideways glance at Peter. "Can you take Savva's bag?"

"Sure."

"Hang on!" Savva protested. "I'm capable of carrying my own bag. There's hardly anything in it, anyway."

Walter shook his head. "No, let Peter take it, we haven't got time to argue and I want you to run. I have a feeling they won't leave it at that. They'll be back to check if there are bodies inside the wreckage."

Savva began to protest but Peter had already taken the bag from his shoulder and had started off along the track.

It turned out that Peter and Savva were both in better shape than the pilot, who was soon reduced to a jog. The road, which must have been built many years earlier as a rainy-season passage across the flood plain, was in dreadful repair. In places the dark red clay was badly eroded, either by the cattle or by torrential rain. Gullies dissected the path and every now and then they came across large boulders that looked as though they had been deliberately placed on the road in order to block the progress of vehicles. They also found cattle pats and tracks from time to time, mostly indicating that the cattle had crossed the road rather than travelled along it.

The distance to the edge of a forest was deceptive and turned out to be much further than they had anticipated. A combination of fatigue and bad road conditions meant that instead of running they were soon reduced to walking. The one benefit of the slower pace, though, was that they began to get a better appreciation of their surroundings. They had indeed been fortunate to have found the road, for at times the *toic* on either side of them turned into large expanses of water in which the higher ground was visible only as a scattering of small islands.

No matter how bad the road appeared to be, to their dismay they saw that some vehicles had still managed to negotiate it. Tyre marks had dried into muddy casts in places and at one point they came across what looked suspiciously like tank tracks. Sometimes the tracks indicated that the vehicles had ventured onto the sloping sides of the road to avoid some obstruction. In the worst areas it was hard to imagine how the vehicles had avoided rolling down into the *toic*. Cattle spoor became more frequent and seemingly fresher as they approached the forest edge, though no one volunteered to prod a cow pat to verify the age.

Once or twice Savva looked back at the now faint wisp of smoke rising from the remains of the plane, but it was hard to judge how far they had come as, from this distance, the raised strip of land had merged into the other islands.

The last few metres before the trees were up a sharp incline and soon the men were on slightly higher ground above the flood plain. Best of all, they were in shade and out of the immediate gaze of anyone searching for them. Their suspicion that whoever had ordered the MiG 23s into the air would not be satisfied with the destruction of the Twin Otter was proved correct a few minutes later. A pair of helicopters appeared behind them in the vicinity of the landing field. For about twenty minutes they watched from the safety of the trees as the machines beat their way up and down the *toic*. Eventually one of them appeared to land near the remains of the plane and the other hovered nearby on guard.

Having rested, the men decided to move on. There was something of the boy scout in Peter Lucas for he soon organised them, spread out, five metres apart.

"Is this the way the army do it?" Savva called from his position at the rear. He was not complaining, in fact it was a relief to have someone else do the thinking for a while.

"No idea. I think I saw it in a movie."

"What? *The Dirty Dozen*?"

"I think *The Filthy Three* would be more apt."

The laughter was cut short by the ever pragmatic Walter.

"I thought the idea was also to move silently?"

Although the humidity was high, the temperature felt as though it was in the mid twenties and walking was quite pleasant. The forest was broken up with some areas of trees and others of tall grasses. Cattle tracks led off through flattened grass, but of the cattle themselves there was no sign. Savva had imagined this area would be teeming with animals and birds yet the forest was quiet and eventually he gave up looking for any wildlife. The road was now flat and covered in fine sand, and for the next hour he kept his eyes down, following the footprints in front of him, aware that every step he took was one step nearer safety.

They heard the jeep long before they saw it. At first Walter thought it was coming towards them, but the trees were playing games with the sound and, as they dashed into the forest and hid behind some bushes, there was no doubt it was coming from Rumbek.

"We should have gone to separate sides of the road," Peter said as he peered up to try to catch a glimpse of the approaching vehicle. "This way, we could all be caught."

"Next time, maybe I should climb a tree? I feel safer up in the air." Walter was dead-pan, until he rolled over and winked at Savva. "You would give me a hand up, wouldn't you?"

"It would be my pleasure." Savva smiled.

A Sudanese officer in combat dress sat beside the driver and, in the open rear, six men armed with rifles. They were intent on getting where they were going in the shortest time possible, if the speed at which they were travelling was any indication.

"If it is a scouting party, then they'll be back," Peter said as he cleared a more comfortable place to sit. "So I suggest we have something to eat and drink here."

"And, if they don't come back?" Savva was not too keen to slow down and end up spending the night in the forest. The fact that he had seen no animals was not enough to convince him that there were none, and he was also aware that this was malaria country. Southern Sudan had cornered the market in rare diseases and he did not relish the idea of becoming a case history for those who study tropical diseases from the safety of a mortuary.

"If they don't come back in half an hour we move again." Walter was fishing through his medical kit. "I like the idea of stopping for a while, but isn't the talk of food a little academic. I do not remember passing a McDonalds in the last hour or so, or did I miss a sign saying one was just up ahead?"

"Where do you think the Government of Sudan troops were off to in such a hurry?" If Walter was going to attempt jokes then, Savva felt, he needs all the encouragement he can get.

"Well, you blokes can go Big Mac hunting all over Bahr El Ghazal as far as I'm concerned. I think I'll start on these."

To their amazement, Peter was holding a plastic bag containing three oranges and several bread rolls. Although dry, they had been severely squashed when he had stepped on his bag in the *toic*.

"I grabbed them from the hotel dining room this morning. It's only bread and cheese. I'm afraid I couldn't find the rest of the ingredients for a 'Quarter Pounder'."

They ate in silence, suddenly aware of how hungry they were. When they were about to start on the oranges, Walter held up a hand to stop them.

"I take it none of you gentlemen mind a little alcohol?"

"I'd kill for a beer. But I'm nervous about drinking with Savva after last time."

"I'm not so discriminating about my drinking companions." Savva pulled a face at Peter and turned back to Walter who was reaching for his medical kit. "But I'm not too keen on medical alcohol."

"Medical, no, but certainly medicinal." He produced a small flask of clear liquid from under some gauze bandages. "This is good homemade kirsch. My brother makes it on his farm."

"You are a man of constant surprises, Walter. You have a brother with an illegal still?"

"You are making fun of me, Peter." He shook his head in mock dismay. "Savva will understand."

"Not a lot I'm afraid," Savva admitted, as he watched the Swiss pilot taking a syringe from its sealed packet and fitting a needle to it. "Are we about to get some new form of anti-malarial injection?"

"No! We don't have glasses so I am going to inject a nip into each orange. It should lift our spirits and aid our digestion."

Peter and Savva could hardly contain their laughter at the sight of this mud-bespattered pilot injecting three oranges with the kirsch. The fact that all this was taking place in the present circumstances added a touch of the surreal to proceedings.

"My brother has cows in the Swiss Alps, so the Swiss Government says he can make kirsch. It depends on how many cows you have as to how much you can make."

"What on earth have the cows got to do with it?" Peter was clutching at his belly with the pain of holding the laughter in.

"In old times, the kirsch was used as a folk medicine for the animals. So it was allowed. A man with a still on the back of his truck goes around the farms each year and distills the fermented cherries for the farmers. Sometimes, if he is your friend, he will double distill. My brother is his very good friend."

"But why," asked Savva, through the laughter, "do you have it in the first-aid box?"

"If you get an infection then you dab this on the wound and the germs get drunk and go away." Walter looked at Savva as though he were stupid. "It is also very nice to drink, Mr Savva, at the end of a long day. Here, catch!" He tossed an orange to each of them and taking a pocket knife demonstrated how they should cut a small hole and then drink and squeeze simultaneously.

For a moment, a small forest clearing in Sudan witnessed the sight of three, very muddy, white men, flat on their backs, squeezing oranges into their mouths as though they contained the nectar of the gods.

High above them and far to the east, they heard an aircraft and, a little while later, what sounded like light arms fire, but it was too distant to cause concern and so they lay there in the shade for almost an hour. Savva's mind, which had for so long excluded any thought of possible futures, wandered down strange paths as he stared up through the leaves to some gentle drifting clouds.

It was as though being in survival mode had kept him sharply focused on the "here and now" and in this moment, with companions to help him along the last few kilometres, he could let go. The very thoughts that had started him on this long journey now seemed wrong. He had left Australia because he felt that a life of inactivity was a wasted life and yet, what he had been doing, even if it meant nothing to the outside world, had been important to him. To have woken up and suddenly discovered that he was old and had contributed nothing had been a real fear, but now it all seemed relative.

The need to achieve something, to be someone, was driven by his need to . . . what? And for whom? Savva pictured the small boy in the Moscow orphanage and knew the answer. The boy wanted to be picked up and told he had done well. To be taken out into the world and have a hand to hold while he explored the images around him, without the need to store those images. To know that each day the doors would be open. Each day he would be allowed out to experience something new and fresh. The years he had spent in Australia had been another orphanage experience. Waiting to be told he could go out and see something important. And all the time he had waited, the conviction that he was not worth activating was gaining ground deep inside him. Well, stuff that! He laughed out loud at the deep-seated games he had been playing within himself.

"What's so funny?" Peter rolled onto his stomach and peered through sleepy eyes at the older man.

"I just discovered that I'm full of shit!" gasped Savva, between the convulsions. "I get one chance in a lifetime to lie on my back and watch an African sky through forest leaves . . . and what do I do? I just ran a do-it-yourself therapy session on myself."

"Oh, is that all. I do it all the time. We all do." He lay back in the grass.

"Speak for yourself. If I wanted therapy I would see a professional. If I saw a professional therapist I would certainly need one," Walter said. "I have been thinking we should go."

"I need a toilet stop first," Savva said as he got to his feet. "I don't suppose anyone brought a toilet roll?"

"Use the leaves. Watch out for snakes."

"Thanks, Peter. I need to relax for this sort of thing, that won't help."

"Check the leaves first for spiders."

Savva ignored Walter's contribution and trotted off across the road in search of a slightly more private location. Just as he found a spot he heard a vehicle coming at speed along the road. He turned and managed to catch a glimpse of what looked like the government troops returning. The vehicle sped past but Savva was left with the distinct impression that a couple of soldiers were missing.

There was no sign of snakes where he squatted, but his mind was soon playing tricks with him. Suddenly the forest seemed alive with the sounds of a marauding animal intent on devouring him. He had read reports of hyenas developing a taste for human flesh after feasting on refugees who, at the point of exhaustion, were unable to defend themselves. One of the reports had gone into graphic detail about the animals' penchant for leaping at the face of their victims.

Savva told himself to stop being so paranoid and that he was probably far more at risk of ant bites. The activity he was engaged in is never particularly relaxed, but when undertaken in unfamiliar outdoor locations that are suddenly found to be swarming with ants, it takes on aspects of an anxiety attack. His attempt to hop sideways was an unmitigated disaster. However the leaves he reached for were, he was relieved to see, both ant and spider free.

As he trudged back to join his companions, some instinct brought his senses to full alert, stopping him just short of the road.

Four extremely tall men were standing in the clearing where he had left the others. They were totally naked, if one does not count a rifle as an article of clothing. From where he was crouching, the rifles looked like rather rusty AK 47s. Were these the so-called friendly Dinka? One of the men was prodding Walter with his rifle while another was frisking Peter in a manner that would have done an airport security guard proud.

It became apparent that none of the Dinka spoke English, for, after a couple of exchanges, they loaded all the bags on Peter's shoulders and marched the two men into the forest. Savva suppressed the desire to go with them, even if that meant walking into captivity. He sat very quietly contemplating his next move. His fear, which the company of the other men had kept at bay, bubbled to the surface and he found himself trembling from head to foot. This was, after all, a war zone and it was highly possible that the government soldiers were still hunting him.

His decision to move on was eventually prompted by the sound of helicopters in the west. They were far away but there was no certainty that they wouldn't start a sweep of the road. If they did, he was fine at present because of the tree cover, but there was every chance that it would not extend all the way to Akot. He cautiously stepped out onto the road and headed east.

Under other circumstances, walking along this particular road would have been a pleasant diversion. The combined effects of the gathering clouds and a relatively cool breeze had taken the sting out of the afternoon sun. For the next hour or so Savva was in and out of the tree cover, but even on the exposed sections of the road he saw no threat of any kind. With every step he was further away from danger and yet he experienced a growing sense of fatalism. Something could and probably would go wrong. He refused to believe he could actually walk away from the last few months. The disaster need not even be major. It was as though he had conquered some great peak and was fated to twist his ankle on a pebble.

With such negative thoughts in his mind the sudden end of the trees came as a real blow to his morale. He walked out of the forest and up onto a vast, raised plain where the ground was covered in grasses and scattered with rocks. Ahead of him, a large river snaked its way from south to north in huge sweeping bends. The expanse of the landscape was breathtaking. From where he stood he could see far to both left and right. To the east, another forest appeared to start on the other side of the river. In other times and under other circumstances, he thought, he would like to have shared this vista with Amelia. The thought had brought him to a stop but it also quickly brought back his desire to survive. Keep moving. There was no cover for him now, but also no alternative to going forward.

After about a kilometre the road began to rise, artificially built up above the surrounding landscape. Maybe there were seasons when even this plain was flooded, but whatever the reason, an enormous amount of effort had been put into building the road. He now had the choice of either walking, fully exposed, on the road, or the more secure route alongside it. Despite the fact that coming down off the road meant that he could no longer see in both directions, he took that option and wandered along the many cattle trails that criss-crossed the landscape.

At one point Savva found himself taken by the meandering trail through the centre of a large cleared area. He realised within minutes that this had been a Dinka cattle camp. A proliferation of small burnt circles marked the fire places and the remnants of makeshift huts were scattered about. He found small piles of ash from what appeared to be burnt mounds of dried dung, so he knew that the camp had been only recently deserted. A slashed sack of grain spilled maize onto the dry red earth. In the middle of the clearing, a vulture eyed Savva and considered him such a small threat that he scorned taking to the air and chose rather to simply hop a couple of metres further away.

There was a depressing emptiness about the abandoned cattle camp and Savva was pleased to be away from it. A few minutes later, as the sun began to dip towards the horizon, he clambered up the embankment to take his bearings. The sight that confronted him had him tumbling back down as fast as he could. Less than a hundred metres away, a single lane bridge spanned the river. On the approaches to it were groups of soldiers. He had only glimpsed them but they looked African, and armed to the teeth. Savva lay still, unsure of how much noise he had made as he fell down the bank. There had been . . . he tried to run the image in front of him, but for the first time in his life it refused to come. There had been . . . soldiers in camouflage gear. Tall? Dinka? He shook his head in an attempt to force the image to clear. The bridge? Iron girders high on either side and . . .

The beating of his heart became confused with the sound of . . . footsteps. Someone was walking along the road. Had he been seen? Every instinct told him to run, but for Savva Golitsyn the running was over. There was nowhere that he could go even if his legs would obey him.

The footsteps were almost above him now, but he could not even turn to face his fear. Behind him he heard someone coming carefully down the bank and yet he still sat, somehow calm, resigned to whatever was going to happen next.

"It is OK, Mr Savva. Your friends told me we might find you here."

Savva managed to turn.

One of the tallest men he had ever seen was towering over him, smiling. He had a rifle slung over his shoulder and was an almost comical sight in clothes that seemed several sizes too small.

"I'm Anthony. I think you should come over the bridge with me."

The man's strong hands helped him to his feet and up onto the road. Savva glanced ahead. At the bridge, some soldiers had positioned themselves behind the girders. On the far side of the river, Savva noticed what looked like a junkyard. The rusted and twisted shells of tanks and armoured cars had been pushed from the road into the swamp, evidence that sometime in the past this place had witnessed several major battles.

"How long have you been walking down there?"

"Beside the road?" Savva was relieved to find his voice. "Since the end of the forest, I think. Why?"

"You are a very lucky man. The GOS troops have littered the place with landmines."

"GOS?"

"Government of Sudan. The Arabs. They do it to keep us on the road, where they can shoot at us better."

Savva shut out the thought of landmines.

"You said my friends told you that I was coming. Where are they?"

"One of our patrols picked them up and we didn't realise that there was someone else until they were taken into Akot."

"You are going to take me there?"

"Well, I don't want to stay out here any longer. This is the front line. Over the bridge you are in SPLA territory. There is a hell of a search going on for you, but they seem to think you are still lost in the *toic*. Finding the road was very fortunate. You wouldn't have lasted the night out there."

It could have been like a movie, walking across the bridge, the last rays of the sun on his back, but whoever was directing mistimed it and the sun vanished just as they approached. The clouds that had been gathering all day finally brought rain and Savva walked across the Na'am River in a wet and very ordinary dusk.

CHAPTER

TWENTY-NINE

INSTEAD of arriving at a village, Savva was deposited in a forest clearing. A camp had been set up and guards were stationed on the perimeter. A doctor, another tall Dinka, who was introduced to Savva simply as Dr Steven, took one look at Savva and ordered him to bed where he gave over to uncontrollable shaking. The doctor came in several times and forced him to drink a sweet warm liquid, and eventually he drifted into a disturbed sleep. In his mind, landmines were exploding all around him. Later he thought he heard Heimo Susijarvi's voice calling something to him in Finnish. Aino's face, Amelia's and that of Primakov emerged from the darkness; only to be replaced by faces he could not recognise. Heimo returned with a glass of ice-cold vodka, but no matter how far he strained forward, Savva could not quite reach it and screamed with frustration.

"Nervous exhaustion."

Steven was standing over him, the morning sunlight streaming through the flaps of an olive green tent.

"Nervous exhaustion. Just as well, for a while last night I thought it might be the onset of malaria."

"I thought we were in Akot. Where are we?"

"In the bush a few kilometres out of town. We decided it was safer in case the GOS decided to try to get you back. They seem very stirred up. It was a good move. You probably heard the bombing last night. Unfortunately that was Akot."

"There was a bombing raid?" Savva vaguely remembered the landmines in his dreams.

"Ten or eleven five-hundred pounders. No damage, as usual. The French give them the Spot Satellite images to aid them but they don't have the technology to take advantage of them. They sent in a couple of Antinovs and hand rolled the bombs out the rear loading bay. They cleared a little bit of forest for next year's crop." Steven peered at him. "How do you feel?"

"Not well. Drained would be a good description."

"Do you feel like eating?"

Savva shook his head. Even the idea of food made him nauseous.

"Well, maybe you can eat on the plane. We need to get you over to the airstrip. There is a special ECHO flight coming in. The Khartoum Government has banned all flights but someone important wants you out now. They are going to try to come in without being detected. Can you be ready in ten minutes?"

Savva nodded.

Five minutes later he was on his feet and after a mug of hot, sweet tea he was feeling considerably more human. The others had gone on ahead to assist with refuelling and around him a group of Dinka women were already packing up the camp. Occasionally they glanced at Savva as though he was an exotic being from another planet. Savva would have liked nothing better than to sit and talk with them, but the doctor was waiting for him in an old Landrover, the motor running.

The road twisted backwards and forwards through several compounds. In each there were two or three, what Steven called *tukels*, circular mud-walled huts on stilts.

"The locals call them 'GOS ovens'; the Sudanese Government troops force the inhabitants up into the top section and then set a fire underneath them. Arabs!" He used the word as an expletive. Savva stared at the huts, the image in his mind too horrible to contemplate.

Coming through a break in the trees they had to slow down as a large crowd of locals had come to see the unscheduled flight. As the people parted to let them through, Savva saw a small dark blue plane with the word "ECHO" in large white letters on the fuselage. Underneath in small letters the acronym was explained as: European Community Humanitarian Organisation. The plane's single propeller started to turn and then fired into life.

To the left of the plane, Peter and Walter were rolling an empty fuel drum away. They waved. Savva was about to go over to greet them when Steven's strong arms propelled him toward the open door of the tiny aircraft.

"What about the others?"

"They will come later. No room now. You have to get out of here as fast as possible," Steven yelled over the engine noise. "Good luck."

"In a moment, I've got to thank them." Not waiting for a reply he broke away and strode through the crowd of Dinkas to the small fuel shed.

"You can't come now?"

"I talked to the UN team in Loki and they think that the GOS will lift the restrictions on flights once they realise they have missed you," Peter said. "Don't worry, I'll catch up with you back in Oz."

Savva turned to Walter, who to his surprise, embraced him warmly.

"Thanks for the ride." Savva was lost for words. "Well . . ."

"Come on." Walter guided him out of the hut. "They just made the final boarding call. And if that plane doesn't get out of here soon the GOS will be back for another crack at you."

The crowd of locals parted for them to get through to the plane where Steven was looking anxiously up at the sky.

"Thanks for your kindness, Steven." Savva was unsure how one farewelled a Dinka, but took the risk and extended his hand. To his relief Steven took it and shook it firmly.

"Now, get on the plane! Doctor's orders!"

"You can stop worrying about me, I'll be fine," Savva shouted above the rising scream of the engine.

"I'm not worried about you. I'm worried about what's left of Akot!"

There was no time to reply as Savva was lifted up the steps by Peter and Walter.

Ducking his head he stepped up into the plane and saw that there was only room for two passengers. The seat at the rear was occupied by a smiling man in a business suit. On the seat in front was Savva's bag. The man had obviously been through it for he was waving two of Savva's passports. In one hand he had the passport of Leon Silbert, Australian citizen. In the other, the passport of Nikolai Trinkovski, Russian citizen. The Jack Zinner passport was on his knee.

"Welcome aboard, sir." The accent was British, but with Australian overtones. "A friend of yours said you would appreciate being met at the airport. You sent a fax from Khartoum?" The man raised his eyebrows, but continued without waiting for a reply. "I'm afraid I'm the best we could do at short notice." He put the passports down and extended his hand. "Malcolm Hennessy, Foreign Affairs."

"Savva Golitsyn. Nothing personal, but I have had enough foreign affairs to last me for a while."

The door was closed behind them and Savva moved in a low crouch to his seat in front of Hennessy.

"Very funny, sir. But I'm afraid we have to decide which of these people you are. I must say that I haven't come across a passport for any Golitsyn. Could you maybe take Silbert for a while? It would save a lot of problems on the forms. Mind you, that's what I'm here for. I'm at your service to put in the full stops and dot the i's."

The man in the rear seat talked for a while before he realised that no one was listening. So he sat back and watched as the ground fell away below them.

EPILOGUE

Hᴇ checked the envelope in his pocket and quietly closed the door behind him. The streets were wind-blown and inhospitable as he began his walk. The pavement felt like no-man's-land. The idea of taking a taxi had crossed his mind, but he needed time to think.

There are many occasions when life obliges with neat endings. When the evil characters are captured or blown to smithereens. There are also times when life stuffs up the plot and the lovers die within centimetres of each other. This story, Savva thought, at he walked slowly through the Melbourne streets, has had a bet each way.

The information he gave Foreign Affairs over three very boring weeks in Canberra had been picked clean of every career advancing opportunity it could afford those who asked the questions. At some point the Americans found an adviser who could spot Jebel Marra on a map and then tried to muscle in with the

408

claim that they had been on the case for years. No one believed them.

In the end, when action was indicated, a lot of people sat on hands, not always their own. Though in a twist that delighted no one but a man who insisted on being called Savva, the only people in a position to do anything about Jebel Marra were the French. Not that they had any desire to do so. However, the acute embarrassment at being found playing with nuclear toys again, no matter how small they might be, was a sufficient lever to insist that they send in a strike force and clean the place out. Of course they could claim it as a victory! Of course they could publicise the raid. If they did not then others would, and in far greater detail.

So one hot evening, a bus carrying refugees from Chad turned off the main road to Nyala and detoured to Jebel Marra and caused a great deal of damage before returning the way it had come, with the addition of several very well sealed containers containing weapons-grade materials. The Gaullist right in the French Military suddenly became very quiet.

Savva felt some concern about the true nature of that silence when he heard a rumour that the man who had led the mission to close down Jebel Marra was Jean-Claude Marchand. The rumour was probably true, after all he knew the area, didn't he?

In St Petersburg, a bus collected its normal clientele, a load of vodka-drunk Finns who sounded as though they would sing their way back to Helsinki. Only one man was silent and anyway, he knew not one word of Finnish. He made the journey hidden under the back seat. Later he travelled first class to a reunion in Australia.

Savva's wanderings brought him to a little cafe where the sudden chill had driven the patrons inside. Only one woman sat, face glowing in the cold, at the pavement table. He smiled and took the packet from his pocket.

"The new passport."

The woman removed her gloves, took out the passport and studied it. After a time she looked up.

"And you promise me this is the only one you have?"

He nodded impatiently. It was very cold. He needed coffee.